"Deep into that darkness peering, long I stood there, wondering, fearing, doubting, dreaming dreams no mortal ever dared to dream before."

-Edgar Allan Poe-

DARK DAYS

C.A. KUNZ

Illustrated By
Robert Kunz

For our family and friends.
We are tremendously blessed to have each and every one of you in our lives.

First Printing

ISBN-13: 978-0615563534 (pbk)
ISBN-10: 0615563538 (pbk)

C.A. Kunz, LLC
Orlando, Florida

Praise For The Childe

"This series opener is a great paranormal story with a dash of mystery that will keep readers guessing...it is a thrilling, unputdownable story."

-RT Book Reviews

"All in all, The Childe was a good read, and the authors are to be congratulated for capturing a potential portion of the teenage vampire market!"

-Readers Favorite "Book Reviews and Award Contest"

"A unique coming of age story and of facing one's paranormal calling, "The Childe" is a charming read that will resonate well with many young readers and those dealing with being 'weird'."

-Midwest Book Review

"I loved this book. It was such a page turner...Carol and Adam have written a WONDERFUL story."

-Mindy Fangedmom from Books Complete Me

"...it was brilliant! I usually stay away from vampire novels...But this was such a fun read."

-Alex from Blethering About Books

"The Childe is an amazing debut novel from mother & son writing duo, Carol & Adam Kunz (C.A. Kunz). Right from the start The Childe had me gripped, I couldn't put it down."

-Megan from Reading Away The Days

"I honestly couldn't find anything wrong with it. It had me eating out of its hand the entire time. Everyone needs to go pick this up!"

-Becky from Book Bite Reviews

------------ Acknowledgements ------------

First and foremost, we would like to thank Robert Kunz, Tim Coleman, Charlie Steffy, Amanda Lynch, Matt Boggs, and Andrew Nocar for being our A-list supporters, dedicated readers, much-needed critics, and editors. We are truly grateful for all of your assistance throughout this whole process.

We also want to thank Robert Kunz for again providing the wonderful illustrations for our book. You are extremely talented, and we are honored to display your art within our art once more.

A huge thank you should go to Lee Wilson who has been hard at work on a truly incredible companion soundtrack for our series. He is an extremely talented musician and we are very lucky to have his help and support on this project.

Very special thanks to our newly gained Twitter and Blogger friends. Every single one of you has helped in ways you can't even imagine! We truly appreciate your words of encouragement and honest reviews of our work. We can't thank you all enough for what you have done for us!

Tremendous thanks should also go to Lisa Surphlis for designing yet another amazing cover for us. You have seriously outdone yourself this time and we're incredibly grateful!

Thanks to *you*, our readers, for reading our books. By performing this simple act you are helping us make a lifelong dream come true and you have no idea how much you mean to us (or Cat).

Finally, we cannot forget to thank all of our wonderful family and friends. Your love and support keep us always moving forward, and for this we are eternally grateful.

Mrs. Rosenbaum's

NAME: CAT COLVIN
ADDRESS: 2626 NEHALEM AVE
PHONE #: 555-1343
EMERGENCY CONTACTS:
- MOM: RACHEL COLVIN
- DAD: SAM COLVIN
EMAIL ADDRESS:
- REDFREAK10@ASTORIA.NET

TEACHER'S NOTES:
* BROTHER IS TAYLOR COLVIN
* BOYFRIEND IS RYAN BECKFORD
* INTERESTING GIRL WITH FIERY RED HAIR

name: elle porter
address: 2620 nehalem ave.
phone #: 555-2628
emergency contacts:
- mom: cindy porter
- dad: Frank porter
email address:
- astoriapanther1@astoria.net

TEACHER'S NOTES:
* THE 'SHY' AND QUIET ONE OF CAT COLVIN'S GROUP OF FRIENDS
* OUR SCHOOL MASCOT, THE PANTHER
* A TAD SOCIALLY AWKWARD

NAME: MATT THOMAS
ADDRESS: 2623 NEHALEM AVE.
PHONE #: 555-3255
EMERGENCY CONTACTS:
- MOM: LILLY THOMAS
- DAD: ALLEN THOMAS
EMAIL ADDRESS:
- DONJUAN13@ASTORIA.NET

TEACHER'S NOTES:
* SISTER IS SARA THOMAS
* ONLY MALE BEST FRIEND TO CAT COLVIN
* SEEMS TO BE YOUR TYPICAL TEENAGE BOY

English Class

NAME:
ADDR
PHON
EM
-
-

Name: Hannah Bancroft
Address: 1113 Hillcrest Dr.
Phone #: 555-8923
Emergency Contacts:
- Mom: Ulla Bancroft
- Dad: Lucien Bancroft
Email Address:
- lonelygirl12@Astoria.net

TEACHER's NOTES:
* ISSAC BANCROFT IS HER OLDER BROTHER AND LEADER OF THE PREPPY GOTH CLIQUE
* HANGS OUT WITH CAT'S GROUP AGAINST HER BROTHER'S WISHES
* THERE IS SOMETHING ODD ABOUT HER AND HER BROTHER'S GROUP

Name: Amanda Stevens
Address: 2611 Nehalem Ave.
Phone #: 555-7108
Emergency Contacts:
- Mom: Aurora Stevens
- Dad: Bernard Stevens
Email Address:
- CravenFanatic@Astoria.Net

TEACHER'S NOTES:
* A PART OF CAT COLVIN'S GROUP OF FRIENDS
* ODD GIRL WHO ALWAYS CHANGES HER APPEARANCE
* VERY OUTSPOKEN AND OPINIONATED

Phon
emergency contac
- MOM: MOLLY
- DAD: STEPHEN
email address:
- KEWL CHICK@

TEACHER'S
* SHE IS A
* LIKES TO
* HAS A GR

Name: Julie Winters
Address: 2615 Nehalem Ave.
Phone #: 555-7204
Emergency Contacts:
- Claire Winters
Email Address:
- JWinters@Astoria.Net

TEACHER'S NOTES:
* SEEMS OLDER THAN SHE IS
* BEST FRIEND TO CAT COLVIN
* ATTENDED PRIVATE SCHOOL (MADISON PREP) WITH CAT

TS:
ALLEN
ALLEN
@ASTORIA.NET
NOTES:
*
*
*

Contents

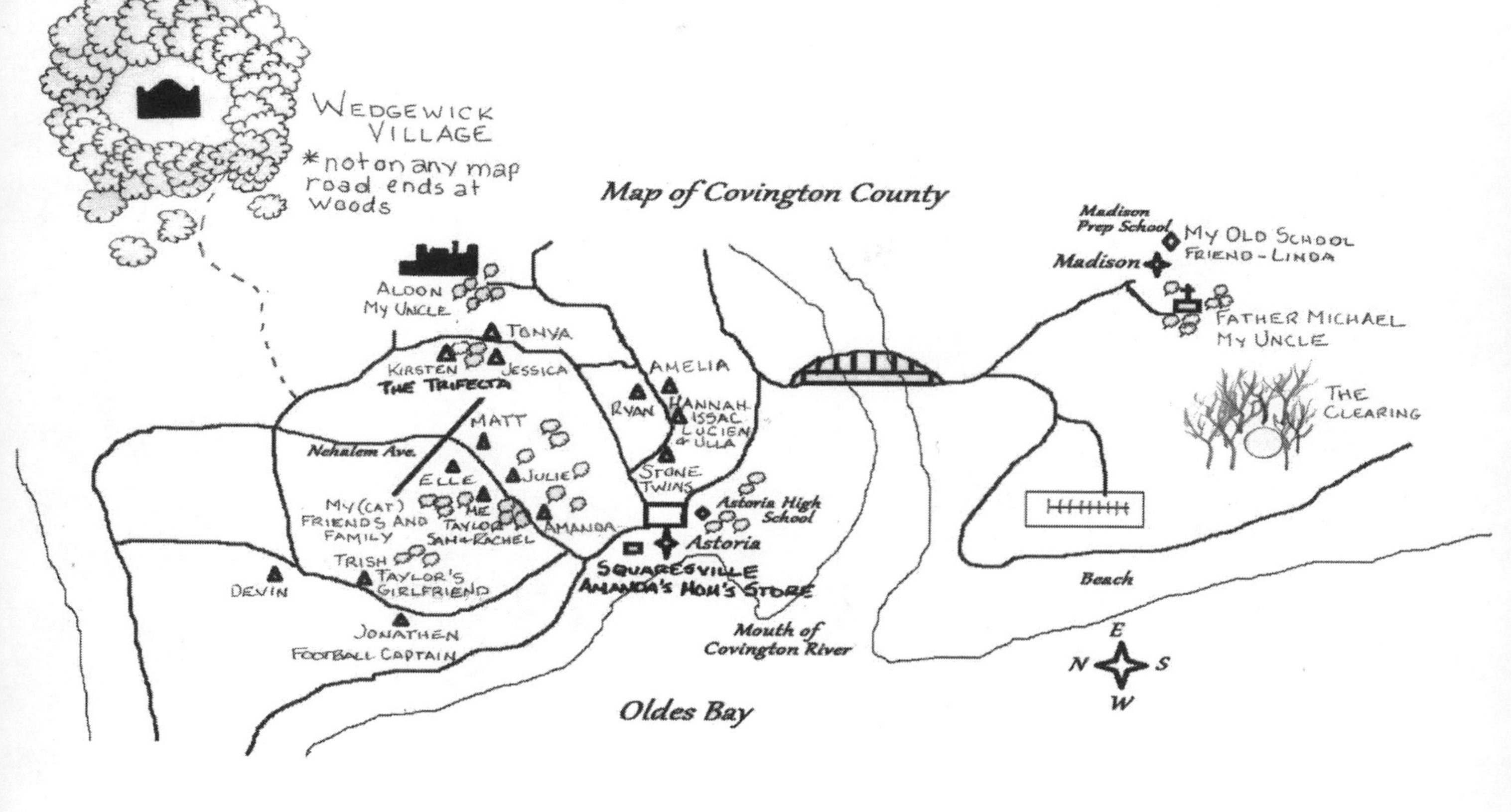

Map of Covington County
WEDGEWICK VILLAGE
*not on any map road ends at woods
ALDON My UNCLE
TONYA
KIRSTEN
JESSICA
THE TRIFECTA
MATT
Nehalem Ave.
ELLE
JULIE
My (CAT) FRIENDS AND FAMILY
ME TAYLOR SAM & RACHEL
AMANDA
TRISH
TAYLOR'S GIRLFRIEND
DEVIN
JONATHEN FOOTBALL CAPTAIN
AMELIA
RYAN
HANNAH ISSAC LUCIEN & ULLA
STONE TWINS
Astoria High School
Astoria
SQUARESVILLE
AMANDA'S MOM'S STORE
Mouth of Covington River
Oldes Bay
Madison Prep School
MY OLD SCHOOL FRIEND - LINDA
Madison
FATHER MICHAEL MY UNCLE
THE CLEARING
Beach
E
N
S
W

1
Summertime Blues

Cat Colvin felt like she was prepared to face many things in her life. Being told she was adopted was definitely not one of them. It had only been a day since she found out, though to her, it had already felt like an eternity. Like an entire lifetime of living a lie. Normally, she was a strong person and could take things with a grain of salt, but this news was tough. It wasn't Mr. Crawley's algebra class tough though, but real life issue tough. Not knowing the truth about her past, Cat found herself questioning everyone and everything.

Cat's cell phone was constantly being bombarded with calls and texts from her friends. So she decided to shut it off and throw it in the top drawer of her desk, putting it out of her mind. She wanted to be alone. No one could console her, not even her boyfriend Ryan, or her four best friends. Cat even tried to watch her favorite Robert Craven horror film, *Red Twilight,* but it too failed to pull her out of her slump.

It was a typical rainy Astoria day, a perfect match for Cat's mood. She spent most of the morning staring out of her attic bedroom window at the rain rushing down the street toward a gutter. Cat wished the rain would wash away her problems just as easy as it was washing leaves and mud off the street and sidewalk.

Cat opened the window and stepped out onto the balcony. In the rain, her bright red curly hair quickly lost its volume. It became plastered to her pale face and framed her eyes, one sky blue and one amber. She began to cry and her tears melded with the rain that was streaming down her cheeks. Cat let out a heavy sigh and firmly grasped the railing of the balcony with both hands. She wanted to scream, yell, anything. Cat raised her eyes to look across the street at her best friend Julie's house. She saw Julie peering through the curtains, looking at her. Julie began to wave, but Cat shied away, and then slouched down onto the wrought iron bench that sat just outside her window.

As the rain intensified, Cat hurried back into her room. She dripped all the way to the bathroom and left watery foot prints across her old wooden floor. After slowly peeling off her clothes, she proceeded to ring them out in the shower, and then draped them over her laundry hamper. She stood in front of her bathroom mirror in just her bra and underwear, looking at her reflection critically. "Who am I?" she asked out loud. "Stupid question Cat, you know you don't have the answer." Pressing her head against the mirror and letting out a sigh, she thought back to the beginning of her freshmen year at Astoria High School. *If I had known that all of this crazy stuff would've happened because of me switching schools, I wouldn't have begged my parentals to let me. I know for a fact that Linda wouldn't be missing now if Julie and I would've walked home with her from Madison Prep like we used to after swim practice.*

Backing away from the mirror, a sparkle in her reflection caught her eye. It was the ring she was wearing on a chain around her neck. A gift from her boyfriend Ryan. Cat smiled, clutching the ring in her hand. *I guess something good did come out of this, but at what cost? By giving me this ring Ryan has driven a wedge between himself and his friends. And even though he acts like it doesn't bother him, maybe it does. So many complications.*

Even after she was showered and dressed in warm comfy pajamas, Cat didn't feel any better. She had taken some comfort however, knowing she took her pill for her blood disorder that morning ensured there were going to be no signs of fainting spells, hearing voices in her head, or strange visions in her near future.

The aroma of freshly made breakfast her mom had placed in front of her door four hours prior had dissipated. Cat's stomach grumbled, reminding her that she was depriving it of sustenance, but she ignored it.

The stairs creaked as Rachel climbed up to Cat's attic bedroom door to see if Cat had eaten the food she'd left. A frown marred her beautiful face as she saw she hadn't. Picking up the plate, she returned to the kitchen. After scraping the food into the trash can, Rachel sat at the kitchen table with her head in her hands. She couldn't wait for Sam to get home from his last day of teaching until summer school. She hoped that he would know what to do. All Rachel wanted was to hug her daughter, but Cat had locked herself in her room, shutting everyone out. She had made it quite clear that she wanted to be left alone when both Rachel and Sam tried approaching her earlier that morning.

❦ ❦ ❦

Across the street, Julie was in the middle of a phone conversation with Amanda.

"Hey Julie, have you talked to Cat today? I've been trying to get a hold of her because we're supposed to go help my mom at Squaresville. I just called the home phone, and her mom said she wasn't feeling well. Did she seem sick to you yesterday at school?" Before Julie could answer, there was a beep on Amanda's line, signaling a call waiting. "Hey, hold on a sec, Matt's on the other line. Be right back, okay," Amanda said while rolling her eyes.

"I'll be here," Julie replied with a laugh.

"Hey Matt, what's up?"

"So I just called Cat's house, because her cell just goes to voicemail, and her mom said she's sick. Aren't we supposed to watch a movie at her place tonight?" he asked.

"I know right? And she hasn't told any of us, not even Julie, who lives right across the street from her. Hold on Matt, Elle's on Skype," Amanda replied with a huff. She set her cell phone on the bed and adjusted her computer's camera. *Why am I always the central hub for communication?* She thought as Elle's face appeared on her computer screen. "I know, I know, Cat isn't answering her phone," Amanda said dryly with a scowl on her face.

With a confused look, Elle replied, "What? No look!" Elle smiled really wide, pulled her lips back, and put her mouth close to the camera to show she no longer had iron-clad teeth. Her braces were gone. "Just got them off this morning! I'm so excited and…wait, what do you mean Cat isn't answering her phone? Is she okay? Cat always answers her phone." Amanda could hear that Elle, the constant worrier of their group, had immediately gone into worry mode.

"Her mom says she's sick. Hey Elle, could you hold on for a sec? I've got Matt and Julie on hold, and we're discussing tonight's plans, sans Cat," she stated. Picking up her cell from the bed, "Hey Matt, I'm back."

"Is Elle worried?"

"Not until I said something, but she called because she got her braces off."

"Amanda! I wanted it to be a surprise," Elle whined.

"Oh sorry Elle," she apologized, looking at her on the computer. "Alright Matt, act surprised when you see Elle without her braces," she ordered. A knock at Amanda's bedroom door startled her. "Mom, I'm busy right now. I know, we need to leave for the store soon!"

"It's me, Julie. Can I come in?"

"Julie? Sure, come in," Amanda replied with slight aggravation present in her voice. *Having four best friends can be such a trial sometimes*, she thought as the door opened, revealing Julie. Her long blonde hair was pulled up in a ponytail and she looked a little disheveled. Amanda felt a twinge of sympathy at how Julie's appearance had changed since Linda, a long time private school friend of Julie's and Cat's, went missing a couple weeks prior. Julie had always been the sensible one of the group. In the past, she would've never left her room, especially her house, looking the way she did now. Though Julie's perfection used to drive Amanda nuts, she desperately wished the old Julie would return.

"I'm sorry. I know I had you on hold for a while, but Matt called, then Elle came up on Skype to show me she got her braces off…oh crap, sorry again Elle."

"Amanda!" Elle reprimanded.

"Julie, go over and tell Elle she looks wonderful without her braces, I have to talk to Matt," she said in an annoyed tone. Putting the phone back to her ear, "Okay, I'm back Matt." Hearing no answer, she looked at the phone's screen and saw he had hung up. "Great! Patience is definitely not one of his virtues!" Another bang came at Amanda's bedroom door. "Mom, I'm coming. Just a few more minutes, please!"

Without even asking to come in, Matt, the token male of their group, burst through the door. Looking more unkempt than Julie, Matt stood there with two different colored socks on, a wrinkled blue t-shirt, and a pair of tan cargo shorts. Though his hair was wet, she could tell he was definitely suffering from bedhead as his dirty blonde hair was pushed all to one side.

"Matt, do you even own a mirror? And what have I told you about barging into a girl's room! There are very private things in here," Amanda yelled, tossing a pillow in his direction.

"You've got nothing here I haven't already seen. Don't forget, I have a sister and a mother."

Suddenly Amanda's mom, Aurora, appeared in the doorway. "Honey, are you almost ready to go?" Aurora asked and then looked at Amanda's computer screen. "Oh Elle, you got your braces off. You look absolutely lovely hun."

"Thank you Mrs. Stevens, got them off this morning," Elle replied sheepishly, pushing her long brown hair from in front of her face.

"Wow, Mrs. Stevens, cool tie-dye dress," Matt commented, admiring the colorful garment.

Amanda rolled her eyes, "Don't encourage her Matt. She'll only want to dress like that more often."

"Oh you hush Amanda Lynn Stevens. Be ready in ten minutes, we have to get going. And thank you Matt, always a joy having you around," Aurora said with a smile before leaving the room.

"Suck up!" Amanda muttered under her breath.

"What do you mean?" Matt asked with an impish grin. "Hey Elle, look at you," he said as he jumped in front of Amanda's computer screen, hogging up the camera. "No more metal mouth! You look great, that must've been some record huh? You only had those babies in about a year!"

"Yeah the dentist said my teeth corrected quickly. Good thing too, I was worried I'd be stuck with them my whole life."

"Alright, I hate to break this party up, but I've got to get ready. So we'll continue this convo, *ON THE PHONE*, later," Amanda stated, looking pointedly around to everyone, clearly annoyed that they were in her room.

"Five minutes Amanda," Aurora called up from downstairs.

"Alright mom!" Noticing no one was paying attention to her, and still chatting with Elle, Amanda rolled her eyes and proceeded to throw on her tennis shoes. "Oh just forget it guys," she said and then laughed to herself as she continued getting ready. *This is what I get for having my friends live so close to me I guess.*

The rain continued throughout the day and into the night, showing no signs of letting up. Cat lay on her bed trying to read, but found herself skimming the same page over and over again. After closing the book, she threw it across the room in frustration. She scanned her room for something else to occupy her mind. Through the sound of the rain pounding on the roof, Cat heard a noise at the window. Knowing Jewels wouldn't be out in the pouring rain, she approached it cautiously. Looking down at the lawn she saw someone's outline standing under the large Sitka Spruce tree. By the light of the Victorian lamp post she could see it was Ryan. He was being soaked by the rain, despite his efforts to try and stay under the cover of the large tree. Cat wanted to talk to him, but she couldn't. She just shook her head and turned away, closing her window curtain. As she made her way back to her bed, Cat sighed as she clutched the ring around her neck.

Ryan was confused as he saw her bedroom light go out. He wondered what had happened within a day to make her act like this. *Did I do something wrong?* He asked himself. He kept looking up at her window, peering through the water-logged strands of dark brown hair hanging in front of his icy blue eyes, and ignoring the rain running down his face. He fought with himself, trying to decide if he should go up there and talk to her or just give her space. *I'm going up there,* he decided. The moment he took a step toward the house he was pinned by the headlights of a car turning into the driveway. *Great, it's Taylor. There's no mistaking that Mustang!* Taylor jumped out of his car, his angry footsteps quickly ate up the distance between them. His large muscular frame was definitely intimidating.

"What do you think you're doing Beckford? Stalking my sister huh?" Taylor asked.

"Hey, is something wrong with Cat?" Ryan's worried voice calmed Taylor slightly.

"Look man, it's none of your business," he replied. "Now go home and leave her alone, alright."

"Your sister's my girlfriend, whether you like it or not, and I want to know what's going on!" Ryan demanded.

"Yeah, you're right. I hate the idea of you being her boyfriend, but I guess I'll have to deal, seeing as how Cat is one of the most stubborn people I know. But you need to give her some space. Believe me, I'm not just saying that to get rid of you," Taylor's eyes pleaded with him to comply.

"Alright, I'll leave her alone…for tonight." As Ryan turned and began walking away, Taylor just stood there in the rain, shaking his head at Ryan's retreating back.

The following morning Cat awoke to the sound of her mom placing another plate of food at her door. Having not eaten for a whole day, her stomach groaned as the smell of bacon drifted underneath the door into her room. Cat waited and listened for the creaking of the attic stairs to stop, signaling her mom was gone. She opened the door and grabbed the plate quickly. Shutting the door with her foot, Cat ran to her bed, scarfing down the food along the way.

Hearing Cat's bedroom door open and close brought a smile to Rachel's face as she stood at the bottom of the stairs. "She's eating again," Rachel said to Sam as she entered the living room.

"Well, hopefully this is a sign that she's coming around," Sam replied, looking at his wife, happy to see a spark in her eyes.

"I hope so Sam. I hope so."

"Oh, and Aldon just called. He said he met with Gretchen this morning."

"Did he find out anything?" Rachel asked anxiously.

"Gretchen apparently didn't give her the journal. It was an entity that resides in her store, whatever that means," Sam replied.

"But, she could've taken it away from Cat. Why did Gretchen let her leave with it?"

"Aldon asked the same question, and her answer was, 'we have no control over the future, and Cat was meant to have that book'."

"Did she say anything about us?"

"Aldon said she reassured him that our secret was safe, for now," he replied with slight worry in his tone.

"So what does that mean?" Rachel's face reflected the concern in her voice.

"I don't know. That's all he said."

Sam and Rachel exchanged glances, and then looked up toward Cat's attic bedroom, both wondering what the future held.

Turning on her computer, Cat noticed she had forgotten to sign out of her TeenSpace instant messenger. She had over fifty messages from her friends. She deleted them all, not reading what any of them said. She didn't know how long she could keep this up. *I want to talk to them, I do. But I just don't know what to say. And I don't want to have to explain everything. It's hard enough as it is,* she thought.

After shutting down her computer, Cat stared out the window toward Julie's house. It was still pouring down rain, and Cat realized she had made herself a prisoner in her own room. So many questions ran through her head. *Who are my real parents? Why can't I shake the feeling I'm more different than just what I see on the outside? Why have I been so sheltered my whole life? Is there more I haven't been told?* Her head began to throb due to the pressure building up. She opened her mini fridge, popped one of her pills, and then washed it down with a gulp of water. Flopping on her bed, she tried to cry, but no tears came. “Must be all out,” Cat said, laughing hollowly. A knock at her door interrupted her thoughts.

“Cat, honey?” Rachel asked.

“Go away.”

“Cat, please talk to me. I’m still your mother, blood or not.”

“Don’t even start with the ‘I’m still your mother’ stuff. You’ve got no right to say that. Not after the way you’ve lied to me my whole life!”

“Catherine Colvin, you open this door immediately! We’ve let you have your space and now we need to talk,” Rachel demanded with her hands on her hips. “We’re sorry we lied, but you have to understand, we did it for a good reason. So that you wouldn’t feel different.” Rachel waited a few seconds to see if Cat was going to open the door. When she didn’t, “Please open the door. All I want to do is talk. If you don’t like what I have to say, then you can stay in your room the rest of the summer. Just give me five minutes, please.”

Cat rolled off her bed and made her way to the door. She hesitated at first, then reached for the handle and turned it, letting her mom in. “You’ve got five minutes,” she announced with her back to her mom. Rachel grabbed Cat in a hug and squeezed. Surprised by the action, Cat stood there trying to take in what was happening. She could feel her mom's tears soaking her shoulder as Rachel shook with sobs.

"Cat, please forgive us. We love you. I love you," Rachel wailed as she squeezed Cat harder. Finally breaking her defensive stance, Cat turned and hugged her back.

"Rachel, it's okay. I just need time. Thanks for the space, but I need to do this on my own terms."

"I know."

"How did you expect me to react? You dump all of this on me, and then what? We all just hug and frolic in fields of daisies?" Gently pushing her mom back, Cat stared intently into her golden brown eyes, which seemed to have lost some of their usual luster. "Put yourself in my shoes and think how it would feel if, one, your best friend goes missing, and two, you find out you're adopted. I mean, hello, scarring much?"

"I know, that's why we didn't want you to find out like this. We had a plan-"

"Yeah, a plan to not tell me," Cat interrupted.

"No, we were going to tell you eventually. I'm sorry you found out this way sweetie."

"Yeah, so am I," she murmured. "So, are we finished here? Because I have some much needed longing and gazing out my window to do," Cat said dryly.

"Well, there is one more thing I wanted to talk to you about," Rachel replied, digging in her pocket. She pulled out a set of car keys, and then showed them to Cat. "Your dad and I were going to wait until you started school again, but we thought that with all we've put you through, maybe this would help a little." Cat's eyes grew wide as she tried not to break her melancholy demeanor. She reached out and grabbed the keys from her mom's hand and saw the logo of the one car she had asked for after she passed her driver's test.

"You got me a Jeep?"

"Yeah, and it's orange too. Your favorite color." Cat hugged her mom again and then backed away.

"You know, you can't bribe me to make everything okay, right?"

"No, we know. We were planning this even before all of this happened. We just wanted to present this now, as somewhat of a peace offering," Rachel explained.

"Oh…well, I was just making sure we're on the same page."

"And starting now, you're no longer grounded. You've been cooped up long enough. Even though it was mostly self-inflicted," she said, smiling slightly.

"Thanks, but I don't know if I'll be heading outside anytime soon. I'm still trying out this whole hermit thing. I'm not quite ready to face my friends at the moment."

"You know they're very worried about you, right? They've called numerous times. You shouldn't punish them for things we've done."

Cat glanced at her mom and then back at the keys in her hand. "Well Rachel, now you know I'm okay. I think I might go back to the whole moping thing, if you don't mind. But it kind of works best when I'm here alone though," she joked. Rachel smiled slightly and then hugged Cat.

"If you'd like to talk more, your father and I will be downstairs. Oh, and dinner will be at seven if you want to join us." Cat didn't answer. She just nodded to her mom as she left the room.

"Rachel?"

"Yes sweetie?" she asked, re-opening the door.

"Never mind."

That night Ryan stood out in front of Cat's house pacing back and forth in the rain, deciding if he should go up to her window or not, especially after Taylor's warning. He had been waiting for about an hour after calling her phone numerous times and leaving several messages. It was eleven o'clock and Cat's bedroom light was still on. Frustrated, Ryan finally decided to try and talk to her. Just as he was jumping up to the balcony, he noticed a golden form dash out from the Sitka Spruce tree. Ryan waited and watched as a cat bolted across the balcony's railing, through the rain, and up to Cat's bay window.

A loud meow sent Cat hurrying to the window. She was shocked to see Jewels out in the rain. Quickly flinging her window open, she grabbed the feline and began drying her off with the towel that was draped over her tri-fold rice paper screen. "You poor thing, you're soaked to the bone Jewels. What are you doing out in this nasty weather?" The feline nestled up to Cat, purring contently, as if thanking her for the wipe down. The stray cat had made a habit of stopping by Cat's bedroom window regularly. She resembled a miniature lioness, complete with golden brown fur. The name Jewels was given to her by Cat, who loved how her eyes always shined like tiny jewels.

Ryan made his way up to the balcony and continued to watch from outside. Suddenly Jewels whipped around, hissing violently toward the window, and staring straight at Ryan. He quickly descended from the balcony and ran toward his car, hoping Cat hadn't seen him.

"What's the matter girl?" Jewels jumped out of Cat's arms and perched herself on the window seat, her hair raised, and looking like she was ready to attack. Cat peered through the curtains and saw a car pulling away from her house, its tail lights glowing through the rain. “Was that Ryan?” Running over to her desk she pulled her cell phone from the drawer and started to turn it on, but then stopped. She had every intention of calling Ryan, but she couldn’t go through with it. *Come on Cat, you can’t block them out forever,* she thought and then tossed the phone back in the drawer. Plopping face down on her bed, Cat moaned. “Ugh! Jewels, why am I so stubborn?” she uttered as Jewels joined her on the bed and curled up.

The next couple of days passed as a blur. The rain still showed no sign of stopping. It had rained a week straight, an Astoria summer record. The front lawn closely resembled a lake. Cat was still not making any effort to communicate with her friends, though it was becoming exceedingly more difficult not to. She also had yet to join her family for dinner, though at every meal, they saved a seat for her, just in case she changed her mind.

A loud banging came at Cat’s bay window and she saw Julie, standing on her balcony, completely soaked and shivering. “Are you going let me in, or not?” she asked loudly. Cat opened the window and Julie stormed in, grabbing a towel from the bathroom.

“What the heck are you doing out in the rain?”

“Well, when your best friend won’t return any of your calls, drastic measures must be taken,” Julie stammered. “Oh, and that lattice by the way is darn hard to climb up when it’s wet, just saying.”

Cat didn’t say anything. She just looked at the ground in shame, and slouched down on her bed. Julie sat next to her, and put her arm around her. “Don’t worry silly, I forgive you. Whatever your reason is, I’m sure it’s a good one. And by the way, I never bought the one your parents were passing around about you being sick,” she said, smiling at Cat. Cat looked at Julie and flashed her a quick smile.

“Hey, Julie? What’s it like being adopted?”

“What do you mean?” she replied, puzzled.

“Well, when you found out you were adopted, what was it like?”

“I kind of always knew, I guess. So when mom told me, I wasn’t really that surprised. Why do you ask?”

Tears began to roll down Cat’s cheeks as she turned to face Julie. “I just found out that…I’m, adopted. That’s why I went all anti-social.” Before Cat could get anything else out, Julie grabbed her in a hug, and for the first time in a week Cat felt a sense of calm come over her. She smiled as Julie squeezed her tight.

“Julie, I have a favor to ask you.”

"Okay."

"You can't tell the others we've talked. I need more time to think about what I'm going to say to the rest of the gang."

"You got it, but please try to make your talk sooner rather than later. You know I'm terrible at keeping secrets," Julie said with a laugh.

Across town, later that day, Cat's uncle Michael was pacing in the church rectory. His heart and mind were heavy as he debated whether he should inform the Colvin's of the letter he received a week ago. As he combed his hand through his short, bright red curly hair, he pulled out his cell phone and began to dial their number, but then wavered. Quickly ending the call, he leaned against the wall and sighed. "Maybe I can persuade Cat's aunt Ròs that taking Cat is not what's best for her," Michael said out loud. "The Colvin's have done so much for Cat. Now it's my turn to uphold the wishes of my dear departed sister." He turned to his desk and retrieved the letter. Re-reading it, as he had done several times since receiving it, he felt his confidence leave him like air from a punctured balloon. *This isn't going to be good, not good at all. I don't think we're ready for this,* he thought, looking solemnly out the rectory window.

2
Roses Are Red

Michael sat in his cozy cottage that was attached to the back of the church. As he was preparing Sunday's sermon, a loud knock at the front door startled him. The thought of it being Ròs immediately crossed his mind and caused his heart to sink. Michael had lost track of time and was surprised that night had already fallen. As he cautiously walked down the darkened hallway, he never took his eyes off the front door. He swallowed hard before pulling the door open. Michael was relieved to see Joe, the church maintenance man, standing on the porch.

"Fixed the leak in the roof. It was quite a doozy. You okay Father?"

"Yeah, just a little preoccupied is all. Thank you Joe. See you at Mass tomorrow?" Michael asked.

"Yep, I'll be there with the wife and kids, as usual," he replied happily.

Michael closed the door firmly. He leaned against it, took in a deep breath, and willed his heart to slow down. While heading back to his study, Michael was startled by another knock at the door. He figured that Joe had forgotten something. Michael was puzzled when he opened the door and saw the front step was empty. He peered out into the lit courtyard, thankful for the street light that had been installed a year ago, and saw no one. He heard a faint squeaking noise, and looked to his right. He watched the slightly broken, old rectory sign sway back and forth in the breeze. The sign had but one sentence:

Enter all ye seeking guidance and comfort.

He had tried to replace the old sign, but the congregation had balked. So there it was, squeaking, as if protesting against the wind's interruption of its peaceful hanging. After closing the door he made his way back down the hallway toward his study. The light in the study was dim, except for the lamp illuminating his desk.

"Hello Michael," a female's voice came from the vicinity of the couch. Startled, he jumped and hit the main switch, throwing the whole room into bright light. A man and a woman sat on the old Victorian couch in front of him, smiling. "I hope you don't mind, we came in when you were talking with your friend. We didn't want him to see us, of course."

"Who are you? And what are you doing in my house?!" Michael asked forcefully.

"You must forgive our poor manners. I have forgotten that we've never met before." The woman said with a smile as she raised herself from the couch. Michael took a step back. She stood taller than him and had beautiful locks of bright red curly hair. Her face was pale and flawless except for a few freckles that adorned her cheeks. Her eyes were sky blue and pierced through Michael as he stared into them. "I am Ròs Aldridge Cowan, and this handsome devil with me is my husband Trevor Cowan," she explained with a deep Irish accent, and then held out her hand to him. Michael took it, and the first thing he noticed was how cold her fingers were. Trevor extended his hand, which was equally as cold, but gave a heartier handshake. "We're sorry it took us so long to get here, but we ran into a little trouble in South America. We wanted to make sure we weren't followed, so we took the scenic route. Why don't we all sit down, you look a little peaked," Ròs said calmly as she took Michael's hand and lead him to the couch.

"I told you we should've called first instead of just showing up," Trevor whispered to his wife. Michael found himself seated beside Ròs and watched as Trevor pulled up one of the heavy oak chairs as if it weighed nothing.

"How's Catherine? Did you tell her about us and our plans yet?" Ròs asked impatiently.

"Let Michael absorb the fact we're here first Ròs. We gave him a wee bit of a shock. Isn't that right Michael?"

"I'm sorry. I'm not being a very good host. Would you like something to drink?" Michael asked, his own voice sounding unnatural to his ears.

"No, actually we'd like to go see Catherine. I don't think the Colvin's will let us in unless you're with us," Ròs explained. "But first things first. Michael, how much information did your sister give you about this whole situation? When she placed Cat into your care?"

Michael closed his eyes and leaned his head back on the couch, and thought back to that day many years ago. "Well first of all, I hadn't seen my sister in years, and had no idea that I had a niece, or that she was married. She told me her husband had recently passed. And that she was leaving Cat with me for a couple of days until she returned. To say the least, I was shocked." Michael leaned his head forward and slouched with his elbows resting on his knees, looking at the ground. "I didn't ask her where she was going or what she was doing. I've often wondered if I had, would things have turned out differently. Instead, I just took my niece in my arms, and grabbed the envelope from my sister's hand. I saw the terror in her eyes and wanted to ask what was wrong, but it was too late. She had run off into the night. And after that, I never saw her again." Looking up into Ròs eyes, Michael continued, "Two days later, I received word that she had passed from an anonymous letter, with no return address. So, I put into motion the instructions that were left in the envelope. And that's all I know."

"It's not your fault Michael, she was only trying to protect you," Ròs said, placing a hand on his shoulder.

"Protect me? From what?"

"Hmm, where shall I begin? You're a man of faith, are you not?" Ròs asked. Michael nodded. "Well, I need you to have faith. Faith that what I'm about to tell you is true. This is going to be hard for you to hear, but…we're different."

"Different? Different how?" Michael looked bewildered, his eyes moving from Ròs's to Trevor's.

"We're what you'd call the, living dead, or…vampires."

Michael's eyes squinted as he looked at Ròs questioningly. "What kind of joke are you playing here?" Michael asked.

"It's no joke, we're vampires," Trevor interjected calmly.

"Please, leave my house! There's no way I'm handing Cat over to two nut-jobs like you," he stated, rising to his feet. Ròs and Trevor both stood abruptly.

"Nut-jobs?" Ròs asked in frustration.

"Now Ròs, calm down, we need not make a scene," Trevor said in a soothing manner.

Ignoring him, "You want proof, here's your proof Father." Ròs said as her fangs descended from her mouth. Michael's eyelids fluttered, as his shaky legs gave way. He collapsed at their feet.

"I told you to be more gentle Ròs. Now look what you've done, the poor man has fainted. Go get a cold face cloth while I put him on the settee," Trevor instructed. He picked Michael up effortlessly as if he were a child, and then placed him gently on the couch in the corner. Ròs put the wet washcloth on his forehead and they both waited for him to come too.

Several minutes later Michael slowly opened his eyes, confused as to why he was laying on the couch. Seeing two sets of sky blue eyes hovering over him, he sprang up into a sitting position, pulled his knees up to his chest, and made a cross with his index fingers.

"Welcome back, you gave us quite a scare," Trevor said with a grin.

"You fell flat like a lead balloon," Ròs quipped, smiling minus the fangs.

"Ròs, stop it," Trevor reprimanded.

"I'm sorry," she muttered. "I just blurted it out without thinking how you'd respond. I know it's not every day you find out you're related to vampires."

"Ròs, that's enough," Trevor said, noticing Michael's eyes beginning to cloud over again, his finger cross wobbling.

"Well, what should I say then?" Ròs replied as she plopped down into the nearest chair and crossed her arms stubbornly. Trevor turned back to Michael, ignoring his wife's little tantrum, and concentrated on the poor man before him.

"Michael, we're not here to harm you. Our main concern now is for Catherine's safety. As far as we know, only a few people know what she truly is, and believe me, the fewer the better. I promise you, we mean you no harm," Trevor explained.

Michael looked into Trevor's eyes and had a feeling in his gut that he was telling the truth. He lowered his man-made finger crucifix. "Are you telling me that Cat…is like you?" Trevor nodded his head.

"Well, she's *kind of* like us," Ròs commented.

"Sorry, but this is just a little hard for me to digest at the moment," Michael muttered, as Trevor moved back to sit in the chair beside Ròs. "It sort of oddly makes sense though. Erika was vague that night, and I knew she wasn't telling me everything. But, vampires? You're truly, vampires?" He watched as Trevor and Ròs nodded their heads in unison.

"I'll go put on the kettle for tea and we can talk some more," Ròs announced, standing up and making her way to the kitchen. "I'm sure you have loads of questions."

"How do you know I have tea?" Michael called after her.

"I noticed some in the cupboard when I was searching for a face cloth," she replied, smiling broadly.

Michael woke up the following morning and stared at the ceiling, reliving the evening before. *Did that really happen…vampires? They really do exist?* He thought, rolling over and sitting on the edge of his bed. The Cowan's had decided to stay at a local hotel. Michael knew he should've offered for them to stay with him, but he still felt nervous about the whole vampire thing. They were coming back that evening so he could escort them to the Colvin's. He knew this meeting would not be a pleasurable experience, and it filled him with dread. The only thing that made him feel comfortable was the fact that his sister obviously loved and trusted these people, and that's all he needed to know.

As night fell, the Cowan's stood on Michael's front door step. When Michael opened the door, both of them let out a sigh of relief as he met them with a huge smile. "Come on in, let me get my coat. We'll take my car. I just have to get my keys and find my other shoe," he rambled, hobbling down the hallway with one shoe on. "Found it," Michael announced while trying to slip on his other shoe as he emerged from his bedroom.

An awkward silence fell over Michael, Ròs, and Trevor as they drove to the Colvin's. Michael made several attempts to start a simple conversation, but to no avail. Ròs seemed to be in deep thought as she stared at a locket that she held in her hand, and Trevor was in the back seat looking pensively out the window. Michael began to wring his hands on the steering wheel as he thought to himself. *I wonder how tonight will go. Are we making a mistake by springing this on Cat?* Looking upward slightly, Michael thought, *I know we've spoken together professionally on many occasions, but this time I have a personal request. Something I've never asked of you before. I'm asking you for some kind of guidance as to how I should handle this situation. My only hope is that by doing this, no harm will come to Cat and that we do not ruin the Colvin family.*

❦ ❦ ❦

The doorbell rang at the Colvin residence, and Taylor, who was on his way up to his room, turned around to answer it. He was surprised to see Michael standing on the porch. “Hey Mike, what’s up?” he asked. Taylor started feeling a little guilty, realizing that no one had yet told Michael that Cat knew she was adopted. He wasn’t going to tell him, that’s for sure. “Mom, Dad, Uncle Mike’s here!” he called out.

“Well don’t make him stand there, let him in,” Rachel replied while coming down the stairs.

“Yes, Taylor let him in,” Sam repeated from his study.

Taylor opened the door wide and Michael stepped over the threshold. “What a pleasant surprise!” Rachel gushed, embracing Michael in a hug. As Taylor began to shut the door, he noticed two people standing on the porch in the shadows. *They’re not human,* he thought.

“Hey Mike, are these two with you?” Taylor asked, looking out the door.

“Oh, yes, where are my manners,” Michael apologized, turning to introduce his two guests. “I’d like you all to meet the Cowans, Ròs and Trevor. And if you would be so kind as to invite them in, we’d like to speak with you.” He hoped he didn’t sound as nervous as he felt.

"Of course, welcome to our home, come in, come in," Sam gestured, wondering why Michael seemed so uneasy. Sam looked over at Rachel and saw that she too had noticed.

"Taylor, weren't you on your way up to your room?" Rachel asked.

"I guess that's a hint for me to leave. Nice to meet you, Mr. and Mrs. Cowan. Later Mike," he said, and then sprinted up the stairs, two at a time.

"Should we move this to the study?" Sam asked, gesturing toward the open door.

"Excellent idea," Michael stated and took the lead into the room. Rachel grasped Sam's hand firmly. They both exchanged looks and were curious as to what was about to take place. As they entered the study, Michael, Ròs, and Trevor sat on the leather couch facing Sam's desk. Sam grabbed his desk chair and rolled it around to the front of the desk, as Rachel sat on the edge of the matching leather recliner to his left. He saw she was biting her lip as she waited for someone to speak.

"I guess I'll break the ice. Rachel, Sam, it is our pleasure to finally meet you both. I know I speak for Trevor and myself when I say, we can never repay the selfless act you both have done for our family." Ròs's thick Irish brogue shook a little as she glanced at her husband for support. Ròs noticed the confused expressions that Rachel and Sam were sending her way. “I’m doing this a bit badly, aren’t I?” she asked, looking back at Trevor.

“What my wonderful wife is trying to say, is that, as Catherine’s Aunt and Uncle, we want to thank you for taking such great care of her,” Trevor said kindly.

“What? You’re who? Is this some kind of joke Michael?” Rachel asked in disbelief.

“No, Rachel it’s not a joke. This is William’s sister and brother-in-law,” Michael answered.

Cat sat on her bed staring out the window. She hadn’t gone down to dinner and now she was starving. Cat hoped she wouldn’t encounter anyone as she quietly made her way down the stairs to the kitchen, making sure to miss the creaky ones. With a plate full of food and a glass of water, she started walking back to the staircase, when she heard voices coming from the closed study door. She moved closer, and was surprised to hear her Uncle Michael telling everyone to calm down. Cat placed her glass and plate on the hallway side table, and bent to listen with her ear to the door.

“What are you two doing here?” she heard Sam ask forcefully. The anger in her dad’s voice startled Cat. Her father was usually a very calm man, and raising his voice was unlike him.

"We've come to take Catherine with us. It's not safe for her here anymore. I know we should've given you some warning, but we knew that we needed to see you in person to talk about this." Cat heard a woman say with an Irish accent. *Not safe? Who the hell is this lady? And why is she here to take me away?*

"She doesn't know about her past yet, only that she's adopted. She only found that out a week ago, and hasn't been dealing with it very well, I can assure you. So for you to add this to the mix, I just don't know what she'll do," Rachel's voice begged.

"She found out a week ago that she was adopted? Why wasn't I told this?" Cat heard Michael ask.

What is he doing here? Cat thought.

"Erika gave Cat to us to care for. We love her as much as if she was our own. You just can't take her from us!" Cat could hear her mom's heart wrenching sobs clearly through the door.

"Rachel, I'm sorry to upset you. Michael has told us what a wonderful job you've done with Catherine. We know she's truly been loved, but Trevor and I feel she needs to be with us. Her own kind. We can teach her what she needs to survive," Cat heard the unfamiliar Irish woman reply.

"You have no idea what she needs!" Sam's angered voice made Cat jump back this time. "She's the only one of her kind alive and nobody knows what she's capable of!"

Before she could even think it through, Cat stepped forward and flung the study doors open. She witnessed the shock on the faces of the five people within as they all looked her way. "It sounds like there are more secrets I should know. So, I think I should hear them now," Cat said quietly, even though she was screaming on the inside. Michael moved first, put his arm around Cat, and brought her to stand in front of the others.

"Cat's right. She deserves to know. So, everyone just calm down and we'll tell her. Now Cat, you ask the questions and we'll answer them, truthfully," Michael stated. Cat looked at the couple seated on the couch and noticed that they had bright red hair like hers.

"Who are you?" she asked them.

"We're your Aunt Ròs and Uncle Trevor," Trevor answered, squeezing Ròs's hand as a solitary tear trickled down her cheek from seeing her niece for the first time. "Ròs is your real father's sister," he further explained.

"My real father? Do you know where he is?" Cat asked, her voice trembling.

"He's passed my dear," Ròs choked out.

"What? How? What about my real mother?"

"Her too, I'm afraid," Trevor replied with a sad look on his face.

"What were their names?" Cat asked, tears welling up in her eyes.

"William and Erika," Ròs replied.

"Oh," she murmured, her demeanor reflecting the melancholy in her voice. Looking up at Michael, "So, who are you really then?"

"I'm Erika's brother. I'm your real Uncle. I was the one instructed to give you to the Colvin's to raise as their own." Michael said, squeezing her shoulder. Turning to Ròs, "Now, Ròs I think it'd be best if you told her the rest."

Rachel stood to intervene, but Sam took her hand and pulled her down onto his lap, holding her tightly.

"Well, our family comes from Ireland, where your mother and father met. They married in secret because most of our kin were against their union. In protest, William and Erika fled in search of a safe haven to give birth to you," Ròs explained.

"Why were they against it?" Cat asked. Ròs looked over to Trevor for help.

"Well that's where things get a little complicated Catherine," Trevor interjected. "In the eyes of our kin, your parent's relationship was forbidden."

"Forbidden? Why?"

"You see, we're different."

"Okay, so you're different, what does that mean?" Cat asked, frustration present in her voice.

"We're vampires," Ròs explained.

"Vampires?" Cat began. "Vampires?" she asked again in disbelief. "Alright, that's it. I've heard enough of this crap. This is ridiculous. I'm not going to stand here and listen to this after the week I've just had!"

"But it's true, every word. Honest Catherine, we're vampires…and so are you," Trevor implored.

"What? Shut up! Rachel, Sam, are you just going to sit there and let them do this to me? Why aren't any of you saying anything? Uncle Michael, how can you, a priest, just stand there and not sat they're lying?! You honestly don't believe what these people are saying, right?" Cat's voice grew shaky as she looked Michael dead in the eyes and realized he wasn't going to tell her it was a lie.

"I wish I could Cat, but it's the truth," Michael replied softly.

Cat laughed fretfully. "I can't believe it. You're just as crazy as the rest of them."

"Catherine," Ròs said as she stood and made her way toward her, "trust us when we say, that you're a *Childe,* half vampire and half human." Cat's eyes widened as she listened to her aunt's words.

"I'm . . . a . . . *Childe*? A *Childe*?"

"Yes Cat, you are," Sam stated with a sigh.

"And on your sixteenth birthday, your vampire side began to take over. That's why we put you on those pills honey. Those pills help keep your other half at bay," Rachel explained.

"So wait, Dr. Bane is in on this too?" Cat asked in a huff.

"Yes, we've all known for quite some time now. Dr. Bane, Aldon, and even Taylor," Rachel continued.

"Do you hear yourselves? You're all flipping insane! What the hell's wrong with you people? I just can't deal with this right now. If you need me, I'll be in my room," Cat said and then began to turn toward the study door.

"Catherine Ròsaline Aldridge! You cannot walk away from this," Ròs growled while baring her fangs. Her eyes turned black as pitch.

As Cat began to turn back around, she asked, "What did you call me?" The moment she finished asking her question, Cat let out a slight scream as the sight before her startled her. Standing in front of her was the physical embodiment of something she thought was only a myth. *Vampires do exist?* Cat thought while staring at Ròs and Trevor's pearly white fangs and jet black eyes. Her knees grew a little wobbly as a wave of dizziness overcame her. "Why did you call me that?"

"Catherine Ròsaline Aldridge is your full birth name. Given to you by your *real* parents," Ròs explained.

Shaking out of her dizzied state, Cat asked, "So…what you're telling me is…that I'm like you…fangs and all?"

"Well, in a manner of speaking, yes. But you're special Catherine," Trevor replied.

"Why wasn't I told this earlier when all of that weird stuff was happening to me? Instead you let me believe I was sick or something?"

"Cat," Michael said, trying to put his arm around her again.

"Don't!" Cat said angrily, pushing away his arm. "Let me get this straight, you just told me that I'm adopted, and now I'm some *FREAK* of nature. Awesome," she remarked sarcastically with a hollow laugh. As angry tears slid down her cheeks, "So, what next? Are you going to tell me that people want to kill me?" Cat saw the shock registering on the faces before her. "People are out to kill me? You've got to be kidding. Right?" No one answered.

"Now Catherine, calm down. That's why we're here. We'd like for you to come with us. We can protect you," Ròs explained calmly with pleading eyes.

"We can take care of her too," Sam stated directly.

"But you don't know-"

"Well you don't know either," Rachel said, interrupting Ròs.

"Stop! You're sitting there arguing and acting like I'm not even here. This is my life we're talking about," Cat yelled. Holding her forehead, trying to ease the oncoming headache, "I need to think. I'm going up to my room, and I want to be left alone." Throwing her hands down to her side and scowling at everyone, "Do you understand? Alone! I'll let you know when I," she said pointing to her chest, "am ready to talk. This will be my decision and no one else's." As she turned and made her way to the door, "I mean it, no one follow me!" she shouted, slamming the door behind her. Hurrying up the stairs, Cat met Taylor coming out of his room.

"What's up Red Freak?"

"Don't start with me," she growled, glaring at him, as she continued toward her bedroom.

"What the hell was that all about?" he muttered to himself. As Taylor walked into the study he felt the tension was so thick he could cut it with a knife. "Okay, what's up with Cat, and who pissed her off?" he asked jokingly. After a few minutes of the adults explaining what happened, Taylor rolled his eyes at the mess they had made with Cat, each one putting the blame on the other for her meltdown. As far as he was concerned they were all responsible.

Hearing the sound of an engine starting and then tires squealing, Rachel ran to the front door, and threw it open. "It's Cat, she's running away!" she cried down the hallway.

"I'll go after her. I think you guys have done enough damage tonight. Don't worry, I'll bring her home," Taylor stated, grabbing his jacket and moving toward the front door.

"I'd like to accompany you, if that's okay? I promise I'll let you handle Catherine alone," Ròs said.

"Whatever, but you better let me do all the talking," Taylor replied, taking his car keys from the rack.

Ryan felt like a stalker. He had no reason to be on Nehalem Avenue at that time of night. He wondered what Cat would say if she saw him on her street. Suddenly an orange Jeep flew around the corner and Ryan swerved to the right as it sped by. He caught a quick glance of the driver. Noticing Cat's distinct fiery red hair, he pulled into the nearest driveway to turn around and follow her. Before he was done, another car sped by and Ryan recognized Taylor's Mustang in hot pursuit.

Cat ran down the steep path toward the desolate beach below. She headed for the trees that sheltered the barren clearing. She sat down heavily on the concrete foundation, visualizing how the cabin had looked from her nightmares.

Tears flowed freely down her face as she realized this was the last place she had been with her mother. Slouching, with her chest down to her knees, Cat rocked back and forth crying for the parents she never knew.

Ryan pulled up quickly into the parking lot as Taylor and a woman with bright red hair, whom he didn't recognize, were opening their doors. He immediately realized what she was.

"Beckford, what are you doing here?" Taylor asked, anger present in his voice.

"What's wrong with Cat?" Ryan ignored his question.

"None of your business, that's what, now just leave!" Taylor's face reddened as he started toward Ryan.

"Now you two, let's settle down. Hello, I'm Ròs Cowan, and you are?" she asked blocking Taylor's path.

"Ryan Beckford. I'm Cat's boyfriend."

"Yeah, but you're not wanted here right now!" Taylor tried to reach around Ròs for him only to have her push him back gently.

"It's a pleasure to meet you Ryan. I'm Catherine's aunt," Ròs said, lightly shaking his hand. "She's just a little upset at the moment. And Taylor needs to go and find her, don't you Taylor?" she asked, looking pointedly at him.

"Yeah, but I'm going alone!" he responded, glaring at Ryan.

"Of course. Ryan and I will just wait here for you, if that's okay?" Ròs smiled reassuringly at Taylor. Without another word, Taylor made his way down the path and followed Cat's fresh footprints in the sand.

"So, you're Catherine's boyfriend, huh? And a fellow vampire I see. Don't look surprised my dear, I can smell it on you," Ròs said as she watched Taylor walking toward the woods. Turning her attention to Ryan, "You care deeply for her, don't you?" Ryan nodded. "I can sense it. You will keep her secret, I have no worries about that. If I did, I would have already killed you by now," she laughed at the look on Ryan's face. "I am only kidding…well, kind of."

"Cat, Cat?" Taylor quietly whispered trying not to scare her. She lifted her head to look at him and Taylor's heart sank as he saw the pain in her eyes. As he joined Cat on the concrete foundation, he pulled her into his arms and held her as she sobbed loudly into his shirt, not caring that it was quickly soaked. He stroked her hair until she was pacified.

"Sorry about your shirt," she whispered.

"Yeah, you should be," he said, and then hugged her to him again. Cat was overwhelmed with the love he was projecting. Never in her wildest dreams had she thought he'd be the one to come and comfort her.

Taylor chuckled. “You know Cat, growing up, I resented Mom and Dad for bringing you into our family. Man was I jealous, and of course I even hated you a little at times. But you’ll always be my little sister. This last week I’ve wanted to just bust into your room and tell you how selfish you were being. But now I realize, you were hurt and feeling alone. I’m sorry I wasn’t there for you.”

Cat leaned her head against his shoulder, “I think I needed that week, especially with what was unloaded on me tonight. I mean, they told me I’m a *Childe*! A half-vampire! How the hell is that even possible? Don’t I scare you Taylor?”

He laughed. “Well, you don’t see me running do you?”

“So you knew? They told you?”

“Yeah, they told me. Oh, and believe me it took me a while to come to terms with it. But I did, because like I said you’re my sister.”

“I can’t believe Sam and Rachel took me in knowing that I was a freak.”

“Well they did, so just deal with it. Now, being half-vampire aside,” he said matter-of-factly, “I know you have a huge decision to make. Ròs and Trevor want to take you away, but we want you to stay here. Whatever you decide, I’ll have your back.” Cat smiled up at her brother. “But know this, if you leave us, a hole will be left. I’m not trying to make you feel guilty. I just want to let you know how I feel. How Mom and Dad feel. So kid, get up and let's go face this together. Tell them you need some time to figure out what *you* want to do," Taylor said, returning her smile. "Give me your hand Red Freak."

Cat scowled jokingly as he helped pull her to her feet. "That's Miss Red Freak to you, buddy." As they walked back to their cars, Taylor threw his arm around Cat's shoulders and pulled her close. She smiled, and swiped away the tear that had trickled down her cheek.

When they reached the parking lot, Taylor was relieved to see Ryan's car wasn't there. Ròs stood by the Mustang, watching the pair warily as they approached. Cat moved toward her aunt, shocking Ròs as she hugged her tightly. Ròs's throat constricted and words escaped her as she hugged back.

As Ròs watched Cat and Taylor settle into their vehicles, a quick vision shot through her head. *An ornate coffin, a gorgeous evil vampire, and the whisper of Catherine's name from his lips.* She gasped. "Cain is going to find out about her," she whispered under her breath. Ròs looked at Cat with worry in her eyes, as she began to drive away.

"Something wrong Ròs?" Taylor asked.

"No, nothing."

"Well come on then, get in. Cat's going to beat us home."

3
I Know What You Are

Cat opened her eyes and it was pitch black. She couldn't see anything. Her breathing sounded louder than usual and seemed to engulf her. Raising her head quickly, trying to sit up, she hit full force into something. "Oww! Damn that hurt!" she yelled in pain, rubbing her forehead. Feeling above her, Cat felt a soft, silky, fabric covering something solid. As she pressed her palms upward, she was met with resistance and couldn't budge whatever lay above her. Kicking to the front and side, she felt she was enclosed within a space. She began to panic. Her breathing grew heavier as she started pounding her fists about, hoping someone would hear. She tried to scream, but nothing came out. Cat began frantically pushing upward using all her strength, but nothing would budge. She took in a couple deep breaths trying to calm herself and then tried to focus. A beeping noise startled her and she realized it was her cell phone indicating a message. Digging in her pocket she found her cell and read the text:

Wake up Cat!

The number was unknown. By the light of her phone, Cat caught a glimpse of something next to her. Slowly, she turned to face it. Piercing jet black eyes bore into hers. The man's cold stare caused Cat to freeze in fear. He grinned, revealing his long fangs. "Catherine," he whispered. She let out a blood curdling scream and began pounding feverishly. He reached out for her, his evil laughter filling her ears.

Cat sat up violently in bed, breathing heavily. Her throat felt raw, as if she had been screaming for hours. She reached over to her night stand, her hand was shaking as she turned on her lamp, which filled the room with a soft glow. "Seriously Cat? Dreams about sleeping next to vampires? Really? I'm so over vampires! I don't care if they say I am one. I'm over it!" She pulled herself out of bed and she made her way to the bathroom. Cat splashed cold water on her face, and then grabbed for her hand towel.

Feeling pressure in her upper jaw, she moved closer to the mirror and opened her mouth wide. By the flicker of the night light she saw two long pearly white fangs descend from her gums. Her eyes widened with shock. “What the?” she exclaimed, flipping on the overhead light, and then realized her mind was not playing tricks on her. She was indeed staring into the face of her vampire side. She moved closer to the mirror, and examined her fangs, pulling her lips back to get a better look.

Hearing a knock at the bedroom door, Cat stiffened, putting her hand over her mouth, shielding her fangs. “One second!” she called out, her fangs causing a slight lisp.

“Is everything alright? I heard you screaming. Did you have another bad dream?” Rachel asked through the door.

“Yeah Mom, I did,” Cat called out. She had reverted back to calling Rachel “mom,” after a long discussion with her parents upon returning from the beach the previous night. On the ride home, Cat realized Taylor was right, that her mom and dad were suffering just as much as she was.

“Could you open the door please? I want to see if you’re okay.”

"Actually Mom, right now is probably not the best time," Cat replied nervously at the thought of her mom seeing her like this.

"Young lady, humor your mother and open the door." Cat tried to figure out what to do, but couldn't think of one good idea. Walking to the door, she kept her mouth covered as she opened it. Rachel looked at her confused with one eyebrow raised.

"See, everything's fine," Cat lisped through her hand.

"Why are you covering your mouth?"

"Severe case of halitosis," she joked, laughing hollowly.

"Oh, I see. Well as long as you're fine."

"Yeah, I'm heading back to bed now. I think I've met my nightmare quota for the night." Rachel scanned the room making sure everything was in place, and then kissed Cat on the forehead. Cat closed the door and leaned up against it, breathing a sigh of relief. She felt her mouth and groaned, realizing her fangs were still very much there. *Great, how will I explain these in public*? She thought as she climbed into bed.

Along with dark circles under her eyes from lack of sleep, Cat's fangs were still there the next morning. "OMG! It's Saturday and everyone's home! What am I going to do? I can't walk around like this!" Even though her family knew she was a *Childe*, Cat didn't feel comfortable showcasing that fact in front of them, proving that she truly was different.

She stood in front of her bathroom mirror and squeezed her eyes shut, concentrating, trying to make her fangs disappear. "Cat honey, it's trash day! Could you take the garbage from the kitchen out to the curb?" Rachel called from downstairs. Cat moaned and tried once more to make her fangs retract with no success. With no other recourse, she covered her mouth and made her way downstairs. Hearing Taylor's bedroom door open, she let out a tiny squeal and rushed passed him.

What's up with her this morning? Taylor asked himself.

Cat grabbed the trash, and peeked around the kitchen door to see Taylor leaving the house. She waited until she heard the revving of his Mustang, and then slowly crept her way to the front door. Sprinting to the trash can at the end of the drive way, she quickly took the top off the can and threw the bag inside.

"Yoo hoo, Catherine! You're starting the day late I see. And still in your pajamas huh?" Maude, Cat's nosey next door neighbor, asked smugly. "You know when I was your age, I wasn't allowed out of the house looking like you currently do. You should always try to look your best in the presence of others dear," she continued lecturing Cat.

Cat wished she could bare her fangs and growl at Maude just to see her either die of fright or run away screaming, tearing at her hair. *Ugh, but knowing her, she'd just say that I'm being weird, or eccentric,* Cat thought as she grinned at Maude from behind her hand.

"You silly girl. What on earth are you doing, covering your mouth like that?" Maude asked, peering through her thick coke bottle glasses.

"Sorry Mrs. Roberts, I've got to go," Cat said muffled through her hand as she ran for the front door.

"Well I never. That girl is so strange. Runs in the family I guess," Maude muttered under her breath as she waved to Sam, who was in his pajamas mowing the tall, soggy grass that was currently their lawn.

Later that night, standing on the roof of their two story Victorian house, Cat swayed back and forth on the edge looking out onto Nehalem Avenue. Staring down at the ground, she wondered what would happen if she jumped. *Will I land on my feet? Can vampires even break bones? Maybe I can float like those vampires in Robert Craven's novels?* She thought, lifting one leg and beginning to step off. Hesitating, she quickly pulled her foot back and sat down, feeling dizzy. "This is totes crazy! I can't be a vampire! They don't exist," she murmured under her breath. Running her tongue along her fangs, she groaned at the fact they still hadn't retracted.

A fat drop of rain landed on the back of Cat's hand and she looked up at the sky. There were no stars. Dark ominous clouds loomed overhead. She saw a quick flash of lightning in the distance, followed by the light rumbling sound of thunder. The storm had come up suddenly. As the rain began to increase, Cat rushed off the roof and made her way through the open attic bedroom window, closing it behind her.

Cat's bedside clock registered midnight and she was showing no signs of being tired. She felt that her body was becoming more nocturnal, thus the reason for her slight insomnia. Of course it didn't help that she had recently gone through two traumatic revelations. Her mind was restless with more questions than ever before. Wide awake, she gazed out her window at the rain, thinking back to what her Aunt Ròs had said. *I can't believe there are people out there that want me dead. I mean they don't even know me, and they want me dead?* Cat remembered the journal that she received while visiting The Purple Door, a unique store in the strange little town of Wedgewick Village. She had only read a couple of entries out of the small and tattered brown journal before it went missing. What she had read though made Cat think her current situation eerily mirrored that of the person who wrote it.

Cat gasped as a huge gust of wind blew her bay window wide open, and swept through the room. Papers went flying from her desk and were strewn about the floor as rain drenched the cushions of the window seat. Cat struggled to close the window against the strong wind. As she reached to latch the lock, a flash of lightning illuminated the balcony outside. She was startled to see a figure standing in front of her and let out a quick scream before she realized it was Ryan. Quickly covering her mouth, "Ryan, what are you doing? You scared the crap out of me!"

"Sorry, are you going make me stand out here all night? Or are you going to let me in?" Cat opened the window and Ryan stepped in, a puddle of water quickly formed at his feet. She grabbed a towel from the bathroom and threw it to him. He thanked her for the towel as he began to wipe his face.

"What are you doing? I mean it's after midnight," Cat whispered while trying to make her hand positioned over her mouth look natural.

"Well, I think it's perfectly normal for a boyfriend to worry about a girlfriend who doesn't return his phone calls."

"Yeah, about that. I'm really sorry. I just needed to be alone for a bit. Figure some stuff out. You know, slay some personal demons and such," she joked, trying to sound genuine, but instead it sounded hollow to her ears.

"Oh, I see. How did that go?" he asked as he began drying his hair.

"Uh, quite unsuccessful really," she replied. Moving forward, Ryan brushed a rogue strand of hair dangling in Cat's face behind her ear. He smiled at her, making her blush. Grabbing her by the waist he pulled her close, the towel now resting around his neck.

"What's with the hand? Kind of makes it hard to kiss you, don't ya think?" Cat moved in closer and nestled up to Ryan's shoulder burying her mouth into the towel.

"Ryan, I've really missed you. And it was really sweet of you to come and check on me. But if my parents catch you in here, we're both dead," she stated, hugging him closer and getting her clothes more wet in the process.

"Cat, I know what you are," he said softly into her ear.

"What?" Cat asked absently. Hearing the attic stairs creak slightly, she glanced at her door. "Ryan, you better get out of here, someone's coming!" Turning back to look at him, her eyes grew wide at the sight before her. Gone were his baby blue eyes, and in their place were jet black ones. Two long fangs framed his mouth as he grinned. Cat screamed involuntarily, and the sound of the creaking stairs grew faster and louder. As her bedroom door flew open, she spun around to see her mom rushing in. Cat turned back quickly to look at Ryan, but he was gone. The window was open and her curtains were billowing in the rain soaked wind.

"Cat, what's wrong? I heard you whispering up here and then you screamed."

"I thought I saw something outside, but it was nothing," she replied, as she rushed forward to shut the window, still stunned about what just happened. Rachel raised an eyebrow at her daughter.

"But it sounded like you were talking to someone. Were *they* here? Tell me the truth Cat," Rachel demanded.

"No, *they* weren't, I swear. I just spooked myself. I'm going back to bed now," she replied, climbing under her covers. Rachel gave Cat one last questioning look and then closed the door behind her. Cat panicked. "Oh crap, I didn't cover my mouth!" she said and then felt her teeth. There were no fangs. *How did I make them go away? Did mom see them? Did Ryan?* Staring at her ceiling, Cat tried to take in all that just happened. *Wait a minute, Ryan's a vampire too? What the hell's going on?* She sprang out of bed and grabbed her cell phone from the top drawer of her desk and dialed Ryan's number. The call failed to go through. She tried to text him, but it wouldn't send. "No bars, damn storm," she huffed.

Frustrated, Cat tossed the cell phone back onto her desk. She plopped back onto her bed, and shivered, realizing that her gown and the sheet she pulled over her, were soaked. Sighing, she yanked the wet sheet off of her and tossed it into the hamper along with her night gown. She put on a pair of comfy pink and white pajamas and hopped back into bed. Cat picked up the tattered copy of *Red Twilight*, written by her favorite horror author Robert Craven, and tried unsuccessfully to occupy her mind with reading.

Cat dialed Ryan's number, and in frustration, threw the phone on her bed when she was immediately sent to voicemail. *So this is what it feels like to be ignored*, she thought. It had been days since the incident where Ryan revealed himself to be a vampire, and Cat had called so many times she lost count. All of her texts went through, but there were no replies. *Maybe this is how my friends feel. I've totally shut them out of my life. I can't keep this up, they don't deserve this. So what if I'm adopted. They can handle that. The other thing maybe not so much, but I'll just keep that to myself,* she thought while picking up her phone to call Amanda. Cat wavered, putting the phone down, and groaned at her stubbornness. Wanting to ease her frustration, she decided to go for a drive. She headed downstairs and was stopped by her dad.

"Where are you off to young lady?"

"Uh, I need to get out of the house Dad. I think I'm coming down with a case of cabin fever. Just going for a quick drive."

"Oh, well aren't you worried that you'll bump into your friends while you're out? You know the ones that you've been ignoring for the past couple of weeks?" he asked, frowning at her. Cat didn't respond. "Honey, you're going to have to talk to them eventually, you know that, right?"

She looked down at the floor and then back to Sam, her eyes filled with guilt. "I know Dad, I will," she sighed. "But right now I need to drive. Is that okay with you?" Sam nodded with slight disappointment on his face, and then headed toward his study to read his daily paper.

"Cat, please be careful," he said over his shoulder.

"Will do Dad."

Cat took the long way to the beach. She needed to clear her head, and driving with the windows down and music blasting did just that. She tried not to think too much about her friends or Ryan and just focused on getting to the beach. When she arrived, it was empty. The sky was overcast and there was a light fog that covered the sand and forest ground. "Not really beach weather I guess," Cat said to herself as she scanned the lifeless area.

She hurried to the barren clearing and sat on the concrete slab, trying to focus. Looking at the trees surrounding her, she began to wonder what vampire abilities she possessed. Spying a large tree to her right, Cat wondered if she would be able to scale it. *If Bartholomew Drake can do it, I should be able to, right?* She thought as she readied herself. “Alright Cat, you can do this,” she stated confidently, staring up at the huge obstacle.

The thought of being a half vampire was surreal and scary, but Cat was trying to embrace it. She needed to begin honing her skills to prepare for what Ròs told her was coming her way. As she stared intently at the tree, Cat tried to imagine herself ascending it effortlessly. This was her first attempt, and she was hoping for beginners luck.

Bolting toward the tree, Cat leapt into the air, catching her footing on the trunk, and propelled herself upward. Digging her nails into the bark, she pulled herself along. She paused, realizing how high up she was and looked down at the ground. “Holy crap! I did not just do that!” Cat panicked as she started losing her grip and began to slip down the tree, her nails ripping along the trunk. She tried to stop herself, but instead lost her footing and fell to the ground, sending a large dust cloud swirling into the air. Dragging herself to her feet, she began to pick the twigs and leaves out of her hair and dusted off her shirt and jeans. “Okay, one more time!” she announced, determined to do it.

An hour flew by, and after many "one-more-time" failed attempts, Cat found herself gazing out onto Oldes Bay from the highest branch of the tree. The wind blew through her thick fiery red hair as she sat there taking in the awe-inspiring scene before her. She wished that she could share it with Ryan and her friends.

Safely back on the ground, Cat gazed at the concrete foundation and thought back to the nightmare she had about a year ago. Hearing a rustling noise behind her, she quickly turned and collided with something, causing her to fall backward. Looking up, she saw it was Ryan.

"Cat? What are you doing out here?" he asked, reaching down to help her up.

"I could ask you the same thing," she said, taking his hand as she stood with his assistance. "And why haven't you returned any of my calls?"

"I guess you know how it feels now, huh Miss Colvin," he replied dryly. "Besides, I didn't know how to approach you after that night."

"Hey, you can't just show your fangs to a girl and then expect her to not freak a little. Plus you ran off without saying a word."

"It was either that, or deal with your mother, no offense," he replied with a grin. Ryan noticed Cat's gaze return to the concrete foundation in the middle of the clearing. "So, back to my original question, what exactly are you doing here?"

"I just came here to think," she answered distractedly, looking at the foundation.

"Well, I can think of a lot nicer places you can do that instead of this run down bare patch of land, with a shoddy piece of concrete at the center of it."

"It's more than that to me Ryan," Cat replied, looking at him.

"What aren't you telling me?"

"This was the last place I was with my mother. My birth mother I mean," she answered quietly.

"Oh, I'm so sorry. I didn't know."

"Last year, I had this dream…well really a nightmare. I saw a weathered cabin in this clearing. Inside was a woman frantically shoving clothes into a bag. She was afraid. I could feel how scared she was. At the same time I could feel her courage. She was protecting something…and that something was me. There were men outside, taunting her. They set fire to the building and watched it burn to the ground. That evil laughter…I don't think I'll ever forget that. It's weird how I'm able to remember something so vivid even though I was only a baby at the time. She escaped through that trap door, there in the foundation," Cat said pointing to it. "I've tried opening it, but it won't budge. The fire probably sealed it or something." Cat paused and Ryan placed his hand on her shoulder. Looking into his baby blues and then back to the foundation, she said, "She was so beautiful Ryan. Truly beautiful."

"So what happened after that?"

"I guess she took me to my Uncle Michael's, and was never heard from again. He received word that she had died, but no one knows how. It's really sad when you think about it." Tears began to well up in Cat's eyes and she quickly brushed them away.

"I'm so sorry Cat."

"Okay, I answered your question, now answer mine. So, what are you doing here?"

"Alright, I'll tell you, but you have to close your eyes," he replied.

"Do I really have to close my eyes?"

"Just humor me. You'll love it, I promise," he said, extending his hand out to her. Cat's eyes narrowed as she glared at him. Groaning, she closed her eyes and took hold of his hand.

"Where are you taking me Mr. Beckford? And how many girls have fallen for this trick?" Cat asked, allowing herself to be led by him.

"You're the one and only. And it's a secret. Don't worry, I'll tell you when you can open them."

"The one and only? So I'm that special huh?"

"Yeah, I like to think so."

Cat felt the ground under her feet go from dirt, to sand, to rock. The sound of the waves crashing against the shore was loud in her ears. They stopped and Ryan squeezed her hand. "Okay, open your eyes." Cat was amazed at the sight before her. They were inside of a large cave. Scanning the area, she saw that it looked lived in. Training and exercise equipment was strewn about, and several pieces of patio furniture sat off to the side of a large, black, tumbling mat in the far corner of the space.

"Ryan, what is this place?" she asked, looking around.

"This is my little hide-away. It's where I come to relax. I also train here."

"Train? For what?"

"Well, you know, I have my skills as a-"

"Vampire?" Cat finished his sentence.

"Yeah, vampire. I train for control. Being a vampire around humans can be challenging. You've got to learn to blend in. Training allows me to rein in my primal urges and be able to hide and control my abilities," he explained as he placed his hand on Cat's shoulder. "I know finding out you're half vampire was a little overwhelming, but-"

"Wait, how do you know that?"

"Well, I always kind of knew you were special, but I just recently found out what you are. Please don't be mad at me, I know I should've told you earlier, but it wasn't my place," Ryan explained. "I really wanted to talk to you-"

"Could you train me? Teach me how to control…whatever it is I can do?" she asked, interrupting him.

"Uh, well-"

"You're the only one I can talk to openly about this. You were a great tutor, I'm sure you'll be a great trainer. I trust you," Cat said, gazing deeply into his eyes. "Besides you kind of owe me for keeping this secret from me."

Ryan pulled her close, kissed her soundly on the lips, and then whispered, "okay" into her ear. "So what would you like to learn first?"

"Uh, how do you control your teeth? Sometimes mine won't retract, and it's a real pain. I had a recent scare with those babies, and with school starting soon it won't be as easy to hide them. I'd hate to think what might happen," Cat said, feeling her mouth.

"It takes a little practice and a lot of thought. Of course sometimes it's near impossible to stop them. Like if you get too angry or too scared. It's like a reflex. Watch." His teeth began to lower and then slid into place. Ryan then closed his eyes, and Cat watched as they slowly retracted as if it took no effort at all. "Now Cat, I want you to think about your teeth. In your mind I want you to see them sliding down. Try it." Ryan watched as she closed her eyes and saw frown lines marring her forehead as she concentrated. He grinned as two white pointed canines descended and touched her bottom lip."

"Wow, that was easy," she said, her teeth slightly getting in the way of her tongue.

"Don't worry, with time you'll lose the lisp. Now close your eyes again and see your teeth sliding back inside your gums. Go ahead try it." He watched as she clenched her hands, tensing her body. "No you're trying too hard," he said, and then Cat gave a sigh of frustration. "Relax, just let it happen." He grinned as her teeth slowly withdrew. "There, see that wasn't so hard was it?'

"I can't believe I did it. Thanks Ryan, I only hope it works that easy when I really need it too," Cat exclaimed.

Ryan laughed. "So, what else would you like to learn?"

"Actually, I have a quick question before we continue," Cat said, studying Ryan's facial features.

"Okay, shoot," he replied, a little perplexed by the look she was giving him.

"How old are you…really?"

"I'm seventeen, why?"

"I thought vampires were old…like, really old," Cat stated confused.

"Well most are, but our coven is kind of different."

"Different how?"

"It's a long story Cat, and I don't want to bore you with the details," Ryan answered, dodging her stare.

"I've got time, it's not like either one of us is immortal or anything," she said sarcastically.

"Later," he snapped, making her shy back with surprise.

"Okay…touchy subject…got it," she said.

"Sorry, I just don't feel like talking about it right now."

"So, could you at least tell me how many vampires there are in Astoria?" she asked hesitantly.

"Well, there are my parents…and a few others." He stopped and looked at Cat.

"What? Don't you trust me?" Cat cocked her head to one side, a smile now missing from her face.

"Of course I do. I'm just not sure if it's my place to tell you about the others," Ryan answered, his eyes not meeting hers.

"Okay, but I think I can guess. Let me see there's Amelia, the Stone Twins definitely, and of course Isaac. But if he is, then that means Hannah is too," she said, the crease in her forehead deepening. “But Hannah’s so sweet. She can’t possibly be a full-blooded vampire.” Ryan laughed and pulled her closer. “What’s so funny?” she asked, playfully pushing him back and keeping him away at arm’s length.

“You. Aren’t you sweet? And aren’t you a vampire?”

“Well yeah, I guess so,” Cat replied.

“Then why are you so shocked about Hannah?” he asked, swatting her hands down and capturing her in a bear hug.

“I guess it’s just weird. I mean there are books and movies where vampires are good, but Hannah? You’ve got to admit it’s a stretch.” Cat smiled, returning the grin on his handsome face.

“What about me?” he asked, resting his forehead on hers.

“I don’t know. You do look a little evil!” Cat giggled as Ryan pulled back, looking at her as if offended, and then silenced her with a kiss.

As the sun began to set, the pair exited the cave. Ryan took Cat’s hand and spun her around to face him. “You might want to hold on tight,” he said with a mischievous grin as he grabbed her around the waist and pulled her close. *I can’t believe I’m about to do this. I hate heights. Imagine that, a vampire that hates heights,* Ryan thought. Before Cat could get in a word, they slowly began to rise into the air. She lunged forward and squealed, grabbing his shoulders tightly. As they rose higher, the low lying sun cast their long silhouettes on the beach. Cat dug her face into Ryan's chest, too scared to let go. "Cat, open your eyes," he whispered softly into her ear. She slowly opened them and lifted her head.

Looking around, "We must be at least fifteen feet up," she said in awe. The ocean breeze gently caressed her face and she smiled. "Ryan, this is amazing!" Cat felt free, almost as if she was floating by herself and Ryan wasn't holding her anymore.

"All you needed was a little push Cat. Look, you're doing it on your own." Cat glanced down at the beach and then back at Ryan. Her smile turned into a look of horror, realizing that she was indeed on her own. She screamed as she began to tumble toward the sand. Ryan plunged down after her. He extended his arm and caught her by the belt just before she hit the ground. Cat was breathing heavily, her face inches from the sand.

"Well, I guess that ends lesson two," Ryan joked as he lifted her into his arms and slowly touched down on the beach. "Are you alright?" he asked while looking at her shocked face. Regaining her composure, Cat scowled as if mad at him and then burst into giggles.

"That…was…awesome!" she exclaimed. Ryan laughed and then put his arm around her shoulders.

As the pair made their way toward their cars, Cat's cell phone beeped. Looking at her phone, "Crap, my mother has called me like a thousand times! She's going to kill me!" Ryan gave Cat a worried look as she pressed speed dial to call home. "Hey Mom, sorry I missed your calls. There was no signal here at the beach. I know, I know, I'm on my way home. I know, curfew. Be there in a little bit. Love you too Mom," Cat said and then hung up the phone.

"She didn't seem that upset, I guess," Ryan commented.

"Oddly, no. Just my *average* worried mother," she joked, smiling at him. "Thanks for this, I really needed it. And sorry for being super flaky recently, but can you really blame me?"

Ryan placed his hand to Cat's chin, gently turning her face to his, "Just don't make a habit of it Red Hot, okay?" Cat smiled, and Ryan smiled back.

On the drive home, Cat was in deep contemplation over what Ryan had said earlier. *I wonder what makes them all so different from other vampires. And why did Ryan snap at me when I asked? And they all eat food too, which is odd because I thought vampires only drank blood. Damn all these secrets! And damn Hollywood for lying to me! Robert Craven, you sure do have it all wrong.*

4
Coming Clean

Picking up her cell, Cat dialed Julie's number.

"Hey Cat, what's up?" Julie answered.

"Um, I need you to do me a favor."

"Of course, name it."

After several minutes of conversation Cat ended the call, and then rushed to the shower to get ready. As she ran down the stairs, her wet hair flew behind her. Rachel exited the kitchen and watched as Cat made for the front door. "Bye mom, going to Julie's. Wish me luck, love you," Cat called out, as she quickly opened the door and shut it before Rachel could respond.

As Cat pushed open the back door to Julie's house, she noticed the kitchen was empty. She quietly made her way through the house to the French doors leading to the family room. Julie had left the doors open slightly, allowing Cat to hear to the conversation within.

"I emailed her this morning, but it was returned. Her inbox was at its max. Then I tried her cell, and it went straight to voicemail again. I know her mom says she's okay and just to be patient, but frankly I'm a little pissed! We're her best friends, and it's not right she's treating us this way!" Amanda's angry voice came through the opening.

"Maybe it's my fault. I must have done something wrong," Elle's tearful voice came next.

"I think one of us needs to just go over there, and, I don't know. But do something," Matt interjected.

"Guys, calm down, it's no one's fault." Julie stopped as she saw the door open and Cat walk in. Three pairs of eyes looked at her in shock. Julie smiled. Elle was first to move, running up to Cat and flinging her arms around her so tightly that she could hardly breathe. Amanda crossed her arms and put on her "I'm angry at you" look, and Matt just stared as if he saw a ghost.

"Hey guys, I think it's about time I apologize. I know I've treated you all like crap, and I'm really sorry. You guys didn't deserve this," Cat stated.

"You're sorry? We haven't seen or heard from you in three weeks! Three weeks! We've never gone longer than a day without at least a phone call. But no, you didn't care that we were suffering. Matt even cried!" Amanda yelled, her face turning red.

"Hey I didn't cry, you did! Just last night in fact," Matt stated glaring at Amanda.

"Please guys, don't fight. Sit down and let me tell you what's been going on." Everyone took a seat except for Amanda, who continued to stand in front of them with her arms still crossed. "Amanda, come sit down," Cat said, patting the cushion next to her on the couch.

Amanda plopped down heavily beside her, "This better be good, 'cuz right now I'm really upset!"

"On the last day of school, when I got home, I walked in on my family talking about me. I found out I'm…adopted," Cat said quietly.

"Aw Cat," Elle murmured breaking the silence. Matt sighed, at a loss at what to say next.

"Is that all?" asked Amanda impatiently. "You put us through all of this hell for that? I can't imagine what you've done to your parents!" Cat turned red with total embarrassment at the truth in Amanda's blunt words. She had hurt her family. She had hurt her friends.

"I know I've been a jerk. And yeah, you're right I've hurt you guys. And I guess I've been selfish too, not thinking about your feelings either, but I want to apologize. I really hope you can forgive me," she pleaded, looking at each one of them. Cat was immediately enveloped in Amanda's arms, and she could feel her shaking. Pulling back a little, she saw tears running down Amanda's face.

"Don't you ever, ever, do this again Catherine Colvin! We love you and will always have your back," she sobbed. Julie and Elle came over and joined the two with tears of their own.

"Geez, girls. Ask me again why I put up with all of you," Matt quipped.

"Because you love us!" Elle reached over and grabbed him, pulling him roughly into the group. Cat swore she saw a tear in his eye too.

"Michael, do you have any garlic? I can't seem to find any," Ròs asked standing in the pantry.

"No, I got rid of it, like I did the crosses. I figured you couldn't be around that stuff."

"Hollywood and their crazy made up myths. For your information the first vampire coven was Italian. Take an

Italian's garlic away, and you'll start a war," she stated looking at Michael's grin.

"I guess I have a lot to learn. I should've realized that. Cat really loves garlic, and she often helps me in the church. I feel like such a fool."

"Don't fret over it Michael. Up until a few days ago you had no idea that we even existed. In real life I mean. Some legends are true though. Old vampires, for instance, cannot be exposed to sunlight, because we receive much more than a tan. Oh, and a well-placed stake through the heart can do us in as well. And there is always the old fashioned burning method. Or, of course there's also beheading," she said matter-of-factly, stirring the pot of delicious smelling marinara sauce on the stove. Michael cringed at the word beheading. "Oh, and don't worry about turning into one of us if we get a little peckish. You'd have to drink our blood after to change," Ròs said and then laughed it off.

Michael laughed nervously. "Well I guess that's kind of a relief…kind of."

Ròs laughed again. "Your dinner is almost ready, and Cat should be here soon. So we should probably start setting the table."

Michael watched as the beautiful woman moved gracefully around his kitchen. For a vampire that didn't eat food, Ròs was a wonderful cook and always insisted on making every meal.

After the first night, Michael had offered for them to stay with him until Cat made up her mind. He really liked the Cowans. They were great house guests, always helping out around his little cottage. He had given Emma, the church's housekeeper, two weeks off to go and visit her family just in case they did anything suspicious. He needn't have worried though, because most of the time he forgot they were vampires, and instead thought of them as mere mortals.

"So Ròs, Trevor, do you still plan on taking Cat from us?" Michael asked, worried about their response.

Ròs laughed. "As if Cat would allow us to just take her. She's quite the strong-willed girl, that one. Just like her parents were. No, she shall make up her own mind and we'll act accordingly," Ròs replied while removing the bread from the oven.

"Besides, she seems to be well taken care of here," Trevor interjected. Michael smiled and was relieved to hear their answer.

"Hello, anybody home?" Cat's voice came from the hallway. She moved into the kitchen and stood in awe at the scene before her. Ròs was standing at the stove with her long red hair tied back, wearing a bright red apron, stirring a pot. Trevor was setting the dining room table for two and Michael was exiting the pantry with a bottle of sparkling apple cider in tow. It looked like a normal family getting ready to sit down for dinner.

"Oh Catherine, don't you look lovely tonight. We're just about ready. Just have a seat and I'll be right there," Ròs's soothing voice had her moving to the nearest chair.

"Do you need any help?" Cat asked.

"No sweetie, your uncles and I have it all under control."

Cat watched on as everyone continued setting up for dinner. The one odd thing that she noticed as she scanned the space was there were blankets covering all the windows. *Hmmm, I guess those block out the sunlight*, she thought. As everyone joined her in the dining room, Cat found herself sitting across from her aunt at the head of the dinner table, with her uncles on either side.

"Cat, you look different," Michael commented as he noticed his niece's happier demeanor.

"Yeah, I finally sat down today and told my friends." Cat jumped when Michael dropped the fork he was holding onto his plate. "Oh, no, I told them I'm adopted, not the other thing. I've kind of been avoiding them since school let out, but they forgave me. I still can't believe I was so stupid."

"Of course they'd forgive you. You're a wonderful young lady who would only surround herself with compassionate friends. I'm so happy you took that step. What about your parents?" Ròs asked

"I'm going to talk to them when I get home. I realize I've hurt them too. And before you ask me, I haven't made my decision yet, please give me a few more days, okay?"

"Of course Catherine. We understand how hard this is for you, and we're very patient. I mean we're immortals after all. Now you two eat. You men just talk too much and the food is getting cold." Ròs and Cat laughed at their dinner companion's puzzled faces.

Two hours later, Cat pulled into her driveway. Her stomach was tied in knots thinking about the conversation she was about to have with her parents.

"Yoo hoo Catherine. You're cutting it a little close to curfew aren't you dear?" a sickeningly sweet voice called out.

"Great, just great! Nosy Maude and little Fredricka, just what I need," she murmured to herself. "Hey Mrs. Roberts. Almost, I've got about 25 minutes still," she said out loud, pasting a smile on her face. Fredricka, her annoying little poodle, lunged forward making Maude stumble. Maude grabbed ahold of the spare tire on the back of Cat's Jeep to stop herself from falling.

"Fredricka, bad girl! You almost made mummy fall," she chastised the small pooch who had grabbed Cat's shoelace, and began pulling it with all her might.

"So who does this belong to, this ugly orange contraption?" Maude asked. Cat knew Maude had seen her driving it and that is was hers, but she just needed confirmation.

"It's mine. Isn't it gorgeous. I love orange, such a warm color don't you think?" Cat replied mockingly.

"No, I think it's positively dreadful. Definitely not a young ladies vehicle, that's for sure. I don't know what your parents were thinking when they bought it for you. It's not even your birthday. And also with you being on restriction and all. That's what's wrong with the younger generation today, spoiled rotten you are," Maude rambled on, not noticing that Cat's attention was centered on the small poodle that was determined to eat her shoe. Cat gently nudged her away, which Fredricka didn't like, and reacted by viciously growling at her and clamping down on the front of her sneaker.

"Fredricka! Leave Catherine's shoe alone," Maude demanded, pulling at the leash, causing the little animal to let go of Cat's shoe and growl at her. "Do we have to go home and have a talking to? You don't talk back to mummy like that, wait until I tell Daddy." To Cat's surprise Maude turned around and made her way back to her house, apparently forgetting Cat was even there. She knew that *Daddy,* Mr. Roberts, could care less about Fredricka's bad behavior.

Cat's thoughts were interrupted by Taylor's car entering the driveway. She smiled as she saw her brother's girlfriend Trish sitting in the passenger seat. The beautiful brunette's usually spunky demeanor was absent, as she stared back at Cat with an uneasy smile. Cat realized she hadn't seen Trish since she found out she was adopted, and not wanting to make things awkward, she knew she had to put her at ease.

"Hey guys, where have you been?" Cat asked as the two exited the vehicle.

"Went to the movies. Hey, what are you all dressed up for?" Taylor asked.

"I was visiting the Aunt and Uncles for an early dinner. You know with the whole curfew and all. We had a really good time."

"What did you guys talk about?" he asked, not sure if he really wanted to know.

"This and that. I was just going in to talk with Mom and Dad, so you might as well join the party."

"I guess I should be heading home right about now anyways. Don't want to interrupt family stuff," Trish said.

"Let me take you home," Taylor stated.

"No that's alright. I just live right around the block, and I've got about ten minutes until curfew. No big deal. This is important Taylor. You should go," she replied and then kissed him on the cheek. As she began to walk away, "I'll see you tomorrow Tay. See you later Cat."

"Bye Trish." Cat waved to her, feeling bad about her walking home alone.

"Well let's get this over with," Taylor replied, as dread settled in his stomach like a huge rock.

As they walked into the house, they heard their parents' voices coming from the study. With Cat leading them, she pushed open the door, revealing their mom and dad sitting on the overstuffed leather couch, Sam's arm was around Rachel.

"I need to talk to you," Cat blurted out, causing worry to spring into Rachel's eyes, and a frown to appear on Sam's face.

"Of course honey, come in and take a seat. Oh Taylor, come in and have a seat too." Taylor sat down next to Sam as Cat leaned up against her dad's desk, willing her legs to stop shaking.

"Today, I decided to fix things with my friends, it was way overdue…I also realized that I've hurt you all the most…and, I'm sorry." Cat saw her mom was about to speak and shook her head. "No, mom, let me finish. When I found out I was adopted, I felt like my life had been a lie. It's hard to explain, but in my head I became an outsider, belonging to no one. I felt alone. I'm sorry it took me this long to figure out what you've done for me. You've given me a home, and so much love, and I've been selfish by shutting you out. All I want is your forgiveness." Cat watched as a tear rolled down her mom's cheek, and her dad swallowed hard as if something was stuck in his throat. The room was quiet and the grandfather clock in the foyer seemed unusually loud. Aided by a gentle shove from Sam, Rachel stood up and put her arms around Cat, hugging her close.

"We love you so much Cat. There's nothing to be sorry for. I wish we had told you the truth sooner. But the real truth is, you're our daughter and always will be." Rachel held her, gently stroking her hair.

"I guess I even like you a lot. Ow, what was that for," Taylor said looking at Sam after he elbowed his son in his side. "Okay, but you know I hate all that mushy stuff. I guess I love ya too," he said, grinning at Cat.

"Cat," Sam began, then took a deep breath, "Oh hell, come here and give me a hug," he demanded, to which she promptly obeyed. They all began laughing as she fell onto her dad's lap and everyone piled on top.

Several minutes later, with Cat sitting between her parents, she cleared her throat. “I want to stay with you. But if it means that it’ll put you all in danger, I’ll go with Ròs and Trevor. I couldn’t bear the thought of any of you getting hurt because of me.” Sam sighed, looking at Rachel over Cat’s head.

“We don’t want you to go, and don’t worry about our safety. We’ll be just fine. I’m so happy. I could just eat a gallon of ice cream,” Sam shouted.

“Now Sam you know it’s bad for your cholesterol.” Seeing his unhappy expression, Rachel said, “Well, maybe half a gallon.” Cat giggled as her dad jumped up and did an impromptu dance in the middle of the floor. The three looked at one another and rolled their eyes as he danced out of the room, on his way to the kitchen.

Taylor asked how Cat’s friends had reacted to her apology and she eagerly told them all the details from when she called Julie until she came home.

The following day, Cat sat in her dad’s study with everyone gathered. All eyes were on her as she stood in front of them. “I’ve made my decision. I don’t want to hurt your feelings, but I can’t come with you,” she said looking at Ròs and Trevor. “I thought long and hard about this, and I belong here. I know by staying, I could place myself and my family in danger, but this is where I feel I belong. Please don’t be mad at me. I'm so glad I got to meet you, and now know where I come from. Of course it'll take a while for me to accept the whole vampire thing, but for right now I'm just plain old Cat. Who has a rare blood disorder, and that's how I want it to be. Do you understand?" Her eyes pleaded with them as she waited anxiously for their answer.

"We knew what you were going to tell us today. I cannot say that we're not deeply disappointed, but we understand. The Colvin's have taken such great care of you, and for that we will always be grateful," Ròs said glancing at Sam and Rachel. "I know if William and Erika were here today, they'd be very proud of you Catherine." Digging in her dark green, leather coat pocket, "I brought something with me that I want to give to you." Ròs handed Cat a small wooden box. Inside she found an ornate gold locket.

"It's beautiful Ròs," Cat said as she examined it.

"Try opening it," Ròs said. As Cat popped the clasp open, she found a picture of an extremely handsome man and a beautiful woman inside.

"Is that-"

"Yes, it's Erika and William." Ròs pulled a gold chain from around her neck and showed it to Cat. "I also wear the same locket. If you look at the back, you'll notice an intricate Celtic knot. That is the sign of our coven in Ireland, the Dearga.

Now, this locket is very special, please take very good care of it," she explained with a smile.

"So, this might be a dumb question, but how is there a picture of my father in the locket? I thought vampires didn't cast a reflection."

"Ah yes, well you're mostly right. A vampire has a way of controlling what they want others to see. Most vampires hate to be seen or known to exist, so they remove their reflection," Ròs explained.

"I wish I would've known that like five yearbook pictures ago."

Ròs laughed. "Oh no, your vampire powers have only fully manifested in the last year or so Catherine. You were still mostly human up until the day you turned sixteen. Besides, a Childe is different from a regular vampire anyway. You generally have no control over what the outward world sees. Your vampire side does, and sometimes you might find yourself fighting it for control. Kind of like a split personality."

"Great, that's all I need right now…a split personality," Cat groaned.

"But you have nothing to worry about because you're on quite the appetite suppressant, or so I'm told. I'm not sure how I feel about those pills they make you take, but if they stop your vampire side from completely taking over, then I guess it's a good thing you take them."

"So, are there any other things that I should be made aware of? You know, just so there are no more surprises?"

"Not that I can think of now," Ròs replied, searching her memory, with her hand about her chin.

"Well we best be off, got a lot of ground to cover you know," Trevor stated while wrapping his arm around Ròs's shoulders.

Cat smiled. "I don't know how to thank you guys. I hope you'll keep in touch with us and come back to visit," Cat said, looking at them hopefully.

"Rest assured Cat, we shall return," Trevor replied.

Cat stood on the porch watching as Michael's car pulled out of the driveway, and made its way down the hill. She felt sad until she turned and found her parents standing in the doorway, looking so happy. *Yes, I've definitely made the right decision.*

Standing in the Parliament's Great Hall, Andrei tried to control his temper and avoid the eruption of his fangs. The impossible woman before him made it a difficult task.

"So when did you arrive back at the castle?" Lisbeth inquired.

"A few days ago," Andrei replied.

"And you are just now seeking me out? So what news do you bring from your trip to Astoria?" she asked, her patience wearing thin.

"I still have no leads on the Childe, if that is what you are asking."

"What do you mean you still have no leads on the Childe? What have you been doing this whole time?!" she asked in frustration, and bared her fangs. Andrei gave her a withering look. "What of my brother Lucien then? Has his condition improved?"

"No, he is still as stubborn as always, and has yet to rid himself of his drinking addiction," he replied with a smirk.

"This is no joke Andrei! You are seriously trying my patience!"

"Now, now, Lisbeth, calm yourself," Valdir said placidly as he strolled up to the pair. His footsteps on the white marble floor echoed throughout the vast space. "There is no reason to shout my dear. Andrei seems to be doing his best to locate the Childe, is that not right Andrei?" he asked looking pointedly at him. Andrei nodded. Lisbeth crossed her arms in anger and let out a huff of annoyance. "See Lisbeth, there is nothing to fret over. Time is on our side. Neither our master Cain, nor The Parliament are aware of this situation. So as long as we keep on top of it, we can rid ourselves of this issue before it escalates."

"But my visions are becoming stronger. This Childe seems to be different," Lisbeth whispered anxiously.

"Yes, and her appearance has not been the same from vision to vision. At first she had black hair and now she has bright red, curly hair. Maybe you are losing your touch old girl," Andrei stated dryly.

"I have had just about enough of you!"

"Silence you two! I tire of your incessant arguing!" Valdir whispered. "Maybe it is time for all of us to pay a visit to our dear Lucien. It would seem that a little persuading is in order."

"I have a plan Valdir, give me a little while longer and Lucien will be compliant with our wishes," Andrei stated confidently.

"What are you playing at Andrei? You have been at this for quite some time now, with no results!" Lisbeth put her hand up protesting Valdir's attempted interruption. "Let me finish! You have always been a little sneak Andrei, and I have never trusted you. You're just lucky that I cannot see into your mind. But trust me when I say, when I do find out, you will no longer be Cain's favorite little errand boy," Lisbeth whispered angrily, glaring at Andrei. Giving a glance to Valdir, she stormed out of the great hall.

"That woman is such a nuisance," Andrei commented, leaning back in the ornate, dark red wood high back chair he was sitting in.

"Quiet Andrei," Valdir muttered as he spun to look him dead in the eyes. "I know what you have been up to in Astoria. For your sake, it better pan out. I am tired of cleaning up your messes! If those girls cause any issues for us, you will be kissing sunlight, understood?" he growled, his eyes turning jet black. Andrei looked at him with shock written all over his face.

"How do you know?"

"Don't concern yourself with that. Just make due on your promise, and bring Lucien back to us. And find the Childe!"

Andrei stormed into his personal chambers, his normally deathly pale face was bright red with anger. "What am I, some kind of servant at their beck and call? I will show them. Yes, I will find the Childe and bring her…directly to Cain. Those bumbling fools will receive no credit for this! The only decision I will have to make is will the Childe be alive or dead when I present it as a gift to him."

Holding a piece of paper in her hand, Linda scanned it from top to bottom. Coming face to face with her slightly fuzzy, black and white picture, she stopped. *I look so happy.* She traced the picture with her index finger and then read the heading on the flyer, “Missing.” *Of course my family is looking for me, why wouldn’t they be?* She thought.

“You really need to stop dwelling Linda,” Becca stated nonchalantly, her voice echoing slightly in the abandoned tunnels beneath Astoria. Many years ago, the tunnels were used for drainage, but now were vacant and dilapidated. The limestone walls of the tunnels were grungy and most of the metal gates, that separated the many chambers connecting the tunnels, were now rusted. They were officially condemned thirty years prior.

“Becca, don’t you ever miss your family…your friends?” Linda asked while still looking at her picture.

Becca thought about it for a few seconds and then said, “Not really. What about you Amy?”

“Like my family really cares about me! Did you see the picture they picked for my flyer? It’s hideous! They only want me back so they can put me back in Juvie. So they know where I’m at all times!” Amy answered as she stared directly at Linda, her eyes turning jet black. “Besides, now we’re vampires. How could you miss being an insignificant human?” Linda didn’t answer.

I wish I could just go home, I don’t belong here with these girls. Damn you Andrei for doing this to me! Linda thought as she continued looking at the flyer.

"Why do you think Andrei took us in the first place?" Becca asked while she thumbed through an old issue of a fashion magazine.

"It doesn't matter why! He just did! And if you don't want to end up like the first girl, then I would stop asking such stupid questions," Amy growled, baring her fangs.

"Geez Amy, you really need to relax, like pronto," Becca murmured while rolling her eyes. Amy ripped the magazine from her hands and flung it down the tunnel, landing it in a puddle of murky water. "Hey! I was reading that." Amy just rolled her eyes and proceeded to plop down on one of the three mattresses lying on the ground.

"I'm bored. We should go cause a little trouble or something," Amy said mischievously.

"I agree, I'm just itching to try out these new abilities we have now that we're vamps," Becca stated.

"I don't think that's such a good idea," Linda said sheepishly, turning to look at them.

"Well, it's a good thing it's not up to you Linda. Andrei left me in charge, remember!" Amy said.

"How could we forget," Linda muttered under her breath.

"What did you say?" Amy asked, her eyes pinning Linda's. "You better start falling in line girlie, or else you'll have Andrei to deal with when he returns."

Linda shied away at the mention of Andrei's name and looked back at the flyer. She clutched the cell phone that she kept hidden in her pants pocket, her only link to her old life. *I wish I could just call my mom and hear her voice again,* she thought.

"Uh Amy?"

"Yeah what?"

"Before we cause a little trouble, could we get some new outfits? I'm not feeling this whole ragged look anymore," Becca said while examining her blood stained and torn clothes.

"Whatever," Amy replied in an annoyed tone.

"Great, because I know the perfect place for a five finger discount," she said with an evil grin.

5
Sparks Fly

A hand shot up from the front row causing Mayor Markus Woods to groan inwardly. As soon as he spoke the words Founder's Day Celebration at the town hall council meeting Markus knew that the self-anointed Queen of Astoria, Debbie Fuller, would have put in her two cents. Correction, make that fifty cents. "Yes, Mrs. Fuller. Do you have something to add?" Markus asked.

"As you all know, my mother Carrie Winthrop has passed the torch of 'Head of the Event Planning Committee' to her only daughter, moi. And with me as your leader, I think this year will be the best Founder's Day celebration we've ever had," Debbie Fuller announced arrogantly while looking around at everyone in attendance. Groans could be heard throughout the assembly as the mayor tried to restore order to the crowd.

"What great enthusiasm Mrs. Fuller. I'm excited to see what you've planned for this year's festivities," Markus replied with an empty smile. Debbie took her seat with a look of pride on her face. "Now, moving on to the topic of ending the curfew. I've spoken with our sheriff, Barry Stokes, and he believes it would be okay to end the curfew effective immediately. However," Markus said, pushing his glasses up off his nose and then cleared his throat. "I'm still asking that we express caution while traveling alone at night, especially since the culprit has yet to be apprehended."

Rachel looked at Sam with slight concern in her eyes over the fact they had yet to figure out who was behind the disappearances. Sam squeezed her hand and smiled. Pulling her hand up to his mouth, he kissed it.

"There's one more incident I'd like to bring before you. A few nights ago, Aurora Steven's store, Squaresville, was broken into. Sheriff Stokes and I feel that it was the work of juveniles, and is being considered an isolated incident. Nothing of major value was stolen except for some clothing. Please keep a watchful eye out for suspicious activity. And if you hear anything, call our local sheriff's office with information. Meeting adjourned," Markus declared, banging his gavel.

"Do you feel that?" Matt asked as the group walked around downtown while on their lunch break from helping at Squaresville.

"Feel what?" Amanda replied.

"Freedom. Glorious freedom," he exclaimed. "No more curfew means we can resume our nightly strolls to the CinePlex for midnight showings!"

"Is that all you think about Matt? Movies?" Amanda asked, rolling her eyes.

"No, of course not. There's girls too," he kidded, and then flinched as Amanda punched him in the arm.

"Will you two behave? We're in public you know," Julie chastised jokingly.

"Yes mother!" The two of them responded in unison, and then Amanda punched him again for copying her.

"My mom is still locking the doors and windows every night, even though the curfew is over. Her trust in people is still iffy at best," Elle chimed in. "And strangely, I felt safer with the curfew in place."

Cat was quiet. She was still unsure of how to act around her friends. Even though she made up with them and things in "friend world" were back to normal, they really weren't for her. She felt terrible for having to hide her true identity away from people she's known all her life. Just the thought of them finding out she's a freak, and not wanting to be around her anymore, was tearing her apart.

"Hey Cat, what do you think about the curfew being over?" Matt asked, breaking into Cat's thoughts.

"Uh, good I guess. I mean, but what about the break-in at Squaresville. Don't you guys feel it was kind of weird that only some girl clothes were taken, and no money was stolen?"

"Yeah, my mom was so happy they didn't take more. And the one night she actually leaves money in the register, we get robbed. I agree it's weird that more wasn't taken though."

Cat began to reply but her attention was turned to a store front window they were passing. A large cardboard cutout of famed vampire, Bartholomew Drake, sat in the window. Cat had to lift her jaw off the floor as she stood staring in awe at the display before her. Her friends joined in. "Guys, look! A new store is opening soon! And they're having a book launch party for Robert Craven's new novel in the Dark Shadow series," Cat exclaimed grinning ear to ear. A sign hung on the building, it read:

Coming Soon:

The Three Penny Brit

Bookstore & Café

"A bookstore café?! About freakin' time we get one of these in Astoria. Seriously, we're so far behind the times here. We don't even have one of those Star coffee places!" Amanda stated.

"I totes see a potential new hang out in our future," Cat said. "We're so coming for the grand opening!"

Amanda's cell phone beeped, signaling a text message. She pulled out her cell and saw the message was from her mom, it read:

Where R U? U still coming back 2 help out n the store? Luv ya!

"It's my mom. I guess we better get back. She's still a little freaked out by the break in," Amanda said as she slid her phone into her pocket. The group pulled themselves away from the store window and hurried down Exchange Street toward Squaresville.

The night of the Founder's Day parade and fireworks spectacular had arrived. Downtown Astoria was blocked off for the parade route, and crowds of people stood along the sidewalks awaiting the arrival of the floats.

"I've got to hand it to Debbie Fuller, this celebration has been the best it's ever been. That lady excels in the art of excess," Rachel murmured to Sam as they stood by watching the parade.

Debbie and Kirsten approached in the Founder's float dressed to the nines with crowns atop their heads. The mother and daughter team were the epitome of over doing it, complete with elbow, elbow, wrist, wrist, royal waves. As the leader of the Trifecta, the three most popular girls at Astoria High, Kirsten reigned supreme as the queen bee of the school. The willowy brunette used to be the star athlete, until Cat's arrival on the swim team, which created a one-sided-Kirsten-only rivalry between them.

Kirsten glared at Cat and Amanda as she noticed them mocking her and her mom's royal waves.

"Taylor sure dodged a bullet by ignoring that one," Cat quipped.

"Yeah, I mean would you look at those two? Seriously? They're totes ridonkulous," Amanda said.

"Well are you really that surprised, I mean they're self-proclaimed town royalty," Cat muttered, rolling her eyes.

"Man she's hot!" Matt exclaimed, wolf whistling at Kirsten as the Founder's float stopped in front of their group. Kirsten sneered at him and then immediately turned her attention to the rest of the crowd, a fake smile plastered on her face.

Amanda smacked Matt across the back of the head. “Down boy, heel!” she joked as Matt glared at her while rubbing the offended area.

“We’ve got funnel cake!” Elle announced excitedly as she joined the group while juggling four plates in her hands. “We got the works of course, ice cream, strawberry topping, and powdered sugar!”

“You guys are life savers! Thanks for braving the crowd,” Cat said while grabbing a plate, and then began munching down the delicious smelling dessert.

The street lamps around the town square dimmed until the only visible lights were that of the illuminations adorning the floats. “Okay Astoria, and now the grand finale!” The announcer’s voice came through the speaker system. The roof tops of the surrounding buildings lit up as fireworks shot from them into the sky. The crowd stared in awe at the spectacle. The fireworks burst into a colorful display, painting the clouds overhead. The floats began moving again at a crawl. As the Founder’s float continued past Cat and her group, Cat saw a rogue firework sputtering toward the large tree the float was passing. It exploded into the tree, making it burst into flames. The crowd gasped as Kirsten and Debbie screamed, scrambling to get out of the way of a burning branch that slammed into the float.

"Kirsten look out!" Cat yelled, pointing at another firework making a beeline for the royal pair. Hearing Cat's yell, Kirsten dropped to the floor and pulled her mom with her. The firework whizzed by and barley brushed Kirsten's crown. It crashed into the back of the float and set it aflame. Confetti and Paper Mache from the float showered down on the street after the impact. Kirsten and her mom leapt from the burning float as the crowd scattered in a panic.

Cat and her group ducked as a firework buzzed over their heads and shattered the store window behind them, sending shards of glass crashing down on the sidewalk. Several more stray fireworks hit random floats, setting each one ablaze and leaving them burnt to a crisp.

The sound of ambulance and fire truck sirens filled the cool night air, drowning out the screams and moans of the injured and scared. Cat and her friends stood by shocked, watching the chaos continue.

"Did you like the show Cat?" A hauntingly familiar female voice whispered into Cat's ear. Whipping around to put a face with the voice, she found no one. Full of concern, she scanned the crowd, looking for anything out of the ordinary. In the distance on a small hill, standing in front of a group of trees, Cat noticed three deathly pale girls. Their skin radiated in the moonlight. One of them she recognized immediately. "Linda?"

she whispered and moved forward trying to make her way toward her. Cat fought against the crowd that was being pushed back by the firemen, and lost sight of Linda and the two strangers she was with. As she made it to the front of the crowd, Cat looked up at the group of trees again, but the girls were gone.

"Cat, what's wrong? You just took off!" Julie asked catching up to her.

"Nothing, thought I saw something," Cat responded, still gazing at the trees.

Laughing wickedly, relishing in the chaos they just caused, the three vampire girls dashed through the tree tops. As they approached a barren clearing, the girls slowed and floated to the ground. Becca waved her hand from left to right and the trap door in the concrete foundation flew open. She giggled, "I never do get tired of that."

"Did you see the look on their faces? That couldn't have gone more perfect!" Amy announced, laughing evilly. "And Becca, great job with the fireworks. Who knew your talents would come in that handy."

"I only wish I could've hit that stupid tramp Kirsten! Ugh! That girl's so annoying," Becca replied, and then slammed her fist into her palm.

"You're just mad because she creamed you at swim regionals," Amy mocked.

"Whatever! It still would've been cool," Becca huffed, crossing her arms over her chest.

"Oh, and nice touch Linda, whispering in Cat's ear like that. You really freaked her out," Amy said with a menacing grin.

"All part of the plan, right? Besides, it's not like I had a choice," Linda remarked. A buzzing sound erupted from Linda's pocket. Pulling out her cell, "It's my mom!"

"Hey, that's not fair! Why does Linda get to keep her phone?" Becca whined.

"She's not supposed to have it," Amy said, glaring at Linda. "Anyway, you can't answer it! That would be against Andrei's rules. He said we have to forget our past. We're vampires now, bloodthirsty killers. There's no room for mortals in our lives!" Grabbing the phone from Linda's hand it buzzed again and Amy saw Cat Colvin's name on the screen. She looked up at Linda with fire in her eyes. "Why is Cat calling you? How does she have your-" as the answer dawned on Amy, she grinned devilishly. "You were friends with her, weren't you? Why didn't you tell us before?"

"Well I was still going through the transition. How did you expect me to remember such an insignificant detail like that?"

Linda hoped her true emotion didn't show as she lied. Amy looked at Linda suspiciously as Becca snatched the phone from her hand.

"Ooh, we could have some real fun with Cat now." Becca smirked looking at the phone. "Let's send our little friend a text, shall we?"

Across town, Cat's phone beeped on her desk indicating a message. She sprang from her bed, threw her copy of *Red Twilight* on to her nightstand, and grabbed her phone. Plopping back on her bed Cat stared at her cell, her eyes full of concern. The text was from Linda and it read:

Guess who?

What's happening? First Linda disappears. Then I see her at the parade, and now a cryptic text from her cell? After she set her phone down, Cat curled up on her bed while clutching her pillow against her chest, and went into deep thought.

A light scratching noise at Cat's window startled her. It was Jewels. Opening her bay window, the feline sauntered in, and then laid down on Cat's bed, swaying her tail back and forth in utter contentment. Cat cuddled next to her, absently stroking her fur as she stared at her cell, trying to make sense of everything.

Linda snuck away while Amy and Becca were feeding. As she trudged along through the tunnels toward her house, sadness enveloped her. She had traveled to her home this way several times before without anyone knowing. Part of her wanted to just turn around and walk away, but she couldn't, she had to say goodbye to her old life one last time. *Why me? Why did Andrei choose me? I had a life, a family...friends. I don't want to live like this! I'm a freak of nature! This isn't fair!* Linda thought crossly.

Finding the manhole leading up to her street in Madison, Linda climbed out. The glistening of the moon in a nearby puddle drew her attention to it. Standing over the pool of water, she stared into it deeply. Seeing no reflection, she stomped into it, splashing the water. As she saw a glimmer of herself through the ripples in the puddle, Linda backed away from it and turned around, coming face to face with her house. The windows were dark with a lack of activity. No lights were on except the faint flicker of the TV in her mom's bedroom. Silently entering the house, she made her way to her room. Her mom hadn't changed a thing. Everything was still as Linda had left it. Looking to the vanity mirror, she saw all the pictures of her and her friends lining it. One in particular caught her eye. It was of her, Cat, and Julie in their Madison Prep uniforms, all hugging each other and laughing. *Happy times*, she thought, and then placed the picture back on to the mirror.

Heading to the next room had her looking in on her brother, Max. He was quietly snoring with Buck, their family Boston terrier, sleeping at his feet. Blowing him a kiss, she made her way to her mom's bedroom and peeked in. As usual her mom had fallen asleep watching TV. Linda saw evidence of the tears that had stained her face, and it made her sadness worsen knowing they were for her.

"Stay tuned for breaking news from Astoria's Founder's Day disaster! Full story coming up in two minutes!" Jillian Brown, Astoria news's top reporter, stated through the television. Linda felt a sense of guilt, even though she had nothing to do with the fireworks. She wished she would've had the strength to stop them, but instead she had stood helplessly by as the carnage unfolded before her.

Quietly lying down beside her mom, Linda stared at her face. She wished she could turn back time when her only worries were what to wear to a school dance, and whether she had studied hard enough for tests. Seeing Cat earlier that night had made the pain that much worse, knowing that her life might be in danger from the very people she was now associated with. Andrei terrified her, the other two completely trusted him, but Linda had this sneaking suspicion they were all just pawns in his plan, and were expendable. Combing back her mother's hair, Linda kissed her forehead. Tears began welling up in her eyes as she whispered, "Goodbye, I love you." Her mom suddenly sat up and began looking around.

"Linda?" Casey asked the empty room. Looking to the left she noticed the window open and the curtains gently blowing in the night breeze. Linda hovered just below the window and breathed a sigh of relief, glad that her mom hadn't seen her. Making her way back to the tunnels, Linda turned around once more to look at the place she had spent her whole life. She couldn't fight back the tears any longer. As they began to stream down her face, she descended into the tunnels, not looking back, finally saying farewell to her past life.

"Where have you been?" Amy's voice called out from the dark as Linda reached a small chamber within the tunnels.

"Just went for a walk, that's all," Linda replied trying to hide her face, not wanting Amy to see her tears.

"A little walk huh?" Becca interjected.

"Yeah, a walk."

"What's that in your hand?" Amy asked. Linda clutched the charm bracelet her mom had made for her. She had grabbed it from atop her dresser, and forgot she was still holding it.

"Nothing," Linda replied, putting the bracelet into her coat pocket.

"Nothing? It looks like something to me. We know where you've been. And if you want Becca and I to keep your secret from Andrei, you'll do exactly what we tell you from now on. Am I understood?" Amy asked with an evil grin. Linda nodded her head. "Oh and I'll let you keep your silly little charm bracelet, I'm feeling quite generous tonight."

How did she know I had that with me? Linda thought. She shuttered. She didn't know who scared her more, Amy or Andrei. But one thing she did know was that Amy never made idle threats.

The next day the doorbell rang at the Brewer residence. Casey sighed, sitting at her usual place at the kitchen table. The table top was littered with newspaper articles about her daughter Linda's disappearance. As the doorbell rang again, an exhausted Casey realized that her son, Max, was not going to answer it and went to do it herself. Standing on the porch, Cat smiled as Casey opened the door. "Oh Cat, what a nice surprise! How have you been?" Casey asked, giving Cat a lengthy hug.

"Hi Mrs. Brewer, how are you holding up?" Cat asked, reciprocating the hug. Cat had felt bad about not visiting after Linda's disappearance. She wanted too, but found it too hard to deal with. Even now she was overcome with emotion after seeing Linda's mom's face.

"Well, I have my good days and my bad days," she replied with a wan smile. "Oh what am I doing? Come in, come in." Scanning the walls of the foyer hallway, Cat saw pictures of Linda and her brother Max, revealing memories of a cheerful past. A feeling of sadness came over her as she watched Mrs. Brewer straighten one of the pictures of Linda hanging on the wall.

"They have no leads," Casey muttered unexpectedly, catching Cat off guard.

"They're still looking, they'll find her. I know it," Cat replied.

"I know she's still alive…that's why I haven't disconnected her cell phone line yet. I had the police try and track her through the phone. But every time they did, there wasn't a signal on her end," Casey responded. "Everyone thinks I'm going crazy with depression or something…but I've seen her." Cat felt conflicted. She wanted to tell Mrs. Brewer that she'd seen Linda too, and that she had also received a text message from her, but knew she couldn't. Cat didn't want to cause more problems for Linda's family, and wanted to wait until she found out what was really going on before she said anything.

"Hey Cat, long time no see!" Max called out as he ran downstairs, interrupting their conversation.

"I think I'm going to go lay down for a bit. It was lovely seeing you Cat. Please don't be a stranger, okay," Casey sighed heavily as she made her way upstairs to her bedroom.

"Sure thing Mrs. Brewer. Take care of yourself," Cat replied as Max put his hand on her shoulder.

"Just between us," Max whispered, "I'm really worried about mom. She refuses to do anything the doctor recommends. And she swears she sees Linda every night. I feel she's losing it. And with her saying that she sees Linda all the time, it makes things harder for all of us. She needs to get out of the house, but won't. Could you ask your mom if she'll plan a ladies night out or something?"

"Sure, I'll talk to her when I get home," she replied after seeing the desperation on his face.

"I really do miss her," he said sadly while looking at the picture of Linda his mom had straightened earlier.

"Yeah, me too," Cat replied.

6
New in Town

"Mom, I look, ridiculous! Tell me again why I have to wear this flower hat thing?" Cat moaned while adjusting the frilly purple flower pot hat that sat on her head.

"It's our new and unique way of advertising the store, plus it looks wonderful on you," Rachel said with a smile. "Julie doesn't seem to have a problem wearing it," she stated, pointing at Julie, who was ringing up a customer. Cat adjusted the hat again as it seemed to want to take a nose dive every five seconds.

"Mom I know I said I'd help out around the store for the rest of summer, but I never signed up for crazy hats. Plus what if someone walks in that knows me? I'll be the laughing stock of Astoria High."

"Oh stop being so dramatic Cat. You only have two weeks left of summer, just go with the flow of life, and embrace the flower hat," she replied while placing the flower pot hat on her own head. "Now hurry along, we've got a busy day ahead of us, and there's no time to dawdle," she said, shooing Cat toward one of the registers. Rachel watched as Cat walked away, happy that things were finally getting back to *normal*. "I won't cry," she mumbled to herself as a tear ran down her cheek, and quickly made her way to the back of the store so no one would notice.

Covered in potting soil and animal excrement, aka fertilizer, Cat and Julie loaded the flower van after closing time. Business had been booming for *Florals by Rach*. Of course it did help being the only floral shop in town

Cat climbed into the driver's side of the van, as Julie hesitantly got into the passenger's side and buckled in. "Cat, are you sure that you're ready to drive this beast?" Julie asked with concern in her voice.

"Of course I am. Why wouldn't I be?" she replied, starting the engine.

"I don't know, maybe because this van is twice as big as your Jeep and you-"

“Oh Julie, you worry too much. I can handle this, it’s just like riding a bike...a really, really big bike.”

“Yeah, but Cat, you still fall off of your bike.” Cat rolled her eyes, put the van into drive, and took off down the road.

Rounding the bend that led to Nehalem Avenue, a completely bare tree caught Cat’s eye. All of the trees around it were full of life, their branches covered in colorful leaves. This one tree though, was dark and muted. No sign of life. *Hmmm, that’s odd*, Cat thought to herself as she suddenly smelled the strong odor of cinnamon coming in from the open van window. Her attention quickly shot back to the road, “Cat watch out!” Julie yelled as they barreled toward a huge semi-truck. Quickly turning the wheel, she barely missed the truck by mere inches. Cat slammed on the brakes, breathing heavily.

“You okay Julie?” she asked apologetically.

Julie laughed nervously. “Yeah, I’m alright. That was a close call.” Cat poked her head out of the window and looked back at the large green truck. The words *International Movers* were written on the side.

“Hey, it looks like we have new neighbors,” Cat announced.

“That would have been a great welcoming, crashing into their moving truck,” Julie said while giggling. “The truck says International Movers. I wonder where they’re from?”

Cat noticed a young dark skinned girl, who looked to be about her age, walking from the house toward the moving truck. "It seems like we'll also be getting a new addition to our school this year," Cat said with a smile as she continued up the street to her house.

Buzz...buzz. "Hey Julie can you get my phone? It's vibrating in the cup holder up front," Cat asked as she gathered several potted plants from the back of the van.

Julie picked up the phone, "Cat it's your mom, do you want me to answer it?"

"Yeah, I kind of have my hands full at the moment," she groaned, struggling to carry all of the plants to the front door.

"Hello Mrs. Colvin, uh huh, yeah, I can tell her for you. Alright, well I guess we'll see you in a little bit then." Just as Julie hung up the phone, she was startled by a crash near the front door. Cat had dropped one of the plants, breaking the pot, and spilled the soil all over the porch. "What happened?" Julie hid her grin, as she realized what Cat had done.

"Oh, I'm just a klutz. Mom's going to flip," Cat murmured while sweeping the soil into a pile with her hands.

Julie chuckled. "I'm sure she'll understand. She still might lecture you though, on how you should make multiple trips instead of one."

"Let's just clean it up before she gets home."

"Oh, and she wants us to put the casserole that's in the refrigerator, in the oven for dinner."

❦ ❦ ❦

"Hello, is anyone home?" Sam announced as he entered the house.

"Hey Dad, glad you're here. I just preheated the oven, so could you please put in the casserole when it beeps. Oh for about 30 minutes or so should do. Thanks Dad, you're the best." Cat gave Sam a peck on his cheek and then she and Julie disappeared out the front door.

"Welcome home Dad. How was your day? Oh Cat thanks for asking, it was wonderful. Sure I'll put the casserole in the oven, I'm good for something right?" Sam mumbled to himself, making his way to the kitchen.

Outside, Cat and Julie both grumbled as they saw Maude Roberts standing by Cat's car. "Hey you two," she called out as she waved to them. She then yanked on Fredricka's leash, who was busy trying to dig a hole in the yard. "Your Dad was in a bit of a hurry, tried to catch him before he went inside. For his age he moves rather quickly. Anyway, have you noticed the moving truck down the street? It seems we have new neighbors." Leaning in closer Maude's voice lowered, "I didn't see any signs of a mother figure, but there is an older man and a young boy. The strange thing is, there's also a young girl who has a really, really dark tan, if you know what I mean. They must be one of those progressive families that I've heard so much about. Not that I'm discriminatory or anything, no siree, I'm equal about everyone."

Yeah you talk equally about everyone, Cat thought. "We're just on our way to welcome them to the neighborhood."

"I'd come with you girls, but I have to start dinner. Do come over after you visit with them, and we'll have a little chat, shall we?"

Julie and Cat nodded their heads and took off down the street trying to hold back their laughter. "Yeah, like we'd really go over and purposefully have a chat with *her*. Not in this lifetime," Cat whispered to Julie.

"Maybe we should wait for the rest of our group before we go and meet the neighbors." Julie slowed down and then stood still.

"Like that wouldn't be totes overwhelming. Matt would probably say something inappropriate, and then Amanda would smack him for it. And Elle would probably be so nervous, she'd immediately ask to use their bathroom. No, I think we should go by ourselves, and then report back to the group."

"Okay, maybe you're right."

"Hey look, what is that thing in their front yard? That looks like one of those wooden training dummies. You know, like they use in karate," Cat explained after seeing the confused look on Julie's face.

"Don't you think it's a little weird that they have one of those?"

"And Matt having a blow-up clown punching bag isn't?" Cat commented.

As the moving men were closing the back door of the truck, a tall, good looking older man stood off to the side holding a clipboard, flipping the pages quickly as his pen flew over them. "Thank you gentlemen," the man said with a distinct British accent, handing the clipboard over to one of the men. "It looks like we're all set here." The three men jumped into the truck and it pulled away from the curb.

Julie and Cat crossed the road and were met by the greenest eyes that either one of them had ever seen. His hair was short and wavy with a mixture of colors from blonde to brown. He smiled when he noticed them. "Well hello young ladies, are you what they call the Welcome Wagon?"

Cat grinned, "I guess you could call us that. We're your neighbors up the street," she said, and then introduced herself and Julie.

"The name's Gerard McNeil, and it's a pleasure to meet you. Oh look, here comes my eldest now. Duffie, come and meet our neighbors, Cat and Julie," he called out. "If my guess is correct you're all about the same age." Julie and Cat watched as a girl matching Maude's description walked toward them. Her smile was friendly. Her beautiful black hair bounced with every step she took, and her long legs helped make short work of her journey to meet them. Her light brown eyes though, they noticed, were guarded.

"Nice to meet ya," Duffie said in her distinct British accent.

"Why don't we all go inside and have some refreshments. I find myself feeling a little parched," Gerard stated, walking toward the front door. Julie and Cat followed them into the foyer and found themselves surrounded by boxes.

"It'll take us a little while to get this place in order, but I know it'll get done. Right Duffie?" Duffie nodded.

Looking into the dining room, Cat saw numerous plates full with cakes, pies, muffins, and other random desserts. "Duffie, what's with all the baked goods? They look delicious," Cat asked gesturing toward the dining room table.

"Oh that. Well, you see my dad has already become quite popular with the women in the area. Especially when they found out he's single," she giggled.

"Leif! We have guests, please come down and meet them," Gerard called up the stairway. A loud sound from above caught their attention and they watched as a young man ran down the stairs. "One day if you're not careful you're going to break something," he chastised jokingly.

"Cat, Julie, meet my daredevil brother Leif," Duffie said dryly, rolling her eyes. Cat and Julie were speechless as their eyes glanced over him. He was tall like his dad and looked sporty in his running shorts and tank top. His hair was bleached blonde and his eyes a bluish green. His grin made their hearts beat just a little faster. Make that a lot faster.

"Hey neighbors," Leif said with a little wave. "So, who's Cat, and who's Julie? No, let me guess." his British accent sounded like music to their ears. He seemed to think for a minute and then pointed to Cat, "You're Cat, right?" Cat felt like she had lost her voice. All she could do was nod.

"How did you do that?" Julie asked.

"It's a secret. Now let's have some refreshments, we stocked the kitchen yesterday. And thanks to our father we have plenty of desserts to choose from," Leif joked, pointing to the dining room.

"Let me apologize for my brother. His ego sometimes gets the best of him. I hope I can enlist your aid in the matter." Duffie's smile lit up her face as her brother gave her a playful shove.

“I tried to raise them civilized. But as you can see they still need some work,” Gerard laughed and then the others joined in.

❦ ❦ ❦

Sitting at the kitchen table, the four became fast friends. Cat knew that there would be a lot of hearts broken by the pair, as Duffie was as beautiful as her brother was handsome.

“Penny for them Cat?” Duffie asked.

“What? Oh, penny for my thoughts? I was just thinking that you two are really going to shake up Astoria High this year.”

“For a second there, I thought you were wondering how we’re related, if Leif is white and I’m black. No? Well if you were to ask, it’s complicated,” Duffie replied with a chuckle.

“So, do either of you have a boyfriend?” Leif asked changing the subject.

“I have a lot of friends that are boys,” Cat answered, not knowing why she was being so evasive. *Why didn’t I just say that Ryan was my boyfriend?*

Duffie grinned. “Well I hope you’ll share.”

“Of course,” Cat laughed. “Well this has been fun, but we have to get going. We should plan something with the rest of our group. They’ll absolutely love you guys.”

“Maybe we could all come over and help you unpack, if you need help?” Julie interjected.

"Sure, maybe," Duffie answered and then Leif gave her a questioning look.

Everyone stood at once, and Julie and Cat were ushered out the door with promises to get together soon. As they were leaving, Gerard waved to them through a wall of boxes that he was busy rummaging through.

The group met in Cat's bedroom the following evening. Fridays were typically their hang out day since they all worked at different places most of the summer. Cat and Julie told them about the new neighbors down the street and how neat their British accents were. Matt rolled his eyes at their description of Leif and how that every girl in school, whether they were a freshmen or a senior, would give him a second and third look. He seemed to perk up though when he heard that Duffie was beautiful. To him, she sounded like that Egyptian goddess from his book of mythology, but the name seemed to escape him.

"So I tried out for the football team. I find out the first day of school if I made it or not," Matt announced to the group.

"You…tried out…for football?" Amanda asked, trying not to laugh out loud.

"What do you mean by that?" he replied, looking offended. Cat nudged Amanda.

"That's great Matt! So what position did you try out for?" Cat asked, nudging Amanda again as she was stifling her laughter.

"Well you really don't try out for a position. They kind of test you out and see what you'll be good at, but I don't care. I just want to be on the team."

"Aren't you scared that you might get hurt?" Elle asked. "I see a lot of damage from the sidelines dressed in that panther costume. And let me tell you, it's dangerous out there Matt."

"Yeah, but think of all the girls that will want me if I'm on the football team," he replied with a grin.

"See I'm right! He does have an ulterior motive for being on the team," Amanda stated and then quickly moved away from Cat so she couldn't hit her again.

"Hey Elle, how are those devil spawn that masquerade as the children you baby-sit?" Cat asked, changing the subject.

"They're not too bad, I guess. They've only locked me out of the house twelve times this summer instead of twenty five like last year."

"What do you mean they're not too bad? They almost burned the house down last year!" Amanda interjected.

"What can I say? I just have a way with children I guess. And it pays well too," Elle joked, making everyone laugh.

Later that night, after everyone was asleep, Cat got up and made her way to the bathroom. Trying to tip toe over her friends, she stumbled, stubbing her toe on her dresser. The ache surged up her leg, and Cat bit her lip to keep from yelling out. A sharp pain stabbed at her bottom lip and she realized her fangs had descended. Closing the bathroom door behind her quietly, she turned on the light to look at herself in the mirror. "Great!" Cat whispered in frustration. "This isn't good."

"Cat you okay in there?" Amanda asked from the other side of the door.

"Yeah, won't be a minute, if you need to, you can use the bathroom downstairs," Cat answered in a soft voice, not wanting to wake the others.

"Amanda what are you yelling about?" Matt asked groggily, raising his head from the futon.

"None of your business, go back to sleep," she barked back testily.

"What's going on?" Elle asked, unzipping herself from her sleeping bag.

"Amanda, please be quiet, you're waking everyone up," Cat whispered urgently through the door.

"I guess I'll just go use the one downstairs, and you guys, go back to sleep," Amanda said annoyed, opening the attic door and stomping down the old, creaky stairs.

Great, just great! Now she's going to wake up the whole house, and I'll never get out of here. I must concentrate on getting rid of these things before anyone else comes knocking! Cat thought, pulling up her lips to get the full view of her pointy teeth.

"Hey Cat are you going to be in there long?" Matt's voice came through the door, making her jump.

"Please go downstairs, I'll be in here for a bit," Cat answered, trying to suppress the frustration from her voice.

"Alright, I hear Amanda stomping back up anyway. Geez, she's going to wake the whole house making so much noise," Matt murmured.

You think? Cat groaned inwardly, and then closed her eyes willing her teeth to retract. Taking in a few slow deep breaths, she concentrated on her task and felt them slide back up into place. *Perfect! Now, what did I come in here for again? Oh yeah how could I forget?* She thought moving to the toilet.

"Hey Cat are you going to be long? I really need to pee!" Elle's voice loudly whispered at the door.

7
School's in Session

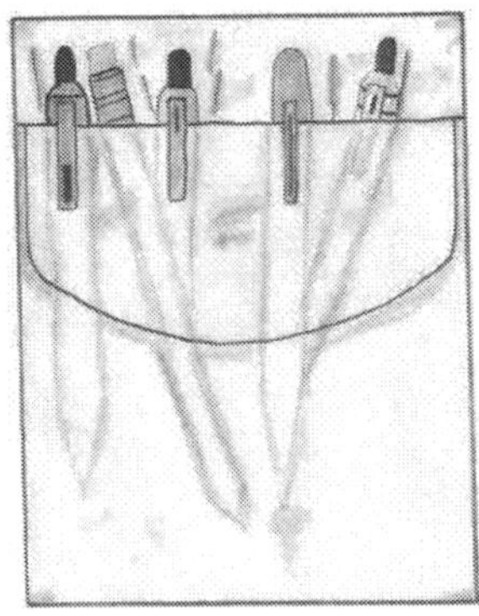

"Excuse me. Do you know where, the biology classroom is?" a man asked distractedly, standing in Miss Amaya's classroom doorway, and fumbling with the papers in his over the shoulder bag. Miss Amaya swept back her wild curly blonde hair as she looked up from her homeroom roster. There in front of her stood a tall, handsome, young, but kind of nerdy looking guy.

"Uhh, it's, d-down the hall. Three doors," she stuttered.

"Thanks," he said, glancing down the hall and then back at Miss Amaya. Their eyes met and it was an instant connection.

"Uhh, I'm M-melvin. Melvin Pierson. The new biology teacher. But you probably already guessed that," he said, and then laughed nervously while running his fingers through his light brown hair.

"I'm Amaya Phillips," she said. As she stood up, Miss Amaya accidentally pushed her syllabi off of her desk and onto the floor. She bent down and began picking them up in a frantic manner.

"Here, let me help you with those," Melvin said as he crouched down to assist her.

"Thank you, but that's not really necessary," she began and then raised her head, almost bumping into his.

"Oh, we almost became a cliché just then. You know bumping heads and all," he chuckled, and then proceeded to gather the rest of the papers off the floor. Miss Amaya smiled as they both stood. "Well, I best be off. N-nice meeting you," he stuttered, handing the papers to her.

"Y-yeah, same here," she replied as Melvin grabbed his bag, and then made his way for the door. Turning to look at her again, he bumped into the wall and then shook it off with a nervous smile in her direction. Miss Amaya giggled, muffling the sound with her hand.

The large wooden double doors at the end of the school's main hallway flew open, and Duffie and Leif strolled through them, oozing confidence. To all who saw, they moved as if they were in a slow motion scene from a movie. As the wind blew into the hall through the open doors, it rustled their clothes and wafted their hair. Duffie walked ahead as Leif stayed close behind her. Most of the girls in the hall were instantly drawn to the gorgeous silent type freshman, but he paid them no attention. Noticing Cat and her friends down the hall gathered at her locker, Duffie waved them down, "Oi!" she yelled at the top of her lungs. In that very instant she tripped over the guy in front of her and fell forward. Leif reached out to catch her but was too late. Duffie crashed into Tonya, who collided with Jessica, sending her bumping into Kirsten, and landing her face first into a trash can. With Kirsten's feet flailing in the air, the hall erupted into laughter. Her two Trifecta lackeys muffled their laughs with their hands over their mouths.

"Help me, you idiots!" Kirsten cried out to her drones. Tonya and Jessica struggled to pull her out. Duffie stood up cautiously with the assistance of her brother, her shocked gaze fixed on the mess she had made. Finally free, Kirsten began pulling trash from her beautiful chestnut brown hair as she vocally expressed her disgust with loud and annoying, "ewws!"

"I'm so sorry, my feet have a mind of their own," Duffie said apologetically, and then stopped as Kirsten put up her hand.

"Seriously! What's your damage? I'm sorry?" Kirsten yelled in frustration. Jessica reached up and tried to pull a piece of trash from Kirsten's hair. Kirsten swatted her hand away, "Stop it Jess! Can't you see I'm trying to be intimidating?!" Jessica backed off and began glaring at Duffie along with Kirsten. Realizing what Kirsten and Jessica were doing, Tonya stopped twirling her gum and joined the two in glaring at Duffie. Getting into Duffie's face, Kirsten pointed her finger into her chest. Leif stood right behind her, staring down Kirsten with his bright bluish green eyes. Just as Kirsten was about to say something, Cat and her group interrupted.

"Kirsten, don't you have better things to do than push your weight around?" Cat asked lazily.

"Well, well, if it isn't Miss Catherine Colvin! Don't you have better things to do than butt into other people's business?" she spat out.

"When you mess with my friend, it becomes my business!" she replied forcefully.

"Oh look, the little kitty has her big girl panties on. I'd watch it if I were you fire crotch," Kirsten fired back.

"Break it up ladies! You two are teammates, you should know better," Coach Hutchins called out as she pushed her tall, athletic frame through the crowd that had formed around them.

Kirsten turned to Duffie, "This is far from over!" Quickly flashing a smile to Coach Hutchins, she snapped her fingers signaling the Trifecta's exit.

"Well that was a great welcoming. What a way to make a grand entrance," Duffie stated while dusting herself off. "Thanks Cat, by the way."

"No problem Duff. I've dealt with her before, you could say that I'm kind of an expert," Cat replied. Leif dropped his guard and was finally able to relax as he gave a relieved look to Cat.

Amanda laughed. "That was great! I couldn't have planned that to go any better myself!"

Isaac and his group made their way down the hall and the sea of students parted for the sharply dressed Goth clique. Ryan walked a few steps behind the group in his letterman's jacket. Even though the whole summer had passed, things were still iffy between Ryan and Isaac.

"Wow! Who's the major hottie walking our way?" Duffie asked, motioning toward Ryan.

Breaking off from his group, Ryan waved at Cat and smiled. The rest of his group glared at him, and then at Cat, except for Hannah who also smiled and waved.

Matt put his arm around Duffie, "Well you see Duffster, that's Ryan. And he's with Cat, so kind of off limits. A no fly zone if you get my drift."

"Oh, I see. Nice catch Cat! Definitely a looker, that one," Duffie said to Cat who was busy intercepting a huge hug from Ryan.

"So Cravenites, craving the new Robert Craven novel coming out soon?" Ryan dryly asked the group.

"Totes, of course!" Amanda exclaimed and then showed off the shirt she was wearing under her jean jacket. It read:

Bite me Bartholomew Drake!

A pair of fangs framed the lettering with droplets of blood dripping from each. Ryan grinned at her, shaking his head.

"You guys are Robert Craven fans?" Duffie asked.

"Umm, in a word, yes!" Cat replied, Ryan's arms around her waist, hugging her from behind with his head over her shoulder.

"Like his biggest fans ever!" Amanda exclaimed.

"You should all come to the grand opening of my dad's book café then! We're having a Robert Craven launch party that night at midnight, for the book's release!"

"OMG! Seriously?" Cat asked excitedly. "Your dad owns that new store opening in downtown, the one with the Bartholomew Drake cardboard cut-outs in the windows?"

"Yep. You guys should come, it'll be lots of fun!"

"Count us in!" Amanda declared to which everyone else agreed.

Cat entered her third period as the first bell rang, and sat in the back of the class. Pulling out her notebook and pencil, she laid them on her desk, preparing to take notes.

"Is this seat taken?" Duffie asked, pointing to the seat next to her.

"Oh hey Duffie! Nope it's all yours," Cat replied.

"Thanks. So, English class in America, huh? This should be interesting," she joked as she pulled her notebook from her backpack. Cat giggled.

"Hey there, lovely ladies! You two look very lonely back here all by yourself. Mind if we join you?" Matt asked with Amanda by his side.

"Really Matt, could you be any sleazier?" Amanda commented jokingly as she hit his arm. Duffie and Cat both stifled their laughter. Rubbing his arm, Matt sat down next to Cat.

"Man Amanda, you're definitely getting stronger, have you been working out?"

"No Matt, you're just getting weaker," she remarked. Matt rolled his eyes and then saw Hannah walk through the classroom door.

"Hannah, back here!" he called out. Hannah blushed as she shyly waved. Brushing her long blonde hair from in front of her face over her ear, she made her way to the back of the class. Hannah took the seat in front of Cat and refused to look back at Matt, her blush deepening. Matt was completely oblivious to how she was reacting, but everyone else saw it clear as day. "So, I guess our teacher is the wife of Mr. Rosenbaum, the art teacher Hannah and I had last year." The mere mention of her name from his lips, made Hannah slump further in her chair, blushing bright red. "She's supposed to be this very strict, and an uptight book worm," Matt told the group.

"Yeah, Taylor and Ryan both warned me about her. From what I hear, she's no Mr. Crawley, but she's up there," Cat commented.

"Who's Mr. Crawley?" Duffie asked.

"Someone you're better off not knowing," Cat replied.

The tardy bell rang, signaling the start of class. The door flew open and in walked Mrs. Rosenbaum. She looked like a supermodel. Her long black hair swayed from side to side with every step in her white patent leather pumps. Her olive skin radiated which allowed for her piercing hazel eyes to be showcased. Her white blouse was open revealing the slightest bit of cleavage. Her legs went on for days and lead up to a tight black mini skirt. The rumors about Mrs. Rosenbaum were proven instantly false the moment she walked into the room. *How did Mr. Rosenbaum end up with her?* Cat thought to herself. Matt, along with the rest of the male population in the class were beside themselves. There, standing in front of them was the physical representation of every one of their pre-pubescent fantasies. A little drool began to run down Matt's chin.

"Matt!" Amanda whispered. "Matt!" she whispered again.

"What?" he slowly replied in a daze.

"Get a hold of yourself, come on you're drooling!"

Matt wiped the drool, his eyes still fixed on their teacher. Hannah turned to look at Matt. Noticing his reaction she slumped even deeper into her chair. *He'll never notice me like that*, she thought to herself.

"She has to know what she's doing wearing a get-up like that. I mean honestly. In England we'd call her a scrubber," Duffie whispered to the group.

"Well in any language, she'd be translated to hot!" Matt interjected.

Facing the blackboard, Mrs. Rosenbaum wrote her name perfectly with equal spacing between the letters. "Class, my name is Mrs. Rosenbaum," she announced, placing the piece of chalk onto the blackboard's ledge, and then walked around to the front of her desk. Leaning back, she crossed her legs at the ankles and pushed out her chest, showing off her assets even more. The guys all swooned and the girls groaned inwardly. "I know that most of you have probably heard I'm strict and mean. That I'm too hard and have never, in my whole ten years of teaching, ever given an A for a final grade. But despite popular belief, I'm not a witch with a capital B as most past students have referred to me as," she said with a hair flip. "And if you all do your work, we should have no problems," she said grinning. "Now, everyone take out a sheet of paper and write your name, address, phone number, cell or home, emergency contacts, and email address. This will serve as a personal database so that if I need to get in contact with you, I'll be able to do so easily."

All the guys in the classroom ripped out a piece of paper as quick as they could and began writing feverishly. Collecting the papers, Mrs. Rosenbaum thumbed through them, stopping on Cat's. She looked up from Cat's paper right at her and smirked. Cat didn't notice.

"Cat! Cat! Over here," A female voice yelled out from the bleachers as Cat walked into her fourth period swim class with Hannah and Duffie. She looked up, startled by the young girl flailing her arms in the air and calling her name. Cat waved, not knowing who she was, but made her way up to her smiling face anyway. "Oh Cat, I'm sooo excited that I get to swim next to such a living legend as yourself!" The girl announced.

"Thanks, but I'm not that good," Cat replied.

"Don't be so modest, you're totes amazing!" the girl exclaimed.

"Sorry, but I'm drawing a blank on where I know you from," Cat said as she took a seat by the girl.

"I'm Shannon Starks! Mt mom's Glenda. You know, the front office receptionist? We went to all of your meets last year! I'm such a fan!" Shannon gushed. Duffie and Hannah looked at Cat, both with an unsure look on their face. "Will you be my swim partner when we pair up? Oh please, please, please?" Shannon asked, her eyes growing wide.

Cat groaned to herself, "Sure, I'd love to."

"Oh look girls, there's Catherine Colvin and her misfit friends," Kirsten announced as she walked up the bleachers with Tonya and Jessica in tow. As she passed, she gave Duffie a slight nudge on the shoulder.

"Hi, my name is Shannon."

Kirsten looked at her with disgust, "Like I care," she replied and then snickered as she took her seat near the top of the bleachers.

"That girl is going to be a pain, I can feel it," Duffie murmured.

"It's okay you two, just ignore her. Robbing her of attention is like her kryptonite," Cat explained as she glared back at Kirsten, who, along with the rest of her Trifecta entourage, was all grins.

After lunch, Matt rushed to the bulletin board located by the gym. He had eagerly anticipated this moment ever since football tryouts. He was sure he had made the team. Scanning the roster with his index finger, he came upon his name. He stopped and stood still, completely motionless. His group finally caught up to him.

"Well spaz, did you make it or not?" Amanda asked.

"Yeah Matt, what position are you playing?" Julie chimed in. Everyone stood there patiently waiting for his response. Slowly, he turned around and met the group with a blank stare.

"Yes!" he suddenly screamed out. "I can't believe I made it!" As he moved away from the roster, Cat and the rest of the group crowded around in disbelief, looking for his name. Next to the position, *team assistant* was: Matthew Thomas. "I'm the new team assistant! I can't believe it!" The group turned to look at him, not understanding his current state of happiness after finding out he was basically the team's new water boy. Not wanting to hurt his feelings, they agreed to not ruin his moment and instead decided to relish in it with him.

"Congratulations Matt, you'll be the best water boy, I mean team's assistant, this school has ever seen," Cat said enthusiastically. Amanda tried unsuccessfully not to laugh at the idea. Hiding behind Cat and Julie, Amanda hid her laugh and bright red face behind her jacket.

"Can you imagine the amount of chicks, I mean women, I'll be able to attract now that I'm on the football team?"

"Oh they'll be all over you for sure," Amanda said sarcastically, laughing out loud.

"Ignore her Matt, you'll be great," Julie assured him.

Jonathen, the captain of the football team, approached the group. His younger brother Brandon, an incoming freshman, was next to him. Brandon was a miniature version of Jonathen. Both had broad shoulders, blonde hair, and an athletic build, with striking good looks and chiseled faces. Like Matt, Brandon had tried out for the football team over the summer.

"Hey guys, you all know my little brother Brandon, right?" Jonathen asked the group. Brandon quickly waved to them and then hurried over to the bulletin board to look for his name.

"I made the team!" he exclaimed, as he high fived his older brother.

"Was there any doubt bro?"

"That's awesome Brandon, what position?" Cat asked

"I'm lead running back for the Freshman team. I can't wait to be second string behind Ryan on varsity next year," he replied as his older brother gave him a quick glare.

"Oh and congrats Matt on becoming the team's assistant. It's a tough job man, I hope you're up for it," Jonathen said with a smile, trying to change the subject.

"I'm the man for the job!" Matt exclaimed and then smiled ear to ear.

Realizing it was only minutes until the bell, Cat rushed down the hall toward her locker after saying her hurried goodbyes. Not wanting to be late, she feverishly dialed in her lock combo and threw it open, grabbing for her biology notebook. Losing her grip on it, it fell to the ground. As she bent down to pick it up a large, polished, black boot stepped down on it. "I kind of need that," she said, trying to wrestle it from underneath the shoe. Letting out a frustrated sigh she stood up and came face to face with Isaac, who was grinning devilishly at her.

"Oh my deepest apologies, is that *your* notebook under my foot?" he asked smugly. Cat just glared at him. Isaac's grin increased.

"Can I have my notebook, please?" Cat asked, anger showing in her eyes.

"Sure, by all means, take it," he replied innocently. Cat bent down and grabbed for it, noticing that more people had gathered behind him. She tried to pry the book from under his foot, but to no avail. Standing up abruptly, Cat glared at Isaac again. This time she was met by the evil stares of not only Isaac, but also Amelia, and the Stone twins.

"Having issues Cat?" Amelia asked condescendingly as the Stone twins grinned and snickered.

"No, actually I was just leaving," Cat replied bluntly. Anger surged through her as she bent down and grabbed for her notebook again. Isaac applied more pressure on it. Cat grabbed his ankle tightly and threw his foot off the notebook, causing him to stumble backward. After picking it up, she glared at Isaac and his group. Isaac stared at her in shock as Cat walked away.

"How did she do that?" Isaac asked confused.

"Why did you let her go?" Amelia asked.

"We thought we were going to play with her," the Stone twins said in unison.

"Well I used all my strength to push down," he replied, anger lacing his voice.

"All your strength, are you sure?" Amelia asked in a whisper.

"Yeah, all of my strength," he replied with one eyebrow raised. The stunned group watched Cat as she hurried down the hall.

The last bell rang as Cat rushed into biology. The whole class turned and looked at her as she stopped dead in her tracks. Looking around the room, she realized that every desk was taken.

"You must be Catherine Colvin," a male voice sounded from the front of the class. She turned to see her teacher holding the class roster in his hands.

"Sorry I'm late sir, locker trouble," Cat replied.

"It's okay, but just don't make it an everyday occurrence, okay?" he said, checking her off as present.

"Got it, won't happen again." Mr. Pierson turned around and began writing on the chalkboard. "Umm, sir, where do I sit?" Cat asked.

"Oh, yeah, sorry about that. They kind of loaded this class up for some reason. Umm, how about at one of the lab tables. I'll get an extra desk brought over for tomorrow's class," he replied with a smile. Cat shyly took her seat on the stool behind the large black topped table, embarrassed that everyone was still staring at her. She saw Hannah sitting in the back row. Hannah waved and mouthed "sorry" to her. "Damn Isaac, and his damn group," Cat muttered to herself.

8
Guess Who's Coming To Dinner

"Lordie, lordie, aren't you a sight for sore eyes," Elsie remarked as she opened the door and saw who was standing in front of her. "Aldon and Druanna are going to be so surprised!" their housekeeper gushed.

"Well Elsie, you have not changed in all these years, in fact you look younger," the handsome and distinguished man replied, bringing a big smile to Elsie's round face.

"Oh Edgar, you big flirt! Now get yourself in here right now, and let me go find those two. I just returned from running errands. I'm not sure if Druanna is back yet. Have a seat in the living room, make yourself comfortable," she rambled, taking his coat.

Edgar Girven watched as her short, round body bounced down the hallway and out of sight. The councilman shook his head, hating the sensation of his silver-laced black hair being bound by a leather strip, instead of being free like he wore it back home. He was fatigued. The trip from Austria had been a rough one. Instead of sitting he decided to wander around the room, admiring the antiques and baubles Aldon had collected during his world travels.

"Edgar, you sly devil. Why didn't you let us know you were coming?" Aldon's huge voice echoed in the large living room. The gray hair, gray bearded giant moved forward to shake Edgar's hand briskly.

"I wanted to surprise you, and apparently I have done a good job of it old friend."

"Yes you have. Druanna is out, but should be home shortly. Hope you are here to stay awhile."

Edgar stretched his arms out wide. "Thank you, I think I will. That trip practically did me in. I don't know how you enjoy traveling so much. Those airplanes are so small and claustrophobic. I like having my feet firmly planted on the ground, and not ten thousand miles in the atmosphere." He laughed, joining in with Aldon's infectious one.

"Would you like a nap before dinner?" Aldon asked.

"No, but what I would like is a drink and a game of pool. You still have the pool table, right?"

"Of course? Just because we are old, does not mean we do not like our toys anymore," Aldon chuckled as he slapped an arm around his shorter friend's shoulder, and escorted him to the billiard room.

"That was absolutely delicious Elsie!" Edgar announced, looking at her blushing face as she began collecting the dinner plates.

"It was just some meat and potatoes with a few veggies thrown in, nothing special," she replied.

"Well it must be that Elsie touch then." He laughed, seeing her face becoming more red by the minute.

"Now you folks move to the living room so I can clear this up. No Druanna, put that down and go converse with the men. They need guidance, they're men after all." Elsie finished picking up the plates and gave Druanna, who wasn't very much taller than her, but a great deal thinner, a little push toward the door.

"Okay bossy, I'm going." Druanna smiled and followed the two men. She heard Elsie humming a tune behind her as she headed into the kitchen.

"So what brings you to our fair town?" Aldon asked Edgar as he sat on the couch opposite him.

"Several things actually. First to see you and lovely Druanna of course," he said, wriggling his eyebrows at Druanna, making her giggle. "I would also like to hold a meeting with the rest of the group about these weird disappearances. And last, but not least, I would like to request a dinner invitation from the Colvin's. The council thinks it is about time one of the members meets this young lady that has been causing quite a stir in our meetings as of late. And I nominated me," he joked.

"Well, all of that can easily be arranged. But I'm warning you to quit flirting with my wife. She doesn't like it," Aldon said sternly and threw back his head, laughing heartily as Druanna smacked his hand.

"Sorry I'm late," Cat announced as she came around the corner to the cave. Ryan silenced her, kissing her senseless until she forgot what she was about to say. His hands brushed through her hair, making her heart speed up, and though the air from the ocean was cool, she felt like she was in a sauna.

"What were you going to say?" Ryan whispered into her ear, sending a shiver down her body.

"I forgot," she murmured as he nibbled at her ear. "Stop it Ryan. Behave! I'm here to train," she stated as she gently pushed away from him, and tried to control the feelings surging inside of her.

"But this is training too. And we can't get enough practice, now can we?" he chuckled, watching her try to pull herself together. Her cheeks were flushed and her hair was messed up, but in a good way.

"Ryan, stop," she said while backing away from him. "Let me catch my breath, you're such a…well, I can't think of what you are at the moment, but you are one," she huffed indignantly. He grinned as he watched her put her hands on her hips and glare at him.

"Okay, you win, we'll train."

"No touching exercises okay, promise?"

"Okay, I won't touch you," he replied while turning around so she didn't see his smirk. *I'm going to make her wish she hadn't promised that, yes I am,* he thought. "Alright, time to train Red Hot. Keep in mind that you asked for this, okay?"

"I'm ready, let's do this," Cat replied. *How hard can this training stuff be? We're vampires,* she thought.

"Okay first we'll start with *shifting*, which is moving quickly from one place to another. Now, watch me," Ryan said as he stood in front of her. Cat blinked and he was gone. Her eyes darted around the area looking for him, only to find him standing at the cave's entrance.

"I didn't even see you move. Do you think *I* can do that?"

"I know you can," he replied with a smile. "Now, let me show you something else, and then we'll practice." Ryan walked over to stand in front of her. "Alright, I want you to attack me."

"Attack you? What if I hurt you?" she asked smugly.

"Do you want to learn or not?" Ryan raised an eyebrow, his baby blue eyes penetrating hers.

"Sorry. So, you just want me to attack you?" Ryan nodded. "Okay, here goes nothing." Cat moved forward and reached out to grab him. Ryan moved so quickly she lost sight of him. All that was left was a faint, black, hazy outline of his body. It looked like his shadow. Feeling a tapping on her shoulder, Cat turned to her left and saw him standing there.

"Alright, one more time. Attack me," Ryan ordered, standing there nonchalantly. Without hesitation, Cat lunged for him. Ryan side-stepped, leaving his faint, shadowy outline in front of her again. Connecting with it, Cat clutched the shadow in her arms, and it dissipated into a puff of smoke when she hit the ground.

"Okay, how'd you do that?" she asked while pushing herself up from the ground.

Ryan chuckled. "It's called *fading*. And you'll find out soon enough,"

"So, I can do that too, huh? What's next?

"Well, I know you're in shape from swimming, but you also have more strength you can tap into. But you've got to be careful to control it, or you could end up hurting someone when you don't mean to. Watch," he stated, moving over to a large boulder buried in the sand and proceeded to lift it up as if it weighed nothing. "Remember, since you're still half human, you always need to stretch before we begin. Don't want you hurting yourself," he said as he threw the boulder off to the side, and then moved over to the cushioned black mat in the corner of the cave. Cat crossed the room and started following his instructions for the exercises he wanted her to do. *This is going to be a piece of cake,* she thought as she bent over to touch her toes.

"I think we've practiced enough today," Ryan chuckled looking down at Cat as she laid face first on the mat.

"Yeah…I think we should…call it a day," she replied, drenched in sweat and trying to catch her breath.

"So grab your stuff and we'll get going."

"Where are we taking off too?" Cat asked with a mischievous grin that quickly turned to a look of puzzlement, as Ryan grabbed his stuff and walked out of the cave. "Gentleman much? No that's okay Ryan, I don't need any help getting up," she rambled to herself as she climbed to her feet.

Every muscle screamed at her for moving. Her legs felt like jelly and her arms not much better. *And here I thought I was in shape*.

"Are you coming?" Ryan asked, re-entering the cave with his back pack slung over his shoulder.

Cat picked up her bag, disappointment running through her. "Okay, so when is our next training session?" she asked, trying to keep her feelings in check.

"I'll let you know at school." Ryan held back a snicker as he watched her face fall. Cat moved ahead of him out of the cave and sped up as she felt him trying to catch up with her.

"Cat, is something wrong?"

"No, why would there be? I just want to get home. I'm cold."

"Have I upset you?" Ryan asked, glad that she was ahead of him and couldn't see his grin. "Cat wait up!"

"I told you, I'm cold, and I want to get to my Jeep. It's not my fault you can't keep up," she huffed.

Ryan let her move further ahead of him, watching her struggle through the loose sand, muttering to herself, and trying to keep her balance. He knew her legs had to be tired after the rigorous training.

In her anger, Cat didn't see the piece of driftwood half hidden in the sand and tripped, falling forward. Ryan shifted to her side and stared down at her.

"Can I touch you now? To help you up of course," he asked finally laughing out loud.

"Ryan, you're such a jerk!" Cat stated jokingly as she sat up and brushed the sand off of her. "I hope you're enjoying yourself," she murmured.

"Well can I?" he asked again his face solemn, all trace of humor gone.

"No, but you can join me," she laughed, grabbing his hand, and pulling him off balance so he fell beside her.

"My pleasure," he smiled as he took hold of her. As Ryan's lips found hers, he laid back, pulling her down with him. Her long fiery red hair draped over his face, smelling like fresh peaches and salty air. "That will teach you never to make me promise not to touch you."

Cat fidgeted in the dress her mom begged her to wear. She wondered who the special dinner guest was that had her mom acting like a spaz. She took one last look in the mirror. "Ugh, whoever designed this should be banished from the fashion world! Hello, would you like a copy of the *Watchtower*? No? Well then have a blessed day," Cat murmured mockingly and then made her way downstairs. Pushing open the kitchen door, she was greeted with the smell of the pot roast simmering, making her mouth water. “Mom that smells delish. Can I have just one little piece?” she asked, watching her mom slicing the meat.

“Go ahead, you’ll bug me until I let you anyway. Oh Cat, be a dear and do the potatoes please?” Cat grabbed the bowl and began mashing them.

“So who’s the mystery guest? Must be someone important. I don’t usually have to dress up,” Cat asked, looking at her mom.

“He’s an old friend of the family and has traveled all the way from Austria to visit. You’ll like him. He’s a little old fashioned, kind of like Aldon.”

“So how long until dinner?”

“They should be here any minute, and we’ll eat soon after,” Rachel answered while pushing back her hair that had fallen in front of her face with her wrist. “Taylor, is the dining room table set?”

“Yes mom, all done.” Taylor replied as he pushed open the kitchen door, nudging Cat’s arm as he went by.

“Hey watch where you’re going dork,” Cat said and then gave him an indignant look.

“You bumped me,” he replied, grinning mischievously.

"You better watch it bud, or you're going to get a hot potato facial!"

"Now children behave. Oh, I think they're here. Let's go greet our guests." Rachel took off her apron, patted her hair down, and pushed her two offspring toward the front door.

Her father stood in the foyer with Aldon, Druanna, and a tall handsome man with shoulder length hair. As they moved closer, Cat noticed his eyes. They were a strange color. *Bronze eyes, how weird is that?* She thought.

"Edgar, welcome to our home," Rachel pushed past them and reached out to hug the handsome stranger.

"Rachel you haven't changed a bit. Sam told me you had become old and dowdy, but I see he was not telling the truth," Edgar joked.

"Oh stop it," Rachel said, pushing him away playfully.

"Taylor, Catherine, I'd like you to meet Edgar Girven, an old and dear friend of mine," Aldon said.

"And also an admirer of beautiful women," Sam chuckled, putting his arm around Rachel.

"Very pleased to meet you both," Edgar said, reaching out a hand to shake both of theirs. Lifting his nose to the air, Edgar breathed in heavily. "Something smells heavenly Rachel. I sure hope you have not been slaving away in the kitchen on my account," he stated, smiling at her.

"No, I just whipped up a little something. No chore at all. Now come on in and have a seat in the dining room. Dinner will be ready shortly. I hope you brought your appetite," Rachel stated as she headed back into the kitchen.

"I did indeed, that has not changed. I still thoroughly enjoy my food," Edgar replied following everyone into the dining room.

"So, Mr. Girven how long does it take for you to get here?" Cat asked when there was a lull in the dinner conversation.

He smiled. "Too long my dear. I loathe flying."

Not too shabby for an older guy, quite charming really, Cat thought.

After dinner, the men retired to the study while Cat and Taylor helped the women clean up. With the dishes done, Taylor gave his mom and Druanna a quick kiss on the cheek and Cat a head rub as he exited the kitchen on his way to meet Trish.

"I'm going to my room to read for a bit," Cat said making, her way up the stairs.

"Okay sweetie, we're going to make sure those three men are behaving themselves," Rachel said.

Opening her bedroom door Cat smiled as she saw Ryan reclining on her couch, reading her newest movie magazine. "Been waiting long?" she asked as he sat up, grinning at her.

"Not long. About fifteen minutes or so. Your parents?"

"They're in the study with my aunt and uncle, and our dinner guest. A rather handsome man actually."

"Handsome huh? So how old is this guest?" Ryan asked casually, though Cat could sense he was tense waiting for her reply.

"Why are you so interested in his age Ryan?" she replied with an eyebrow raised. Ryan looked pointedly at her. "Okay he's really old. As old as Aldon is," she laughed as he jumped up and grabbed her around the waist.

"Good, so if I have to fight him, I should have an edge," he whispered in her ear.

"I don't know. He's quite tall, and looked like he could hold his own," she replied innocently.

"Bet he doesn't kiss as well as I do."

"You might just win that bet," Cat said as he moved in to prove his point.

"So, I understand Catherine has been told she was adopted, and also that she is a Childe. I am sure you know the council had reservations about her finding out all of this. But she seems to have adjusted to the news pretty well," Edgar said, reclining in the overstuffed chair in the study.

"Not at first, I'm afraid. When she found out she was adopted it didn't go as well as we hoped. Then a week later she was hit with the fact she's half vampire. It has taken a while, but we feel she's coming around," Sam sighed, leaning back and putting his arm around Rachel. Rachel nodded in agreement.

"She has no idea about us though, right?" Edgar asked.

"No. We feel she has enough on her plate at the moment. And her safety is the main priority here," Rachel replied, unconsciously biting her lower lip after she finished talking.

"Do you think that is wise? Not telling her?" Edgar asked Sam, much to Rachel's relief.

"Yes, we do. Aldon and I have discussed the matter thoroughly and have agreed, as Rachel stated, she has enough to contend with at the moment."

"Good, that is how the council sees it as well. I shall report back to them that I find Cat a most charming young lady. You should be proud of her and Taylor too of course. This was not an easy task for you to take on, but you seem to be handling it quite well. But, if she is ever made aware of us, the council will have its say. You do understand this? It will be for your safety and ours," Edgar explained. Everyone nodded in agreement. "Now onto the next matter. Aldon informed me that thankfully, no other girls have disappeared. But it does worry me that there is no sign of what has happened to the three that are still missing. Tomorrow I have a meeting with

Lucien to discuss his feelings on the subject. Then I will return to the council with my findings."

"Would you like some more to drink?" Rachel asked noticing Edgar's empty glass.

"Certainly, how about another refill of that fine wine we've been enjoying. It is quite exquisite. Truly good indeed," he said, smacking his lips.

❧ ❧ ❧

"Sire, my humble apologies for the interruption, but there is someone at the gate wishing an audience with you. He is quite the bold individual. Pue almost took his head off, but he insisted on speaking with you about a very important matter. It is from his mistress. What do you wish I do with him?" Andrei's servant Tal swallowed nervously, waiting for his reply.

"Send him in. If this information is lucrative, he will live, if not, we shall feed," Andrei sneered as his servant hurried out of the room. He arrived back a few seconds later with a tall, slender, regally dressed individual who was holding a letter in his hand. His face was stoic. "Who sent you?" Andrei demanded, shocked when the stranger met his eyes straight on, with not a hint of fear in them.

"I serve Councilwoman Blanche Calder, and she has instructed me to deliver this letter to one Andrei Lazar. I assume that is you?" the man stated coldly.

"Give it here!" Andrei demanded, holding out his hand. Examining the envelope, he was confused when he saw the red wax seal bearing the mark of the Varulv Council, a V inscribed over an A.

"I shall wait outside for your reply," the stranger stated.

"If I have one!" Andrei growled as he watched the man turn and make his way out of the room. Breaking the seal, Andrei began reading the flowery script.

Andrei Lazar,

It would seem we have a common enemy. I wish to arrange a meeting with you to discuss a temporary truce. Both sides working together toward a common goal. I know you will want the information I possess. I believe you are seeking a Childe, am I right?

Andrei looked up from the letter and grinned. *A Childe? This meeting could prove quite important*, he thought. Before he could call the stranger back in, the man re-entered the room and stood in front him. The edges of his mouth were curled up in an evil smile.

"Well?" The man asked.

"You tell your councilwoman she has her audience," Andrei replied, glaring at the smile on the man's face.

"Very well, I shall inform her immediately."

The meeting between Blanche and Andrei was held in a secluded forest just on the outskirts of Budapest, Hungary. They had decided on neutral meeting grounds between Romania and Austria, with an equal representation of both parties present. Though Andrei seemed to have a calm demeanor as he approached the forest tree line, he was still on his guard. He was meeting with a very influential person of his enemies after all. "Are you sure we can trust her?" Tal asked in a whisper, as Blanche, surrounded by three henchmen, came into view through the trees ahead.

"It is a little late for thoughts like that now, is it not Tal? We shall hear her proposal from a safe distance. No rash moves, until I say," Andrei replied, trying to sound calm, as he smoothed back his thick dirty blonde hair.

"As you wish sire," he stated.

As Blanche noticed Andrei and his men approaching, a menacing grin formed on her mouth. Outstretching her arms, "Andrei, so happy you could join us," she stated in a sarcastic, sickeningly sweet tone. Andrei nodded, glancing at the three men around her, all staring with penetrating glares in his direction. "Do not fret vampire, we wish to form a truce. Oh and forgive this rag tag group of individuals beside me. They are only for show. You know, in case you had some not so bright ideas," she said with an eye brow raised.

Andrei laughed to himself slightly. “What is this plan of yours?” he asked impatiently.

“So you are a get-right-down-to-business type? I like that,” she quipped with a smirk.

“I do have one question before we begin though. Why do you want to be rid of this Childe? I thought your kind wanted to protect them.”

“I have my reasons Mr. Lazar, do not concern yourself with them,” she stated with slight anger in her voice. “So shall we begin?” An hour later, the insight Andrei gained from the meeting delighted him, and a truce was formed.

Nestled behind the large ornate wooden desk in his study, Andrei was in deep thought about what he learned. *Catherine Colvin, I knew she was different. This shall be my little secret. The Parliament will not be told. When all is said and done, Cain shall grant me whatever I desire.* “Tal, ready the car. It is time I returned to Astoria!” he ordered his servant. Searching through one of his desk drawers, Andrei didn’t see the person who slipped into his study.

“Heading back to Astoria, eh?” Lisbeth asked snidely, sneering at Andrei when he popped up to look at her.

“Maybe. What does it matter to you?” he replied.

"Just curious is all. I have my eye on you Andrei. You will slip up, I know it. And when you do, I will be there to revel in it."

"Give it a rest Lisbeth, I must be on my way. This delay is not worth my time, nor energy," Andrei said, continuing to look through his desk drawer.

"We shall see Andrei, we shall see," she smirked. "Oh, and please do give my regards to my dear brother Lucien, will you?" she called out as she left the room. Andrei huffed, slamming the desk drawer shut. *I wonder if Valdir told her what I have been up to. No, he wouldn't...would he?* He thought.

"Your car is ready sire," Tal called into the study.

"Very good, we shall leave at once!" he shouted.

A slight rain, just enough to make one miserable, was falling as Andrei arrived in Astoria. Making his way down the muddy tunnels, he heard the three girls talking before he saw them. Stepping into the cavernous central chamber, he chuckled as they turned and looked at him with surprise in their eyes. "I see you girls have bonded like I hoped you would."

"We're practically sisters, aren't we girls?" Amy replied, looking pointedly at Linda.

“Yes, and we’ve been totally bored with you gone,” Becca added, pushing her hair out of her eyes.

“Have you now?” Andrei lifted one eyebrow and smirked as he watched Becca and Amy’s eyes fill with excitement. “Something I will be happy with I presume, from the look on your faces.”

“Well I’m sure you know we caused a bit of trouble. Misdirected a few fireworks, but no one was killed though. We just wanted to stir up a little chaos,” Amy finished with a flourish. “Linda though, was a little reluctant. But she’s finally come around. Haven’t you?” Amy asked, smirking at her.

“And I know you’re just so excited to learn that our girl Linda here used to be best friends with Cat,” Becca piped in. Andrei schooled his features as not to reveal his shock at this information. *It worked! They truly believed that while I was gone, I could read their thoughts,* he laughed to himself.

“You have no idea how delighted I was to find out this news,” he replied. “This little detail shall fit into my plans perfectly.” Andrei reached out for the girl’s hands. A cold shiver ran down Linda’s spine at the look on his face, wondering what his plans were. “In fact, I feel this is cause for celebration. Shall we feed? I find that suddenly I have a very sizable appetite.”

9
Three's A Crowd

"That's awesome you made the swim team Duffie! I'm not surprised though, you're really good," Cat said and then smiled at her while stretching her arm across her chest.

"You're not too shabby yourself Cat," Duffie replied, putting on her swim cap.

Kirsten and her usual Trifecta entourage of two sauntered into the locker room, their heads held high. Spotting Cat, Kirsten walked over and stood in front of her, her hands on her hips. "Look girls, it's the three amigos," she said snidely. Cat,

Hannah, and Duffie all looked at each other, and then at Kirsten with a confused look.

"Was that supposed to be an insult or something?" Cat asked.

"It sounded more like a compliment. I would've said something like, 'hey look it's the three stooges'," Hannah replied, grinning at Kirsten's obvious frustration.

"I just meant that you always hang around each other. Whatever!" Kirsten yelled and then stormed off.

"Daft cow," Duffie murmured. Cat and Hannah both giggled, knowing that Kirsten heard the insult.

Turning abruptly Kirsten yelled, "What did you call me?"

"Nothing. I didn't say anything," Duffie replied innocently. Cat and Hannah, along with a few other girls, snickered off to the side. Just as Kirsten was about to respond, Coach Hutchins entered the locker room.

"Alright ladies, head out to the pool," Coach Hutchins ordered. Noticing the tension in the room, "Everything okay here?" she asked, singling out the Trifecta and Cat's group.

"Everything's fine Coach. Just a little discussion between us girls," Kirsten replied with an empty smile.

Coach Hutchins looked at Cat, "Is that true Cat?"

Kirsten glared at Cat, mouthing the words "you better not." Coach Hutchins quickly turned back to Kirsten, who immediately slapped the same empty smile back on her face.

"Yeah, we were just talking about swim strategies for this year," Cat replied, hating the fact she lied to her coach, but didn't want to involve her in such petty issues.

"Uh, huh," Coach Hutchins responded unconvinced. "Well, come on and hit the pool already, we don't have all night!"

Standing by the pool waiting for their turn on the blocks, Cat thought about how her vampire abilities would work in water. *I wonder if I can swim faster. It wouldn't necessarily be cheating. It's only practice,* she thought trying to convince herself. Coach blew her whistle and shouted "next!" Duffie emerged from the pool and Coach Hutchins called out, "Way to hustle Duffie! That's what wins competitions around here!" Cat smiled at Duffie and mouthed "good job." Waiting for the second whistle, Cat bent down into starting position. She watched the water glisten with a glow from the fluorescent lights above. *Alright, just this once. Let's give this a try, shall we?*

"Go Cat! You can do it!" Shannon yelled from the sidelines. Cat smiled at her and then groaned. *Wow, that girl's something else. I mean she's nice and all, but look at her frantically waving at me. It's kind of weird.*

The next whistle had them all diving into the pool. Cat began swimming normally and then quickened her pace little by little. Touching the far wall, she kicked off and propelled herself like a torpedo through the water, causing a slightly larger wave than usual.

Duffie stood by watching with wide eyes. "What the?" she whispered to herself. Finishing miles ahead of anyone else, Cat climbed out of the pool and was greeted by Coach Hutchins.

"Keep that up Colvin, and you should have no problems retaining your regional title!"

"Thanks Coach," she replied. *So I can swim faster.*

"How did you move so quick?" Duffie asked.

"Yeah Cat, that was amazing," Hannah followed up.

"I don't know, I just dug deep I guess," Cat replied, wiping her face with a towel. When Cat wasn't looking, Duffie glanced at her with questioning eyes.

"OMG Cat! I so wish I could swim like you! You're totes amazing!" Shannon gushed as she linked arms with her.

"Thanks Shannon," Cat said, and then mouthed "help me" to Duffie and Hannah.

Walking up behind Cat's group, Kirsten discreetly reached up and ripped out some straggling hairs poking out from underneath Duffie's swim cap.

"Oww! Bloody hell!" Duffie exclaimed, turning around to face Kirsten. Kirsten gave an innocent look and shrugged her shoulders. Duffie glared, watching as Kirsten rejoined her group and then turned her focus back to Cat.

"Watch this," Kirsten whispered to Jessica and Tonya. Nonchalantly, Kirsten walked over to the pool, and dunked her hand full, that was full of Duffie's hair, into the water. "Ewww! I found some of Duffie's trashy weave in the pool!" she cried, pulling her hand out of the water so everyone could see. Snickers could be heard throughout the area. A tense Duffie scowled at Kirsten as she stood there with an evil grin and the strands of weave in her hand. Duffie began to move toward her, but then was gently pushed aside by Cat who proceeded to storm over to stand toe to toe with Kirsten.

"What's your deal?" Cat asked forcefully.

"Oh look, it's a freak standing up for her freak friend!" Kirsten replied with a laugh and then glanced over at her group. Without hesitation Cat shoved Kirsten into the pool just as Coach Hutchins emerged from the locker room. The girls were startled by the deafening sound of the coach's whistle as it filled the pool area.

"Cat! Kirsten! In my office, now!" Coach Hutchins roared. Cat glared at Kirsten splashing around, screaming for her two lackeys to pull her out. After two failed attempts Kirsten muttered, “useless,” and pulled Tanya and Jessica into the pool.

Sitting in the Coach’s office, Cat fidgeted with her swim suit while Kirsten put on a nonchalant attitude, staring at her manicure. Coach Hutchins closed her office door and then sat heavily in her chair behind her desk. “Now, what’s going on between you two? And don’t tell me nothing,” she said, pointing at them. They both sat in silence dodging her stares. “Okay, if that’s how you want it. You two can stay after practice and swim laps!”

“Coach, that’s so unfair!”

“I think it’s a fitting punishment,” Kirsten said sweetly, looking at Cat.

“Oh Kirsten be quiet! Save your ass kissing for someone else,” Coach Hutchins fired back. Both girls slouched in their chairs, crossed their arms, and looked away from each other.

Reaching the wall, Cat and Kirsten both came up for air and looked at their Coach. “Another!” she yelled at them and then blew her whistle. Cat’s arms and legs were tired. She was really beginning to regret pushing Kirsten in the pool. Her breathing had become labored and her muscles ached, as she reached out again for the wall.

“Okay, hit the showers you too! Maybe now you’ll act more like teammates!” Coach Hutchins ordered. Pulling themselves out of the pool, both girls walked to the showers, feeling like their feet were encased in concrete. Cat went into the first set of showers and Kirsten walked to the last set, too tired to make a snappy comment at Cat as she passed. Turning on the hot water, Cat let it wash over her to massage her aching muscles. Toweling herself off, she headed toward her locker.

"Kirsten, I'm sorry for pushing you in the pool," Cat said begrudgingly. She waited for an answer. "Kirsten?" A shiver of fear ran down Cat's spine at the silence. "Kirsten?!" she shouted loudly, her voice echoing through the dimly lit locker room.

"What?!" Kirsten answered, popping out from behind a few rows of lockers ahead of Cat and startling her.

"Nothing," Cat replied.

"You're such a freak," Kirsten said smugly, rolling her eyes while still towel drying her hair.

"Whatever," Cat murmured. Opening her locker, Cat grabbed her clothes and pulled them on quickly. Her cell phone beeped signaling a message. Grabbing her cell from her messenger bag she read the text:

I thought Cats hated water!

Her eyes grew wide when she saw the text was from Linda. Cat called out to Kirsten. There was no answer. Quickly making a beeline for Kirsten's locker, "I really think we should-" Cat began and then stopped as she heard Kirsten talking. Rounding the corner, she saw her busily getting dressed and a curly haired blonde was sitting on the bench behind her, her back to Cat. "Kirsten?" Cat asked cautiously.

"What now freak?" Kirsten replied smugly. The blonde girl slowly turned around and smirked at Cat. It took her a few moments, but Cat eventually realized who the girl was. Her picture was plastered on many of the flyers posted about town. It was Becca, one of the missing girls. "Don't mind her Becca, she's a weirdo!" Kirsten said, rolling her eyes. Two fangs descended from Becca's gums adding an evil touch to her grin. "So Becca, what are you doing here anyway? You're not still pissed about what I did at regionals two years ago are you?" she asked absently.

"Kirsten I think we should leave," Cat said nervously. Ignoring her, Kirsten kept rambling.

"Because I won that race fair and square!" Kirsten said while digging through her locker. Becca rose to her feet, anger filling her face. She moved up behind Kirsten and growled. "Gawd Becca, you should really get that checked," she said as she continued rummaging through her locker.

"Kirsten, run!" Cat yelled.

Kirsten turned, "Cat I'm really getting tired of your-" Becca grabbed Kirsten by the throat and slammed her up against the locker. "Let go of me you psycho!" she shrieked. Seeing Becca's fangs glistening in the fluorescent lights, Kirsten let out a blood curdling scream. "Cat, help me!" she cried. Cat moved forward to intervene, but then Becca turned to her and hissed, waving her index finger back and forth. Two more figures emerged from the shadows, stepping into the light. Cat saw it was Amy, the other missing girl, and Linda. Amy was dragging something behind her. It was a body. Tightening her grip on the body's shirt, Amy brought it up effortlessly with one hand, and threw the person at Cat's feet.

Cat gasped. "Coach!" she cried out as she knelt down and felt for a pulse. She was still alive. Standing up Cat glared at the three girls, her fingernails digging into her palms. She noticed that Linda was not looking as blood thirsty as the other two, in fact she avoided eye contact with Cat altogether.

"Tag! You're it!" Becca yelled, tossing Kirsten forcefully at her. Cat caught Kirsten and struggled slightly to help her stand upright. Grabbing hold of Kirsten's hand, she took off running away from the girls. Wicked laughter echoed throughout the locker room.

"What's going on?" Kirsten asked breathlessly, trying to keep up.

Cat paused and looked around for a place to hide. “You wouldn’t believe me if I told you,” Cat replied hurriedly. The sound of finger nails lightly scratching on lockers seemed to grow louder and louder.

“Cat…Cat…we’re coming to get you,” Amy whispered eerily.

Spying the sports equipment cage, Cat dragged Kirsten over to it. “Hide in here, I’ll come back for you when it’s safe.”

“No! Forget it, I’m staying with you! There’s no way you’re putting me in a cage, while you get to run around!”

Cat palmed Kirsten’s face, “sorry, but this is for your own good,” she said apologetically as she forcefully shoved Kirsten into the cage, causing her to crash into the shelves holding the basketballs. The shelves toppled over and Kirsten fell to the floor unconscious. Cat apologized again, and then locked the padlock on the cage door. As she turned around, Cat came face to face with Amy, who was grinning menacingly.

“Fetch!” she yelled as she back handed Cat, sending her flying down a row of lockers, slamming into the ones at the far end. Cat looked up wearily, groaning, her vision blurred. “Aww, I’m sorry. Was that too hard?” Amy asked as she ran her hand along the side of Cat’s face. Suddenly Amy was thrown backward. Cat could hear a struggle happening before her in the distance, but couldn't make out anything. She heard something smash into a locker, making it squeak under the pressure. Hearing the painful grunts that followed, Cat tried to focus on what was going on, but her vision blurred again, and then nothing, just darkness.

"Cat? Cat?!" A muffled voice called out to her. Blinking, Cat slowly opened her eyes. "Cat, you alright?"

"Yeah," she strained out, smiling wobbly when she recognized Ryan's voice. Her eyes focused and she was happy to see those baby blues staring back at her.

"What the hell happened here?"

"Did you…fight them off?" she asked.

"Who?"

"The three missing girls."

"What? Exactly how hard did you hit your head?"

"No, they were here Ryan…they're vampires…even Linda," she murmured, trying to shake the dizziness she was feeling.

"Cat, are you sure they were vampires?"

"Totally sure," she replied. Ryan carefully helped Cat to her feet. Pressing on the locker, he tried to smooth out the dent she had made, slowly molding it back to its original shape…somewhat. Standing, Cat put her arm around Ryan's shoulder as he helped her sit down on the bench. "What are you doing here?"

"Hannah told me that you had a fight with Kirsten. And Coach Hutchins made you stay after practice. So, I decided to wait for you. Then I heard all the commotion, like someone fighting, and rushed in to find you here," he explained.

Cat's eyes grew wide, "Oh Coach…and Kirsten! We need to check on them!" Helping her up, they both scrambled over to the sports equipment cage to find Kirsten. Breaking the lock and opening the cage door, Ryan and Cat saw movement under one of the shelves that had fallen over. Ryan lifted up the shelf with one hand and tossed it aside. A quiet groan came from the pile of basketballs. Reaching in, Ryan pulled Kirsten out. She slowly opened her eyes. Looking around, Kirsten realized she hadn't been dreaming, and began freaking out.

"Vampires! Where are the vampires?!" Kirsten asked frantically. Ryan glanced at Cat with a look of concern.

"There are no such things as vampires," Cat replied, chuckling nervously.

"What do you mean? We were just attacked by them, just before you pushed me into this cage…hey! You pushed me in here!" she stated angrily.

"No I didn't. You must've fallen in the cage and knocked yourself out. We came running when we heard the crash," Cat lied, as Kirsten looked at her with questioning eyes.

"Ryan, what are you doing in the girl's locker room?" Coach Hutchins asked as she came around the corner, rubbing her head.

"Uh, well," Cat began to explain, but then Ryan put his hand on her arm and squeezed gently. She turned to look at him and he shook his head. Moving toward Coach Hutchins, Ryan looked deeply into her eyes and whispered something Cat couldn't hear. Coach Hutchins nodded and walked back toward her office, looking as if in a trance.

"What did you say to her Ryan?" Cat asked.

"I took care of it okay, don't worry," he replied, smiling reassuringly.

"Will someone please explain to me what's going on here?" Kirsten asked in frustration.

Ryan turned to her, his eyes jet black. "Everything's fine Kirsten. You had a little accident and we came to help you. Get your things and go home," he said. Kirsten stiffened up, her eyes glazed over in a trance. She gathered her stuff from her locker and left, not looking back.

"You totes just used your vamp mind tricks, didn't you?!" Cat asked in disbelief. Ryan looked at her with a trickle of blood running down from his nose. "Ryan, your nose, it's bleeding!" He smirked and then wiped the blood away.

"I guess it is. I might have overdone it a bit," he replied and then stumbled, falling into her arms. Propping him up, Cat sat him down on the bench next to the equipment cage.

"Ryan are you okay?" Cat asked with worry in her voice. He nodded while rubbing his head, trying to ease the pressure. "Well this is a switch, huh? I'm usually the one getting all light-headed and falling on the floor," she remarked, giggling softly. He began to chuckle but then groaned.

"I've never done that before…it was kind of intense. We're actually forbidden to control someone's memory like that. But I had to…there was no other choice," he explained. "Unfortunately, we have bigger problems than stopping Kirsten from spreading our secret," he continued, looking at Cat with concern in his eyes.

"I'll say," she responded dismally. Reaching into his pocket, Ryan withdrew a small silver canister. He popped the top off with shaky hands and dumped a large blood red pill onto his palm. "Hey, that looks like the pills I take."

"Yeah, remember how I said our coven here is special, well this *little* baby is the reason," Ryan stated, examining the pill, holding it up to the florescent lights. In the light it had a deep red glow to it. "Dr. Bane has all us vampires on it. So it doesn't surprise me that you take them too,"

"And if you don't take them…then what?" Cat asked.

He chuckled. "I don't know. That's never happened before. All I know is they curb our appetite, and that my mom is very adamant about us taking them."

"Hey Ryan, how is it you and your coven can walk in the sun? I thought sunlight was like a vamp's kryptonite? I mean, I know why I can, because I'm still half-human."

"Well just between you and I, these pills we take, are like some kind of blood steroid. It makes us like the living undead…if that makes any sense?" Ryan replied.

"Kind of...but, then that would mean you're just-"

"Like you?" Ryan completed her sentence. "Yeah, that's our secret. None of our brethren know that our whole coven here in Astoria are all like the Children they want to destroy. Actually, no one knows that us youngsters even exist. Our parents have hidden us away from our brethren, in hopes that we can all lead *normal* lives. Which is why you can't tell anyone what I've told you, okay?"

"Scouts honor, my lips are sealed," she replied. "This is all just so crazy! To think I thought none of this existed, but here it all is, right here in Astoria," she continued, slightly laughing.

"Yep, this place is like one big cornucopia of the supernatural," he joked.

"Ryan, have you ever…you know, drank blood?"

"You mean like bite someone? No, why?" he replied and then popped the pill in his mouth.

"Just curious."

❦ ❦ ❦

"Mom, dad! I'm home!" Cat announced walking through the front door.

"So, laps for fighting huh?" Taylor smirked, shaking his head. Rachel and Sam came into the foyer, both looking disappointed. Cat dodged their glares.

"Catherine Colvin! I thought we raised you better than that?" Rachel reprimanded. "And Kirsten? Of all people to fight with."

"Mom, I can explain-"

"There's no explanation for this Cat. I want you to march up to your room and think about what you've done," Rachel said, crossing her arms over her chest.

"Cat you really should be more careful. You don't need to be drawing unnecessary attention your way. The last thing we need is for someone to find out what you are. Especially a gossip queen like Kirsten," Sam explained while cleaning his glasses with his shirt. Cat giggled at the fact her dad used the phrase gossip queen, but then quickly apologized, putting on a serious face as no one else was smiling.

Rachel pointed up to the stairs and Cat slouched with a slight huff, as she made her way up to her room. Closing the bedroom door behind her, Cat kicked off her shoes, threw down her messenger bag, and flopped down on her bed exhausted. Rolling over, she looked up at the ceiling thinking about what could have happened if that person hadn't intervened. *I wonder who helped me?* Hearing a faint squeak outside of her window, Cat sat up quickly. She heard the sound again and moved cautiously toward it, grabbing a shoe off the floor along the way. Peering out the window, Cat saw Ryan sitting on the bench just outside. He seemed to be in deep thought while he studied the forest as if waiting for something. Opening the window, "Ryan, what are you doing? Have you been here this whole time?"

"Yeah. I thought I'd sit watch for a while," he replied, smiling at her, his beautiful eyes glistening in the moonlight.

"Need some company?" she asked, returning his smile.

"Don't you need to get some sleep?"

"Not really, I've kind of become an insomniac."

"Yeah, that happens. It comes with the whole being a vampire thing," he said with a chuckle and then patted the bench. Cat sat down next to him. He wrapped his arm around her as she snuggled up close, burying her head into his shoulder. "You know, I was really worried about you tonight. We really need to be careful Cat. Cat?" he asked when he heard quiet snoring coming from her. "Insomniac huh?" he joked. Scooping her up into his arms, Ryan carried Cat into her room, her body wriggling slightly as if to protest. Kissing her forehead, he tucked her into bed.

"You really do love her, don't you?" Taylor asked from Cat's doorway. Ryan tensed, looking up at him in shock.

"How did you-"

Taylor tapped on his nose, "keen sense of smell, remember?"

"Oh. I was just leaving by the way," he replied, turning to the window.

"Hey, you didn't answer my question!" Ryan turned back to face Taylor.

"Yes, I really do love her," he whispered, as Cat tossed and turned slightly in bed.

"Well, you know what will happen to you if you ever hurt her, right?" Taylor asked.

"I do. But I'll never hurt her, or let anything else hurt her either," he replied.

"Good, we're on the same page then. See you at practice tomorrow. And you're going to need to hustle more, or Brandon will take your spot next season," he joked, grinning.

Ryan smirked. "Will do."

Taylor walked out of the room closing the door behind him. He looked down the staircase to see Rachel and Sam standing together. He signaled to them that everything was fine and made his way down the stairs.

"I'm so proud of you dear. You handled that like a true older brother," Rachel gushed. Sam put his arm around him and smiled.

Ryan looked at Cat, a slight smile on his face. Turning off the bedside lava lamp, he exited through the window. Sitting back down on the wrought iron bench outside, he waited, watching for any signs of movement in the forest which was illuminated by the moon above.

10
Three Penny Brit

"Ryan, you've been sitting outside my window, watching over me for the past two weeks, and nothing has happened. Don't you think that if they were going to try something again, they would've by now? Besides, your mom will begin to dislike me if I occupy all of your time like this," Cat said, staring intently into his eyes while both of them lay on her bed.

"You're right," he replied, and then grinned after seeing the offended look on her face. "I'm only kidding. But Cat, there's something that you need to know about newly turned vampires. They're unpredictable, more dangerous, and less controlled. The fact that they haven't attacked again can be one of two things. Either the person who fought them off gave them a good beating, or they're planning something bigger." Ryan combed his hand through Cat's hair, pushing the wayward strands over her ear while returning her deep gaze. "I hope it's the first reason, but we can't be sure."

Cat bent her head up and kissed him softly on the lips, her hand caressing his chest. "You better get going, your mom's going to text you soon to get your butt home, I can feel it," she murmured jokingly as she playfully pushed him away, trying to break his serious demeanor. Ryan laughed softly and then kissed her again before he made his way to the window.

"Don't do anything reckless tonight, okay?" he said as he turned around and flashed a grin before he made his exit.

"Hey Ryan?"

"Yeah?" he asked, poking his head back through the bay window.

"Are you ever going to use the front door?" she inquired with a grin.

He just laughed, and said, "Good night. And I mean it, nothing reckless."

Cat didn't want to tell Ryan, but she was worried about staying home by herself with only Taylor. She didn't want him to worry. She knew that Ryan had to go home, and telling him would just have thrown that idea out the window.

Snuggling up in her bed, cuddling her pillow, Cat tried not to react to every strange noise that she heard outside. "Come on Cat, there's nothing there. They haven't tried for two weeks, why would they all of a sudden strike again?" she tried to reassure herself. *Ryan did say that they could be unpredictable though.* Cat heard her cell beep, breaking her train of thought. Opening it, the message read:

Got home safe. Call me if anything happens k. Ttyl luv you! Nothing reckless! Lol

Cat smiled at the message and was about to reply when a loud resounding knock came from the front door. It echoed through the entire house, sounding slow and powerful. Warily, Cat opened her bedroom door. She made her way down the old attic's spiral staircase, which creaked with every step she made, making her feel more uneasy. "Hey Cat, could you get that?" Taylor asked, hearing her pass outside his bedroom door.

"Alright," she replied hesitantly. Rachel and Sam were at a town hall council meeting which meant Cat was at Taylor's beck and call. Creeping down the stairs in her old pink ratty robe, she made her way to the front door. It was night time, and looking through the eye hole, all she could see was a faint outline of something outside. Flipping the switch by the door illuminated the front porch. Looking through the eyehole again, she saw no one. Opening the door slightly, Cat peeked through the crack. "Hello? Is anyone there?" she asked, her voice shaking. There was no answer. Opening the door all the way, Cat spied something lying on the front porch. It was a small square package tightly wrapped in brown paper and tied with a thin tan string. Written in bold letters on the package was: *For Catherine Colvin.* So many thoughts ran through her mind. *Who left it? What's inside? Is this a trap? Should I take it?* Cat crept out onto the porch toward the package. "Hello?" she asked once more into the night. She scanned the front yard to see if anyone was there. Seeing no one, she bent down and picked up the package.

"Cat, what are you doing? Who was at the door?" Taylor asked behind her making her jump. Stuffing the package into her robe, she spun around to face him.

"Holy crap Taylor! A little warning next time would be nice, thanks!" she joked. "Oh and strange thing, no one was at the door. Must've been some kids or something." Taylor looked at her suspiciously and crossed his arms over his chest.

"Well then get your butt inside. Mom and Dad would kill me if anything happened to you!"

Cat rolled her eyes at him. "I can take care of myself you know. I'm half that which shall not be named, remember?" she whispered at him.

"Whatever, you're still my younger sister and they'd kill me all the same," he replied, and then motioned for her to get back inside. Cat rolled her eyes again and then rushed passed Taylor, up the stairs and into her room, slamming the door behind her. Taylor shook his head as he closed and locked the front door. "That girl's a strange one. Special indeed," he quipped to himself.

Jumping onto her bed Cat pulled out the package and laid it out in front of her. She studied it, not sure if she wanted to open it. *It could be from the three girls! Maybe I shouldn't open it. Maybe I should wait for Ryan,* she told herself. "Ahhh, what the heck," she said aloud, tearing off the wrapping. Layer by layer, she peeled back the brown paper until she reached the contents. It was a book. Seeing the back cover, Cat turned it over and her eyes filled with surprise. She read the title eagerly:

The Cleansing
By Robert Craven

Cat could hardly believe that she was holding the book in her hands. "OMG! This is Craven's new novel! It's not even out yet!" she squealed. Opening the book she noticed some writing on the first page, it read:

To my #1 Cravenite! Thank you for all the support. I hope this book helps.

-Robert Craven-

"This, is, totes, awesome!" Cat exclaimed in a whisper, grabbing for her cell phone.

"Hey Cat, what's up?" Julie answered.

"You'll never guess what was just left on my doorstep!"

"What?"

"A signed copy of Robert Craven's new novel, *The Cleansing*!"

"Really? That's amazing!" Julie replied cheerfully. "Who left it?"

"Well, it was so weird. Someone was at the door, and then when I answered it, they were gone. And all that was left was the book," Cat explained excitedly.

"Hmmm, that is weird," she replied.

"Well what's weirder is he signed it to his number one Cravenite. But on Craven's fan site, I'm like number 4,000 or something on his list of top fans. So maybe he sent it to the wrong person," Cat sighed, flopping back on her bed.

"Maybe…but either way, I don't think you should tell anyone else about this, especially since the book hasn't come out yet," Julie said in a concerned motherly voice.

"I know right? But you have to admit, this whole thing is really cool!"

❦ ❦ ❦

Miss Amaya entered the teacher's break room and noticed Melvin Pierson standing next to the coffee maker, watching the coffee drip slowly into the pot. His hair was disheveled and his wrinkled shirt was half-way tucked in. *Hmm, he's usually impeccably dressed,* she thought. "Good morning Melvin, rough start to the day?" she asked with a warm smile. Turning his head to face her, he grabbed the pot of coffee, and stretched for his mug that was just out of reach.

"Oh, Amaya Phillips, hi," he replied distractedly as he began pouring the coffee, not paying attention and instead getting lost in her gaze. "Oww, crap!" he exclaimed, missing his mug and sending hot coffee splashing on the counter top and onto his gray pants and white shirt. "Great!" he continued, beginning to wipe his clothes off with paper towels. Miss Amaya tried not to giggle.

"Are you okay? You look a little worse for wear," she stated, handing him more paper towels.

"Yeah sure, why do you ask?"

"Oh, no reason really. Just that you look like you rolled out of bed with those clothes on."

"Well, I kind of did. I'm really behind on grading papers and getting my lesson plans together. I was up late last night. I feel so disorganized, and this is usually not like me. I think I might need a teacher's assistant," he joked, but sounded defeated.

Miss Amaya thought intently for a moment. "If you're serious about this, I might have the perfect student for you."

"I guess it wouldn't hurt to have some extra help. Who'd you have in mind?"

"How about Catherine Colvin? I'm sure she'd love to help you out. She's a hard worker. Plus she thinks you're a great teacher," Miss Amaya explained.

"Oh that would be great, do you really think she'll be up for it?"

"Sure do. You should talk to her today after seventh period."

"Thank you so much for the idea Amaya, I'm really going to consider it," he said, smiling at her. "Well I best be off. Got to clean up and make myself look presentable before my first class," he said with a chuckle. Grabbing his half full coffee mug from the counter, Melvin made his way to the door.

"See you later Melvin," Miss Amaya called out. Melvin held up his mug, toasting toward her as he made his exit. She waved to his retreating back with a longing look in her eyes.

Standing by her locker, Cat was showing everyone the signed copy of Robert Craven's new novel. "To my number one Cravenite! That's awesome Cat!" Amanda whispered trying not to draw any attention to their group.

"I can't believe you brought it to school Cat, especially after our talk last night," Julie reprimanded.

"Oh Julie, you and I both know that I'm terrible at keeping secrets. Especially when it's a secret like this," Cat said. *Well I guess that's not completely true,* she thought to herself after she said it.

"Can I hold it?" Elle asked with her eyes full of envy. Cat placed the book into Elle's outstretched hands and she began scanning it as if it were a bar of gold. "So Cat, have you read any of it yet?"

"Of course not, we have a pact don't we?" she answered.

"That didn't stop you before," Matt interjected.

"Matt, that's so unfair. It was only that once," she replied.

"So what are you all plotting?" Mrs. Rosenbaum asked, standing behind Elle and looking over her shoulder. "Is that the new Robert Craven novel? How do you have it? It hasn't come out yet," she asked excitedly. Matt gulped as he stared at her slightly unbuttoned blouse. Amanda noticed what he was doing and stomped on his foot, making him yelp.

"Cat is Craven's number one fan, so he sent her a signed copy," Amanda said.

“Amanda!” Cat groaned at her as she grabbed the book from Elle and shoved it in her messenger bag. Amanda turned to her and shrugged, mouthing, “What?”

“Very interesting,” Mrs. Rosenbaum replied. “You must tell me how it is Cat. I’m a huge fan. See you in class everyone.” As Mrs. Rosenbaum walked away, Duffie and Leif approached the group.

“Hey guys!” Duffie called out as Leif waved to everyone, semi-hiding under his gray ski cap.

“Hey Duffster,” Matt said, still distracted by Mrs. Rosenbaum’s exit.

Leif’s eyes filled with panic as he looked down the hall. “Uh, I’ll, see you guys, later,” he muttered, and then took off the opposite direction he was looking. Moments later a parade of females blew past them, obviously hurrying after Leif.

“What’s that all about?” Cat asked, watching the girls scurrying after him.

“This kind of happens all the time,” Duffie explained while giggling. “Leif is, how we say, popular with the ladies.”

“Hey Matt, you could take some pointers from him,” Amanda joked, patting him on the back. He glared at her and then she smiled innocently, making the group laugh.

“So, you’re all coming to the grand opening of my dad’s store, right?” Duffie asked.

"Definitely, wouldn't miss it," Cat replied.

"Can we dress up?" Amanda asked with a gleam in her eye.

"Sure, why not. I'm sure there will be gobs of Craven fans there dressed up as well," Duffie explained. Amanda smiled mischievously and everyone looked at her, wondering what she was planning.

"Can we bring a guest?" Elle inquired, causing everyone to stare at her in disbelief.

"I don't see why not," Duffie replied.

"A guest, other than us?" Matt asked with narrowed eyes.

"Well, yeah-" Elle began to reply.

"Who is it Elle?" Amanda probed.

"Uh, um, well," she answered sheepishly, dodging their stares.

Ryan came up from behind Cat, grabbed her around the waist, and squeezed her in a hug. "Oh brother, all right everyone, that's our cue to leave the happy couple alone," Amanda groaned. Cat rolled her eyes at Amanda. As everyone dispersed, Cat turned to Ryan.

"So how's mom?" Cat asked jokingly.

He smiled at her and replied, "fine."

"Got any plans for this Saturday? Want to come with us to the grand opening of Duffie's dad's store? It should be fun."

"I'm busy Saturday night."

"Oh really? Should I be jealous?" she asked with one eyebrow raised.

"Yeah, maybe. No actually I've got a family thing, a meeting really," he replied. Cat looked deep into Ryan's eyes and knew that something was up, but didn't want to pry. She just said, "okay" and then kissed him softly on the lips. Pulling away slightly she gave him a quick smile as the school bell rang and then they headed down the hall hand in hand.

After swim practice Cat made her way to Mr. Pierson's classroom. He had asked her during seventh period if she could spare a couple of minutes to talk to him at the end of the day. She held back a giggle at the sight of him sitting in his chair, his hair sticking up from running his hands through it all day. He was so focused that he didn't realize she was standing in front of his desk until she cleared her throat.

"Oh Catherine, sorry, have you been standing there long?" he asked, putting his pen in his pocket protector, and adjusting his glasses, which were slightly crooked on his face. *He's so cute,* Cat thought, *in a geeky sort of way.*

"No, just got here. What's wrong? You look a little frazzled?"

"So much work. But that's actually why I asked you to stop by. I need a teaching assistant, or TA as you youngsters call it."

Cat held back another giggle as he didn't look much older than her. "So Amaya, I mean Miss Amaya said you'd be perfect for the job." He looked pleadingly at her.

"She did, did she? Well I'd be honored." She watched as he slumped in his chair, relief written all over his adorable face.

"That would be wonderful. I'd only need a few hours of your time a week. I know you have swimming, and I'm here until all hours anyway. But you just show up when you can. I'll be eternally grateful."

"I'm available most days, except for the ones I have swim meets on. Do you need any help tonight? Practice went short, and my boyfriend Ryan is still in football practice. So tell me what you need me to do." Cat watched in delight as a huge smile erupted on his face. Mr. Pierson dug into his bag and withdrew a huge stack of papers, plopping them down in front of her. Cat looked at the stack with wide eyes as she grabbed a chair and pulled it up to his desk.

Ryan watched from a nearby tree as Cat and her friends walked toward the Three Penny Brit. He snickered at Amanda's outfit. It was a cross between, *Elvira Mistress of the Dark*, and a punk rocker. Her tall and bushy black hair made him laugh harder. *Seriously Amanda, a punk vampire?* Honing in on Cat, *you know she'd be really pissed off at you for spying on her,* he thought, hoping that the three girls wouldn't be making an appearance.

As Cat entered the store, Ryan scanned the windows and saw a large cardboard cut-out of Bartholomew Drake, famed vampire of Robert Craven's *Dark Shadow* series. *It amazes me that she's still a fan of his novels, even now after knowing what she is. I wonder if she's figured out all of his books are based on our kind's history.*

❧ ❧ ❧

Cat looked around the trendy book café. The store resembled a highly polished British pub with rows of book shelves. The walls had a dark wood finish, as did the floor. It was definitely one of the coolest places in downtown Astoria.

"Oi! Over here guys!" Duffie called out, standing next to a display of Robert Craven's new book, *The Cleansing*, and waving to the group. She wore a layered maroon cocktail dress and knee high black boots. Her beautiful, wavy, black hair was set back with a maroon hair clip.

Matt wolf whistled, "Duffster, you clean up nice!"

"Oh grow up Matt," Amanda chastised as Duffie just laughed off his comment, shaking her head.

"Great costume," Duffie said while looking Amanda up and down.

"You really think so?"

"Yeah! Punk rock vampire, right?" Duffie replied.

"Wow, finally, someone who gets me!" Amanda exclaimed as she grabbed Duffie in a bear hug. Duffie gently patted Amanda's back while smiling awkwardly. Over Duffie's shoulder, a concert stage in the back corner of the café caught Amanda's eye. A sign next to the stage read:

Playing Tonight:
The Damianic Bombshells

"The Damianic Bombshells are playing here tonight? They're like totes the best thing that's come out of our school, ever! They're awesome!" Amanda announced eagerly, releasing her grip on Duffie.

"Yeah, my dad heard they had a darker feel to them. And that they'd blend well with our theme tonight. Their lead singer is intense though. She's nice, but just a tad eccentric," Duffie said with a laugh.

"But Bridgette's soooo hot! She can be all the eccentric she wants to be! Just as long as she wears those skimpy outfits, and sings the way she does," Matt commented with an impish grin.

Amanda smacked him across the chest. "Matthew Ian Thomas, could you please keep your hormones in check for like two seconds?!" she asked glaring at him.

Matt rubbed his chest, "I guess that's my signal to head on over to the refreshments," he joked.

“They’re just over there,” Duffie said, pointing to the coffee bar where her father Gerard was setting up samples of his signature café drink. Gerard waved to the group. “He’s so silly sometimes. It’s interesting how into all of this he gets. He kind of gets a little geeky. But he’s my dad so I’ve got to love ‘em,” she chuckled.

Matt rejoined the group with a plate piled high with food. “Hey Duffster, what’s this I’m eating?” Matt asked, holding a pastry up to her.

“It’s a sausage roll,” she replied.

“Man, its delicio-” Matt stopped, his mouth gaped wide open, and his eyes fixed on the store’s entrance. The bit of food that was in his mouth rolled out onto the floor. “Is that Elle?” he asked, pointing with his fork. Elle walked toward the group, her arm linked with Brandon Esham’s, the captain of the football team’s younger brother.

“Hi guys,” Elle said shyly.

“When did this happen?” Amanda asked bluntly. Elle giggled at Amanda’s costume, and found it hard to answer her seriously. Matt was too stunned to say anything. Elle looked beautiful. Realizing Elle and Brandon were there together, Matt glared at him, pointing his plastic fork in his direction.

“You!” was all Matt could get out.

Pulling Matt's hand down, "Sorry Brandon, Matt gets a little overprotective sometimes," Cat explained.

"He's really harmless," Amanda quipped, ignoring Matt's glare.

"Am not!" Matt defended himself.

"Anyway, Brandon, how's practice going? My brother isn't being too hard on you is he?" Cat asked, trying to ease the awkwardness.

"Don't change the subject Cat. We've got a right to know what's going on here!" Matt declared, puffing out his chest.

"We're just out on a date Matt, okay?" Elle replied, feeling embarrassed.

"Next thing you know he'll be asking what Brandon's intentions are," Amanda mocked.

"What *are* your intentions?" Matt asked, raising his fork to Brandon again.

"My intentions are to go get some drinks Matt. Why don't you come with me and we'll talk," Brandon said, and then winked at Cat.

"Alright, but I'll be watching you," he murmured, following Brandon toward the refreshments.

Waiting until the boys were out of earshot, Duffie, Amanda, and Cat all turned to Elle. "Well?" Amanda asked eyeing her.

“What?” Elle responded evasively.

“The Boy!” Amanda replied.

“Your date,” Cat added.

“Spill the tea,” Duffie chimed in.

“Well what can I say, he likes the panther,” she stated plastering a huge smile on her face. All four girls squealed while jumping up and down and holding hands.

A loud guitar rift sounded as The Damianic Bombshells took the stage. Bridgette, the lead singer, raised her hand into the air as she looked out at the crowd gathering before her. Slowly bringing down her hand, she put her finger to her lips, signaling for the crowd to quiet. As silence fell, Bridgette motioned for the drums, tapping her foot along with the thunderous hypnotic beat while looking menacingly out at the crowd. Cracking a smile, she began to sing their song, *Complicated.*

Amanda had run to the front of the stage when she heard the band starting up. Matt joined her, gawking at Bridgette’s chest in her torn black shirt held together by safety pins. Brandon returned to what was left of the group alone, juggling refreshments for the remaining three girls.

“Everything alright Brandon?” Cat asked.

“Yeah everything’s copacetic,” he replied, passing out the drinks.

"Oh good, glad to hear all's fine in boy world," she joked.

"Hey, where's Julie and Ryan?" Duffie asked loudly, trying to talk over the music.

"Well Julie said she had to do something with her parentals tonight. And Ryan was busy too," Cat replied.

"It looks like the band has a few crazy groupies," Elle commented, pointing at Amanda and Matt who stood mesmerized in the front row. All four of them laughed at the pair.

"Is that Mrs. Rosenbaum in the crowd over there?!" Cat asked in a shocked tone.

"Where?" Elle asked.

"You can't miss her, she's the only adult over there," Cat said loudly.

"It is!" Duffie yelled back. "She did say she was a huge fan of Craven's."

"And with that outfit, she's not leaving much to the imagination," Cat commented, looking disgusted. "You know, I don't get it. Something's up with her. How could I hear horror stories about her as a teacher from my brother, and now all of a sudden she's this buxom beauty? And by the way, where's Mr. Rosenbaum?" Cat and Duffie looked at her suspiciously.

"People change Cat. I mean look at me, I too was once a caterpillar, and am now a beautiful butterfly," Elle explained dramatically with her hand across her chest.

"Can't argue with that statement," Brandon agreed.

"Aww you both are too cute for words!" Cat exclaimed. "And I guess you're right Elle, but I'd still like to know where Mr. Rosenbaum is."

As the Damianic Bombshells finished their last song, *Friend Me Or Die*, the crowd dispersed. "That was, hands down, the best concert ever!" Amanda declared as she rejoined the group, clutching a band shirt in one hand and their demo CD in the other. "They just gave us this stuff for free! For free!" she exclaimed.

"I think Matt's a little love struck," Elle said, waving her hand in front of his face.

"Ya think? She had two legs and boobs! Of course he's love struck," Amanda said dryly.

Breaking out of his trance, "hey, I resemble that remark," he replied with a grin.

Cat left the Three Penny Brit with a ton of Robert Craven swag, which included one of the cardboard cut-outs of Bartholomew Drake, under her arm. Matt and Amanda followed behind Cat toward her Jeep, toting their swag with them as well. "What a night!" Amanda declared as she settled into the passenger seat, her Damianic Bombshell t-shirt over her Robert Craven one. Too tired to respond, Cat and Matt just sighed contently in agreement as they pulled out of the parking lot.

Ryan watched as Cat drove away. Lifting his nose to the air, "What's that smell? Cinnamon? That's strange, it's really strong," he said. He then noticed the Damianic Bombshells packing up their van while talking to Mrs. Rosenbaum. *Hmm, interesting*, he thought.

11

Are You A Good Witch Or A Bad Witch?

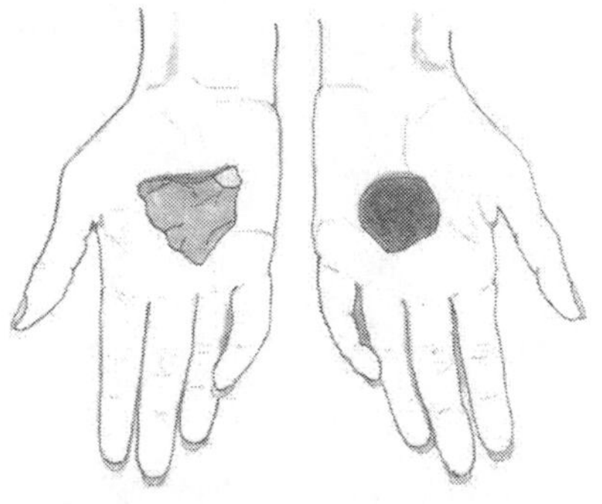

"Cat please slow down and chew your food," Rachel said, looking sternly at her daughter. She grinned when Cat groaned.

"Mom, I need to get going," Cat replied as she shoveled another spoonful into her mouth.

"And where are you off too this Hallowed night?" Sam asked, taking a huge bite of pumpkin cheesecake and then closed his eyes as the delicious taste filled his mouth.

"I told you at dinner on Monday that Miss Amaya invited me to an All Hallows Eve festival at Wedgewick Village. I decided to go, remember?" Cat watched as her dad seemed to sift through his memory, apparently coming up blank. "Anyway I've got to run. And don't worry Mom I've got a jacket in the car, so I'll be warm enough. See you sometime later tonight. I won't be too late, promise," she said quickly when she noticed the frowns appear on both their faces. Giving them both a quick kiss, Cat rushed out of the kitchen.

"Cat, are you going by yourself?" Sam asked to the closed door. Scratching his head he turned to Rachel. "Do you remember discussing this on Monday night?"

"No, but that doesn't mean she didn't mention it, does it?" Rachel's puzzled look met his.

"Well I guess it's too late to stop her now. I thought she was spending the night with Amanda and the rest of the gang like they normally do on Halloween."

"So did I," Rachel replied, picking up the empty dinner plates and putting them in the sink.

Cat felt the cold as soon as she stepped outside. *It's freakin' freezing*, she thought. She rushed to her Jeep, not realizing someone was sitting inside until she opened the door. "Julie what are you doing here?!"

"I'm coming with you. Wherever that is. Do you think after all these years together I wouldn't see past the little untruth you told the others? So you could have the night free to do…whatever you're doing? I can't believe you tried to skip out on us tonight," she chastised, watching Cat look away ashamed.

"Okay so I lied, a little. I'm just taking a minor detour." She saw Julie smile mischievously.

"So where are we going? And don't say I'm not invited, because that's just tough. I'm going. And hurry because a certain snow-woman is making her way across the yard to converse with us," Julie said, pointing to Maude Roberts who was bundled up in a ghastly white coat and a black ski hat.

"Too late, she's blocked us in! How the heck does she move so fast?" Cat sighed, grabbed her flannel, faux fur lined winter coat, and put it on before she rolled down the window.

"Catherine, where are you off to tonight? Don't you and your little friends usually get together on Halloween, and watch those trashy movies you young people like so much?"

"Oh hello Mrs. Roberts. How are you?" Cat tried to keep a straight face as she heard Julie giggling quietly behind her.

"Why thank you for asking. Well, my arthritis is acting up something fierce, and I've had a pain in my neck for a couple of days. Those stupid doctors can't find anything wrong. Don't know how they can feel justified in taking my hard earned money for nothing. No help at all," Maude grumbled as she struggled to pull back her pooch's leash. "Fredricka leave those tires alone! Bad girl, stand over here by Momma." She pulled hard on the leash making the little dog turn and grab it with her teeth, tugging with all her might. "So where are…yo…u off…to?" she finally got out, her face turning red from the effort of trying to get the leash out of the little dog's mouth.

"Have to run Mrs. Roberts, I think Fredricka needed to pee." Cat's face was strained trying to hold back the laughter as Maude realized Fredricka was peeing all over her shoe. Maude could swear the little dog had a defiant look as Fredricka stared up at her while squatting down over it.

"Oh my! You little devil! You just wait until we get home and I tell your daddy! He won't be happy, no sir. Bye girls," Maude called out as the Jeep backed down the driveway and took off up the road. Cat and Julie burst out laughing so hard that Cat had to stop the car and wipe the tears from her eyes. When they had regained their composure, Cat looked to Julie.

"Alright, you can come, but this is our secret. Number one, I don't want to hurt the others' feelings. And number two, I don't want them to know where we went. Understood?" Cat watched as Julie nodded. Quickly looking in all of her mirrors, Cat slowly pulled back onto the road.

"Boy that was hysterical. Poor Fredricka! Did you see the jacket she had on? It matched Maude's. And those little doggy boots! I bet she feels like a real freak. So where are we going?"

"You'll see," Cat replied, keeping her eyes on the road. Julie was silent until they turned down a lane, making their way toward the woods.

"I've never been this way before, are you sure you're not lost?" Julie asked as they entered through an archway of large, bare, and ominous trees that towered over them.

"No, we aren't lost. It's just a little further. Now Julie I want you to keep an open mind tonight. This place we're going to is hard to explain and you might see things that don't make any sense. And the people are also a little different than your usual Astoria native, but they're good people. So please be nice."

"When am I ever not nice?" Julie turned and looked at Cat trying to keep a straight face.

"Sometimes you can be a little blunt and you know it," Cat laughed, seeing her friend's stern mouth break into a grin.

It seemed like they had been driving through the forest forever with no sign of exit. Cat slowed the car and pulled off the trail. "Damn, I forgot, I can't get in without the words,"

Cat murmured to herself. *Listen to me. I can't get in without the words? I sound like a crazy person. Who would have thought all of this exists. Magic, vampires, witches, what's next?* She thought.

"What? What's wrong?" Julie asked confused.

"Oh nothing, I just need to make a call real quick," Cat said, pulling out her cell. "Great, no reception! Now how are we supposed to get in?" Just as the words left her mouth a car pulled up beside them. Inside, a round face with frizzy hair beamed at them, her face slightly illuminated by the soft glow from the car's inside lights. As they watched, she rolled down her window and gave them a kind smile.

"Forgot the password have we dearies? Don't worry. I do it all the time. Just follow me," she laughed pulling ahead of them. As Cat followed the car, suddenly the forest opened up and they were bathed in the moonlight. Sneaking a look at Julie, Cat saw that her mouth was gaped wide open.

"How…did…that entrance wasn't there before?" she stuttered.

"Now Julie, I told you that you'd see things tonight that might not make sense. This is one of them. Just go with it. Okay?"

"Okay…I think," Julie muttered while shaking her head.

“Look, the road is lined with carved pumpkins. There must be hundreds of them!” Cat said, distracted by the sight before her.

“Cat keep your eyes on the road,” Julie preached, even though Cat saw she was just as astonished as her, looking on with awe at the sight before them.

❧ ❧ ❧

“Where’d she go?” Duffie asked Leif, who was sitting next to her in the car. He shrugged his shoulders.

They had followed Cat and Julie from Nehalem Avenue. At lunch the day before, Cat had made an excuse why she would be late to Amanda’s horror movie fest. Duffie couldn’t figure out why she was the only one who knew Cat was lying, especially since these people had known Cat all her life. She thumped her hand on the steering wheel in frustration. *Something’s strange about Cat. And Julie’s another mystery*, she thought. “I guess we’ll just wait in the woods until they come back out,” Duffie muttered while backing up the car and settling into the darkness.

❧ ❧ ❧

Wedgewick Village’s town square was bustling with activity. Taking on a very traditional Halloween feel, it definitely looked different from the last time Cat visited. Julie grabbed Cat’s arm, determined not to lose her in the crowd. Cat was amazed at the transformation the village had undergone. The cobblestone streets had changed as well, and were now black instead of the pristine reddish-orange color they were before. Festive Halloween flags were hung from every store front, and the window decorations were full of color and little macabre touches. Old style lanterns with a faint, ghostly light emanating from them, illuminated each store sign.

"Wow! They really went all out for Halloween, look Julie!" Cat exclaimed while admiring all of the decorations. Julie felt Cat stop every few seconds to take in the sights, "This is so awesome! Hey look at that store," Cat said, pointing to *SPELLS ARE US*. Its store window had a large black cauldron, which was bubbling furiously with a putrid, green smoke flowing from it.

Next door, within the window of *FAMILIARITY: A STORE FOR FAMILIARS,* a black cat rose from its nestled position on a dark purple velvety cushion. As the feline arched its back into a stretch, it gaped open its mouth in a yawn. The cat's bright green eyes found Julie's. A look that resembled a smile appeared on its face.

"Come on Julie, people are saying there's a parade starting soon," Cat said, interrupting Julie's staring contest with the cat.

"Why is everyone wearing witch hats?" Julie asked.

Cat looked around and realized that Julie was right. Every man, woman, and child had a pointy black hat perched atop their head. The strange thing was they weren't wearing costumes, but rather normal clothes.

"Yeah that's a little strange, but hey this place is a little out there," Cat laughed slightly. "Hurry Julie, let's see if we can find a spot to watch the parade from."

"Off the street please! Off the street! Parade's going to start! Please, off the street, and that means you two." The pair turned and found a tall, thin man dressed in a black tuxedo, his face painted ghostly white with his hands on his hips, staring at them. The large frilly black and white bow-tie completed his look. "I need for you young ladies to please move off the street. The show is about to begin. Oh, there goes the bell now." A loud sound filled the air and people scrambled from the street until there was only Julie, Cat, and the man left standing in the middle.

"Sorry sir, we'll move. I think your costume is great by the way," Cat beamed as she saw the man puff out his chest, flashing them an evil grin.

Squeezing their way onto the sidewalk, Cat and Julie watched with the crowd in anticipation. Two figures on stilts came into view first. Lurching by, each one wore a pumpkin head mask with eyes glowing bright orange, like candles flickering inside of them. Their mouths were carved into frightening smiles. To the crowds delight, they would swoop down quickly in front of random spectators, startling them. Several more stilt walkers, dressed as ghouls, had masks so lifelike it made Cat and Julie take a second look. Their hands were gnarled and greenish brown with disgusting wart like bumps and realistic pus filled boils. Cat giggled as one of the ghouls reached out for her, but seeing that she wasn't afraid, it shrugged its shoulders and moved on.

Fire eaters, scantily clad men and women juggling sticks of fire, came next. They stopped periodically to eat the deadly flames without any apparent harm. The crowd *oohed* and *ahhed* at their dangerous tricks. After the beautiful fiery display, a dazzling colorful group came into view. Figures dressed as flowers danced gracefully around massive tree-looking creatures as they slowly lumbered by.

Small dainty figures resembling fairies shortly followed. As they pranced down the street their delicate wings illuminated in a range of colors as they fluttered in the light breeze. Their pointed ears and almond-shaped eyes made them look mysterious and ethereal.

In the distance an eerie thunderous sound erupted, heralding a crowd of men holding drums. Every man wore a dark red robe with a hood that hid their eyes. They drummed in a hypnotic rhythm. Listening to the beat, Cat felt a strange connection to the group, especially when the drumming stopped and the men began to hum. They continued eerily humming as they passed by, resuming their drum beat several seconds later. "Wow Julie, that was awesome!"

"I know! It was like they were talking to us through their drums. Does that sound odd?"

"No, I know what you mean. I couldn't have described it any better," Cat replied, turning her head back to the parade as the crowd cheered.

A long jet black hearse with ornate silver accents slowly made its way down the cobblestone street, driven by a skeleton dressed in a black top hat and tails. A couple sat in the seat attached to the roof. The woman had long white hair adorned with a crown of blood red roses, matching her dress. Her face was angelic. Her dark eyes and eyebrows looked strange against her white hair and the paleness of her skin. She smiled, and her angelic demeanor was ruined by two perfect fangs protruding from her mouth. Her partner wore a black tuxedo accompanied with a brilliant white shirt. The only splash of color on his outfit was the blood red rose attached to his lapel. A top hat and a black cane, with a silver bird for the handle finished his look. His face was monstrous with huge red scars and disgusting black lumps. His yellow teeth, revealed when he smiled gruesomely at the crowd, matched his eerie yellow eyes. The sign on the hearse door read:

All Hail!

The King And Queen Of All Hallows Eve!

Please Stop By Later For A Bite!

A few people laughed as they read the sign, others just looked on in awe at the realistic monster couple. The hideous looking man suddenly stared directly at Cat. "I want you," he mouthed, accompanied by a chilling smile, making her shiver.

"What a gruesome couple," Julie stated rather loudly, making Cat jump.

"That's an understatement," Cat replied, rubbing her hands up and down her arm, trying to ease the goose bumps. To Cat's relief the hearse passed by and the chill she had felt began to dissipate.

"Too bad the others couldn't have come with us. They would have really enjoyed this!" Julie remarked.

Cat bit her lip as she remembered the lie she had told them. *Yeah, some friend I am*, she thought.

"Well that was interesting," Julie said, interrupting Cat's thoughts. "What's next?"

"Come on Julie, follow me." Cat grabbed Julie's hand, pushing her way through the thickening crowd. Every step forward seemed like two steps back as the crowd seemed to carry them back toward the town square. Seeing a small opening, Cat lunged for it, pulling Julie through before it closed. Relieved, Cat saw The Purple door a few feet away, and trying to not step on anyone's toes, continued to push her way through the sea of people. Standing in front of the store they saw huge cobwebs covering the front window, and rather large realistic looking spiders making their way up and down them.

"Are those spiders real?" Julie asked.

"I don't know, they look it don't they," Cat answered as she pushed open the door. The melodic door chime announced their arrival.

"Cat, I'm so glad you were able to join us this fine evening!" piped Gretchen. The lovely store owner was beautifully dressed as a fairy godmother. Her long silver hair shimmered as if it was dusted with crystal iris glitter. She moved quickly through the crowd and enveloped Cat in a big hug. "Amaya mentioned you might be coming. And I see you brought your friend Julie. What a wonderful surprise," she gushed turning to her. Gretchen smiled at the shocked look on their faces. "So ladies help yourself to a cup of pear cider and a pumpkin cookie, or one of those ghost popcorn balls. I'll be with you in a minute," Gretchen said, pushing them gently toward a table filled with delicious treats.

“How did she know my name?” Julie whispered, watching Gretchen welcome more people into the store.

“You’d be amazed what she knows. First time I met her I thought she was actually reading my mind. It kind of gave me the wiggins, I’m not gonna lie,” Cat replied, grabbing a pumpkin cookie. “Julie you got to try these! Mmmm, so good!” she continued, placing a cookie into Julie’s open palm.

Giving Cat a nudge with her elbow, “There’s a little person heading our way, waving at us. No don’t look, but she’s dressed like the good witch from that movie,” Julie whispered and then took a bite of the cookie.

“Hello Catherine, and Julie, welcome,” Annie said as another shocked look came across Julie’s face.

“Hi Annie, I just love your costume. You make such a good good witch,” Cat commented as Annie blushed.

“Thank you, I thought it might be a little over the top, but Gretchen said it was fine.”

“Hey, where’s Aylah?” Cat asked.

“She had to run an errand for Gretchen. She should be flying in soon though.” Annie put her hand over her mouth, realizing what she just said. “Uh, I’m going to go help Gretchen. You girls enjoy yourselves. Now, let’s see if I can make it through this mess without getting trampled,” she laughed, vanishing into the crowd.

"Okay so this is getting really weird Cat. Two people have known my name without me telling them. Creepy much?" Julie asked.

Before Cat could reply, she felt a hand grab her shoulder. Turning, she looked into the smiling eyes of Aylah. She was dressed as a harem girl. Her beautiful long brown hair was pulled up into a high ponytail, held in place by a jeweled clip. Aylah gave her a hearty hug.

"Catherine, I'm so happy to see you! And Julie, it's wonderful that you could join us as well," she laughed, noticing Julie's expression as she moved forward to hug her too. "I'm Aylah, and yes Julie, we know who you are. I'm sure Cat has told you of our special little village. And what a glorious night to visit. Everybody's celebrating on this wonderful holiday. Samhain is one of my favorites."

"Your village is truly fascinating," Julie said, still a little awed.

"Now I know you're here because you have questions you need answering, right?" Aylah asked and then Cat nodded. "Well, then I shall go relieve Gretchen so that she may speak with you. Why don't you two make yourself at home? And don't forget to say goodbye before you leave." With a little wave, Aylah made her way into the crowd, which parted as if she was gently pushing them aside.

"Alright, I'm a pretty open minded person, but now that's three people who have known me. What is this place? I mean how do they know my name?"

"They just do. I told you this place would be different." Cat saw Gretchen pointing to the back of the store. "Sorry Julie, but I need to leave you for a few minutes. Have a look around. This store's really neat. I'll be right back, promise."

"You better be," Julie replied, and then watched as Cat followed Gretchen through a door.

Violet candles illuminated the room they entered. Cat noticed as Gretchen closed the door, the noise from the crowded store had completely diminished. There was only silence. "Have a seat Cat," said Gretchen, gesturing to a chair across the table. A deep purple cloth covered the table and a huge crystal sat in the middle of it. Gretchen sighed and placed her hands on the table.

"Before we begin I'll need to place a protection spell. This is Samhain after all, when anything can happen." Gretchen reached out for Cat's hands. After Cat placed her hands in Gretchen's, she murmured a few words which Cat couldn't understand. "Now, open your hands Cat." Gretchen held up a smooth round blue stone and a rough jagged black stone, placing them in Cat's left and right hands respectively, and then closed them into fists. "I ask that you hold onto to them tightly. No matter what happens, do not let them go until I take them from you, Okay? It's very important you heed these words."

"Okay, but what could happen?"

"Don't worry about that. I just like to take precautions."

"*Ask her, ask her, oh please ask her,*" Spirit said in Gretchen's ear.

Gretchen turned around looking behind her, acting as if arguing with someone. "Okay, okay, I'll ask her. I told you I would! You're such a pain sometimes Spirit," she muttered, and then focused her attention back to Cat. "Spirit would like to speak with you directly, if that's fine with you of course?" Cat began to think it over. "Does he have your consent? You don't have to if you don't want to. Quiet Spirit, I'm not trying to talk her out of it," Gretchen said teasingly.

"I'd like to speak to, um, Spirit. It's okay, really Gretchen," Cat answered, not knowing what to expect.

"Well here goes nothing," Gretchen said as she closed her eyes and placed her hands on the large crystal. The Crystal beamed with a brilliant light as Gretchen gasped, taking in a deep breath. The light from the crystal dimmed, and Gretchen's body became limp, her head hung low, mimicking a marionette. Suddenly Gretchen's head and body sat straight up in her chair, her eyes wide, staring directly at Cat.

"*I will behave*," A strange voice said through Gretchen, who was now looking to the side. Gretchen turned her head to look at Cat again, "*Oh Catherine, it's so nice to finally get a chance to chat. Do you mind if I call you Cat*?" Cat nodded while biting her lip, trying not to giggle at the semi-masculine voice erupting from Gretchen's mouth.

Did Spirit just take over Gretchen's body? This is getting totes bizarre! Cat thought.

"*It's great to finally see you clearly. In my spirit form, it's like I have this ghastly haze over my eyes and everything looks fuzzy. And might I say you're quite the looker, and that hair is to die for*!" he said, as Cat blushed from the compliments. "*Oh and your complexion, peaches and cream for sure*." Spirit commented, and then Gretchen's head cocked to the side again. "*What? Hush Gretchen! I'm just making small talk, give me a break. It's boring just talking to you all the time. This is my show, and I'll run it, thank you. So just butt out. Yeah you heard me, butt out*!" Spirit argued, looking behind him. "*So, Cat where were we, before we were rudely interrupted? Questions, right? Well fire away*."

"Well, um," Cat began, trying to compose herself while containing the laughter bubbling up.

"*Since the cat's got your tongue, I'll begin. I see you found out you're adopted. With love you find it's not all that bad really, is it? Hmmm, you know you're a Childe as well, pointy pearly whites and all. Special indeed. And now one of your best friends is hanging around with a pair of evil chicks, right*?" Cat quickly closed her mouth when she realized it had been hanging open for a couple of seconds, as the spirit had counted off each item with Gretchen's fingers.

"Yes, you're right. But how-"

"*How do I know all this, come on Cat, for real? Like I don't know all? Shut it Gretchen! Maybe not all, but enough to know why she's here*," Spirit huffed. "*So, you want to know about Linda and whether you can save her*?" Spirit asked. Gretchen looked in deep thought with her hand about her face. "*I'm told she's salvageable, but you have to destroy the one whose blood made her. Strange...Linda hasn't met this being, but how can that be*?" Spirit asked confused. "*I'm puzzled by this, and let me tell you, this doesn't happen very often*." Gretchen's head looked off to the side, "*Hey! What are you doing? Who are yo-*" Cat watched on, stunned as Gretchen's eyes rolled back, and her head fell forward, slamming into the table.

"Gretchen? Gretchen?" Cat shook her, forgetting about the stone in her right hand, and dropped it on the table as reached out for her.

"Gretchen's not here, try again," A sinister female voice came from Gretchen's mouth. Sitting up she raised her head. A trickle of blood ran down Gretchen's forehead. Cat sank back in her seat scared by the look of hatred glaring at her from Gretchen's eyes. They were dark red with just a hint of black surrounding them. *Those aren't Gretchen's eyes*, Cat thought. Her gaze was drawn to the smirk on her mouth. "Ms. Colvin, you silly little girl. It seems you've dropped something." Cat looked down at the table and saw the jagged black stone sitting there. As Gretchen's hand reached for it Cat snatched it up quickly and brought it close to her, clutching it tightly. Gretchen laughed evilly. "Stupid girl! Do you think a little stone will protect you?" Cat felt the stones had power and trusted in Gretchen that they would keep her safe. "Oh goodie, we have company, come to save your precious *Childe*." Cat turned toward the door, surprised to see Aylah standing there. "Come in Aylah, and join the party."

"No I think I will pass Quintance. I do not think your sister will approve of your actions here."

"Like she has a choice! She was foolish enough to let that silly Spirit take over, giving me the chance to…visit. Oh how I miss our visits." Gone was Gretchen's face and in its place was a face similar, but ghastly in appearance. Cat cringed at the dark smile Quintance projected at her.

"Cat, I need for you to stand up and come to me," Aylah said quietly. Cat tried to stand, but her legs became wobbly and she fell back in her chair.

"I think the poor child's scared out of her wits, don't you Aylah? Ah, it would seem we have another eavesdropper. We are so popular today." Quintance moved her hand sending the door flying wide open. "Come in child. Julie is it? Don't be shy my dear. Ohhhh, you're interesting now aren't you?" Quintance asked, examining Julie who was framed in the doorway. "What can you be? Oh, you're a-" Gretchen's head fell on the table with a sickening thud. Aylah rushed over and gently helped Gretchen up.

"Aylah…could you…fetch me…a glass of water?" Gretchen's weak voice asked.

"Certainly. Julie come with me, everything is okay now." Julie gave one last worried look to Cat and then followed Aylah out of the room.

"You can let go of the stones now Cat, I'm back." Gretchen tried to give a reassuring smile, but her pale face filled Cat with concern. Gretchen reached out and patted her hand. "Sorry I couldn't formally introduce you to my sister…my twin to be exact. As you can tell, Quintance took a different road than I did, I'm afraid." Gretchen paused as Aylah set a glass of water in front of her. After taking a sizable gulp, "Thank you Aylah. Please go look after Julie, make sure she is okay," Gretchen said with a smile. As Aylah left the room, Gretchen turned her focus back to Cat. "My sister was not always like this. No, there was a time when we were much alike. But something happened and she changed for the worse. I haven't seen or heard from her for years now. I should've been more aware that this could happen, especially tonight."

"Annie is making you some herbal tea to give you back your strength," Aylah stated, poking her head back through the doorway.

"Thank you Aylah."

"Gretchen, are you sure you're okay?" Cat asked.

"I am my dear. A little weary, but I'm fine." Gretchen's eyes became serious as she looked at Cat. "I need to tell you something. Since my sister knows of you now, I fear she will only add to your ever growing number of issues. I will not lie to you Cat, she is a very powerful dark witch, and you must be extra careful now that she knows what you are." Gretchen stood, making her way over to an antique dark wooden cabinet. Opening one of the drawers she drew out a small vial that contained a pale purple liquid. "I'm going to give you this to keep on your person at all times. When you feel yourself in danger, open the vial and it shall dispel even the most powerful of dark magics. The stone Amaya gave you should also be worn constantly now, as it will add another layer of protection. Oh, and Miss Amaya forgot to tell you this, but your moonstone is also your entry item. It allows you access to our village. Just say these words, *Revealius Indrogorum*, at the forest entrance while holding your stone."

Cat felt the moon stone that was resting on her chest with her hand.

"Yes, child it was much more than just a present. Now I need to rest, I feel a little light headed. I will bid you farewell for now," Gretchen said weakly and then disappeared, leaving behind a purple smoky haze.

Cat rubbed her eyes and then gave a startled look to Aylah who had returned with a tray that held two tea cups.

"Don't worry Cat, she's fine. Gretchen would have never made it home the normal way." Aylah helped Cat up from her chair and walked with her toward the door. Cat held up the small glass vial hanging from a thin leather band and stared at it.

"That is a very special item you hold in your hand Cat. It will protect you and others around you. Don't hesitate to use it." Cat nodded and slid the vial into her jean pocket. "Hone your senses and listen to your intuitions, they will never steer you wrong," Aylah explained, leading Cat out of the room. "I'm truly sorry that your visit was not a pleasant one. But next time we shall more than make up for it. Peace and love go with you."

Cat turned to look for Julie. After spotting Julie by one of the book shelves, she turned back toward Aylah, "So what about-" Cat stopped when she saw that Aylah was no longer there. A single large white feather caught Cat's eye as it drifted down in front of her. She placed her hand out as it slowly floated down, settling on her palm.

"Cat, you okay?" Julie asked, coming up behind her. Dazed, Cat turned to see her friend wringing her hands with worry.

"Yeah, I'm fine. You?"

"Okay, I guess. Hey where did you get that?" Julie asked, pointing at the feather.

"It was just here."

"Well, come on Cat, I think we need to get going. I've had enough weird for the night, that's for sure." Cat agreed. Julie glanced at the back room and saw it was empty. *What's with this place,* she thought. Leaving the store, they made their way to Cat's Jeep.

The drive home was quiet, and neither Cat nor Julie noticed the car following them. Duffie and Leif watched as they had flown by in the forest, and then followed them back to Nehalem Avenue, wondering what had transpired.

Spying their three friends standing by Cat's front door, Julie and Cat groaned in unison. "This is not going to be good," Cat muttered.

"So where have you two been?" Amanda's angry voice rang out as Cat and Julie got out of the Jeep. "Just going to be a little late, huh? It's been more than three hours!"

"I'm really sorry guys. I had something very important to take care of," Cat tried to explain, but she felt it fell on deaf ears. None of her friends looked happy.

"You were supposed to spend the night with us. But instead it seems like you made up some lame excuse so you and Julie could go off together," Amanda huffed, crossing her arms.

"We're your friends too! Why couldn't we have come with?" Elle's hurt tone came through loud and clear.

"Yeah, what's up with that?" Matt added.

"I'm sorry, what else can I say?" Cat was at a loss for words. She never thought they would find out. She looked at Julie for help, but she just shrugged her shoulders hopelessly.

"Well I hope you guys have a nice Halloween together. Come on guys, let's go make popcorn. Robert Craven is calling." They all stormed off. Elle looked back over her shoulder at Cat and Julie with sadness filling her face.

"Great, just great. This is the last thing I needed right now," Cat murmured to Julie who just stood by watching as the three headed down the street toward Amanda's house.

12
Sadie Hawkins

Hannah watched from a distance as Matt sifted through his locker. *Just go over there and ask him already,* she told herself. Pushing away from the wall, Hannah made her way over, passing under two students struggling to hang a banner for the Sadie Hawkins dance. Matt spun around as she tapped him on the shoulder.

"Hey Hannah, what's up?" he asked with a smile.

She melted at the sight of his green eyes and dimples. She was unable to talk, she just stared. Taking a deep breath,

"Yeah, umm hey. So do you, have any plans-" she began, but was interrupted when members of the varsity football team came down the hall, calling out Matt's name. Hannah looked away defeated, pushing her long blonde hair over her ear.

"Hey, guys!" Matt said coolly and then turned his attention back to Hannah.

Taking another deep breath, with a lot less confidence, she asked, "So yeah, umm. Has anyone, asked you to the uh, dance yet?" Looking intently at Hannah, Matt finally realized how nervous she was.

"Yeah, actually someone just asked me," he replied with a serious face.

"Oh," she said, her tone filled with disappointment.

"I'm kidding Hannah. Don't look so upset. I meant you," he said, chuckling as she flashed him a hopeful smile. "I'd love to go with you to the dance," he continued, placing his arm around her shoulder. As the pair walked down the hallway toward their English class, Hannah blushed at the stares they were receiving from the many students gathered in the hall.

Isaac glared at his sister as she walked away. "What the hell is she thinking? First Ryan, now Hannah! This has got to end!" he said in a frustrated whisper.

"Easy Isaac," Amelia said slyly as she massaged his shoulders. "There will be a time for that baby. We need to be smart about this." Turning to look at the Stone twins, Amelia grinned evilly. "I think I've got a plan to get both Hannah and Ryan back in line." The twins returned her evil grin.

After school, Miss Amaya paced back and forth in Melvin Pierson's biology class, talking to herself, and awaiting his return. "So Melvin, has anyone asked you to the dance yet? No, no that won't do!" she murmured, continuing to pace. "So Melvin, I like to dance, how about you? No, that's not right either!" Turning and fixing her gaze on his desk chair, "Melvin it would be an honor if you would escort me to-"

"Miss Amaya, what are you doing?" Cat asked while staring confused from the doorway.

"Oh nothing," Miss Amaya quickly replied as she plopped down into Melvin's chair.

"I guess I never realized how much you love…chairs," Cat said jokingly.

"Oh, you saw that huh?" she queried. Cat nodded, grinning broadly.

"So, I was just on my way to practice and I thought I'd stop by and see if Mr. Pierson needed help with anything. Where is he anyway?"

"Haven't the foggiest. I was here just waiting for him to return so I could-" Noticing Cat's inquisitive look, Miss

Amaya continued, “I mean, I wanted to see if he was doing okay as well.”

“If you see him, could you please tell him I stopped by?”

“Will do. Oh and Cat,” Miss Amaya started as Cat began walking away, “they’ll forgive you, just give it time dear.” Cat poked her head back into the doorway. “Your friends, they’ll forgive you.”

“How do you know my friends aren’t talking to me?”

“Call it woman’s intuition,” Miss Amaya joked.

“Thanks, I needed that,” she said in a hopeful tone. “And I hope you’re right.”

Walking into the locker room Cat was immediately ambushed by Shannon. “Aren’t you like totes excited about this weekend’s swim meet? It’s going to be epic!” Cat just nodded as she looked for Duffie and Hannah over Shannon’s head. “So hey Cat, I think I may need some pointers on my back stroke. It’s still a little wobbly, and I know that I’ll be swimming in that meet this Saturday,” Shannon rambled on. Cat looked down at her.

“I’ll give you a quick lesson before practice, okay?” she replied, watching Shannon grin from ear to ear.

“Thanks Cat, you’re like the best ever!” she squealed, grabbing Cat in a bear hug. Finally letting go, Shannon moved toward her locker. Shaking her head, Cat made her way to her locker to get suited up. "Cat! I can't wait for our lesson!" Shannon shouted, causing Cat to turn around and look at her. Not paying attention to where she was going, Cat suddenly bumped into someone. She saw Kirsten standing in front of her.

"Oh I'm so sorry Cat, I didn't see you there. Please forgive me," Kirsten said with a huge smile. She then signaled for her two lackeys to follow her out to the pool area.

"Well that was freakin' odd. No psycho flip out like usual?" Duffie asked, coming up behind Cat.

"I know right? It's like she's broken or something," Cat replied with a laugh. *Yeah, broken indeed. Ever since Ryan did that mind control thing, Kirsten's been uber bi-polar. One minute she's mad at me and the next she's my BFF. Just as long as she doesn't remember anything from that night we're all good,* Cat thought, watching Kirsten leave the locker room. "So, you going to the dance after the meet on Saturday?" Cat asked, turning back to Duffie.

"Nah. Got things to do. Plus my dad has this whole rule that if Leif doesn't go to dances or on dates, then neither can I," she replied.

"Eww, that sucks. Kind of archaic if you ask me," Cat remarked.

"Yeah, I guess you could say he's a little old fashioned," Duffie joked. "But in all honesty though, with Leif's *situation* lately, it's probably for the best."

Cat laughed. "I'm surprised he hasn't taken the last two weeks off because of his little fan club. They've been trying to ask him to this dance constantly. But he amazingly manages to escape them all the time."

"Yeah and he's becoming quite popular with the guys here too," she said sarcastically.

Hannah rushed up to her locker next to theirs, her face flushed as she tried to hurry into her swimsuit. "Hey guys," Hannah said while trying to hide her face.

"What has you so flustered?" Cat asked.

"Oh nothing," she replied, smiling sheepishly and fiddling with things in her locker.

"I know what that look is. That's the look of a woman in love," Duffie interjected. Hannah didn't say a word as her blush deepened and her smile grew.

"Hannah? Who is it? Who's the lucky guy?" Cat whispered excitedly.

"It's nothing guys, really," Hannah replied as she tucked her hair into her swim cap.

"Uh-huh," Cat and Duffie said in unison, totally unconvinced.

"Alright ladies, let's hit the pool!" Coach Hutchins called out into the locker room.

"Don't think you're out of this convo girlie," Cat quipped. "We're finishing this later." Hannah just grinned.

❦ ❦ ❦

The doorbell rang at the Colvin residence sending Taylor rushing down the stairs. He flung open the front door. "Oh, it's only you," he said dryly, seeing Ryan standing there. "Cat, your date is here!" he called up the stairs. Sam and Rachel, hearing Taylor's yell, came into the foyer to greet Ryan. As Cat descended the stairs all eyes were on her. She was dressed in a pretty little yellow cocktail dress with shoes to match.

"Wow!" Ryan said stunned. "Shall we?"

"We shall," Cat replied. After giving hugs to everyone, she took Ryan's arm as he led her outside.

Julie stood next to Ryan's car, looking pretty in a lilac colored dress. "Hey guys thanks for letting me tag along."

"Of course, the more the merrier," Cat said with a smile, but Julie could see the hurt in her eyes.

"I don't see why those three are still giving us the cold shoulder. It's so weird. They never used to be like this. Usually we're all quick to forgive," Julie commented as they piled into Ryan's car.

❦ ❦ ❦

As the trio entered the school's gym, their ears were filled with the sounds of the Damianic Bombshells rocking out on stage. Cat immediately spotted Matt and Hannah sitting at a table with Elle and Brandon.

"Should we go over there and attempt a hello?" Cat asked Julie loudly, trying to talk over the music.

"Sure, it couldn't hurt."

"I'll be right back," Ryan said, squeezing Cat's hand. He then moved toward his group who were busy playing the parts of ominous wallflowers. Cat felt Isaac's and Amelia's cold stares, obviously not amused by her and Ryan arriving together.

"We should get over there before they try to get up and dance," Julie said, tugging at Cat's hand.

"Yeah, let's go," she replied, distractedly watching Ryan talk with Isaac.

"Are these seats taken?" Julie asked, approaching their friend's table.

"Hey Cat, Julie," Hannah called out as Matt just looked at Cat and then turned away, ignoring her. Brandon lifted his hand to wave, but Elle grabbed it, resting back on the table.

"Amanda might mind you two sitting there, but lucky for you, she's hanging out with the band," Elle said coldly.

"You can sit there if you like, I guess," Matt added as Hannah looked at him confused.

"What's going on here? Did I miss something?" Hannah asked.

"Why don't you ask them?" Elle said, nodding her head toward Cat and Julie.

"This is ridonkulous guys! We said we're sorry, what else do you want from us?" *If only I could use my mind control powers on them and not feel bad about it afterwards!* Cat complained to herself.

"Well whatever happened, it couldn't have been bad enough to ruin a lifetime of friendship, right?" Hannah asked, looking around at everyone at the table.

"Hannah we should go dance," Matt said, bringing her to her feet.

"Oh okay, but I still think you all should make up," she replied.

"Later, but now let's dance," he said, pulling her toward the center of the gym. Hannah looked back at Cat and mouthed "sorry."

"Well, are you guys happy?" Elle asked abruptly, pushing back her chair, and then made her way to the refreshments. Brandon sheepishly followed after her.

"So, that was an epic fail!" Cat murmured as she slouched in her seat. Julie nodded and sat down next to her.

"Just give them time. Hopefully they'll come to their senses and forgive us," Julie said while rubbing Cat's shoulder.

"How'd it go?" Ryan asked, coming up behind the pair, and taking a seat next to Cat.

"Not good. Hey Julie, would you mind if Ryan and I went for a dance?" Cat asked.

"Not at all. Actually I think I hear the refreshments calling. So if you need me I'll be over there," she replied with a laugh.

The current song ended and Bridgette, the lead singer of the Damianic Bombshells, grabbed the microphone. "This next song is a new one, and was written by our honorary band member, Amanda Stevens!" The crowd erupted into cheers.

Cat looked at the stage in awe, seeing Amanda standing next to Bridgette with Bridgette's arm around her shoulder. "The song is titled, "*Backstabber*!" Bridgette yelled and the crowd went wild again. Cat couldn't help but think the song was about her and Julie. "Are you ready?" Bridgette cried out as Amanda exited stage left. "All right! One! Two! One, two, three, four!" she yelled and then began singing. The energy on the dance floor became frantic, mirroring the energy on stage. Cat found it hard to dance to the fast beat of the song. Her gaze was fixated on Amanda, who had a smile plastered across her face, obviously pleased at how well the song was being received.

"Hey Ryan, I'm going to head to el baño. I'm not feeling very well, be right back," Cat said into his ear.

"Do you need me to get you anything?"

"No, I'm fine," she replied with a faint smile.

"Alright, well hurry back," he said, giving her a serious look.

"Don't worry, right back," she said, kissing him on the cheek.

As Cat walked into the bathroom down the hall, the fluorescent lights above her head began to flicker. *Great, the lights are acting up again,* she groaned. Looking at herself in the mirror Cat proceeded to blot her face with a wet paper towel. *Well you've really done it now Cat,* she told herself. When she heard the door to the bathroom open, Cat quickly headed toward the nearest stall, wanting to avoid whoever had walked in. Closing the door, she locked it and sat down on the toilet. *Come on Cat, get a hold of yourself. They'll forgive you, and things will be back to normal soon. Well as normal as they can be.*

Light scratching on the stall next to her caught Cat's attention, causing her to jerk up. The sound of muffled giggling followed. The lights overhead flickered again, and then went out, plunging her section of the bathroom into darkness.

"*Catherine…Catherine*," a menacing female voice slowly whispered, echoing in the vast empty room. Cat was torn between using her vamp abilities, or hiding and keeping silent. As a loud bang sounded at her stall's door, she covered her mouth, stifling a gasp. The strong smell of cinnamon filled her nose, causing her to gag. The lock on the stall door slowly began to unlatch and then stopped. Cat withdrew the tiny vial Gretchen had given her at the Purple Door from her yellow clutch, and gripped it tightly. The lock suddenly blew off and the stall door flew open. Cat couldn't see anything in front of her except for a black smoky haze. She still heard the sound of giggling, only louder this time, sending chills down her spine. Cat screamed as a hand with long, sharp, black fingernails reached out from the thick black smoke.

Opening the vial, Cat watched as a pale purple liquid gracefully flowed from the vessel. It engulfed the black form in front of her, and then dissipated it. The liquid quickly sucked back in to the vial, which re-sealed itself. Cat heard the door to the bathroom slam open.

"Cat, Cat? Are you okay?" Ryan called out as he ran up to the stalls.

"Yeah, I'm fine. The stupid lights went out and startled me, that's all," she replied, trying to hide her true emotions. Cat didn't want to worry Ryan any more than he already was. She knew that if she told him what really happened, he'd immediately go straight into uber protector mode. "Hey, how did you hear me?"

"Umm, don't be mad, but I kind of followed you. And I'm glad I did," he replied as he grabbed her hand and pulled her to her feet.

"Yeah me too," Cat said, hugging him.

Ryan knew Cat wasn't telling the truth, but decided to let it go for the time being. He was just thankful she was okay. *I wonder if what happened to Cat has anything to do with this awful smell of cinnamon?* Ryan thought.

While making their way back to the table, Cat saw Amanda and the Damianic Bombshells sitting there with the rest of her friends. Julie was nowhere to be found. "Hey, did you like the song?" Amanda asked, glaring at Cat. Bridgette giggled under her breath. Cat returned Amanda's glare and then grabbed Ryan's hand, leading him out onto the dance floor.

"That wasn't very nice Amanda. I know Cat made you upset, but she didn't deserve that," Elle reprimanded.

"I know, I know. It kind of just slipped out," Amanda replied, looking ashamed.

❦ ❦ ❦

Ryan held Cat close, gently swaying to the music. "So I guess that song was about me," Cat murmured.

"She's just mad Cat. She'll get over it, don't worry," Ryan said, trying to reassure her as tears began welling up in her eyes. Sighing, Cat buried her head into Ryan's shoulder.

As they continued dancing to the music, Cat thought to herself about what just happened in the bathroom. *What the hell was that? And what was with that stuff that came out of the vial Gretchen gave me? I need to go find Miss Amaya like pronto. Maybe she'll know. This is all getting too crazy!* "Hey Ryan? Ryan?" Cat asked. Feeling something was wrong, Cat's head jerked up and instead of Ryan standing in front of her, it was Isaac's cold eyes that she met. At first she thought it was another strange vision, or hallucination, but something felt very real about this. She tried pushing herself away, but Isaac grabbed her wrist, not letting her go. Cat searched the crowd and saw Amelia and one of the stone twins dragging Ryan away as he struggled to get free. Isaac turned Cat's chin forcefully with his hand, making her face him. She glared at him and then again tried unsuccessfully to pull away.

"You're a feisty little kitty, aren't you?"

"Let me go Isaac!"

"I think not," he growled, his hand tightening around her wrist. He grinned at the look of pain on her face as he pulled her close, forcing her to dance with him.

"Ow Isaac, you're hurting me! Let go!"

"First, I want to know, what are you? I thought you were a normie, but I was wrong."

"What are you talking about? Let go of me!" Cat hissed, and then finally ripped free one of her hands.

He quickly grabbed it back, "uh, uh, uh, you aren't playing fair," Isaac's cold hand gripped tighter than before.

"I'm warning you Isaac! You're gonna want to let me go," Cat said, her anger increasing.

"Or what? Come on Cat, let's see that fire. Let's see what you really are," he replied, trying to bait her.

You have to stay calm Cat, don't get angry! Your teeth, remember your teeth, she thought. Cat saw a hand reach out and grab Isaac's shoulder.

"Can't you see that I'm busy here?!" Isaac growled.

"Let her go Isaac!" The sound of his younger sister's voice made him look over his shoulder.

"Hannah, go away! Your turn will come next!" he replied shoving her back while still holding tightly onto Cat.

"I know she's your sister Isaac, but I can't just sit by and let you push her around!" Matt said fiercely, approaching him.

"And what are you going to do about it?" Isaac scoffed, rolling his eyes at Matt.

"I'll show you what I'm gonna do!" Matt roared as he reeled back, readying to throw a punch. Isaac smirked and easily dodged Matt's attack, pushing him to the ground. As Hannah went to Matt's side, Ryan finally freed himself and rushed over to the commotion in the center of the dance floor.

"What the hell do you think you're doing Isaac?" Ryan asked, looking him square in the eyes, his way blocked by the other Stone twin.

"Stay out of this Ryan! This doesn't concern you!" Isaac snarled.

"Well you're messing with my girlfriend and her friend, so I'd say it does concern me!" he fired back.

"You know what? I'm sick and tired of you defending these people against your own!" Amelia yelled from behind Ryan.

"Yeah, back off Ryan! If you know what's good for you!" The Stone twins said in unison. Cat stopped struggling and pulled Isaac close to her.

"I'm not scared of you Isaac! Let me go, now!" Cat demanded, noticing Miss Amaya shoving her way through the crowd toward them.

"Why is it, that this lot is always the center of attention at every school function?" Miss Amaya asked loudly. Everyone turned to look at her. "I don't know what this is all about, but it ends now! If you can't coexist and enjoy the rest of the dance, you need to leave! And from what I can see Mr. Bancroft, Ms. Colvin doesn't want to dance with you!" Isaac immediately released his grip on Cat and slowly backed away, his group joining him.

"Everything's cool here," Isaac stated calmly, but still obviously angry.

"Yes Miss Amaya, everything's okay," Cat said, returning Isaac's glare.

"Good, glad to hear it," Miss Amaya gushed.

The Damianic Bombshells took the stage again and began playing their next song as the gym erupted into cheers.

"Thanks," Cat said turning to Matt.

"I did it for Hannah," he replied coldly.

"Oh, well thanks anyway."

Hannah squeezed Matt's hand, not saying a word, flashing a worried look at Cat.

"Whatever," he replied, leading Hannah away from the dance floor.

"I just can't win," Cat murmured to Ryan and Julie.

"What was that all about anyway?" Julie asked.

"I don't know, just Isaac being Isaac! I think I've had enough for tonight, let's go home," Cat said, sounding defeated.

Isaac and his group watched as Hannah got into Matt's car and drove away. "This isn't over by a long shot. He's going to pay for this. My sister will never be with a normie! Ever!" he growled furiously.

"We'll come up with another plan babe, don't worry," Amelia said, turning toward the Stone twins.

Pulling into the driveway at the Bancroft residence, Matt put his car in park and sighed.

"I understand if you don't want to be around me anymore," Hannah said somberly.

Matt turned to her and smiled. "Don't be silly, I'm not going to let your brother stand in the way of this. I like you too much for that to happen," he replied. Hannah leaned over, kissed him quickly on the lips, and then exited the car.

"Thanks for tonight, I really enjoyed it," Hannah said with a shy smile.

"I had fun too," he replied, grinning foolishly, still reeling from the kiss.

"See you Monday," she said.

"Yeah, see you Monday," he said and then pulled out of the driveway with a huge grin still on his face. *Wow, my first kiss!*

He thought. Turning on the radio full blast, he rolled down the window, not caring that it was eleven thirty at night, or that it was lightly snowing. Dogs began barking and neighbors could be seen coming out of their houses to see what all the noise was about.

Driving up the icy, winding, narrow road, Matt rolled up his windows as the cold wind began to bother him. He smiled as he grabbed the phone from his pocket and began texting a message to Hannah. A deer darted out in front of him and he swerved, dropping his phone. “Crap! Damn animals!” he groaned, feeling around the floor for his cell while trying to keep his eyes on the road. Hearing a light tapping on his driver’s side window, Matt sat up startled, but saw nothing there.

“What the hell was that?” he asked out loud, clutching the steering wheel, and checking all the windows. “Great, now I’m hearing things,” he said, resuming the search for his cell. A louder knock caused him to sit up quickly. His eyes grew wide with shock as he saw a girl flying next to his car, holding on to the side view mirror. Matt instantly recognized her as Becca, one of the missing girls. He couldn’t mistake those golden locks of hair that were plastered on missing flyers everywhere. He yelled as she bared her fangs and hissed violently. Swerving the car left and right, Matt tried to shake her off.

Becca raised her finger to her lips making a shushing sound. She grinned wickedly and then slowly pointed to the road ahead. Following her finger's direction, Matt was startled to see Linda standing in the road in front of him. He stepped hard on the brakes causing the car to slide on the treacherous ice. Trying to regain control of the car, Matt watched on in horror as he barreled in to a tree.

Groggy, Matt lifted his face off the steering wheel as blood ran down his forehead and onto his cheek. His first thought was, *great the air bags didn't deploy.* His head ached and his chest felt heavy from the pressure of hitting the bottom of the steering wheel. *What the hell just happened?* He thought as he wiped the blood from his cheek and felt the knot that was developing on his temple. Matt's eyes flew open as the realization of what just happened hit him. He quickly pressed the button for the automatic locks on his car door and was relieved to hear the locking sound. He frantically looked around for the girls, but couldn't see them.

Matt realized his foot was still on the accelerator after hearing the sound of the tires spinning in the snow. He applied the brakes, and then threw the car in reverse, only to find out it wouldn't budge. After several attempts, he hit the steering wheel in frustration and turned the car off. He noticed the glow of his phone's screen out the corner of his eye and saw that it was lying on the floor in front of the passenger seat. Relieved, he grabbed for it and then felt his whole car shake as if something had crashed onto the roof. Hearing light scratching followed by giggling had Matt quickly dialing 911. “Dammit! No Signal!” he said, and then slammed the phone down into the cup holder. *CLICK...*Matt stared with wide eyes at his car door’s lock as he realized they had disengaged. He hit the automatic switch again, trembling as another evil giggle came from above. He gasped as the locks all disengaged once more. After locking the doors again, Matt reached around into the back seat and grabbed the hammer on the floor that his dad had told him to leave in the car. “Thank you dad,” he whispered, pulling it close to him, preparing to swing at anything that came near.

Slowly his left back seat window began to roll down. He rolled it back up and then hit the window lock button. Slouching back into his seat, Matt gripped the hammer even tighter with fear in his eyes. Everything went silent. Looking around frantically, Matt searched his surroundings for any sign of the girls. Suddenly his car door was viciously ripped from it hinges and tossed aside as Amy grabbed Matt and pulled him from the car.

“You made this entirely too easy,” Amy said evilly. She yanked him up by his neck and dangled him above the ground.

"Why doesn't Matt want to come out and play with us girls? Huh?" she asked, looking back at Linda and Becca.

"What do you want from me?" Matt choked out.

Amy laughed. "Do you hear that girls, he wants to know what we want from him." Becca covered her mouth as she giggled. Linda stood by, avoiding Matt's stare in her direction.

"Linda why are you doing this?" Matt asked hoarsely.

"Matt just be quiet, this will all be over soon…please," Linda pleaded with him as she fought back the tears and tried to keep a stoic face. Matt gripped the hammer tight and mustered enough strength to take a swing at Amy. She moved her head out of the way and swatted the hammer from his hand.

"Now that's not very nice. Didn't your mom teach you not to hit girls?" Amy asked. She tightened her grip on Matt and threw him forcefully through the air.

He hit the ground with a sickening thud and skidded to the other side of the road into a ditch. He lay there still, the pain coursing through his body. He tried to move his left arm, but couldn't, it was broken. Linda started toward him, but was yanked back by Amy.

"You want to join your little friend, then keep going. If not, stay back!" Amy growled. Linda stood still, watching helplessly as Matt tried to move.

“Amy I think he’s scared enough. I think he’s got the message,” Becca said, seeing the crazed look in her eyes.

“Who gave you permission to think?” Amy growled, causing Becca to back up. Turning her attention back to Matt, “Now, where was I? Oh yeah, we want to send a big message to your little friend Cat. Not verbally of course. It’s more like a visual one,” Amy stated arrogantly, walking over to Matt as he struggled to prop himself up against a tree with his uninjured arm. Every part of his body felt like it was on fire. He watched as Amy moved closer to him and crouched down. “So how many tears do you think Catherine will shed over her little friend’s demise?” she whispered menacingly. Matt shuddered as she giggled. Through his blurry vision he watched Amy rear back with her fangs bared. He resigned himself, waiting for her attack, and then to his amazement she abruptly flew out of view. He heard sounds of a struggle close by, but his vision was worsening and he couldn’t make out what was happening. Then there was silence.

He heard a soothing but muffled whisper, “It’s okay Matt, you’re safe now.” Matt mustered a relieved smile, and then felt someone scoop him up, gently cradling him close in a fireman’s carry.

13
Blood Thinner Than Water

Hannah stuck to the shadows, moving quietly, relieved that the grounds of the hospital were silent. It was after visiting hours, and as she spied the window she needed, Hannah ascended the building. Landing on the window's ledge, she peered into Matt's room. She gasped, seeing him lying there in the bed, pale against the bright white sheets. His arm was raised in a sling and several bandages were wrapped around his forehead. She could hear the numerous machines he was hooked up to beeping periodically.

A nurse walked into the room and fiddled with one of the machines, oblivious to the fact she was being watched. Hannah focused her eyes, concentrating on the nurse. As if in a trance, the nurse turned around, made her way to the window, and opened it. The nurse then retraced her steps and left the room, closing the door behind her. Hannah climbed in and moved quickly to Matt's side. Taking his hand, she shivered at his lack of warmth. She thought back to the end of their night together.

How happy Hannah was when Matt had dropped her off at home. Even Isaac's cold expression as she walked into the house hadn't fazed her. As she reached her room, Hannah took out her cell and dialed Matt's number, disappointed when she was sent straight to voicemail. She laid on her bed, counting down the minutes, realizing that he probably had his phone off because he was driving. A slow hour had gone by before she tried to call again. A strange voice answered, "Hello, may I ask who is calling?"

"May I speak to Matt please?"

"I'm sorry, but he can't come to the phone right now. This is Deputy Kim Burkins, of the Astoria sheriff's department. There's been an accident. He's been admitted to Astoria General."

"What? Is he ok?"

“May I ask who I’m speaking to?”

“This is Hannah Bancroft, is Matt ok?”

“Oh Hannah, he’s doing fine from what I understand. He was a little banged up, but…hold on, let me find out what room he’s in so you can go visit him tomorrow, okay,” Deputy Burkins said. Hannah shook as she waited in anticipation for more details. “So, he’s in room 221.”

“Thanks,” Hannah said quickly and then hung up the phone.

Now by Matt’s side, tears stung Hannah’s eyes as she scanned his body. When she looked up, she was startled as Matt’s cloudy gaze met hers.

“Matt?” she blurted out, her throat restricted with emotion.

“Hannah,” Matt murmured, smiling crookedly.

“Oh Matt, how are you feeling? I was so worried about you!” her words rushed out.

“I feel better…was in a lot of pain before…but now I feel like…I’m just floating on a cloud.”

“How would you know what that feels like?” Hannah giggled slightly, squeezing his hand a little tighter.

“I just do…what are you doing here? Did you come with someone?” he asked.

“No, I came alone. Matt what happened?”

“You shouldn’t…have come alone.”

"Why not?" Hannah felt a sense of dread, not really wanting to hear his answer.

Matt gripped her hand tightly, "There are monsters…vampire looking people out there. You should be safe at home. I saw them Hannah…vampires!" He shivered, reliving the attack.

"Matt, are you sure?"

"Hannah you need to go home…I'm getting sleepy…Hannah I want you safe…worried." Hannah's eyes turned jet black as she stared intently into Matt's.

"Matt you need your rest. You'll remember nothing from the accident. It'll all be a blur to you," she said, and then her eyes returned to their natural light blue. "I'm so sorry. I can't believe they did this to you!" Matt slowly closed his eyes as Hannah gently laid his hand down and bent over, softly kissing him on the cheek. "I'll be back later, I promise, but I must go now," she murmured, turning one last time to look at him before slipping out the window.

Reaching her car, Hannah opened the door and sat heavily in the driver's seat. She knew she had broken a sacred rule. It was forbidden for her to erase a human's memory, but she didn't want Matt to remember his attackers. She would confront Isaac and his group. *This has gone far enough! Being mean is one thing, but causing harm is quite another!* Hannah thought, as she pounded on the steering wheel.

"Now, I know it's past visiting hours, but I feel your friend needs you right now. He's in a private room so there should be no problem with you spending the night," Dr. Bane explained as he led Cat and her friends into Matt's room. "No loud talking. And I don't know how comfortable you'll be in these chairs, but you'll have to make do. Alright, goodnight ladies," Dr. Bane grinned, closing the door on the four people standing in the room. Amanda and Elle's tear streaked faces, and Julie's melancholy expression tore at Cat's heart. Moving forward she grabbed them all in a hug. Immediately arms came around her, hugging her back.

"Oh Cat, Julie, we've missed you so much," Elle sobbed.

"Yeah…me…too," Amanda sniffled, squeezing harder.

"We've all been dumb. It's terrible that something like this has to happen for us to realize how stupid we've been," Julie whispered quietly.

"I'm so sorry guys. Maybe if we hadn't fought, Matt wouldn't be laying there," Cat replied, looking pensively at the pale figure lying in the bed.

"We can't blame ourselves. We just have to be here for him now, and make a pact that we will never ever let this happen again. Whatever happens from now on we'll stand together okay. I can't go through this again. These last few weeks have been just awful, right Amanda?" Elle looked at Amanda who nodded, too overcome with emotion to comment.

The four friends moved to stand around Matt's bed. The monitors beeping and tubes protruding from his body made the group speechless as they held hands, each sending non-verbal encouragement to him.

"Isaac? Isaac where the hell are you?!" Hannah's angry voice echoed through the empty foyer. "We need to talk, now!"

"What are you blabbering on about? Still mad at us for earlier?" Isaac smirked at the angered look on her face as he exited from the living room. Amelia and the Stone twins stood behind him grinning like fools. Hannah clenched her fists, desperately wanting to knock the grins from their faces.

"How could you do this to him? What has he ever done to you all to deserve this? You could've killed him. All because I asked him to a stupid dance! I asked him, he didn't ask me. If you needed to take your anger out on someone, it should've been me," Hannah shouted, poking her finger in to Isaac's chest, while brushing away the angry tears with her other hand.

"What are you talking about? And quit poking me! Have you gone crazy? Who's hurt?" Isaac asked, confused at his sister's current emotional state.

"Don't try to look innocent. I know you caused his accident. He's lying in the hospital, tubes hanging out everywhere, in pain, because of you being a complete and utter ass!" she poked even harder, as she enunciated every word.

"Hey, stop that! We haven't hurt anyone. Now calm down, who's in the hospital?"

"Matt! He said he saw you!"

"Wait a second, Matt's hurt? Well it wasn't us. We haven't seen him since the dance."

"He said monsters, vampires came after him, and that just about describes you guys to a tee now, doesn't it?" Hannah glared at them.

"Hannah, Isaac's telling the truth. We left the dance and came straight here. We didn't touch your little boyfriend," Amelia huffed. Isaac started to move toward his sister.

"Stay away from me. I'm going to tell Mom and Dad about this. And you better have a good explanation for hurting an innocent." Hannah stomped up the stairs and slammed her bedroom door.

"Well that was entertaining," Amelia quipped.

"Quiet Amelia, someone or something hurt that boy. And since it was definitely not us, who did it? We're the only ones of our kind in this town that cause trouble, but we never hurt anyone, scare them yeah, but-"

"I don't know why you're so upset. You liked the idea of someone stirring up trouble last year," Amelia sneered, covering up her hurt feelings after Isaac snapped at her.

"Not while we're getting the blame for it," Isaac replied. "Anyway, Hannah's right. Our parents do need to know. I'm going upstairs to try to convince her we had nothing to do with this. You guys go to your parents. They must still be at the meeting. I'll catch up with you later," Isaac said, moving quickly up the stairs.

Cat sprang up in her chair when she heard moans coming from Matt's bed. She saw his eyes open, looking bewildered as he scanned the room. He began panicking as he saw the tubes hanging from his arms.

"Shhhh Matt, it's okay. You're safe, you're in the hospital. You had a little accident, but you're going to be alright," Cat whispered, patting his hand.

"What…happened?" Matt's gaze held Cat's as he waited for her answer.

"You were in a car accident. You were the only one hurt. The police said you must've lost control on the icy roads or something. Do you remember anything?"

"No, the last thing…I remember, is driving away from Hannah's house."

"Hey dork, what did you go and have an accident for? We've been here all night watching your butt sleep instead of being in our own warm, comfy beds. You're lucky you've got friends like us," Amanda's voice sounded normal, but her face revealed her true feelings.

"Sorry…why didn't you all go home? Cat what are you doing here? We haven't been…talking lately," Matt grimaced.

"Go back to sleep Matt, we'll fill you in when you feel a little better. See this button? It's for pain. Do you want me to push it?" Matt barely nodded. Cat heard the beep as she pressed down. "Now that will make you feel better. Close your eyes and relax, we'll be right here if you need us."

"Thanks," Matt mumbled and then closed his eyes.

As Cat and Amanda turned around to return to their seats they saw Julie and Elle staring up at them. "He's fine, we should see if we can get some sleep ourselves," Cat said wearily, plopping down in a chair, and then stared out at the darkness beyond the hospital windows.

"Ow," Cat said, sitting up from the uncomfortable position she had slept in all night. Touching her bottom lip she pulled back her finger and it was bathed in blood. *Oh crap, my fangs are out. Fan-flippin-tastic!* She thought. Cat covered her mouth and looked from side to side. She was relieved to find everyone was still asleep. She concentrated and tried to make her fangs retract, but they wouldn't. Glancing at the bed she noticed a new IV pole with a bag, filled with a red substance, hanging from it. *Of course, blood,* Cat thought realizing that the coppery smell must have triggered her fangs. W*hen was the last time I took my pill? Stupid Cat, just stupid. I've got to get out of here!* She told herself as she quietly made her way past the sleeping bodies. Carefully opening the door, Cat slipped out into the corridor, still covering her mouth with her hand. It was brightly lit and people in colorful scrubs moved in and out of rooms lining the hall. Cat stood outside Matt's room wondering what to do next.

"Cat?" Dr. Bane's voice seemed loud in the quiet corridor.

"Dr. Bane I need your help. I'm kind of having an *issue* at the moment. If you know what I mean," Cat whispered, removing her hand from her mouth, revealing her obvious predicament.

"I'd say you are. When was the last time you took your pill?" he asked as he took her arm leading her down the hallway to a closed door marked Personnel Only.

"I don't remember," she lisped, covering her mouth again.

"Well you're too far gone now for the pills to have effect. We need to get you some real blood," he whispered as he unlocked the door and flipped on the light switch. Three refrigerators stood in front of them surrounded by cabinets labeled with their contents. "Have a seat in that chair Cat, and let's see what we can drum up for this condition of yours." Dr. Bane opened one of the refrigerators, and Cat saw rows and rows of labeled bags filled with a red substance that she assumed was blood. In the door were several bags sitting by themselves. Dr. Bane grabbed a few of them and shut the door. Holding them up to the light, "Well these bags don't seem to have labels. They're probably excess. I'm sure it'll be okay for you to have these," he said, handing one of the bags over to her.

"What do you expect me to do with this?"

"Okay, I'm going to need you to bite the bag, and let your fangs do the rest."

"Ewwww! I don't want to drink it. Please tell me there's another way." She scowled when he shook his head.

"Open up Cat, and place the bag to your teeth. Come on, be a big girl and take your medicine."

Opening her mouth, Cat closed her eyes as she felt the cold plastic bag caress her lips. She cringed as her teeth pierced it, feeling the blood entering her teeth. Cat was amazed that there was no taste. Dr. Bane's handsome face broke into a smile. "Not bad, huh?" Cat shook her head and watched as the bag emptied. Dr. Bane took another bag and held it out. Pulling the other one gently from her teeth, she pushed the second bag in.

"I think two bags should be enough to suppress your appetite. It's a good thing this happened here. The last thing we want is for you to have to find a warm bodied blood supply on your own." Cat silently chuckled as she visualized herself trying to feed from Fredricka, getting a mouthful of fur in the process.

Cat suddenly began to feel dizzy, her vision blurring slightly. She felt an uncontrollable urge to giggle out loud, but the plastic bag stuck to her fangs made it difficult. *I better keep this bag in my mouth. I wouldn't want to get blood all over me. They'd call me Bloody Cat, or blood sucking Colvin, or undead Cat if I did,* she hysterically thought. As Dr. Bane removed the bag from Cat's mouth, she let out a loud giggle and then hiccupped

"Cat are you okay?"

"Yes," she said, followed by another loud hiccup. "Yeeeessss, I'm just great Doc!" she giggled again at the alarm she saw in his face. Bringing the second bag up to his nose, Dr. Bane immediately realized the cause of her strange behavior. The blood was tainted with alcohol. *Great, how did Dr. Gregg's experimental blood get put in here?* Then he remembered the broken refrigerator down in the lab. *Fantastic, now she's drunk! How am I going to explain this?* He thought.

"Doc, do you…know how many feeeeeeeemales…drool over you. Even my mom…thinks you're hot!" Cat laughed, lying back in the chair. She would've slipped out of it if Dr. Bane's reflexes hadn't been so quick. Holding on to her, he grabbed his cell, and pressed a few keys.

"Aldon we have a slight problem. I need you to meet me at the hospital's back entrance. Yes, as soon as you can. Thanks, I'll explain when you get here." He hit the end button and then caught Cat as she suddenly leaned forward, planting a big kiss on his lips.

"Mmmmmm wait until I telllll everyone I kissed the hunky doctor. Of course I can't do that…Ryan would be soooo maaaadd. Cause he loves me. He's so sweet." She frowned, looking into Dr. Bane's eyes, "You won't tell, him, will yoooou?" she loudly whispered and then hiccupped again.

"No Cat I won't. In fact we won't tell anyone okay? This will be our little secret."

"Soooooo mannnny secretssss I keeeeeep. I-" Cat's head fell forward as she passed out. Dr. Bane sighed, pressing numbers on his phone again.

"Carol, it's me, please meet me on the 2rd floor of the hospital. I have a little issue that I need you to help me with. Yes, and bring me a wheelchair. I'm in the temporary blood room. Thanks. And please hurry." Hanging up the phone he knew in the next few hours he'd have a lot of explaining to do.

Half an hour later Cat was safely buckled into Aldon's back seat. As Carol took off with the wheelchair, Dr. Bane watched Aldon pull out of the back parking lot, merging into the traffic. Sighing, he made his way back to Matt's room preparing an explanation for Cat's absence.

⸙ ⸙ ⸙

Rachel placed a cool washcloth on Cat's forehead, and grumbled worriedly at the fact her sixteen-year-old was lying in front of her inebriated. She thought back to when Aldon had called during breakfast.

"Drunk?" Sam had asked after answering the phone and hearing what happened. "But she's staying in Matt's room with the others, how did she get drunk? Oh, I see. We'll see you soon then."

"What? Cat's drunk? How?" Rachel exclaimed.

Taylor laughed. "Way to go *Red Freak*! Little sis is looking to be grounded for life."

"Quiet Taylor, Cat didn't drink on purpose. It seems our little girl forgot to take her pill. And Dr. Bane had to improvise by giving her blood bags. I guess a few of them were tainted. Aldon's on his way here with Cat. She's unconscious, but okay," Sam explained

"She's gonna have one heck of a hangover though. Hey, does this mean I can drink too?" Taylor asked, trying to look innocent.

"No young man it does not. This was an accident," Sam said, and then Taylor jumped up to answer the door when the bell chimed through the house.

"Let's go take care of our little drunkard," Sam joked, smiling as he grabbed Rachel's hand, leading her out of the kitchen toward the foyer.

❦ ❦ ❦

"So my little ones, tell me again of this cloaked figure who has thwarted you for a second time," Andrei said, leaning back in the chair while crossing his legs, with a puzzled expression on his face.

"We have no idea. They come out of nowhere," Amy complained.

"Out of nowhere?" he asked.

"And they're really strong too, like super strong!" Becca chimed in.

"Well girls, it would seem that we have a little issue that needs to be dealt with. But for now, I think we should plan for something a tad bigger, and see if we can't draw this person out. Yes Amy, I see your hand is raised, what do you want?"

"I think we need a cow, because cows give us milk, and we really need milk," she snickered, causing Andrei to roll his eyes.

"Okay ladies, we shall find you a cow. Has to be a strong one though. One that's able to sustain you three."

"Andrei, I think I know just the perfect person," Amy's sinister smile caused Linda's stomach to churn, dreading who Amy had in mind.

14
M.I.A.

Sitting on the bench just outside her oval bay window, Cat fiddled with the locket her aunt Ròs had given her. As she studied the pictures within, Cat felt a sense of sadness overcome her. "I look just like her," she said to herself in a reflective tone, tracing the picture of her mother with her index finger. *He looks so regal, and I definitely know where I get my fiery red hair from*, she mused, gazing at her father's photo. Tears formed in her eyes as Cat clasped the locket shut and clutched it tightly in her hand. Looking up into the night sky at the full moon looming overhead, she tried to ward off the oncoming flow of tears.

Staring down at the locket once more, Cat noticed the Celtic knot on the back of it was now flush with the face, and not raised like before. Examining it further, she found herself turning the symbol one full rotation, trying to reset it. With the Celtic knot back in place, Cat set the locket down on the bench beside her. Standing up, she leaned against the balcony railing, closed her eyes, and let the frigid wind caress her cheeks and tussle her hair. She turned around abruptly when she heard a clanking noise behind her. Cat watched in awe as the locket bounced along the bench. She moved forward and it stopped. As she reached out to pick it up, the locket moved away and began to glow with a faint violet light. “What the heck?” Cat asked, her eyes wide with shock.

The locket suddenly popped open and the violet light shot into the sky. Watching its path, Cat saw the light intersect with a trail of purple smoke making its way toward her house. It seemed like it was coming right at her, but at the last minute switched directions, heading for the widow’s walk at the top of the roof. Cat hurried up the icy ladder, her Ugg boots giving her traction. Reaching the widow’s walk, her eyes met her aunt Ròs’s.

"Catherine, Catherine, what's wrong?" Are you in trouble?!" Ròs asked in a panic, pulling her up on to the roof, and grabbing her in a hug.

"I'm fine. What are you doing here?" Cat's voice was muffled, being smothered by Ròs.

"Well you called me!" she replied, pulling Cat away to look at her.

"Wait, I did?"

"The locket, you used it right?"

"I called you with that?" Cat asked.

"I guess I did not explain that properly. Well you see it's enchanted with witch magic. A transportation spell to be exact." Noticing Cat's confusion, Ròs said, "It's a long story."

"Of course it is. Why wouldn't it be?" Cat joked. *My life keeps getting weirder and weirder.*

"You have to be careful with that locket. Its *magics* are very sensitive," Ròs explained.

"I'm really sorry," she apologized.

"Oh, it's okay. Just try not to use it again unless it is a dire emergency," Ròs said with a laugh.

"Got it," Cat replied.

"Well since I'm here now anyway, how are things? Has anything interesting happened lately?" Ròs asked.

Oh, if only you knew, Cat thought. "No, not really. Just trying to survive high school," she chuckled. Cat didn't want Ròs to know about what was really going on. She didn't want to be forced to leave the Colvin's, her friends, and most of all Ryan. She knew lying to Ròs wasn't right, but she was willing to do so in order to not jeopardize her "normal" life more than it already was.

"Survive high school?" Ròs sounded confused.

"Yeah, you know," Cat began and then realized Ròs was from a different world than hers. "Oh, I guess you don't. Well, you have your bullies, horrid teachers, and gawd awful homework! Plus peer pressure, and the list goes on," Cat explained.

"Sounds positively dreadful," Ròs replied.

"Yeah well, so goes the life of a teenager," she drawled unenthusiastically.

"Well as long as you're okay, that's all that matters," Ròs stated, putting her hand on Cat's shoulder.

"Yeah everything's fine, no worries here," she replied with a slight smile.

"Alright then, I'll be off. Oh and try not to tinker too much with the locket, unless it is a true emergency. The ride is quite intense, never really liked it in the first place. But it is a quick way to get somewhere," she explained and then laughed. "I love you Cat, please be safe."

"Love you too Aunt Ròs, and I will be, don't worry," she replied.

"Oh, and one more thing before I go. Please do call on me if you are in trouble. Don't be afraid to confide in me," she said with a slight smile and a look of concern.

"Will do." Ròs winked at Cat and then leapt off the roof, disappearing into the night. *Man, if Robert Craven knew about my life, he'd have another best seller on his hands for sure!* Cat told herself.

"Cat? Are you going to make the incision? Ugh, I can't do it," Hannah moaned, completely disgusted at the sight of the frog stretched out in front of them. Cat looked down at the poor thing lying there motionless, and then glanced over at the scalpel in her hand.

"I don't think I can do it either," she replied, gagging at the thought.

"Problem ladies?" Mr. Pierson asked, approaching their lab table.

"Uh sir, is all of this really necessary? You know the whole frog massacre thing?" Cat asked with a disgusted look.

"Oh come now ladies, it's not that difficult." Mr. Pierson chuckled as he took the scalpel from Cat's hand and put it to the chest of the frog. As he began to make the incision both Cat and Hannah put their hands to their mouths trying not to gag. Thankfully the bell rang, and Mr. Pierson placed the scalpel down on the table. "Okay class, we'll pick up where we left off tomorrow. Please read the chapter in your lab book about frog dissection, if you haven't done so already," Mr. Pierson said smiling, his dimples adding the final touch.

After swim practice, Cat sat in Mr. Pierson's classroom, helping him organize his files. "So, I probably shouldn't be asking a student this, but what do you think of Amaya Phillips?" he asked, sifting through some papers, avoiding eye contact with Cat.

"I love Miss Amaya. She's amazing," Cat stated. "Why, what's up?"

"Oh nothing. Just curious is all," he replied with a grin, and then pushed his glasses up off his nose. "Oh and by the way, thank you so much for helping me stay organized, I know what kind of stigma can come from being a teacher's assistant."

"It's been cool, plus no one's really given me a hard time anyway," Cat replied. "Hey, Mr. Pierson?"

"Yes Ms. Colvin?"

"I don't mean to be rude, but what's with the pocket protector?"

“Oh this?” Mr. Pierson asked drawing it from his shirt pocket. “Well, it’s kind of my security blanket. Don’t leave home without it.”

“Why?”

He chuckled. “Let’s just say, I had a little pen incident once, and this keeps that from happening ever again.”

“I see.”

“I know, you probably think I'm this super nerd or something,” he began.

“No, not at all. I’ve got a security blanket too, kind of. It’s the book, *Red Twilight*, by Robert Craven. I’ve read it a million times.”

He laughed. “Oh yeah, he’s that horror writer right? The ever elusive man.”

“That’s the one,” Cat replied. “So, now back to Miss Amaya.”

“Well with that said, it’s getting late and you should probably get home, I’m sure you’re tired after practice and looking through files here,” Mr. Pierson rambled, frantically putting some papers into his over the shoulder bag, and trying to avoid the subject.

Cat groaned. “Alright then, see you tomorrow, for our…dissection.”

"Yeah see you tomorrow," he replied with a slight laugh. Watching Cat leave his classroom, Melvin began sifting through more papers.

An hour later, Melvin finished organizing for the night and put the last of his files into his bag. Turning off the lights he closed the door behind him. The hall was empty and Melvin's footsteps echoed through the school's corridors. A loud bang came from behind him. Startled, he spun around and saw one of the janitors coming out of a classroom, picking up his mop that had fallen through the door into the hall.

"Sorry 'bout that, mop's got a mind of its own," the janitor called out.

"Tis all right, just gave me a little-" Melvin began to reply and then realized the janitor had put in his earphones. Shaking his head, he turned and made his way to the exit.

Reaching the parking lot, Melvin noticed that his and the janitor's cars were the only ones left there. "Too bad I don't get paid by the hour," he joked. Making his way to his car, Melvin drew his keys from his pocket. As he inserted them into the lock his car alarm went off, surprising him, and causing him to drop his keys into the muddy snow. Groaning, Melvin bent down to pick them up only to find them gone. "Great, just great! They must've gone under the car," he muttered in frustration throwing his bag on the trunk. Getting down on his hands and knees, he peered into the blackness under the vehicle, with the annoying sound of the alarm still ringing in his ears. Unzipping his jacket, Melvin drew a penlight from his pocket protector. The light's beam caused the keys to shimmer, and Melvin realized he would need to stretch to reach them. *How did they get so far under the car?*

Over the sound of the screeching alarm, Melvin heard a muffled bang as the whole car shook. Springing up, he scanned the surroundings seeing nothing unusual. The street lamp in the parking lot gave off quite a bit of light, but he still couldn't shake the feeling that someone was watching him from the shadows beyond it. "Get a grip Melvin, it's just that stupid alarm driving you nuts. Just get the keys already," he muttered, getting back down on the ground and shining the penlight under the car. "What the hell?" he asked out loud when the light's beam failed to reveal the keys. He jumped to his feet confused. *They were just there, where could they have gone?*

The sound of the car alarm shutting off and the doors unlocking broke his train of thought. Melvin hesitantly reached out for the handle and the door locked again. Hearing giggling behind him, he spun around, but saw no one. "Hello? Is someone there?" he asked, taking a few steps away from his car, the snow crunching under his feet. "If this is a joke, it isn't funny in the slightest...hello?" he asked again into the dark.

Hearing no reply, Melvin rubbed the back of his neck, trying to ease the goose bumps that were rising up. Turning back around to face his car, his eyes grew wide when he saw a pale teenage girl sitting on his car's roof, her straight black hair falling over her face.

"Mr. Pierson right? Are you looking for these?" she asked as she dangled the keys from her finger. Slowly raising her head, Amy flipped her hair back, her jet black eyes challenging his. "Remember me Mr. Pierson?"

"Uh, yes…I do, but what are you doing here Amy?"

"Do you remember how you failed me in biology, even though I had begged you not to? Oh how the tables do turn!" Amy grinned, revealing two long white fangs. Melvin's eyes filled with fear as Linda and Becca popped up from behind the car with their fangs bared as well. "This is the part where you run," Amy said menacingly. Melvin took off running back toward the school's main entrance, yelling at the top of his lungs. Pulling on the doors wildly, he realized the janitor just locked them. He could see him walking away down the hall, oblivious to his yelling. Banging feverishly on the door, Melvin continued yelling, trying to get the attention of the janitor. *He can't hear me! He has those damn things in his ears*! He thought and then was viciously ripped away from the door.

❦ ❦ ❦

Early the next morning, Cat strolled into Mr. Pierson's classroom and was surprised to find Miss Amaya sitting at his desk, flipping through his lesson planner. "Hey you're in here a lot, aren't you?" Cat asked her jokingly. Miss Amaya looked up at Cat with worried eyes and a half smile. "So, where's Mr. Pierson?"

"I don't know. He hasn't called in sick or anything yet, but being late just isn't like him."

"Huh, well if he doesn't come in, who will take over his class?"

Miss Amaya lifted up the notebook containing Mr. Pierson's lesson plans, "you're looking at her."

"Oh, I'm sure everything's fine. He'll be here, don't worry, okay," Cat said reassuringly, placing her hand on Miss Amaya's shoulder.

"I know, but I just have this weird feeling in my gut," she said as she looked weakly into Cat's eyes.

"I know what you mean," Cat replied, suddenly concerned.

❦ ❦ ❦

Cat hated being late to class. Even with a tardy pass in hand, she still rushed to her locker. Flustered, she mis-dialed her combo and had to start all over again. She heard someone walk up beside her and turned to face them. Cat groaned inwardly when she saw it was Isaac. “What do you want? Stalking me much?” she asked snidely.

“We need to talk,” he replied with a cold stare.

“I have nothing to say to you,” she answered as she pulled her books from her locker and then slammed it shut.

“It’s about Hannah.”

“I already told you that I’ll be friends with whoever I want, and so will your sister. So the quicker you get that through your thick skull, the better off we’ll all be!” Cat stated bluntly. She went to move away, but instead was blocked by Isaac’s imposing form. “Really? Intimidation doesn’t work, remember? I’m not scared of you Isaac,” she said, staring at him and was shocked to see the usual sneer lacking from his face. In fact he almost looked human to her.

“Cat will you just listen for a second! I’m not here to fight, alright!”

“Okay, that’s a new one. You have five seconds Bancroft, and that’s all you get,” she said, raising an eyebrow to him.

“I want to…uh,” Cat waited as he fumbled for the words. She almost smiled seeing him like this…almost. She thought about teasing him, but decided against it. “I want a truce,” he blurted out.

“A truce?” she asked.

"Yeah, you know we don't mess with you, you don't mess with us. A truce," he whispered quickly.

"Hey, let's get one thing straight. You're the ones who mess with us," Cat stated.

"Whatever, do you want a truce or not?" Isaac asked in frustration.

"What brought this on?"

"Hannah," he replied, looking away shamefully.

"When have you ever cared about what she thinks?" Cat asked smugly.

Isaac slammed his hands on the lockers on either side of Cat, and then brought his face right in front of hers. "Do you want a truce?" he roared.

"Sure, truce," Cat replied, and then extended her hand for his after he backed away. Just as Isaac went to shake her hand, Cat pulled hers back. Isaac glared at her, she returned it. "What about the rest of your group?"

"I'll take care of them, okay!"

"Alright, truce," she said, shaking his hand. Isaac immediately stormed off down the hall, not looking back. "Wow, I can officially add that to my ever growing list of things I didn't see coming," Cat mumbled.

Sitting in her sixth period chemistry class, Kirsten began to nod off while listening to her teacher, Mr. Thompson, ramble on about the properties of water. "Blah, blah, blah, water, blah, blah," Kirsten murmured to herself. She stretched and yawned, leaning back in her chair. "Chemistry…most boring class ever." Looking over to her left, she saw Tonya doodling in her notebook. *An elf, riding a unicorn? Really?! Why do I even hang out with her?* Tonya looked up from her drawing at Kirsten and smiled, giving her a little wave. Faking a smile, Kirsten turned her attention back to the teacher, rolling her eyes.

"Psst…Kirsten," Jessica whispered.

"Jessica, do you have something you want to say to the whole class?" Mr. Thompson asked.

"Uhh, no. I just wanted to talk to Kirsten," Jessica replied blankly. Mr. Thompson stared at her with one eyebrow raised and his arms crossed. "Oh, right, class," she said, slouching back into her desk.

"So glad you remembered Jessica. Now, where was I? Water, right," Mr. Thompson stated. Kirsten rolled her eyes again shaking her head.

The class seemed to be lasting forever, and Kirsten was having a hard time keeping her eyes open. Resting her head on the cool desktop, she slowly drifted off to sleep. Opening her eyes, Kirsten looked around and saw nothing but rows of lockers. "Why am I in the locker room? I'm supposed to be in chemistry," she asked out loud. Out of the corner of her eye, she noticed a basketball bouncing toward her from the equipment cage. After grabbing the ball on its last bounce, Kirsten headed over to the cage, and placed it back on the shelf. As she turned around, she was stopped cold by Cat, who was frantic.

"Kirsten, you have to hide! They're coming!" Cat spat out.

"What are you talking about?"

"There's no time to explain! Hurry, hide in there!" Cat ordered, putting her hand on Kirsten's shoulder, and shoving her slightly toward the equipment cage. Kirsten pushed Cat's hand off of her.

"I will not, until you tell me what's going on!"

Cat looked away, "Shhh…they're here."

"Who's here?" Kirsten asked anxiously.

Cat slowly turned her head back to face Kirsten, her fangs bared. "Vampires," she said and then lunged for Kirsten's neck.

"No Cat!" Kirsten screamed, waking up in class. Everyone was staring at her. Scanning the room, Kirsten became more and more embarrassed as she noticed all the looks she was receiving. *What the hell was that?* She thought.

"Looks like someone has a lesbian crush," A girl called out from the back of the class.

"Who said that?" Kirsten asked angrily, eying the two back rows. No one answered.

"Kirsten, I'm going to need you to stay after, to discuss this little episode of yours," Mr. Thompson ordered as the bell rang, signaling the end of class. Kirsten moaned and slumped in her desk.

Walking into her biology class, Cat expected to see Mr. Pierson sitting behind his desk with his usual glasses nestled just off the bridge of his nose, his prized pocket protector proudly displayed, and his light brown hair disheveled from running his fingers through it all day. Instead she was met with a somber and tired looking Miss Amaya.

"So I'm guessing he called in then?" Cat asked. Miss Amaya shook her head and proceeded to cross names off the roll call sheet.

"So class, today we shall pick up where you left off on your frog dissections. Everyone please proceed to your lab tables and begin prepping your areas," Miss Amaya said, forcing a smile. She walked over to the cabinet where the frogs were being kept. Opening it she was hit by the stench of formaldehyde. *Ugh, this is such a foul smell!* She thought. As she distributed a frog to every lab table, Miss Amaya cringed at the sound of each one plopping onto their trays.

"Miss Amaya?" Cat called out, holding the scalpel to the frog's chest.

"Yes dear, you have a question?" Miss Amaya asked, covering her mouth with her lavender scarf to protect herself from the smell.

"Well, Mr. Pierson was in the middle of showing us how to make the first incision yesterday, and then the bell rang. Could you show us?"

"I guess, I could," Miss Amaya replied, hesitantly taking the scalpel that Cat handed to her. With one hand firmly holding the scarf over her mouth and nose, Miss Amaya placed the scalpel to the frog's chest. Pressing the scalpel down, using only two fingers as to not accidentally touch the frog's slimy skin, she began to make the incision. The sound of the frog being cut open caused her to squint and turn her head away. Suddenly a liquid shot out from the opening causing Cat, Miss Amaya, and Hannah to scream. Miss Amaya's eyes rolled in to the back of her head as she collapsed, fainting to the floor. Her scarf slowly floated down to the ground after.

"Miss Amaya?!" Cat yelled.

Waking up in the nurse's office, Miss Amaya blinked open her eyes and felt her head. A groan of pain followed. "You took a nasty little fall there Amaya," the school nurse said, patting her arm.

"How long have I been out?"

"Not long. The school day is almost over though," she replied with a smile.

A few moments later the school bell rang. The door to the nurse's office flew open and Cat ran into the room. "Miss Amaya! They found Melvin's car in a ditch by the Covington River! There's no trace of him anywhere!" Cat's voice wobbled.

"What?!" Miss Amaya sprang up, forgetting her headache. "Do they know what happened?" she asked with worried eyes.

"No, they have no idea! Principal Landers just made the announcement like fifteen minutes ago. She wanted to let us know personally, and not have to find it out on the news."

"I was shocked when I heard. Such a nice man, I hope they find him soon," the nurse commented. Miss Amaya stared at Cat in disbelief, Cat stared back. A tear rolled down her cheek as Cat embraced her in a hug. No more words were spoken.

15
Mind Your P's And Q's

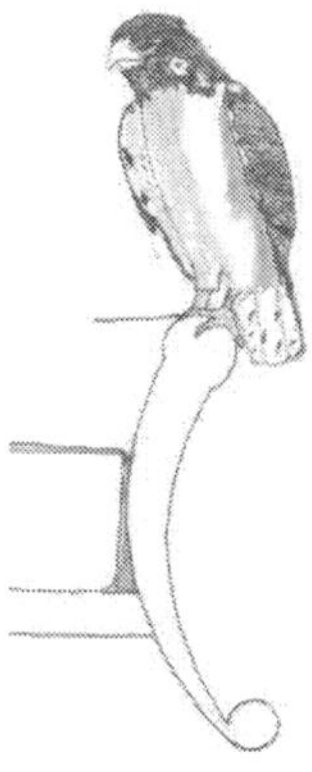

The school's winter open house was a packed affair. As Cat and her mom entered her biology classroom she was overcome with sadness. She missed Mr. Pierson's smile. Miss Amaya stood by his desk greeting the parents and students, not looking any happier than Cat.

"Mrs. Colvin, Cat, welcome. And thank you for braving this dreadful weather to be with us. I'm still getting used to this room." Her eyes began tearing up as she turned to point to a sheet of paper lying on the desk. "Please sign in, and as soon as the bell rings we'll begin."

Cat reached over and squeezed Miss Amaya's hand, relieved at the little smile she received back.

"Welcome parents and students. I'm Miss Amaya and this is Biology 101. If some of you haven't heard, I'm Mr. Pierson's temporary replacement. On the board you'll see what we have in store for the remainder of the school year. We recently dissected frogs, not one of my favorite things, I can assure you," she smiled as several people laughed at the disgusted look on her face. "Now, feel free to look around the room at some of the projects your children have been working on. And if you have any questions don't hesitate to ask."

After walking around the classroom, Rachel sat down in one of the many student desks, trying to keep her attention on one of Cat's project folders. Instead, she was distracted by her daughter's focus on Miss Amaya. Cat had informed them of the affect Mr. Pierson's disappearance had on her usually happy teacher. Out of the corner of her eye, Rachel watched as Ulla Bancroft's ugly glare focused on Cat who was talking with Hannah.

"Miss Amaya looks really upset," Hannah said gloomily.

"I know. I wish we could help her. She really liked Mr. Pierson, and he liked her," Cat whispered, glancing over at Miss Amaya.

"I can't believe they found his car in that ditch. It's strange that they didn't find him too, don't you think?"

"Yeah and why was he out that way? He lives on the other side of town. It's really weird." Cat shook her head and then froze, as she met Ulla's cold stare over Hannah's shoulder. "Your mom doesn't look very happy," Cat whispered. Hannah turned her head and sighed as she looked at her mom.

"I've got to go Cat. That's her 'come-here-right-now' stare. I guess I'll see you tomorrow," she murmured, making her way to her mother's side.

"Mom what's up with Mrs. Bancroft? She's always giving us the evil eye."

"Just ignore her. Ulla has always been like that. I think she thoroughly enjoys making people uncomfortable. Oh, there goes the bell. Let's go find your Dad and Taylor."

Rachel stood and moved to the front of the class to say goodbye to Miss Amaya, not seeing that Ulla was also moving forward. "Miss Amaya, thank you for taking over the class, even though it's under such tragic circumstances. Cat is especially grateful that you did," Rachel said reassuringly.

"So this is how you get the witch into your corner!" Ulla's menacing whisper made Rachel turn quickly.

She glared at Ulla, and was thankful that they were the only ones left in the classroom. "I see you still haven't worked on your manners Ulla," Rachel replied.

"How dare you talk about my manners you filthy mutt! I loathe that my children have to go to the same school as your offspring. You keep your Cath-"

"Ladies, please for your children's sake, cease this behavior." Miss Amaya's eyes met Ulla's with a warning.

"Sorry, you're right. This isn't the time, or the place. Please forgive me. And thank you again for everything," Rachel said and then shook Miss Amaya's hand before leaving the room. Without a word, Ulla scowled at Miss Amaya and then followed Rachel out.

Outside in the parking lot, away from the crowd, Trish's parents, Roland and Anna Digby, were in a heated argument with the Stone twin's parents, Tegan and Meredith.

"I don't believe you!" Roland said, standing toe to toe with Tegan.

"I don't care what you believe! Our children did not attack that boy!" Tegan shot back.

"It seems strange that after the incident at the dance, Matt has an accident. If we find out that anyone in your group caused this, things will change in this town, starting with you all leaving! It was a bad idea for Aldon to allow it in the first place! You better just keep an eye on your children, and what they're up to!"

"Are you threatening my kids? If so, you better watch your back!" Tegan growled, shoving Roland who in turn pushed back.

"Stop Roland! Let's not do this here. Somebody might see us. Please honey, let's go," Anna pleaded.

"Yes, I agree Anna. Tegan, look, here come the twins, let's leave," Meredith said, pulling Tegan toward the car.

"Meredith, we need to resolve this, otherwise it will only get worse," Anna said while gently taking her arm.

"Anna I know the boys can cause a little trouble, but they'd never hurt anyone, please believe me," Meredith replied.

"Don't grovel to those animals Meredith, let's leave!" Tegan roared, his teeth elongating. Meredith sent another pleading look to Anna and then turned to follow her husband.

Anna and Roland watched as the Stone family got into their car. "Roland, I think we need to have a meeting. If they're telling the truth and it wasn't them, we have a serious problem on our hands," Anna said, clutching her husband's arm tighter as they made their way back to the school to find their daughter Trish.

"What a game! I lost count how many times I held my breath. Those last seconds were so tense! I thought I was going to lose my mind! That final pass Taylor threw to Ryan was amazing. I can't believe we won State! I can't wait to see Taylor! I just wish I didn't have to go home and change, darn soda. I'm glad you guys are giving me a ride though." Trish finally took a breath and stopped talking, causing the three others in the car to burst out laughing.

"What are best friends for? Oh, and are you sure you don't want someone to drive to the Colvin's with you?" Beth asked, looking at Trish through her rear-view mirror.

"No that's okay, you guys go ahead. I'll meet you there. I think I might be a little while anyway. I don't want this soda stain to become permanent. I'm just so excited!" Everyone laughed again as Beth pulled the car into Trish's driveway. "Okay, I'll see you guys soon. Way to go Panthers!" she yelled as she shut the car door and made her way to the front porch while fumbling for her keys. Beth beeped the horn and then backed out of the driveway.

Trish smiled as she heard, "*We are the Panthers, the mighty mighty Panthers*," coming from the open windows of the car.

The house was dark and quiet. *Oh yeah, I forgot my parents went to the game with the Colvin's*, Trish thought. Hurrying up the stairs, Trish's cell phone rang and she grinned as she heard Taylor's ring tone.

"Hi Taylor!"

"Hey, sorry about the background noise. This locker room is insane! I can't wait to see you, I love you! Sorry, I can't hear if you are talking back, but I just wanted to let you know I can't wait to see you. I know I just said that, but it's true. So hurry, but be careful and get your cute butt over to my house. I'll meet you there. Love you!"

"Love you too Taylor!" Trish yelled into the phone before he hung up. Trish beamed as she removed her stained jersey, an exact replica of Taylor's, and pulled an identical one out of her closet. *I'm so glad I've got this back up,* she thought. While pulling the jersey over her head, she heard a strange noise coming from outside her window. Looking through her curtains, she saw nothing but snow covered trees illuminated by the Victorian streetlamp outside. Retrieving her jacket from the floor, Trish started down the stairs, her keys jangling in her pocket. As she reached the bottom of the stairs, the doorbell rang. "Who is it?" Trish asked jokingly, thinking that it was her friends at the door. There was no answer. Opening the door, "Guys, I told you I-" Trish stopped as she noticed no one was on the front porch. "Guys?" she asked unsure. Shrugging, Trish closed the door behind her and locked it. She walked to her car with a bounce in her step, excited at the thought of seeing Taylor soon. *What's that smell?* She thought turning her nose up to the air. Hearing a low growl, Trish turned on her heel coming came face to face with long teeth and jet black eyes.

❧ ❧ ❧

The Colvin residence was jam packed full of people. Cat sat with her friends in her dad's study trying to avoid the chaos that was currently her house. "It's amazing what breaking your arm will do for your popularity, huh Matt?" Cat commented jokingly, looking at all of the signatures on his cast.

"I know, it's awesome! My year is definitely looking up! I made the football team, and received many a girl's sympathy," he replied with a goofy smile.

"You horn dog!" Amanda stated. "What about Hannah? How does she feel about all the attention you're getting?"

"Hey I can't help that girls want to sign the cast, okay. Besides Hannah doesn't seem to mind."

Oh Matt you're so oblivious to how Hannah feels. I don't think that girl knew what she was getting herself into when she signed up for you, Cat thought.

"Hey Cat, where's Ryan? The rest of the team is here," Brandon asked, his arm around Elle.

"I don't know-"

"Cat Honey, could you help me for a minute in the kitchen?" Rachel called through the study door, interrupting her.

"Be right there mom," she replied. "I'll be back," she told everyone in an irritated tone. Cat made her way through the mass of bodies toward the kitchen. Reaching the kitchen door Cat felt two arms wrap around her waist, pulling her backward.

"I finally found you," Ryan whispered in her ear.

"I didn't know I was lost," Cat whispered back as she turned to look into his shockingly blue eyes. "You're lucky I didn't use one of my training moves on you just now." Ryan laughed. "So, where have you been?"

"I had something to do real quick. Do you want to continue this conversation upstairs?" he asked and then gently kissed her mouth.

"Maybe," she answered, slightly pushing away from him. "But first I've got to go see what help my mom needs. Why don't you go to my room, and I'll be up soon."

"Okay, but be quick. I've barely seen you all day," he replied, looking at her forlornly.

"Oh don't pull that poor puppy dog look on me Mr. Beckford. I saw all those cheerleaders hugging you after the game. I couldn't even get close," she replied flippantly.

"Yeah, but all I could think about was the beautiful redhead I spend most of my time with."

"Well this redhead needs to go. So let me finish what I've got to do, and I'll see you in a bit," she said as she pushed away from him and giggled, and then made her way into the kitchen.

Several minutes later, on her way upstairs, Cat was brought up short by Julie. "Hey Cat, where are you going?" Julie asked from the foyer. "The gang's waiting for you to watch *Darkness Awakes* on DVD in the study."

"Oh, I'll be down in a sec. I just have to run up to my room for something," she replied. Julie could sense Cat wasn't telling the truth.

"Well hurry up, because someone has to keep Amanda from breaking Matt's other arm," she joked.

Cat laughed. "Will do."

Reaching the top of the stairs, Cat saw Taylor's door open and watched as he emerged from his bedroom. "Hey Taylor what are you doing up here? The action's downstairs. And what's with the frown, you should be ecstatic."

"I would be if Trish were here. Or at least answering her phone. You didn't happen to see her downstairs did you?" Cat shook her head. "Beth said they took her home to change. That was over two hours ago. I didn't realize it had been that long until somebody mentioned what time it was. I just can't understand what could be taking so long. Maybe something's happened," he rambled on worriedly.

"Don't worry Taylor, she'll show up. She's probably getting all dolled up for the party. You know how girls are. It takes us forever to get ready. I bet she's down there right now. So get your butt in gear and go find her," Cat said, gently pushing him toward the stairs.

"Thanks Cat," he replied with a slight smile. Hurrying up to the attic, Cat pushed down the twinge of worry she was feeling herself.

Reaching her bedroom door, Cat saw it was slightly open and the room beyond was dark. *Silly boy*, she thought moving through the doorway. Two hands grabbed her gently, "Is that you Ryan?" Cat asked mischievously.

"Where's that training move you were talking about?" Ryan mocked. Cat grabbed ahold of Ryan's arm and flipped him over her shoulder onto the floor.

Straddling him, "You mean, that one?"

He laughed. "That was pretty good."

"Learned from the best," Cat smiled as she leaned down to kiss him. Pulling back, Cat stared at him suspiciously. "Hey, it just occurred to me, you're a vampire that plays football against humans. Isn't that a little unfair, especially since you guys won state now and all. Don't you feel a little ashamed of yourself?" she joked.

"For your information, my talent comes from training and discipline. And I've never used my *special* skills on the field, thank you very much."

"Not even once?" she asked with a mischievous grin.

"Okay maybe one time, but we were about to lose, and it-" Cat silenced him with a kiss, both of them grinning.

A tapping sound came at Cat's bay window, interrupting the pair. "Did you hear that?" she asked and then pulled away from him, listening for the sound. "There it is again."

Ryan stood and made his way to the window. Opening the curtains, the moon revealed a large white falcon sitting on the window sill tapping its beak against the glass. *Oh wow, it's that bird I keep seeing everywhere*, Cat thought.

"Be careful, you don't know where that thing's been."

"Don't be silly," she replied, pushing up the latch and opening the window. The falcon flew into the room and perched on the front edge of Cat's sleigh bed. "You're a pretty bird aren't you?" she asked as the falcon ruffled its feathers as if it understood the compliment. "So, what do we do now?"

"I don't know. You were the one that let it in."

"What do you think it wants?" Cat asked. Suddenly the falcon let out a loud screech, nodding its head toward the window. Taking flight it retraced its path out and perched on the balcony. Cat and Ryan moved forward and looked out at the bird. It screeched again, left the balcony, and swooped downward. They looked over the railing and watched as the falcon flew low to the ground, then disappeared around the side of the house.

"That was weird," Ryan muttered. Cat nodded as she watched for the bird to return.

Hearing the falcon screech again, "I think it wants us to follow it," she said.

"Okay bird whisperer," he joked.

"Come on Ryan, I'm serious. We can climb down the lattice," Cat said, pulling at his shirt.

"Or we can do it the easy way." Ryan put his arms around her and proceeded to float them both down to the ground.

"Oh yeah, I forgot about that," she commented as they touched down softly in the snow. "It's freezing out here. I'm totes not dressed for this," Cat moaned as they rounded the corner. The falcon sat on the wooden banister that wrapped around the front and sides of the house, with its wings spread wide. It was peering at something on the snow covered ground. "Oh I hope it didn't kill something. I know it's the circle of life and everything, but I hate seeing Mother Nature all up close and personal," Cat stated, hesitantly following the focus of the bird's gaze.

"What is that?" Ryan asked. The pair approached the shape cautiously. It took a couple seconds to register that they were staring at a body. Bending down, Ryan swiped the hair from in front of the person's face, "It's Trish!"

"What?" Cat yelled, looking down at her pale face and torn bloody clothes. A large piece of paper was pinned to her coat.

NO ONE IS SAFE. WHO WILL BE NEXT?
DON'T KNOW? WELL I GUESS YOU"LL BE
SURPRISED!

"Is she alive Ryan?"

"Yeah, her breathing is shallow though. Hurry and get Dr. Bane!" he answered urgently. Cat ran to the front door, the snow crunching under every step she took. Not stopping to wipe her feet, she entered the house and moved as quickly as she could through the mass of people. *This is all my fault, I'm putting everyone I love in danger. I should've left with Ròs and Trevor when I had the chance. Trish has to be okay, I couldn't live with myself if she's not!* Cat thought. Finally she spied the handsome doctor talking with her parents and pushed her way forward, excusing her rudeness as she went.

"Cat what's wrong?" Rachel asked.

"I'm fine. Dr. Bane I need you to come with me! Don't ask why, just please hurry!" she pleaded. Puzzled, the three adults followed her outside. Aldon saw the group leaving and felt their tension, especially Cat who seemed very distraught. He hurried after and found them bent over a still figure lying in the snow.

"What has happened to her?" Rachel's voice shook.

"Her pulse is weak, and it looks like she's lost a lot of blood. Sam here's my cell. Press and hold seven, it's a direct line to emergency services," Dr. Bane explained and then lifted Trish's eyelids to check her pupils. "Aldon, please go and fetch her parents, we need to get her to the hospital quickly!" Scanning her body, "I don't see any fresh blood, but I can't tell how badly she's hurt until I can examine her."

Trish's mom let out a cry as she moved quickly to her daughter's side. Cat moved to allow her access, and Ryan pulled her to him, watching on silently.

The sound of sirens filled the air as the ambulance came into view. The front yard was suddenly lit up by the lights of the emergency vehicle. People began spilling out from inside the party, wondering what was going on. Sam moved to calm everyone, trying to get them back inside. "What's going on Dad?" Taylor asked as he pushed his way through the throng. Sam intercepted him and whispered in his ear. Cat watched as pain filled her brother's face. "Trish!" Taylor yelled, pulling out of his father's arms and moving quickly toward her. Rachel moved away so her son could take her place. Rachel felt a hand patting her shoulder and turned to find Aldon behind her and a worried Druanna by his side.

Cat took Taylor's arm as they watched Trish being loaded into the ambulance. "She's going to be okay. Her parents and Dr. Bane are going with her," Cat said, trying to comfort him.

"Come on youngsters, pile in. Druanna and I will take you to the hospital," Aldon said as Druanna gently lead Cat and Taylor to their car. "Follow us when you're able to," Aldon called out to Rachel and Sam.

"I'll call you later Ryan. Please tell everyone where I am," Cat yelled as she slid into Aldon's car. Ryan waved to her, sending a heartening look her way.

Rachel put her arm around Ryan, "Now to get rid of all these people," she said, looking out onto the front lawn at the growing crowd.

The next night a secret meeting was held in the back room of Astoria's town hall. Aldon had arranged for the local vampire coven and his group to meet on neutral ground.

"Thank you all for coming tonight," Aldon solemnly addressed the assembly. "As you know, last night one of ours was attacked by something unknown. Her injuries were numerous and quite substantial. But the most heinous act was that the poor girl was strung up and almost bled out entirely. Dr. Bane reports that she will thankfully make a full recovery.

But that still leaves the question of who would do such a thing." Pulling a piece of paper from his coat pocket he held it up so everyone could see it. "A note was left, and I have made copies, which are now being passed around the room. If anyone has any idea who did this, please step forward," Aldon said, his voice booming in the small space. Everyone looked around expecting someone to stand up, but no one did.

"Aldon, if I may speak?" Lucien Bancroft asked.

"You may," he assured him.

"First of all, I would like to send our sympathies to the parents of the young girl in question," Lucien said with a slight bow in the direction of the Digby's. "I also want to express how disgusted we are over this horrible act. Our coven has dedicated itself to change by blending with human society, and we implore that you believe me when I say we had nothing to do with this. We shall help you by any means and find who has committed this foul deed." Aldon Scanned the room, and made eye contact with everyone in attendance. "We all have children, and as parents we would not wish this ordeal the Digby's have gone through, on anyone." Looking directly at the Roland Digby as he spoke, "No one in our coven shall rest until we find the responsible party. You have my word on this, and I do speak for all of us. I know we have had our differences in the past, but I want us to work together. I fear that *all* of our children may be at risk."

"Thank you Lucien. I do believe in your coven's innocence. Though I am not ruling out the possibility a vampire was responsible for this act. I hope you do indeed follow through on your word and help us end this plague on Astoria. It is *our* home that is being threatened. This meeting is adjourned!" Aldon announced and then nodded to Lucien as the others silently filed out of the room.

❧ ❧ ❧

"My old friend, it is so pleasant to see you again. And can my eyes be deceiving me, you look well. Whatever could have brought this change about, I wonder?" Andrei's sneer confirmed the lies in his words.

"I would ask you to sit, but you won't be here long. I just need one question answered. What knowledge do you have of the recent attacks here in Astoria?" Lucien asked coldly.

"Now what would possess you to ask me this question?" Andrei replied, looking offended.

"Andrei, whatever crazy game you are playing at *shall* stop, or there will be dire consequences. This is my home and you are trespassing! I want you away from here! And I do not just mean this house, or this town, but this country. Go home, or else!"

"Or else what? Who will make me? You and your insipid group? I think not! You have become too humanized and are not strong enough to challenge me! I would crush you with ease!" Andrei's eyes turned jet black, his face full of anger, as his teeth descended rapidly. Towering a half a foot over Andrei, Lucien's eyes were also jet black, his teeth sharp and ready.

"Do you find these threats wise? Is your memory so lacking that you have forgotten the past so soon? I am not the man you saw last time you were here. So if you were smart, I would leave now before my anger worsens!" Lucien's voice bellowed throughout the quiet house. "Oh, and do give my regards to my sister the next time you see her." Lucien grinned as Andrei stormed out of his study and disappeared.

Filled with rage, Andrei stomped through the old, abandoned, complex tunnel system that ran under Astoria. "How dare that drunk talk to me that way! He does not intimidate me!" Though his words said otherwise, Andrei shuddered as he thought back to the day long ago when Lucien had bested him.

Reaching the tunnel system's central chamber, he spotted their human "cow" unconscious and chained to the far wall. His clothes were new, as the ones he had been captured in had grown disgustingly ripe after so many weeks in captivity.

Andrei's anger increased as he saw the three girls lying on the mattresses strewn about, each fast asleep. "Wake up!" he yelled, his voice echoing off the barren walls. The three jumped up, trembling at the viciousness in his voice. "How many times have I told you three idiots that you must not drink until your food passes out? You also need to keep him fed! Or else we lose our supply. And how can he eat if he is always unconscious? Imbeciles!" he growled. "Now, go and find him some sustenance. And then please, someone wake him up!"

Without a word the three girls scurried from his presence. Andrei plopped down on one of the mattresses and stared at the still form of Melvin Pierson, the missing Biology teacher.

16
Howl At The Wolf Moon

Cat shivered as she opened her bedroom window and watched the snow fall softly from the sky. It seemed time had flown by since the night of Trish's attack. Christmas had even come and gone, and so had the New Year. *I can't believe Trish doesn't remember what happened to her. It's probably for the best though, given what she went through*, Cat thought.

Looking up in the sky, Cat saw the moon peeking out from behind the snowy clouds. She wondered how Linda was and where she was hiding. Cat had yet to tell anyone other than

Ryan about her encounter with the three girls. For his sake, she wished she could unload her burden on someone else other than him. Ever since Trish's attack Ryan had become even more protective of Cat. He was convinced that the three girls were behind it and was worried she was the next on their list. Cat wondered if that was true. *Are the girls behind Mr. Pierson's disappearance too? Why Linda? Why are you doing this?*

As the wind picked up and the snowfall began to thicken, Cat quickly latched her window and jumped into bed, shivering as she pulled the covers over herself. Reaching up quickly, she turned off the lamp on her nightstand, and then bundled up again. As she stared up at the ceiling, Cat let the many questions she had run through her head.

Cat awoke the next morning to the delicious smell of bacon. Rushing downstairs she flung open the kitchen door and saw her mom standing at the stove humming to herself.

"Morning Mom! Mmmm, smells so good!" Cat commented, reaching around her mom and grabbing a slice of bacon.

Rachel chuckled. "Morning sweetie, fix yourself a plate. Your Dad should be down in a minute, and I heard Taylor in the shower. So you better grab some while you can." Cat quickly piled her plate full of food and then plopped down at the kitchen table. "I'm still a little wary of you staying home by yourself tonight. I wish you'd stay with Julie, like you normally do."

"I told you that we're all going to an early movie, and after that I've got to study for my test tomorrow. And you know that I won't get any studying done if I spend the night with Julie. I'll be okay tonight. Don't worry Mom," she said with a huge smile.

"Don't worry what?" Sam asked, entering through the kitchen door.

"Mom's just worried, as usual, about me staying home alone tonight. I can take care of myself, you know. It's not like I'm a half vampire or anything," Cat said sarcastically. "I pity the fool who messes with me!" she announced jokingly, thrusting her fork into the air.

"That's not the point Cat. Something's going on in our town and it isn't as safe as it used to be. Your mom is just worried like the rest of us are," Sam replied, smiling reassuringly at Rachel.

"Oh no, she's gotten to you too Dad?" Cat joked as Rachel rolled her eyes. "I'm just kidding. I know that everyone's kind of walking on egg shells right now, but I'll be fine."

"Uh oh, serious faces, what's this discussion about?" Taylor asked, standing in the kitchen doorway. Cat was glad to see that her brother was joking again, and in better spirits. He had taken Trish's attack the hardest of anyone.

"Hurry up and get a plate before the food gets cold," Rachel ordered Taylor.

"So is this a secret then?" Taylor asked, spooning some eggs onto his plate.

"No, Cat just wants to stay home alone tonight," Rachel replied.

"Uh uh, no way! Are you actually considering it?" Taylor asked, looking at his mom and then his dad. "Why isn't she staying with Julie?"

"Hello? I'm right here. Did everyone miss the memo of me being a half vampire? I mean I have super human strength and quickness. Does that not ease your worries just a little?" Cat asked, looking around to all of them. No one said anything. They all just shared knowing glances.

"Alright Cat, you can stay home alone. Taylor, Sam, if Cat says that she'll be okay, then she'll be okay. Now let's all eat before the food gets cold," Rachel stated and then swallowed hard, realizing what she had just said. Cat held back her smile as she shoveled a fork full of eggs into her mouth.

"So we all agree that movie sucked! Whose idea was this anyway?" Matt griped as they headed back toward the parking lot.

"Wasn't it yours?" Elle asked, laughing at Matt's feigned puzzlement.

"I don't think so, I think it was Hannah's," Matt replied innocently, his arm pulling Hannah closer to him.

"It was not, I didn't even know *Zombie Massacre 3* was even a movie! I just came along with you guys," she answered and then giggled as Matt gave her a peck on the cheek.

"Face it Matt, you're the king of picking terrible movies! If Amanda was here, your good arm would be sore by now. I even had to wake Ryan up twice," Cat laughed as she felt Ryan squeeze her hand for tattling on him.

"I don't know about you guys but I'm freezing," Elle moaned as they rounded the corner of the movie theater, and a gust of frigid wind blasted them. Rushing to get out of the cold, they ran to their cars, occasionally sliding on the slick pavement. Goodbyes were hastily said as everyone piled into their respective vehicles. Ryan jumped into Cat's jeep as she started the engine. She began rubbing her hands together in front of the air vents, waiting for the heater to kick in.

"Aren't you cold?"

Ryan laughed. "Yep, fully cold blooded." Cat rolled her eyes at his vampire humor. "I wonder why Hannah didn't ride with us. Won't Matt have to backtrack after taking everyone else home?" Ryan turned at Cat's laugh.

"Please, like he really minds. Especially since they'll have all that alone time on the way to her house. Anyway, I thought I was the practical one in this relationship," she giggled.

After Cat dropped Ryan off, she decided to take the long way home. As she slowly made her way along the slick icy streets, Cat saw car tail lights ahead of her weaving back and forth. Suddenly they swerved off the road into a grove of trees. Passing by the car, Cat recognized it was Dr. Bane's black BMW. She quickly slammed on the brakes, causing her Jeep to skid to a halt. She watched as Dr. Bane staggered out of the vehicle and then moved quickly into the dense forest. Alarmed, she unbuckled her seat-belt and rushed from her car. "Dr. Bane? Are you okay? Dr. Bane?" she called out, following his footsteps in the pristine white snow.

"Damn, Damn, Damn, I knew I should've left before now! But that baby wouldn't have survived if I'd left! I just need to get deep enough into the woods, and hope no one notices my car! Stupid cell phone! I can't even let anyone know!" Harold Bane murmured to himself, drawing out a syringe from his bag as he trudged deeper into the thick foliage. He winced, plunging the syringe into his arm, "This will keep the beast at bay until morning." The tranquilizer immediately kicked in and Dr. Bane didn't notice the person approaching him until she spoke.

"Dr. Bane, are you alright?" He turned, shocked to see Cat standing only a few feet away.

"Catherine, what are you doing here?" he dumbly asked, as it was apparent she had seen him pull off the road and followed him. "You need to leave immediately!" he spat out and then groaned as he felt the change approaching.

"What's wrong? You don't look very well, can I help?" she asked, reaching out to place her hand on his shoulder. As the full moon rose above the trees, its bright light glistened off the sweat rolling down Dr. Bane's face. He ripped away from her.

"Cat, please get back…ahh…please leave…I can't hold out much longer!" Backing away slowly, Cat watched on, horrified, as the doctor began jerking back and forth as if he was a puppet on a string. She could hear cracking noises, and cringed as he moaned in severe pain.

"Dr. Bane?" Cat asked hesitantly and reached out to him again, but then jerked back quickly as his eyes met hers. His golden brown eyes were glowing. He growled as his hands crackled and began to elongate. His nose and mouth extended into a wolf snout filled with razor sharp teeth. Dr. Bane fell to his knees as his growing body mass tore his clothes. Hair began to sprout all over his body. Cat was frozen, shocked by the transformation happening before her eyes. She wanted to run, but she knew deep down she was not the one in danger if she left him; he would be. She saw the syringe lying beside him and watched as the man who looked more like a beast now, sank further into the snow, his eyes closing as his body continued its metamorphosis. The werewolf lying in front of her was still Dr. Bane.

Sure he's hairier, has large claws, and big bad teeth, but he still saved my life, and I can't leave him like this. If the werewolf legend is true, then all I have to do is wait until morning and he'll transform back. Cat told herself. *Wait…he's going to be naked! Like really naked! I better get something to cover him up with.* "Dr. Bane, can you hear me?" The creature didn't move a muscle. The only way Cat knew he was still alive was by the low growling noises coming from his mouth. "I'll be right back. I've got a blanket in my Jeep. Don't worry I'll take care of you," she whispered. *I can't believe werewolves exist! My life is a Robert Craven novel!* Cat thought, running through the woods back to her vehicle.

At least twenty minutes had passed since Cat left Dr. Bane's side. During that time she pulled both vehicles further off the road so no one would notice them and come snooping around. She trudged back through the snow with the blankets and beach towels she had retrieved from the back of her Jeep. Luckily she had bundled up before going out with multilayered clothing and her winter Ugg boots. After wrapping Dr. Bane in two fleece blankets, Cat gently lifted his head placing a stack of towels underneath. Leaning back against a huge tree trunk, Cat wrapped her arms tightly around herself to keep warm and pulled the hood of her coat up over her head. "Everything will be okay Dr. Bane," she said, watching him sleep soundly. *I guess I'll be winging that test tomorrow, huh?*

Dawn was breaking and Cat could see the shape of Dr. Bane lying in front of her. He was considerably smaller in size and shivering uncontrollably. She rose stiffly to her feet and made her way to him, relieved when she saw fingers instead of claws peeking out from under the blankets. *What should I do? Should I wake him up? Or leave him and hope he doesn't remember I was here? But I have sooo many questions!* Cat argued with herself.

"Dr. Bane? Dr. Bane, it's Cat. You need to get up or you're going to freeze to death out here." She jumped back as he moaned and started to sit up. Cat quickly turned her back to him, embarrassed that he was very naked under the blankets.

"Catherine, what? Why…oh, I didn't. Yes I did." She heard his anguished voice as he remembered what had happened.

"Don't worry. Your secret's safe with me. I won't tell a soul. I promise. Now, do you have any clothes? I didn't see any in your car. But then again, I didn't check your medical bag though. Maybe you've got some in there?" she rambled on, keeping her eyes averted as she reached into his bag. She sighed, relieved when she found a pair of scrubs inside. “Here put these on, and then we’ll get out of here.” He grabbed the clothes from her hand, her eyes still averted.

“I didn’t hurt you did I?”

Cat shook her head.

“I must say you’re taking this rather well.” He put his hand on her shoulder and gently turned her around. She was relieved that he was now dressed, barefoot, and all goose-pimply, but dressed none-the-less.

“Please, Dr. Bane. I found out I’m adopted, a half vampire, have to take blood pills every day, and have a white witch for a science teacher. So what’s the big deal about you being a werewolf?” Her smile wobbled as he raised her chin so her eyes met his.

“I always thought you were a tough young woman and now I’ve proven myself right. Thanks for watching over me. I was careless. We’re only forced to change once a year on the Wolf moon, but last night I had an emergency, and I cut it pretty close…really close.”

“We? There are others? Of course there are. You wouldn’t be alone, that wouldn’t make sense. Wolves travel in packs, right?”

"I guess the cat's out of the bag. Excuse the pun. But I guess you had to find out at some point, huh? I just wish it had been under more controlled circumstances."

"Yeah, people keep telling me that," Cat joked.

Dr. Bane laughed. "Now, I'm freezing and my feet are numb, so let's go and straighten this all out." He took Cat's arm and they made their way to the cars. "Leave your Jeep, I'll send someone back for it. I think there are some people you need to see." Cat buckled herself in the passenger seat and felt grateful when he set the car's heater to full blast.

Uncle Aldon's mansion looked like a fairytale castle with all the brilliant white snow covering the turrets, roofs, and gardens. Dr. Bane drove his car up the freshly shoveled driveway and parked by the large arched heavy oak front doors. Puzzled, Cat took his hand as he held her car door open and pulled her to her feet. "Why are we here?" Cat began to shake, not from the cold, but from fear of what she might learn behind those doors. "I don't think I want to go in and see Uncle Aldon right now. I think I need to go home," she said. Her voice shook as bad as her whole body.

"It'll be fine Cat, trust me." Dr. Bane's beautiful golden brown eyes met hers and she felt a warm feeling come over her.

"Harold! We were worried sick! What happened?" Aldon's voice came from the doorway behind Dr. Bane. He turned and Aldon saw Cat standing there.

"Aldon, it would seem we've waited too long," Dr. Bane said resignedly.

"Yes, I see that we have. Well let's get this over with. Come on in Cat. You'll catch your death of cold out here," his warm robust voice washed over her. Cat allowed Dr. Bane to lead her into the foyer as her eyes stayed glued to Aldon's worried face.

"I really need to get home and get ready for school. I've got a test today, and I haven't studied, and I know I'm going to fail, and my car is back in the woods, and Dr. Bane is a werewolf, and I haven't taken my meds, and…I think I need to sit down," Cat rambled and then felt her legs give out from under her.

Dr. Bane quickly reacted and picked her up, carrying her through the ballroom door which was being held open by Aldon. The first thing Cat noticed was that the ballroom was quiet despite the crowd of people standing before her. She saw several members of the football team, their parents, and even her high school's principal, Ms. Landers. *I can't believe all of these people are werewolves. What the hell's going on!* Cat thought crossly. Dr. Bane held Cat tighter as she gasped when she saw Sam, Rachel, and Taylor moving toward them. As her Dad reached out to take her, she shied away from him and clung closer to Harold. Realizing the truth, a sudden rush of anger swept through Cat. *How dare they do this to me again*!

"Dr. Bane please put me down," Cat said quietly and felt herself being lowered to the floor. She straightened out her clothes and then looked up. Everyone stood there like statues. "So let me get this straight," her voice echoed through the room, "this past year I thought I was losing my mind, seeing weird things, and fainting a lot. Which, I was told was due to a weird blood disease. Then I found out I was adopted. Told I'm half something that I thought was only a myth! Then you tell me there are people, or whatever, out there who want me dead. Then I realize that my boyfriend is kind of like me, and, to top it all off, I secretly trained really hard to be able to protect all of you. Only now I find out you all don't need my protection! You can do fine on your own! Because you're all freakin' werewolves! Well I think…I think…oh hell, I don't know what to think. But wait, I'm mad. Really mad! And right now I don't want to get in to this. So, Dr. Bane you're going to drive me back to my Jeep, and then I'm going home. And if I don't wake up in my bed and find this was all a dream, I'm going to school. No, don't say a word, don't follow me," Cat stated, staring everyone down. Turning to Trish, "You too? And Aunt

Druanna?" They both nodded their heads. "Oh this is too much, I need to go home. Harold, I'll be waiting in the car. I think after what I did for you last night, you could do this one thing for me," she said. Cat walked out of the room and found Elsie standing by the front door. Moving quickly passed her, Cat wrenched open the door before Elsie could.

Sitting in Dr. Bane's car, waiting for him to come out, Cat let herself slump into the seat. *My whole life's been a lie*. She watched as Dr. Bane came through the mansion's front door and made his way to the driver's side of the car. His handsome face was strained. Aldon stood in the doorway a forced smile on his lips. "Sorry about the Harold bit," Cat blurted out. "I'm usually not so disrespectful. I hope you can forgive that."

"Of course Cat. I only hope you can find it in your heart to forgive us. Aldon wanted you to have this back, and I think-"

"Take me home please. I don't have time to discuss this right now. I need normal." She heard Dr. Bane sigh as he started the car. They rode the rest of the way in silence with Cat holding tightly onto the journal, that she thought she had lost, in her lap.

Arriving home, Cat entered the empty house feeling sadness instead of anger. She wanted her life back. The way it was before she started high school. *How could they have kept this from me? How am I going to face them? All of them? Not to mention the fact werewolves and vampires don't get along. At least not in any of the books or movies I've ever seen.* Everything began to dawn on her. The tension between Isaac's and Taylor's group, and the way Ryan had acted when she first brought him home. Little memories came back of things that hadn't quite made sense before, but now made perfect sense.

Where do I go from here? Act like everything's alright? I know they were just trying to protect me. That they love me. But how? Werewolves can't possibly love a half vampire. But they knew when they adopted me, and yet they took me anyway. Look what they've given me, and how do I act? How do I show my thanks? By acting like a moron. A total immature moron! Cat stood up from the stair she had been sitting on and started for the front door with the intention of having Dr. Bane take her back to Aldon's to make amends. She was surprised when the front door opened and her family stood in front of her, their anxious faces waiting for her to respond. Cat lunged forward and put her arms around them, bursting in to tears. She sobbed as they hugged her tightly.

"It's going to be okay Cat, I promise," Sam said quietly.

Cat stayed home from school that day with the reassurance from Dr. Bane that she would be able to make up the test she would miss. Between the lack of sleep from her night's vigil over Dr. Bane, and the emotional scenes that followed, her parents had declared it a "Cat needs a break at home" day. She was alone in the house. Taylor was at school, her mom and dad at work, and Cat lay in her bed going over the events of the last few hours. She couldn't sleep. Spying the little brown journal lying on top of her dresser, she got up and retrieved it. Opening it, she began to read.

I don't know what day it is. We are still running and hiding and I am getting so very tired. The barns we stay in are drafty and John tries his best to keep us warm but we are both miserable. I am worried about my mother and what my father has done with her. John knows I cry at night. I am silent when I cry, but he looks at me with pity in his eyes the next morning. I told him today that maybe I should just give up and face THEM. He shocked me with how upset he became at my suggestion. As he paced the moldy old barn from one end to the other, he informed me that over his dead body would I do that. He was responsible for my safety and that was that. No more arguments. I had to bite my lip from laughing at his attempt at an angry frown. He wouldn't cease until I promised him I wouldn't do anything rash.

John caught some rabbits and roasted them in a pit he dug in the earth. My mother would be proud of the person she chose to protect us. Today we are going to travel along a river that John says will lead us to a small village he knows of. He's hoping that he can find someone who will help us leave the country. I don't want to leave without my mother but I do not say so out loud.

Next Day

We have made it to the village and John found someone who gave us the name of a woman who could possibly help. John wanted me to stay outside the village, but I was adamant that I go with him. We made our way to a huge house on the outskirts. The sun had barely set as we arrived at the door. Upon knocking, a strange looking small man answered and ushered us in. I didn't quite trust him, but John grabbed my hand and pulled me through the doorway. The hallway was dark, so dark that I stopped walking therefore making John stumble into me. The little man lit a torch on the wall, with what, I do not know, as I saw no fire in his hands when it was being lit. John gently nudged me forward and we walked down the now lit hallway to a pair of closed large wooden doors. The little man knocked and a voice called from within to enter. The first thing I noticed was the lovely roaring fire and was instantly drawn to it. John stopped me from moving forward and I noticed he was staring off to the side. I moved a little to see what had caught his attention. I gasped as I saw the most beautiful women, besides my mother, I had ever seen sitting in a throne like chair. Her long hair was silver. Her eyes were smiling as were her lips as she studied us. She welcomed us in and told us there was nothing to be frightened of. She led us to the roaring fire encased in a beautiful ornate fireplace. She called the little man Dun and told him to fetch us hot cider to warm us. She told us her name was Gretchen and she assured us we were safe. I felt a slight twinge of distrust but it was immediately gone as Dun came back with a tray filled with heavenly food and the most delicious hot cider.

Next Day

I don't remember much from last evening. I remember eating and drinking, but I have no idea how I ended up in a wonderfully soft feather bed with silk sheets. Now it is daylight. I am sitting at a pretty writing desk putting down these words. I have bathed and a fresh set of clothes that miraculously fit are now on my body. I peeked out my bedroom door but the house is quiet so I decided to write. I wish my mother was here to share this with me. I feel so alone. Where is John? I wish John would come for me. I don't feel right about exploring the house by myself. In the daylight that nagging feeling that something is not right plagues me.

It has been a couple hours since I wrote last. I was interrupted by a knock at the door and a tall, thin, pinched face woman with matted hair carried a breakfast tray into my room and placed it on the desk, all without saying a word. There was so much food. I fear I made a pig of myself and now I am pleasantly stuffed. I peeked out the door a few times, but the halls are still silent. There is still no sign of John anywhere. I can't believe he has stayed away so long since we have been together all these weeks now. It is after noon and the sun is low on the horizon. I think I will go and explore. I can't stand being alone.

I don't have much time. I have barricaded my door with the ornate heavy wooden chair by the desk. What I fear has happened. I have been betrayed, by John no less. I heard him talking to Gretchen and they are waiting for someone to come take me away. My guess would be my father.

They're here! My father and his followers have entered the house demanding my return. I must try to escape. I hope someone reads this and maybe can help me. I don't know what my father has planned for me, but at least maybe I will be reunited with my mother. I hear them coming up the stairs. They are pounding on the door. I guess this is

17
Seeking Answers

"Revelus Indiedroman!" Cat announced, clutching her moonstone. The village entrance did not appear. "Revelilus Androgormen!" she said with slight frustration while holding onto the stone, but still nothing happened. "How could I forget the words again?" Cat asked out loud, her Jeep idling on the forest road. "I know you're there Wedgewick Village," she groaned and then placed her forehead on the steering wheel.

The hair on the back of her neck suddenly stood up as she felt someone was staring at her. Slowly lifting her head, she yelped at the wizened face looking at her through the driver's window. Grey wiry hair sprouted from underneath his tall, floppy cap. His ears were *pointy*, yeah *pointy*, was the only word Cat could think of to describe them. *He looks like one of those garden gnomes in Maude's front yard,* she thought, giggling. He broke into a huge smile and motioned for her to roll down the window. Cat hesitated, but then felt foolish as the little man seemed to mean her no harm, so she pressed the button.

"Hello me darlin', didn't mean to give you a scare Catherine dear, but you looked a little frustrated." The strange little man's voice had an accent that she determined was Irish.

"Hi, I'm sorry but do I know you? Have we met?" Cat asked, pretty sure she hadn't met him before, but wanted to be polite.

"No, I don't believe we have, but everyone in Wedgewick Village knows of ye Ms. Colvin. And it's my pleasure to finally meet ye."

"Thank you, I guess. Could you possibly help me? I seem to be having some trouble getting in," she said, pointing ahead of her into the never ending archway of trees.

engulfing Cat. “Annie may we have some calming tea please?” she asked quietly, missing Annie’s vigorous nodding. As Gretchen was closing the door Cat heard the customers quietly murmuring to each other.

“Please, have a seat. I know you’re very angry and I don’t blame you. Spirit told me this morning that you had finished reading the journal.” Gretchen sighed as she sat down across from Cat. “I want to tell you the truth about what you read. Please allow me the chance to finish, and then I’ll answer any questions you might have. First of all, I never met the young person from the journal. If I had, maybe things would have turned out differently. As you’re probably aware of, I’m very old Cat. I’ve been around for many centuries.” Gretchen cocked her head to the left, “Hush up Spirit, I’m trying to explain! You can stay, but only if you can keep your mouth shut!” Turning back to Cat, “Now, where was I?”

“*You were saying you were old, very old. Oops sorry, shutting up now,*” Spirit whispered in Gretchen’s ear, causing her to glare to her side again.

“Even though I may be old, that does not mean I’ve always been wise in my years. I’ve trusted the wrong people, and made my fair share of mistakes. But Cat you must trust that it was not I who betrayed this Childe. It was Quintance. All those years ago when this Childe met my sister they thought they were meeting a kind older woman. But of course they were wrong. To this day I still cannot believe Quintance can be so evil. And all of the acts she performed during The Cleansing horrify me. This youngster was not the only unfortunate that came her way though. There were many."

"The Cleansing? You mean like the new Robert Craven novel?" Cat asked.

Gretchen fumbled with her words, "No, no my dear, that's a mere coincidence," she lied, feeling Cat was not ready to handle that side story. "The Cleansing is why you were put into hiding. Why your mother gave you to the Colvin's for safe keeping."

"*Tell her about the prophecy already*!" Spirit yelled in Gretchen's ear.

"Oh Spirit, if you don't be quiet, I'm going to have you cast away! I'm getting to the prophecy!" Gretchen shouted while looking behind her.

"The prophecy?" Cat asked confused.

"Well you see, your kind was foretold to bring ruin to the vampire race," Gretchen explained.

That was written in the journal Mildred gave me, Cat thought, remembering the passage.

"But the problem is no one knows the origin of this prophecy, or whether it was based on facts or lies. But still it proves quite dangerous that such a main conspirator in The Cleansing now knows of your whereabouts. That is why salting has become a daily ritual around the village. Quintance will not get through so easily next time. What am I saying? I hope there is no next time," Gretchen said with a wobbly smile as she took Cat's hands from across the table. "I'm truly sorry that you have so much to bear Cat. But I promise that we're going to do everything in our power to protect you. In fact, last night Amaya salted your house. Now no one associated with dark magic can cross into your home unless you allow it."

"What would Quintance, or any dark witch want with me anyway?"

"Well, dark witches are collectors, and a Childe is like a priceless treasure to them. You see, during the Cleansing it was commonplace for your kind to be used as a form of barter to gain an upper hand against the vampire race. The vampire Parliament used to be the ruling body until the Cleansing lost them a great deal of power and control due to Childe trading. It was the vampires that sought to destroy your kind at any cost, and many took advantage of this by trading Children for their own selfish means."

"So what you're saying is that vampires are out to kill me, and dark witches want to collect me?" Cat asked, and then leaned back into the chair with a grim expression on her face.

"And I wish I could say that my sister, her coven, and the vampire Parliament were the only forces out there you have to contend with. But I'm afraid there are many things out there that you have yet to encounter. And of course, as you know, there are things happening in your own backyard. Those poor misguided girls. I know you wish to learn about Linda, but I can't see what will happen to her or the others. I still only know that the one whose blood transformed her must be destroyed. You must be vigilant Cat. Trust your intuition and it will not steer you wrong." Gretchen could sense Cat had a question. "There's something else you want to know isn't there?" Cat hesitated.

"You knew my family were…werewolves, didn't you?" Gretchen nodded. "Why did you keep it a secret?"

"We all have our secrets dear. Besides, it was not mine to tell. There are things that one needs to find out for themselves. If your family had meant you harm I would have told you, but all I saw was the massive amount of love they have for you. You're a very lucky young lady to have them behind you, but you already knew that, didn't you." Gretchen sat back in her chair, "Now that we're being honest. I have one other little tidbit to let you in on."

Cat groaned, "Please don't tell me that *you* aren't what you seem? I don't think I could handle that."

"No my sweetest, I am what you see. It is Aylah." As Gretchen spoke her name, a falcon flew into the room and perched on the back of the chair next to Cat. "Cat, I think you know my falcon, Aylah."

"Your falcon is named Aylah too?" Cat asked, watching the majestic bird shake its feathers. Her mouth gaped open and her eyes grew wide as she saw the bird transform into Aylah, the woman.

"Definitely didn't see that one coming," Cat blurted out.

Gretchen chuckled. "Cat, Aylah is my familiar."

"Your familiar?"

"Her guardian animal to be exact. I have been with her since she was a young girl," Aylah explained.

"So, do all witches have a familiar?" Cat asked.

Gretchen laughed slightly. "For the most part yes, but technically anyone can have a familiar my dear.

"Huh," Cat replied. Turning to Aylah, "So, when Amy said that you'd be flying in shortly, she really meant it?"

Aylah giggled. "Yeah, it's kind of our running joke around here."

"I told Ryan you were a smart bird," Cat said and Aylah smiled at her. "I don't know what to say. I feel so stupid now. Especially since I was coming here today to blame you for what happened to the Childe in the journal. And I was so scared of the fact that I'd have to hate you. Which is definitely not something I'd like at all. But thank you for telling me the truth."

Gretchen stood up from the table, as did Cat, and she opened her arms to give Cat a huge hug. Aylah wrapped her arms around them as well and squeezed.

"I think I'm going to cry," Spirit said in Gretchen's ear.

"Well if you're going to cry, could you do it in someone else's ear," Gretchen groaned.

"What?" Cat asked, looking up at her.

"Oh no not you dear, it's Spirit. He's quite the drama queen you know," Gretchen remarked, squeezing Cat and Aylah tighter in the hug.

A knock came at the door and a red faced Annie peeked into the room. "Uh Gretchen, about that calming tea, we were out. So I went and searched the whole village. It was all used up, remember? Trouble at the big witch convention last month? I hope friendship tea will be okay, because that's all we have," Annie rambled on.

"That will be just fine Annie, just fine," Gretchen said with her arms still around Cat and Aylah.

On the drive home, Cat missed the car parked on the side of the road. She wouldn't have recognized it anyway. The occupants yes, but not the car. Duffie and Leif watched as the orange Jeep moved further down the forest road.

❦ ❦ ❦

February 2nd, Cat's birthday, was sunny but very cold. She lay in her warm comfy bed not wanting to leave it. Cat wished that it was Saturday or Sunday instead of a school day. Grumbling, she threw back the covers and made her way to the bathroom to get ready.

Bounding down the stairs a half an hour later she found her family sitting in the kitchen, all grinning from ear to ear. Nothing like last year when she thought everyone had forgotten her birthday. It was supposed to be a surprise, but then she ruined it all by passing out and missing her party.

"Good morning birthday girl," Sam greeted her, standing and giving her a big hug.

"Happy Birthday Cat," Rachel said, pushing Sam aside and pulling her close.

Taylor smirked, "Yeah, happy b-day Red Freak. Hope this one turns out better than last year."

"Of course it will. We're doing it my way this year…no surprise," Rachel replied. She let go of Cat and swatted at Taylor's hair. "He really does love you, you know," she continued, smiling at her.

"I know he does," Cat grinned as Taylor made a face at her behind their mom's back.

"So, how does it feel to be seventeen?" Sam asked, as Rachel filled Cat's plate with food.

"No different than 16, I guess. Except I don't feel weird…er," Cat answered.

"You look weird though. Okay mom, leave the hair alone. I'm sorry," Taylor complained. Standing up he gave his mom a kiss on the cheek, fist bumped his dad, and tugged on Cat's hair as he flew out of the room before she could react.

"I swear, boys never grow up! I mean look at your father. Prime example," Rachel commented, pushing Sam away as he tried to pull her hair. "Now off to work with you. And please act like a grown-up while you're there. I don't want to have to go and speak with the dean about you again," Rachel giggled as Sam reached out to grab her and missed as she ducked, moving to the other side of the table.

"I'm off to school so you guys can have some alone time together," Cat joked. She chuckled at the shock on her mom's face as her dad grabbed her and went in for a kiss. Putting on her coat, Cat smiled at the laughter coming from the kitchen.

The cold wind tore through her as Cat opened the door to the Jeep. Julie came sprinting across the road, bundled up so that her eyes were the only part showing.

"Darn, its sooooo cold! I wish we were in Florida right now," Julie moaned, climbing into the passenger side.

"Yeah it's a little nippy huh?" Cat rubbed her hands together as the heater finally kicked in, sending them much needed warmth.

"Happy Birthday Cat! You have to wait for your present until tonight though. I can't believe a year has passed since your last birthday."

"Don't remind me. I'm still mortified that I passed out in front of everyone and missed my cake. This year I feel great, and I'm going to get some cake. Even if I have to eat it as soon as the party starts. I want cake!" Cat giggled as Julie rolled her eyes.

"So you don't even want presents? Well then I'll take mine back. Or better still, I'll just keep it. I want one anyway."

"Want one what?" Cat asked innocently.

"I may be cold Catherine Colvin, but I won't fall for that. You'll just have to wait and see."

"Okay I'll wait, but we better get a move on because here comes you know who and her little monster. And the last thing we need is to be late for school."

"Put your foot on that gas girl and let's go! That lady drives me nuts," Julie said and then cheered as the Jeep took off down the driveway.

"Silly girls driving so fast! Parents should have a strong grip on them and not let them act like wild animals. Thank goodness you don't drive Fredricka. Now pee, so mummy can go inside. It's colder than the dickens out here. Not on mummies boot you naughty girl! I swear, you need glasses," Maude Roberts reprimanded, dragging the little pooch behind her.

That night Cat's birthday party was in full swing by seven. The young ones had taken over the living room forcing the grown-ups into the kitchen and study.

"I think Cat looks wonderful, given what she's gone through. I'm so glad Dr. Bane found out what was causing her illness. Last year was just awful," Amanda's mom, Aurora, stated.

"Yes, it was. And of course it doesn't hurt that Harold Bane is such a hunk," Matt's mom, Lilly, whispered which caused everyone to laugh.

"Quiet, he might hear you. We don't want him getting a bigger head than he already has," Rachel giggled, watching the door. "And we definitely don't want any of the kids to hear us. Even though you're absolutely right. Though I will say, Harold has some competition now with Gerard McNeil in town."

"Oh I know, and isn't his English accent to die for," Lilly stated.

The men heard the women laughing from the kitchen and wondered why.

❦ ❦ ❦

"You must have half of Astoria High here for your birthday," Duffie shouted over the music.

"Yeah, Taylor hates that all of his friends love me," Cat joked. "Hey, where's Leif?" she asked, looking around the room.

"He's hiding over there in the corner. He heard that two of the girls who've been driving him bonkers are here. He's just trying to avoid them," Duffie replied.

"I don't blame those girls. If I wasn't already hooked I'd probably join them," Cat replied and then jumped as two arms came around her waist.

"Join who?" Ryan asked close to her ear.

"Oh nothing, just girl talk. And didn't you learn anything from the last time you startled me from behind?" she asked with one eyebrow raised. "And where have you been? The birthday girl has been neglected and-" Cat didn't get to finish her sentence before he twirled her around.

"Sorry, but I had to hang out with the guys for a bit. But now that I've done my duty, I'm all yours." Ryan's smile made Cat melt.

"You're forgiven. Now please go and fight that crowd and get us something to drink. Everyone's threatened me with birthday spankings, even though I've told them I'm too old for that. So I'm trying to keep my back to the wall."

"Your wish is my command ladies. I'll be right back." Ryan slightly bowed and then plunged into the crowd.

"Cat if you didn't already have your claws in him, I'd give you a run for your money," Duffie sighed. Cat laughed, linking arms with the gorgeous dark-skinned Brit.

"Uh oh, here comes Amanda and she doesn't look happy," Cat murmured.

"So somebody needs to give the water-boy some serious tips about dating," Amanda stated. "If I was Hannah, I'd leave his arse."

"So what travesty did Matt commit now?" Cat asked.

"Well, you see that girl he's dancing with over there?" Cat and Duffie nodded. "That's the third girl, other than Hannah, he's danced with tonight. I mean, he did ask her if it was okay, but still. Ugh, men! They're all pigs!" Amanda's anger subsided as a mischievous look came across her face. "I know what I'm going to do. I'm going to find a guy to ask Hannah to dance. Let's see how Matt likes that," she stated defiantly and then walked off.

"Amanda's definitely an intense person huh?" Duffie asked.

"Uh, yeah, just a little," Cat joked. "At least now she's kind of found her niche with the Damianic Bombshells. She used to be all over the place. We never knew which version of

Amanda we were going to get. At least now there's some consistency," she continued with a laugh.

"Hey why aren't Bridgette and her band here tonight?" Duffie asked.

"Maybe were not cool enough for them to show up. Their loss."

"Just between you and me, there's something off about them. And what's with Mrs. Rosenbaum being their fan girl. Kind of weird if you ask me," Duffie commented.

"Alright I've got refreshments here. One fruit punch for my birthday girl and one pink lemonade for the Duffster," Ryan stated, handing the pair their drinks. They both thanked him and Cat gave him a quick peck on the cheek.

"Cat you have a phone call," Rachel announced, coming up behind her, and competing with the music.

"Who is it?"

She laughed. "I didn't ask. I'm not trying to play the part of nosy mother here."

"You mom? No, never," Cat replied sarcastically.

"You hush. It's probably someone wanting to wish you a happy birthday," Rachel said, gently guiding her in the direction of the foyer.

"Maybe you should give my father some advice on that subject Mrs. Colvin," Duffie joked.

"Oh, where is Gerard? I did invite him," Rachel asked.

"He's doing inventory at the store and scheduling some local author book signings. He said he might stop by later though," she responded with a smile.

Picking up the phone in the front hall, "Hello, this is the birthday girl," Cat said. There was silence. "Hello?" she repeated again.

"Happy last birthday to you...happy last birthday to you...happy last birthday dear Catherine...happy last birthday to you!" An eerie chorus of voices sang.

"Who is this?" Cat asked forcefully. The caller hung up and all she heard was the dial tone. Her hand shook as she placed the phone back onto the receiver. *It was them, I know it,* Cat thought.

"Hey, Mom sent me to tell you it's time for presents," Taylor called down the hall. Noticing the look on her face, "Something wrong?"

"Oh, no, nothing's wrong," Cat replied, forcing an unconvincing smile.

"Well come on then. Presents are waiting!"

"Alright Cat, spill it," Ryan said while lying on her bed later that night.

"Spill what?" she asked.

"Who called you? Your mood changed considerably after you got off the phone."

"How do you know me so well?" she asked, looking deep into his blue eyes. Ryan gave her a questioning look with an eyebrow raised as she tried to change the subject. Cat shied away, "I think it was the three girls."

"What? And you waited until now to tell me?!"

"Hey, it's my birthday, and I just wanted one day to be *normal*, and not have everyone freak-out like you're doing now."

"I'm sorry, but these girls are dangerous. You need to come to me when this kind of thing happens. We're in this together, remember?" Ryan said, combing his hand through her fiery red curly locks.

"I know Ryan, I know," she replied, snuggling up close to him and burying her head into his firm chest.

The next day after school, Cat followed Ryan to the cave in her Jeep. He had insisted on an emergency training session, wanting Cat to be fully prepared for what may lay ahead. As they made their way down to the beach holding hands, Cat pulled him to a stop. She sighed. "Why can't we just be a normal couple walking along the beach?"

"Because life doesn't always turn out the way we want it to Cat. Growing up, I often thought that way myself, craving to be normal. I could only truly accept myself when I hung around Isaac and my fellow brethren. But Cat, do you really think anyone has a *normal* life? Not everything is as it seems."

"Yeah, that's one heck of an understatement. Here I thought you were just a normal math tutor, but now you're my vampire trainer," Cat stated.

"I hope that's not all I am to you," he said, pulling her close.

"No, you know what I mean," she said, giving him a love tap on his chest. He grinned as she giggled softly. "I mean what does a person like Kirsten have to worry about? Her hair being out of place? What outfit to wear to school? I don't see her training because people are out to kill her."

"Kirsten's shallow and insecure. A cloned, hollow shell of a person. You, at least, are special."

"That's what I'm told anyway. But can you really blame a girl for sometimes wanting to be just like everyone else?"

"Come on, let's go get your aggressions out," he said gently guiding her toward the cave.

"You should be scared Mr. Beckford, I've got a lot of pent up emotion just waiting to come out," she joked. "Let's do this!"

"Now that's the Cat I like to see!"

Debbie Fuller ran down the long hallway toward her daughter's room after being awoken by her blood curdling screams. Flinging open the door and turning on the light, she made her way to Kirsten's side. Kirsten was sitting up in bed, her eyes wide with fear and her knees tucked up against her chest, "Honey what's wrong?"

"Oh mom, it was horrible…those eyes, those jet black eyes!"

"What sweetheart? Did you have a nightmare?"

"I had the most horrid dream about Cat Colvin again," she huffed while rubbing her head, trying to ease an oncoming headache.

"Who's Cat Colvin?" Debbie asked blankly.

"She's just a girl at school, on the swim team."

"Who are her parents, I don't recollect that name?"

"Her mom is Rachel who owns the flower shop in town, and her dad Samuel, is a professor at the college," Stan Fuller replied, coming up behind his wife.

"Oh, *those* Colvins! I swear that woman needs a makeover, and he looks like your typical dowdy professor. Dull people, no wonder they didn't ring a bell. Now sweetie, why are you dreaming about this insignificant girl?" Debbie asked, giving her daughter a puzzled look.

"I don't know…anyway back to me. I keep having these awful dreams about her and her teeth. Long white teeth and weird black eyes. It feels like a memory, not a dream, but I can't seem to remem-"

"Hush now, of course it's just a dream. I've seen people in this town with crooked teeth, but none with long teeth and weird eyes. But then again, I'd probably avoid such individuals."

Stan rolled his eyes at his wife's blatant snobbery. "Your mother's right Kirsten. It's just a dream and you need to keep telling yourself that."

"Now honey, do you want me to ring for Gracie to heat up some milk for you?" Debbie asked.

"Yuck mom, I haven't liked hot milk since I was little."

"Well we could go and make some cocoa for you, couldn't we Deb?" Seeing her open her mouth to protest, Stan continued, "Why wake up Gracie when we're perfectly capable of boiling water. Will you be okay honey until we come back?" Kirsten nodded.

"I guess we could. Ooh maybe we have some of those little marshmallows to add to it." Debbie stood up from the bed and made her way to the door. Her daughter's distress was completely gone from her mind, and she was now focused on making cocoa.

"We'll be right back. I'd stay, but I don't think your cocoa will taste very good if I leave it up to your mother." He chuckled and then bent over to kiss Kirsten on the forehead. Kirsten watched her tall and handsome father leave the room.

"It does feel like a memory, I don't care what anyone says," Kirsten whispered to herself while pulling the covers up to her chin.

18
Be Mine, Valentine

A huge snowstorm hit a few days following Cat's birthday. The white snow quickly turned into dirty mush a couple days later. Hurrying to his car, Sam shivered in the frigid February wind. Tearing off one of his bulky gloves with his teeth, he put his key into the rickety door lock. He had endured much teasing over his antiquated car, but he loved his old dependable Volvo. His heater made a gurgling noise as the cold air turned warm and then blissfully hot, thawing him out. Pulling out of his parking spot, he made his way cautiously out of the parking lot.

With the condition of the roads he figured it would take about twenty minutes to reach Aldon's. Sam had received a text from him asking if he would swing by before heading home. “It must be something important for him to want to see me in person. I only hope it’s not something about Cat again. Last month was enough.” He laughed, “Look at me talking to myself. Next I’ll be answering, and then they’ll lock me up for sure.”

Arriving at Aldon’s mansion, Sam saw Elsie holding the front door open, ready to take his coat from him as always. “Good to see you Sam. He’s in the study. Hot chocolate coming right up,” Elsie said as she hung his coat in the foyer closet.

“Oh Elsie, you know me well,” Sam replied with a smile. Elsie just laughed softly as she headed toward the kitchen, leaving Sam to make his way to the study.

“Sam, thank you for coming by. I do hope my text was legible. Druanna insists I get up to speed with all these newfangled devices, but I think speaking on the telephone is a better way to go. Even though, my preference is still the good old face to face meeting.”

“I know what you mean Aldon. It took me forever to figure out my dang computer and it still baffles me at times. So what is so urgent?” Sam asked, taking a seat across from Aldon’s desk.

Aldon leaned back in his chair, “We’ve been summoned by the Varulv council. We must leave for Austria tomorrow.”

“Tomorrow? What’s this about?”

“Some of the council members are worried about the ramifications of our Catherine knowing what we are. They have requested an audience with us to help clear the air of their concerns. I know it is short notice, but I feel we must abide by this summons. We surely do not want a bunch of rogue Varulvs coming our way and causing more trouble.” Sam gave Aldon a strained look. “Don’t worry. It will be fine. We shall convince them all is well and quell their concerns.” The door to the study opened and the clanking of tea cups announced Elsie’s arrival. “Elsie, lifesaver that you are, is that homemade hot chocolate I smell?”

“Yes indeedy,” she replied.

“Mmmm good. Come Sam, let’s enjoy.” Sam cracked a smile but feared things were not going to go as smoothly as Aldon believed.

✦ ✦ ✦

“So Dad, when will you be back?” Cat asked at breakfast the next morning.

“Hopefully I’ll only be gone about three days,” Sam answered, trying to keep the worry out of his voice.

“It’s because of me, this council thing I mean. They must not like the fact you adopted a half vampire huh?”

"Let's get this straight Ms. Catherine Colvin. Whether they like it or not has nothing to do with what we want. What you have to remember is that we're your parents and we love you. And we'd love you even if you had three heads and fifteen toes! Got it?" he grinned at Taylor's expression.

"Hey wait a second, if she had three heads and fifteen toes, I'd seriously have to rethink this whole brother bit. I mean it's bad enough she's red-headed, left-handed, and pale as a ghost, come on! Oww, Mom!" Taylor moaned as Rachel swatted him with the newspaper.

"You, young man better hurry and eat, with less talk. Your sister is beautiful." Rachel laughed as Taylor made a face then took a big bite from a piece of bacon.

"Everything will be fine Cat, no worries. Now I have to go and pack. You two be good for your mom, and I'll be back before you know it," Sam said, leaving the room. Mounting the stairs he mentally crossed his fingers, hoping that he was telling the truth.

Cat walked into Biology and immediately realized that her usually calm and collected teacher looked frazzled. She was reading the Biology textbook with her fingers drumming on the desk beside it. "Good afternoon Miss Amaya," Cat said softly so as not to startle her.

"Oh, I didn't hear you come in."

"What are you reading?" she asked.

"Nothing, just…the next chapter. I'm going to practice on your class today. I really didn't sign up for this you know. I'm sure Melvin…Mr. Pierson would've handled this just fine. But I know I'll just make a mess of it. Ugh," Miss Amaya groaned and put her head in her hands as Cat leaned over and read the chapter heading: *Sexual Reproduction.*

"Ah, I see…well-" Cat stopped as the rest of the class began to trickle in. Taking her seat, Cat watched as Miss Amaya rose to her feet. She noticed her knees were a touch rickety.

"Now, for today's class I have a little movie to show you. Dustin, the lights please?" She turned on the projector and nothing happened. Tapping it a few times, Miss Amaya became more flustered when it still wouldn't turn on. "Dustin, turn on the lights please." *I don't understand! It's plugged in! This was the last projector too! What am I going to do?* Miss Amaya complained to herself. Looking around the room at the students faces, "It would appear I'm having technical difficulties at the moment, we will begin shortly." *Well, I guess I'll just have to use those darn show and tell diagrams in the closet,* she thought as she continued to fiddle with the projector, trying to make it work. Cat felt bad for her teacher. She was so flustered and the class could sense it. Cat hoped the students would behave themselves, but figured that was a long shot.

"Okay, now here we have a diagram of the…uh…female body," Miss Amaya stammered, her face slightly flushed.

"Where's the ta-tas?" a muffled voice came from the back of the class, along with a few snickers.

"Jeremiah Karns! The *BREASTS* are not shown on this poster. No more questions until *after* my presentation, please. Now where was I? Yes, the female body is made to house a fetus for about nine months-"

"How did the fetus get in there? And is it true that Valentine's Day is the best day for a fetus to start?"

"Jeremiah, that is quite enough. Silence please. And no, Valentine's Day has nothing to do with fetuses. It's just a holiday next week."

"If it's a holiday, then why do we have to come to school?" Jeremiah asked with a big grin on his face.

"I don't know. You'll have to ask the school board next time they meet. Alright, Cliff Notes version. Male sperm meets female's egg. Egg grows into a baby and nine months later it's born. Any questions? No? Well then we're done," Miss Amaya said, ignoring the numerous hands in the air. "Turn to page 300 and read the next ten pages. Quiz tomorrow." Moans filled the room. "That will teach some of you to act better in class. And for all the others who didn't act up, I'm sorry." Miss Amaya plopped down in her seat and buried her face in the textbook.

Cat's eyes filled with tears as she tried to suppress the laughter wanting to come out.

Sam came home three days later. He practiced his smile on the drive home. The meeting with the Varulv council had been rocky. Most members were supportive and backed Aldon's reassurance that Cat was no danger to their existence. A small faction though, wasn't happy with the results and had made their voices heard. The verdict was that as long as Aldon and Sam kept control of the situation in Astoria, no intervention would be necessary. During the flight back, Aldon finally broke his positive demeanor and revealed his true feelings to Sam. "I lied Sam. I lied to the council," Aldon said softly with a sigh.

"I know, we both did Aldon," Sam replied.

"We have to get a handle on things. Thankfully no one has told the council of what has transpired in Astoria. And they can never find out. Our future depends on it."

"What should we do?" Sam's worried eyes met Aldon's.

"I don't know. For the first time, I just don't know."

Opening the front door Sam was met with a welcoming party. His family acted like he had been away for years instead of days. *It's good to be home,* he thought embracing them all in a hug.

"Leif, what are you doing behind the bleachers?" Cat asked, peering underneath them.

"Cat you've got to help me. I'm being hounded by a thousand girls all bearing presents for Valentine's Day! It's all a bit too much. I just can't handle it." Leif whispered urgently, relieved it was only her that found his hiding spot. His voice was shaky, but his British accent was still delightful to Cat's ears. She would've laughed if Leif hadn't looked so stricken.

"You can't hide in there all day you know. Come on, I'll protect you from those vicious vixens," Cat joked, reaching her hand out for his.

"No thank you. I don't feel like being punched in the face by the school's famous running back today," he stated.

"Come on lover boy," she said as she grabbed his arm, and pulled him out in the open. "We're just two friends taking a stroll down the hallway to your next class. Nobody will dare mess with you I promise."

Opening the door to the gym, Cat and Leif made their way down the hallway without incident.

"See you after class Leif," Cat said loudly as she walked away. Turning around she found Ryan in front of her with an eyebrow raised.

"Did I just see what I think I saw?" Ryan asked.

"No, you didn't. You saw one friend helping another friend who's being harassed by half the female population at this school."

"I was just teasing. I actually kind of feel sorry for him. That was cool of you to help though. And that, Red Hot, is why I love you." Ryan kissed her and then jogged off toward the gym.

"You what?" Cat called after him, but her voice was drowned out by the bell ringing. "Crap! I'm late!"

After class Cat was still mulling over Ryan's remark as she made her way to her locker. *Did he really say that he loves me?* Pulling open her locker, she blinked. A bundle of black roses greeted her.

"Hey Cat what's up?" Matt's voice came from over her shoulder. "Cool, black flowers. Who left you those?"

"I don't know," Cat replied blankly, thinking they could have possibly been from the three girls.

"Is that a new trend or something? If so, I wonder if Hannah would like them. Uh, I don't know. If it's a cool trend she might though. But-"

"Matt, please be quiet. It's neither a trend nor cool. Not cool at all."

"Are those black roses? Why would anyone give someone black roses?" Elle's voice came up from her right side.

"I was just wondering the same thing," Cat replied, still distracted by the sight of them.

"Hey, what's with the flowers?" Ryan asked, coming up behind her.

"If this is someone's idea of a joke, it's not funny," Cat said, picking them up.

"Are they from *them*?" Ryan whispered to Cat, out of Elle and Matt's earshot.

"I don't know, maybe." Her wobbly tone worried him.

"Here let me have those. They belong in the trash!" Ryan stated, noticing the bewildered look on Cat's face. Grabbing the roses, Ryan dumped them into the nearby garbage can.

"Well that was a perfect way to end the day," Cat said sarcastically.

"Yeah, well if I find the creep who sent them, they'll wish they hadn't," Ryan stated, putting his arm around her and trying not to act suspicious.

"Even if it's your buddy Isaac?" Elle asked.

"No, he's too cheap. Just ask Amelia," Ryan answered with a chuckle.

"I guess I won't be buying Hannah any. I get the feeling it's not cool," Matt said to himself, and then realized the others had moved down the hallway while he was still looking through his locker. “Hey guys wait for me!”

“Mr. Thomas!” A teacher shouted from down the hall.

“I know, I know,” Matt said, seeing the teacher giving him a stern look. “No running in the halls. Got it.”

“So Cat, do you and Ryan have anything special planned for tomorrow?” Rachel asked as they ate dinner.

“Huh? Oh, I don’t know. We haven’t really talked about it.”

“Cat you seem distracted. Something wrong?” Sam asked, a frown marring his forehead.

“Nothing really. Just a weird thing happened at school today, and I guess it shook me a little,” Cat answered nonchalantly.

“What happened?” Rachel asked, seeing through Cat’s ruse.

“After school I went to my locker and there were black roses inside. It was kind of creepy, and gave me the wiggins. But Ryan took care of them, so no worries.”

“Do you have any idea who might have put them there?” Sam asked.

“No. But it was probably just someone playing a joke or something,” she said, shrugging her shoulders.

"Is there someone who likes you but you don't like them?" Rachel asked, looking at Sam who gave her a comforting smile.

"No. Not that I know of. Oh well, it's really nothing right?" Cat asked.

"Of course, a gag I'm sure. Just keep an eye out for anyone acting funny, okay," Sam replied.

Cat laughed hollowly. "It was probably Kirsten or somebody from her group. She's still kind of being a pill." Sam and Rachel looked at each other, hoping that was the answer.

❦ ❦ ❦

Valentine's Day arrived with a bright sun and temperatures warmer than usual. Cat opened her front door to find Ryan standing there with a bundle of pink roses, a box of chocolates, and his lips exaggeratedly puckered waiting for a kiss. "How long have you been out here?" Cat asked surprised, a huge smile on her face.

"Uh, just long enough to see your neighbor check me out like five times, and have an awkward conversation with your father on his way to work," he joked, his lips still puckered up.

"You should've just rang the doorbell," she said, trying to hold back a giggle.

He laughed. "Well then it wouldn't have been a surprise now would it? Are you going to kiss me or not?"

"Oh Ryan! They're beautiful!" she exclaimed, taking the flowers from him and then grabbing him in a hug, kissing him soundly. "Thank you, I really needed this!"

"Well I had to make up for yesterday."

"Let me just go put these in water," Cat said as Ryan followed her inside.

"Randy, Randy, you're never going to believe what I just saw! A boy just went into the Colvin house with Catherine. Without parental supervision," Maude exclaimed.

"And?" Randy replied flipping through the morning paper.

"And? And? Didn't you hear me? No parental supervision! On Valentine's Day! He's luring her with flowers and candy. Someone has to put a stop to this right now," Maude announced as she headed for the front door.

"Leave 'em alone Maude. It's none of your business anyway."

"Darn, I'm too late," Maude murmured, ignoring Randy's comment. "They've left. You better believe that Catherine is going to get an earful when she gets home."

"Everyone always gets an earful with you my dear," Randy said under his breath as he turned the page of the paper. *Great she remembered it's Valentine's Day. I guess I've got to go get her something now. Damn holiday!* Randy thought.

After driving her to school, Ryan left Cat at the gym entrance with a quick kiss. The hallway was deserted except for a few stragglers. As Cat made her way to her locker, the warning bell rang, but in her current mood she didn't care. When she opened her locker, Cat came face to face with a huge paper heart hanging there.

Something was attached to the heart with a large paper clip. Cat's heart sank when she saw it was a pocket protector. She gasped, realizing it was not just any pocket protector, but Melvin Pierson's. His name was written in bold print on the back. Beginning to tremble with worry, Cat grabbed both items and rushed to the biology classroom. Everyone looked up as Cat burst through the door. Whispers began flowing through the class as she just stood there in shock.

"Class, please begin reading page 401. I'll be right outside, no talking," Miss Amaya instructed. With a gentle push she guided a stricken Cat back out into the hallway.

"Cat what's wrong?" Without a word Cat held up the paper heart and Melvin Pierson's property, with tears filling her eyes. “This is Melvin’s. Where did you get it?” Miss Amaya clutched the pocket protector tightly.

“It was in my locker. Yesterday I got black roses. Today I got this. He always had this on him. It was his security blanket. He’d never be without it.” Cat stared at Ms. Amaya’s hand, “Do you think he’s still alive?” she whispered as a teacher walked by.

Ms. Amaya raised her head to look at Cat, “He might be. I have to talk to Gretchen. Don’t tell anyone about this until I do. This is our secret. Oh Cat, I hope he’s alive,” she answered with tears in her eyes.

Cat was relieved when the school day ended. Everyone was caught up in the Valentine’s frenzy and thankfully no one noticed how quiet she had been. Rounding the corner leading to the sophomore locker hallway, Cat spotted one of the janitors standing in front of a locker, appearing to be in a daze. Walking up to him, “Are you okay?” she asked.

“Huh?” he replied startled, breaking out of his trance-like state. “Oh, yeah…I’m fine, I think,” he mumbled out. Without another word, the janitor turned away from Cat, and headed down the hall. *Why am I in the sophomore hall with the master key to all the lockers? I don’t remember how I got here. Now, what am I supposed to be doing?* The janitor thought.

"That was odd," Cat stated, watching him walk aimlessly out of view.

"Hey who's the jokester that put this in my locker?" Matt asked loudly to the others standing beside him. He pulled out the paper heart, and began reading it aloud. Cat's heart sped up as she approached him.

What Would You Do If I Cut Your Heart Out
Would You Scream, Would You Shout
Or Would You Enjoy The Pain
As I Watch Your Blood Drip Down Like Rain.

"Eww! That's sick! Who'd you piss off?" Amanda grimaced, opening her locker. "What the hell? I have one too!"

You Think You Know It All
Yes You Do, This Much Is True
But Your Heart Will Stop Beating
Once I Get Through With You.

"Alright who put this in my locker? I'm about to kick someone's ass!" Amanda shouted into the crowded hallway while waving the Valentine about.

"Wait…I have one," Elle's shaking voice made everyone turn toward her.

They Used To Call You Metal Mouth
You Were Happy When They Came Out

And Now You're Quite The Social Butterfly
I Should Pull Your Wings Off And Watch You Die

This is too creepy! Who gave these to us? They even used my nickname," Elle's worried face met the others.

"I don't know, but we need to show these to someone. I mean this is just messed up!" Matt's voice was laced with anger.

"Shhh, Matt, give them to me. I'll take them to Ms. Landers. Now guys, we don't want to give whoever did this the satisfaction of seeing us upset." Cat gave a sigh of relief as they all handed their valentines to her. Making their way down the hall Amanda glared at everyone they passed, thinking the sender could be any one of them.

Later that evening, Cat phoned Julie to see how she was doing. "So how are you feeling? Missed you at school today."

"I've been better. So anything interesting happen? What did I miss?"

"Oh you know, a quiz in English, terrible lunch, Amanda beating up on Matt, and sick valentines. Just your average day at Astoria High."

"What do you mean sick valentines?"

"Sorry Julie, could you hold on a sec? Miss Amaya's on the other line."

“Miss Amaya? Why is she calling you?” Julie asked.

“Oh…uh…I was helping her research something for bio, and she’s just getting back to me,” Cat replied, hoping it sounded legit. “Just one sec, okay?” Cat switched calls, “Hi Miss Amaya.”

“Hello Cat, I hope this isn’t too late for me to call.”

“No, it’s fine. I’ve been waiting to hear from you. And why weren’t you in biology today?”

“I left right after our conversation to speak with Gretchen.”

“Well what did she say?” Cat asked with urgency in her voice.

“I’m afraid the three girls are the ones responsible for Melvin’s disappearance. Spirit couldn’t see if he was alive though. But I feel in my gut that he’s still with us,” Miss Amaya choked out.

“We’ll find him, I’m sure of it,” Cat said, trying to console her.

“Cat you must be careful. Spirit said that you are their main target. I know you don’t want to tell your parents, but I think it’s time to. You will need their aid, if what spirit fears does indeed come to fruition. We’ll talk more tomorrow. Goodnight Cat, and please be safe.”

“I will, don’t worry,” Cat replied, and then took a deep breath before switching back over to Julie.

After talking with Cat for a few minutes, Julie hung up the phone and turned to her mother Claire, who was standing by waiting to hear what had happened.

"Things are escalating," Julie murmured.

"Are you going out again tonight?" Claire asked.

"Yes, I think I need to," she replied, pulling on her boots.

"Did she believe you were sick?"

"Of course. I've had a lot of practice lying to her."

"But it's for her own good. It's a part of your *focus*."

"I know, but it doesn't make lying feel any better," Julie replied, exiting out the back door.

"So what did she say?" Matt asked Cat the next day at their lockers.

"What did who say?" Cat replied puzzled.

"Ms. Landers, when you gave her those creepy valentines," Matt answered, getting testy as Cat obviously was not paying attention to him.

"Oh, that. She said she'd look in to it."

"Yeah right!"

"What do you mean by that?" Cat asked defensively.

"She probably just thinks it's a prank. But I know better. Something's not right, and I'm going to find out what," Matt said. He turned on his heel, and then stormed off.

"What's with him?" Elle asked from behind Cat.

“I don’t know, I guess he’s off to fight windmills,” Cat quipped, remembering Don Quixote from summer reading last year.

19
Come To My Window

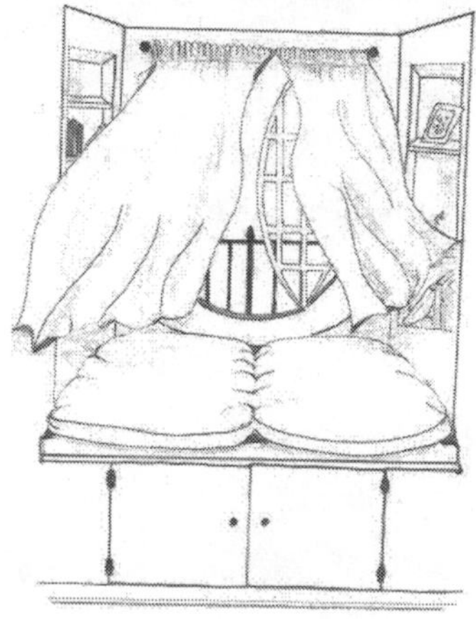

Cat was worried. It had been a few weeks since Valentine's Day and nothing had happened. She found herself jumpy and easily startled. Her days and nights were plagued with thoughts of what the three girls were planning. Cat knew the next attack was drawing near. This was far from over and she had to be ready, ready for anything. She felt guilty that she still hadn't told her parents, and ignored Miss Amaya's advice. She didn't want them to even think about sending her to be with Ròs and Trevor.

A scratching noise at the window pulled Cat away from her thoughts. *Jewels! Just what I need right now*, she thought with a smile. *Somehow talking to that cat always just makes me feel better*. Walking to the window she saw no sign of her, but could hear a faint meowing. *She must be on the roof waiting for me*, Cat thought, opening the window. She pulled her robe tighter as the biting wind hit her. Glancing up at the roof, Cat didn't see the feline. "Jewels? Here kitty, kitty, kitty. Where is she?" Cat began to ascend the ladder up to the widow's walk, but then stopped as she heard a clicking noise. Looking down at her window, she saw it had closed. After climbing down, she reached for the handle and was confused when it didn't turn. It was locked.

"Here kitty, kitty, kitty," a female voice sounded from down below. Cat looked over the balcony and there stood Amy, with a toothy grin. "Can kitty Cat come out and play?" She asked, spreading her arms wide.

"What do you want?" Cat answered stiffly.

"We want to play, don't we girls?" Cat saw two more figures emerge from behind the Sitka Spruce tree.

"Linda misses her little Cat, don't you Linda?" Amy asked, turning to Linda, who had moved forward to stand by her. Linda stared up at Cat, her face bleak. She jumped when Becca elbowed her.

"Amy asked you a question, Linda. Answer her!" Becca grinned up at Cat, her elongated teeth gleaming in the moonlight.

"Linda don't listen to them! Please come back to us," Cat pleaded, watching her friend's face as it went from sad to angry.

"Bit late for that, huh Cat?" Linda spat out.

"It's not. Let me help you," Cat answered.

"Hey, enough of this little reunion. So, how's Matt doing after his little accident? And he was *supposed* to die, for your information," Amy remarked. Cat scowled down at her. Amy laughed evilly, "Oh, and did you like the roses and the beautiful valentine hearts we sent you? We worked really hard on those poems. Hallmark quality really."

"Amy, don't forget about Melvin," Becca reminded her.

"Oh yeah, I almost forgot about dear Mr. Pierson. He's such a hoot at mealtimes. I think he's beginning to enjoy it. What? No response? Cat got your tongue?" The three's wicked laughter filled the air.

"I thought it was you guys. And those poems sucked!"

Amy let out a low growl and clenched her fists as Cat spoke.

"What do you want? If you have a problem with me, deal with me. I'm the one you want right? Then what are you waiting for? I'm right here. Come and get me." Cat grinned coldly as she saw the indecision on their faces. She rose up over the balcony and floated gracefully to the ground. "You want to play? Let's play!" Cat rose back up into the air and floated to the nearest tree.

The three girls looked at each other, "What are you looking at me for? Get her!" Amy's voice shook with rage. Linda and Becca just stood there looking up at Cat in the tree. "You imbeciles! Why are you just standing there? Go get her. Or do I have to do everything myself?" she yelled.

"But Amy, I thought we were only instructed to scare her. And to me she doesn't look very scared," Becca whined.

"Fine. You two stay here," Amy hissed. She floated up to the Sitka Spruce tree branch that Cat was perched on. "Nowhere to run now Cat." Amy grinned and then lunged for her. Cat dodged her and shifted to the next branch up, out of Amy's reach.

"Kind of slow aren't you Amy," Cat taunted, moving gracefully between the large tree's branches.

"I'll show you slow," Amy replied angrily while shoving a few smaller branches from in front of her face as she talked. Bounding up several tree limbs, Amy chased after Cat in hot pursuit. Cat managed to stay one step ahead of her, always shifting from her grasp at the last minute.

"Alright that's it. No more fooling around," Amy whispered angrily. She gripped the tree's trunk firmly and began rocking back and forth, shaking the tree with her brute strength. The tree swayed uncontrollably which caused Cat to lose her balance. She fell, but caught herself on the tree limb she had been standing on. As she struggled to pull herself up, she felt long fingernails dig into her shoulders, feeling like needles as they punctured the skin.

"Doesn't that feel good Cat?"

"No, not really," Cat replied and then pushed her head forward and then shoved it back quickly, head-butting Amy in the nose. Amy lost her grip on Cat and began to fall, but then grabbed onto Cat's ankle, and pulled her down with her. Both girls slammed hard on to a large tree limb just below them.

"Didn't count on that, now did you?" Amy stated with an evil grin as she sat up. "You may be quicker, but I am much stronger!" Cat pulled herself to her feet and got into a defensive stance while Amy dusted herself off. "One more time then little kitty?" Cat just waited there, staring her down. Amy dove for her and then screamed as something flew into her face, wildly scratching her. Cat watched on in amazement as Jewels seemed to appear out of thin air, causing Amy to tumble to the ground. Becca and Linda hurried to her side to help her up.

Jewels landed gracefully on her feet, hissing loudly at the three girls. “Becca! A little help here would be nice!” Amy barked. Becca nodded and then concentrated on Cat up in the tree. Moving her hand from left to right, she sent a tree branch hurling toward Cat. Cat ducked out of the way and dove to the next branch, tearing her robe in the process, and catching a fist full of twigs and leaves in her hair. The sound of the branch beginning to crack under Cat startled her.

Becca concentrated on the branch Cat was lying on and squeezed her hand in to a fist. The branch snapped from the tree and sent Cat tumbling down with it, crashing through layers of foliage before hitting the ground. As she struggled to make it to her feet, Cat glared at the three girls the whole time. She noticed Amy eying Jewels with a smirk on her face. Worried for her feline friend, Cat tried to shift over to her. Amy lunged for Jewels before Cat could reach her. Jewels easily moved out the way, and Amy’s momentum sent her flying by, skidding along the ground. The feline turned and Cat could swear she was grinning.

“So Cat has a kitty to fight her battles for her,” Amy growled, pulling her face up from the soggy grass.

“Maybe she thought I was outnumbered and came to help,” Cat said, shrugging her shoulders and sending the girls a huge grin.

"You wouldn't be so cocky if our master was here," Becca said smugly.

"You have a master? So what, you're like slaves or something?" Cat asked.

"We're not slaves, we're-"

"His army!" Amy roared, finishing Becca's sentence.

"An army? You guys? Ha, like that scares me! I want you to stop this! Let Mr. Pierson go, and get the hell out of Astoria! You've got no idea what you're dealing with here!" Cat yelled. Then Jewels hissed again at the three.

"We don't know what we're dealing with?" Amy chuckled. "Did you hear that girls? We don't know what we're dealing with! Well, kitty Cat, I don't think you know what *you're* dealing with. Our master wants you, and he'll have you when the time is right!" Amy's jet black eyes seemed to flash red in the moonlight.

Suddenly the yard was illuminated by the front porch light. Alarmed, Cat's focus turned to the front door. When she looked back at the three girls, they were gone. Jewels was sitting there all alone, licking her paw. As Cat heard the front door begin to open, she shifted to the side of the house. Sam stepped out onto the porch and scanned the yard. He lifted his nose to the air, "Vampires?"

Great, how the hell am I going to get inside now? My window is locked, and dad's at the front door. Oh, I can wake Taylor up! Cat thought and then floated up to his window. She knocked but there was no answer. She knocked again harder, and was relieved when a figure came into view. Taylor's sleepy face peered out at her and then his eyes opened wide with shock at the sight of her floating in the air.

Taylor flung open the window and asked, "What are you doing? And why do you look like crap?"

"It's a long story, and it's freezing! Do you mind moving so I can come in?"

"So this is what it looks like when a vampire floats, huh?"

"Really funny Taylor, really funny. Just go back to bed and pretend this was a dream."

"More like a nightmare. You should see your hair," Taylor laughed.

"You should see yours, Alfalfa!" Cat remarked, opening his bedroom door. As Cat checked to make sure no one was around, she saw the foyer light go out, and then heard her dad coming up the stairs toward her. She hurried toward her attic bedroom and floated up the stairs so not to make them creak. As she closed the bedroom door behind her, Cat sighed, relieved that she was safe in her room. *What was I thinking, taking on those three? I mean I could've been killed*, she thought as a shiver of fear ran through her. Hearing the creak of the stairs, Cat flopped on her bed, and pulled her comforter up to her chin, pretending to be asleep.

Sam opened her bedroom door and looked around. He smiled when he saw Cat asleep in her bed. “Goodnight Cat,” he whispered and then shut the door.

Cat waited until she heard the creaking of the stairs cease before she headed to her bathroom to clean up. As she began to open her bathroom door, a knock came at her window, startling her. “If you’ve come back with reinforcements just forget it! I’m not in the mood,” Cat whispered angrily, throwing the curtains open. She was surprised to see Ryan standing there, a frown on his face.

“So, an exciting night huh?” Ryan asked as he stepped into the room, looking at the leaves and twigs still stuck in her hair. “And I see you’re wearing the latest fashion,” he continued, pointing at her dirty and torn robe.

“Yeah, really exciting. You just missed it. You could’ve joined Jewels and I in a little game of tag with the three vamp girls,” Cat said over her shoulder as she made her way to the bathroom to see the damage.

“They were here?” Ryan asked and then a muffled shriek came from the bathroom.

"No wonder I scared Taylor, I'm hideous!" Cat moaned, pulling the leaves out of her matted hair.

"I think you look fine," Ryan said, coming up behind her.

"You really need to review your definition of looking fine. Either that or get glasses," she groaned. "Then again, maybe leaves in hair could be a new trend. And since we have so many trees in Astoria we totes could cash in."

"Cat we need to get serious for a moment. These girls are dangerous," he replied, turning her around to face him.

"Don't you think I already know that? Hello, physical evidence here," Cat stated, pointing at her hair and robe. "It also seems like they're not working alone. They have a master."

"What? They said that? I wonder who it is. We need to talk with Mr. Bancroft immediately. This is getting too far out of hand." Ryan's forehead creased with worry.

"Maybe you're right. I'm just so tired of everything though. I just need normal! Is that too much to ask for?" she sighed as Ryan took her in his arms.

"Don't worry Cat, we'll work this out. You need to get some sleep though," he said as he laid her down on the bed and tucked her in. Kissing her forehead, "I'll be right here when you wake up, okay?" Cat yawned slightly while nodding her head.

"Eww, I feel so gross. I really should take a shower, but I'm too exhausted," she moaned. As she rolled over, Ryan laid next to her and wrapped his arm about her waist.

What are we going to do? Ryan thought as he removed a small twig from Cat's hair.

❦ ❦ ❦

"So did you come through my window last night or was that a nightmare?" Taylor asked Cat as they made their way to their cars.

"I have no idea what you are…oh hi Mrs. Roberts such a lovely morning, isn't it? I'd love to stay and chat, but we're running a little late," Cat said rapidly as Julie ran up the drive and jumped into the Jeep, giving Maude a little wave.

"Well dear you run along and I'll just chat with Taylor about the strange noises I heard last night." Taylor groaned inwardly and glared at Cat as the Jeep started backing down the driveway.

"Well young man did you hear anything last night?" Maude inquired.

"Nope, can't say that I did. Sorry, but I'm kind of in a hurry too. They kind of frown upon us being late for school," Taylor quipped without waiting for her response.

Watching Taylor pull away from the driveway, Maude yanked on Fredricka's leash and made her way back to her house. "Something's not quite right about that family, and mummy intends to find out what it is. I know I heard voices and strange noises last night. Darn it, I wish I hadn't left my glasses down stairs so I could've made out what on earth was in that big tree! Oh well, from now on my glasses will be right beside my bed. I'll be prepared next time." Maude opened her front door and made her way inside, as Fredricka was busy attacking the leash.

The school day seemed to drag on forever as Cat was anxious to get the meeting over with Mr. Bancroft. Before first period she had found Miss Amaya and told her about the night's events. She informed Cat of a sealing spell that she could place on her house. Unlike salting, which only wards off dark magics, a sealing spell would prevent the three girls from crossing her house's threshold. Cat didn't mention the part about Lucien Bancroft, wanting to see how the meeting would go first. She hated keeping secrets from Miss Amaya.

The final bell rang and Cat quickly grabbed her things and made her way to her locker. Ryan was standing there looking troubled.

"What's wrong?" Cat asked before dialing her locker combination.

"I couldn't concentrate today. All I kept thinking about was what happened last night, and that I wasn't there to help you. It scares me that I can't be there all the time. If anything ever happened to-"

"Listen Ryan, I'm okay, really," she said, emptying her messenger bag into her locker. "Now let's go talk to Mr. Bancroft." Cat took Ryan's hand and lead him down the hall. "There's Julie, let me give her my keys, and then I'll meet you at your car." She gave him a quick kiss before making her way across the parking lot. "Thanks so much for doing this Julie. I'll come by your house and pick up the keys later, okay?"

"No problem. Have a good time," Julie called out as she opened the Jeep's door and got inside.

"Thanks again," Cat yelled back, smiling. Julie watched as Ryan drove away and then hit speed dial on her phone.

"Yes, I know," she told the person on the other end. "I'll take care of it." Julie sighed as she pondered her night ahead. "I guess my English homework won't get done tonight," she muttered as she pulled out of the parking lot.

Sitting beside Ryan, Cat suddenly became nervous. She had only seen Lucien Bancroft from a distance. With his short black hair, his pale skin, and piercing green eyes, he reminded her of Isaac. She hoped he wasn't as mean as his son, but more like his daughter. Ryan seemed to feel her tension as he reached across and took her hand in his, keeping his eyes on the road.

"What's he like?" Cat asked.

"He's cool, nothing like Isaac. Isaac may take after his dad in looks, but his personality is all his mom's doing."

"Yeah, I know what you mean. My mom and Mrs. Bancroft don't get along very well. And she just loves me to pieces," Cat joked.

"Well don't worry. Lucien said she won't be home when we get there."

Cat sunk back in the seat realizing she was holding herself so stiff and tense that her muscles had begun to ache. She had forgotten to show Ryan the journal that she had tucked away in her bag. She remembered it that morning while getting ready for school. Cat brought it with her to show Mr. Bancroft, with the hope he might know who wrote it, and what happened to them. Ryan had told her, though he was only seventeen, the vampire parents that lived in Astoria were each well over a hundred years old.

Cat took a deep breath as Ryan pulled into his driveway and turned off the car. Before they could get out, the front door opened and Ryan's mom walked to the end of the porch. Making their way up the stone path to the front door, Cat's tension increased when she noticed the frown on Christine's face.

"Ryan, Mr. Bancroft is waiting in the living room. He said you were to meet with him at his house, but plans have changed. So, now he wants to talk to you and Catherine here. What's this all about?" she asked, her eyes pinning her son's.

"Come inside mom, and we'll tell you," Ryan said, touching his mom's arm, trying to soothe her nerves.

"Hi Mrs. Beckford," Cat said, staying behind Ryan.

"Oh hello Catherine. Sorry I'm so rude, but it's not every day that I'm kept in the dark about things I should know about," she said, attempting to smile as Ryan put an arm around her shoulders.

"Mom you were gone this morning when I got up, so I didn't have a chance to tell you," he replied.

"Well I guess I'll get us something to drink then. Go have a seat in the living room and entertain Lucien until I return," she said and then hurried down the hallway to the kitchen.

Cat followed Ryan into the living room, all the while focusing on the Large A on the back of his Letterman's jacket, trying to ease herself. As Ryan stepped aside, she looked up. She watched as Lucien rose to greet them with a warm smile.

"Miss Colvin, it's my pleasure to finally meet you. My Hannah talks about you endlessly. And of course Ryan, I hear, is quite fond of you as well. I am sorry we haven't met before now, but it seems that we should have. Please have a seat and let us talk." Lucien beamed, pointing to the couch opposite the chair where he had been sitting in.

"It's nice to meet you Mr. Bancroft, and I consider Hannah one of my best friends."

"Just Hannah, not Isaac?" Lucien chuckled at her discomfort. "You must excuse me Catherine. I know my son is difficult. But deep down inside he is a good boy." Cat smiled back, trying to envision Isaac being good.

"Here are some refreshments. I know I'm thirsty and I hope everyone else is too," Christine said, placing the tray down on the coffee table. She passed out the tall glasses of lemonade, her hands were visibly shaking.

"Now that we are settled, I think we should get your mother, how do you say, up to speed? Ryan you have the floor," Lucien said and then leaned back in his chair, taking a long drink.

Ryan proceeded to fill his mom in on everything up to that point. She gasped as Ryan said Cat was a Childe, and looked to Cat for her reaction. He told his mom that she already knew, and continued. As Ryan finished, he looked anxiously at his mother, whose normally pale face had become shockingly white.

"I think I need a drink," Christine said, staring blankly.

"You have a drink, right there mom."

"I mean something a little harder than lemonade."

"Mr. Bancroft, the three girls mentioned a master. Would you by any chance know who it could be?" Lucien shook his head, dodging Cat's stare. "Are you sure Mr. Bancroft? This master is clearly after me because I'm a Childe. At least that's what I've guessed from what I've heard and read."

"What do you mean read?" Lucien's penetrating stare made Cat shudder.

"I have this journal, about a Childe," Cat stated, fumbling with her bag, oblivious to the look of devastation on Lucien's face.

"I'm home, where is everyone?" A voice came from the foyer. Christine jumped up from her chair and met the tall good looking man standing in the doorway.

"Hello Lucien, what brings you by this afternoon?" Ivan Beckford asked, not looking at Lucien, but instead fixing his ice blue eyes on the two young people sitting on the couch.

"Dad this is Cat, Catherine Colvin," Ryan announced, relieved when he saw his father smile.

He laughed. "I know who she is son. And might I say it is an honor to have you in our home. What am I missing? Was I supposed to be here for this? I'm sorry I forgot, if I was."

"No good friend, this was hastily planned. In fact we were supposed to meet at my residence, but Ulla came home and this is not a matter I want her involved in."

"What matter? And why does everyone look so stressed? Honey I must say you look ill. And if I may say Lucien, you also look worse for the wear." Ivan's puzzled eyes met theirs.

With everyone's attention on Ivan, Cat was the only one that noticed Lucien glancing over to her lap where she held the little brown journal. *Why are his hands shaking? And are those tears in his eyes?* She thought. "Is something wrong Mr. Bancroft," Cat asked quietly, breaking the silence that had fallen on the room.

"Um, it seems Lucien is upset at what you have sitting in your lap. Right old friend?" Ivan asked. Lucien sighed and looked around the room at its occupants.

"I am afraid you are dead on Ivan. I wondered where it had gotten to," Lucien said, pointing at the journal. "I thought I had misplaced it. But how it came into your possession is beyond me." Lucien's head fell forward and he covered his face with his hands. Cat was the first to respond. She stood and walked to the obviously distraught man and put her hand on his shoulder.

"This belongs to you? So you know who wrote it?" she asked, her voice barely above a whisper. Lucien nodded.

"It was my daughter's," he choked out.

"Your daughter's? Hannah wrote this? But she couldn't have, she's as old as I am. This was written over a hundred years ago." Cat's forehead creased deeply as she tried to wrap her mind around the situation.

"No, no my dear. My first daughter wrote it. Her name was also Hannah, and that was her journal. May I hold it?" Lucien's voice shook slightly. Cat took the book and placed it in his outstretched hands. He raised his head and Cat's heart sank as she saw the despair and sadness in his eyes. Tears made their way down his handsome face, and without thinking, she bent down to his ear.

"It might help if you talk about it." Her gentle voice seemed to calm his trembling and he wiped at his tears, giving her a slight smile.

"Thank you Catherine. It is just that it has been buried so long, and the pain of it has sometimes been too much for me to bear." Lucien cleared his throat, his hands tightly clutching the journal as if it may disappear again. "A long time ago I fell in love with a mortal, as did many of our kind. Our leader, Cain, was immensely displeased by the actions of his brethren. Even more so after offspring were miraculously produced from these unions. Cain sought the advice of a seer to find an answer for how this was possible. The seer told him of a prophecy, that your kind, Cat, would bring ruin upon us," he explained. Cat's eyes narrowed, staring intently at Lucien. Just as Cat was about to speak, "Wait, before you judge me harshly because of what you read in the journal, let me tell you my side of the story. I, along with Ivan, and your real father," Lucien said pointing to Cat, "were all prominent figures within The Parliament, the governing body of the vampire world. We were in charge of implementing our leader's orders. Though we didn't agree with the prophecy, and felt there were inconsistencies, we could never disobey the words of our leader. And thus *The Cleansing* began. Even though my daughter was a Childe, I loved her unconditionally. Your father, Ivan, and myself all devised a plan to save her life and the lives of many others, but it failed. We tried to trick our leader, and I ended up paying the ultimate price." Lucien's mind became haunted with visions of the past.

"I loathed The Parliament and Cain for what they made me do. But they did show me mercy and allowed my leave. So I decided to move my coven here to Astoria. I have lived with the guilt ever since." Lucien looked at Cat and Ryan who both sat stunned by his story. Ivan moved and put his hand on Lucien's shoulder. He looked up and attempted a smile. "If it hadn't been for my good friends, I don't know if I would still be here today."

"It's true, every single word of it," Ivan said.

"Mr. Bancroft, I'm so sorry for your loss, but it wasn't your fault, it was your leader who ordered this!" Cat blurted out, startling herself by doing so.

"So kind of you to say. Unfortunately my heart doesn't seem to agree." Lucien paused, and then stared directly into Cat's eyes. "Catherine Colvin, I pledge that I will do everything in my power to keep you safe."

"Why would you do that? You don't even know me," Cat replied.

"I must right the wrong doings of my previous life, and protect you, as I failed to do with my dear Hannah, and your father."

Cat sat silent for a moment, overcome with emotion, before she spoke again. "Do you think Cain is this master the girls told me about?" Cat asked.

"No, these actions here do not reflect Cain's style. I feel someone else is responsible for this. We shall have another meeting between our groups to discuss our strategy. Since now we have a better understanding of what we are dealing with here."

"I guess I better tell my family before you do Mr. Bancroft. I'm afraid they don't know about my little adventure last night," Cat stated. She felt Ryan's warmth as he moved closer to her.

"Yes, I think that would be wise young lady. Knowing all about your family now, you must realize they have powers too," Lucien said kindly.

"I swear, did everyone know about them? I mean was I the last to know? Like I'd freak out or something? Give me a break, I'm Robert Craven's biggest fan after all," Cat rambled on missing the interchange of looks between Lucien, Ivan, and Christine at the mention of that name.

"Well, I believe this meeting should be adjourned for now. I will get in touch with Aldon. But first, I will give you some time to speak with your parents Catherine," Lucien stated.

"Thank you Mr. Bancroft," she said, returning his smile.

"And if it is alright with you," Lucien said, looking to the Beckford's, "I believe Ryan should stay close to Cat until we get this settled."

"I think his mother and I would be in total agreement with that." Ivan looked to his wife who nodded her head.

"Catherine, thank you once again for your kind words," Lucien said, holding the journal out to her. Cat shook her head, keeping her hands at her side.

"It belongs to you," she said quietly.

Cat's talk with her parents went smoother than expected, especially with all the secrets she had been keeping. Instead of tears, Rachel shocked everyone by becoming a wild woman, swearing she would tear this 'master' limb from limb when she got her hands on him. Sam tried to calm her, but failed. He then tried to convince Ryan that Cat would be fine until the morning and that he could pick her up for school, to which Ryan grudgingly agreed.

Later that evening the Colvin household was rudely awakened by a loud deafening bang that came from the front door. Sam, Cat, and Rachel were stunned to see Taylor lying in the foyer on his back, breathing heavily.

"Son, what in the world is the matter? Are you drunk?" Sam asked in a stern voice.

"No, but you aren't going to believe what I just saw!" Taylor looked up at the three who were staring at him intently.

"Well why don't you enlighten us," Rachel said, sniffing the air to see if she smelled alcohol.

"Mom, stop, I'm not drunk. I just ran into those missing girls! They came out of nowhere and tried to bite me! They're vampires!" Taylor yelled, looking back at the open front door. "As I ran into the house, they were blown back when they tried to follow me! It was like they hit a force field or something!"

"I guess Miss Amaya's sealing spell worked," Cat commented.

"Sorry mom, I think I gave them the finger. But you've got to let me go on that one. First I was happy I wasn't vampire bait, and second I did own up to it, right?" Taylor rambled, but then stopped as he realized they weren't surprised by what happened. "Hey wait! What sealing spell? What have you been keeping from me?" Taylor asked, looking bewildered.

"Come on big bro, let's go into dad's study. We need to have a little chat with you. I don't think you're going to like what we have to say," Cat said, leaning down and helping him rise to his feet. *He's going to be so pissed when he finds out those girls were behind Trish's attack.*

20
Trouble A Brewing

As Cat and Ryan drove home from school the next day, she filled him in on Taylor's attack. "I thought Taylor was going to have to be restrained after we told him everything. He went totally berserk, I could swear he was growling."

"Well he is a Varulv after all," Ryan joked.

"You know what I mean," Cat replied, giving him a love tap.

"So, I guess the big meeting is tonight," Ryan said, glancing over to her.

"I just hope something comes of it. I'm kind of tired of this whole let's-protect-Cat game," she laughed, but it sounded hollow. "You know, I'm really worried about Linda, even after all that's happened."

"I know. It must be hard to have your best friend become an enemy like this."

"That's just it though, I don't think she's like the other two. I know there's still good in her, I can feel it," Cat replied quietly, looking down at her twiddling thumbs. She sighed and Ryan reached his head over to smack a kiss on her cheek while they waited at a red light.

"Things will work out. The grown-ups will handle it, and this will all just have been a bad dream." Cat stared out the window and watched as fat raindrops fell from the sky, hoping he was right.

Several hours after the final school bell rang, Miss Amaya was still sitting at her desk watching the sunset. She was exhausted. She had lost track of how many spells her and Gretchen had cast over the last couple of days. And now she was waiting to finish the last one, a complicated binding spell. One that if done correctly, would suppress the power of the three rogue vampire girls. Miss Amaya was more determined than ever to end this and get Melvin back.

"Miss Amaya?" a voice at the side of her made her jump in her seat.

"Oh Julie, it's you. What are you doing here at this time of night?"

"Sorry I startled you. I just wanted to ask-" Julie stopped, seeing movement outside of the classroom windows. "We need to leave now!" Julie said firmly, grabbing her teacher's arm and pulling her to her feet.

"What is it?" Miss Amaya asked, noticing the earnest look on Julie's face.

"Trouble," Julie replied tersely, dragging her teacher behind her toward the doorway.

"Okay, I get that, but what, or who?"

"The threesome, I saw them outside the window. We've got to go," Julie said, moving her along down the semi-dark empty hallway.

"Julie, what threesome?"

"Shhh! I think I heard something," Julie replied, hearing a door open from behind them.

"Where oh where is the witch? That wicked witch, oh where has she gone? We want to show you our gratitude for the spells you've been casting on us," an eerie voice echoed in the corridor.

"Don't worry we'll find you. And soon you'll be reunited with your honey bear Melvie. He's sooo delish! We just can't seem to get enough of him." Another voice giggled wickedly from somewhere in front of them.

Seeing the door to the janitor's closet, Julie rushed over and was relieved when it opened. After the pair slipped inside, Julie closed the door quietly behind them.

"I need to put an invisibility spell on us, so please stand still," Miss Amaya commanded, closing her eyes, and mumbling words from an ancient language. Julie began to feel a tingling sensation throughout her body as she stood still listening.

"Miss Amaya? I'm beginning to think this whole spell thing was a bad idea."

Miss Amaya's eyes opened. "What do you mean?" she asked and then noticed Julie wasn't in front of her.

"Uh, down here," Julie said.

Dropping her eyes, Miss Amaya looked at her feet. "Oh my, Julie. I'm so sorry. I must've used the wrong spell. You're all furry," she apologized, seeing a cat that resembled a golden miniature lioness in front of her.

"No, your spell worked. It just revealed my true form in the process."

"True form?"

"Yeah, I'm a familiar. Cat's familiar to be exact," Julie meowed.

"Cat's familiar? Wait, you're Jewels? Her stray cat friend? Interesting, you know I always felt there was something special about you."

"Yep, this is my secret. Wait…shhh. I think they're just outside," she whispered. The door to the janitor's closet was suddenly flung open, and the three girls burst into the room.

"Wrong again Becca! She's obviously not in here. You and Linda were right behind her. Tell me again how you lost her? I swear if I want something done right, I have to do it myself."

"Well I-" Becca began to explain.

"I was being sarcastic. I don't really want your input. Now let's split up. We need to find that witch! Andrei will be so upset if we screw up again!" Amy slammed the closet door shut and took off down the hall. "You two idiots, move it!" she yelled, keeping her back to them as she moved quickly out of sight.

"Who died and made her boss! She really irritates me. Come on Linda, let's go back to the bio classroom, maybe the witch has come back for her stuff." Becca's voice became more distant as she moved down the hall.

"Okay Jewels, I mean Julie. I guess we should stay awhile until they leave. Do you want me to try and turn you back?"

"No," Julie's voice purred. "Just give me a little while, and I'll turn back on my own…I hope."

"I guess we should have a seat, we might be here for a bit. You think they'd have a couch or something in here, at least a chair to sit on," Miss Amaya rambled on, missing the rolling of the feline's eyes at her words.

"How'd she get past us? I mean really?" Amy growled, meeting up with Linda and Becca in the woods behind the school.

"She may have gotten away, but lookie what we found," Becca stated, holding a cell phone in her right hand.

"Tell me it's the witch's," Amy said, her eyes brightening as Becca nodded with a wicked grin.

"Huh, so you two aren't so useless after all. This will be perfect. Let's call Cat. Oh this is going to be so much fun, and Andrei will be very pleased."

Cat lay on her bed staring at the ceiling wondering how the meeting was going. She was told to stay home and not leave the house under any circumstances. Taylor was downstairs with Trish, and Cat knew that it had been her parent's idea to have them babysit her. Even Ryan was attending the meeting, which she felt was so unfair. She flinched as her cell phone rang at its full volume. Seeing Miss Amaya's number on the screen she quickly answered. "I'm so happy you called. I'm going crazy waiting for this meeting to be over and find out what's going to happen. It's not fair that my parents think I can't handle this. If they only knew how much I've dealt with, they'd be shocked." Cat paused waiting for a response.

"What meeting is that Ms. Catherine Colvin?" Amy's voice came through the phone.

"What are you doing with Miss Amaya's phone?" Cat asked angrily, her eyes narrowing.

"Well wouldn't you like to know," Amy taunted.

"I wouldn't have asked if I didn't!" Cat grounded out through clenched teeth.

Amy giggled evilly. "If you want to know that badly, why don't you come join the party? We're having so much fun here."

"If you hurt her I'll-"

"You'll what? Come now little kitty and play with us at the clearing by the beach. I know you know where it is. Oh, and one itsy bitsy request."

"What?!"

"Come alone!"

Cat heard a beep and realized Amy had hung up. Quickly slipping on her tennis shoes, Cat grabbed her jacket and left through her bay window. Looking over her balcony and seeing no one around, Cat floated down to the ground and made her way to the shed to retrieve her bike. Sticking to the shadows as best as she could, she was unaware she was being followed. Duffie and Leif rode silently behind her, keeping a safe distance between them, but not losing sight of Cat.

Matt was taking his time heading home after helping his dad at the Port Astoria docks. It was his turn to do the dishes, and he never looked forward to the chore. Peddling up a steep hill, he cursed his car again for stalling out on him earlier. Pulling up on Nehalem Avenue, he noticed three figures dart past him in the distance. As they sped under the street lights, he could see Cat's fiery red hair leading the pack, with two others following a good distance behind her. *Is that Duffie and Leif following Cat? What the hell? They're definitely in a hurry,* Matt thought. "I guess the dishes will have to wait," he said taking off after them. Matt almost yelled out to them, but something told him that they didn't want any attention.

Deep in the tunnel system below Astoria, Amy began prodding Melvin Pierson. "Wake up, you're going to miss the show, and it's going to be great. Wait, I think I hear the master now. Surely you're not still scared of him," Amy giggled as Melvin shivered, his glassy eyes filled with fear.

"Well girls, I assume she's on her way?" Andrei wasted no time asking as he approached them.

"Yep, she is!" Amy said triumphantly. Becca and Linda nodded in agreement.

"We need to ready our other guest, he's not feeling very well I fear, but the show must go on," Andrei said. "Linda do you have a question, my sweet?" Andrei's fangs descended as he talked.

"Is it safe for us to be around him, I mean will the chains hold him?" Linda's voice trembled.

"Don't you worry your pretty little head. He's heavily sedated my dear," Andrei said calmly.

"Yeah, but weren't the chains made of silver before? To keep him from changing? Linda replied.

"All part of the plan Linda. Now, let us go prepare for our guest shall we?" Andrei gestured for them to walk ahead and Amy moved quickly to take the lead. In the next chamber, a shape was slouched over, quietly moaning. Andrei squatted down beside the figure and pulled its hair back revealing their face. "Ah Edgar Girven, old friend, and noble Varulv councilman. Not feeling so well huh? Don't worry it will all be over soon." Andrei let go of his matted hair. "Okay ladies, let the show begin. Make sure you hurry to the clearing and show our honored guest the way to our little trap. I'm dying from anticipation," he said, rubbing his hands together, piercing his lip with his fangs in his excitement. "Mmmm that reminds me,

I haven't eaten. And I shall not meet our guest on an empty stomach. Mr. Pierson, ready or not here I come." His laughter echoed though the tunnels.

As Cat reached the clearing she immediately saw the trapdoor that she was unable to open before, propped open. Throwing her bike on the ground, she rushed over to it and peered into the dark hole. Cat retraced her steps to her bike, removed the headlight from the handle bar, and turned it on. Taking a deep breath, she slowly descended into the floor of the concrete foundation. *I'm absolutely nuts for doing this! But I can't let them harm my friends! Buck up Cat, you can do this!* She thought as she reached the bottom of the stone steps. Making her way down the winding tunnel, Cat wrinkled her nose at the damp and moldy smell. The bottoms of her shoes were taking on water as she trudged forward. She shuttered at what she might be stepping in. Coming to a fork in the tunnel, "Left or right?" Cat asked out loud and then waited to see if she got an answer.

"Leeeeeefffffffttttttt," an eerie voice came down the tunnel, causing goose bumps to erupt on Cat's body.

"Okay you can stop with the dramatics! I'm here, show yourselves!" Cat yelled, but received no reply. "Damn cowards, like I'm scared," she said out loud, trying to sound confident. *Come on, you can't let them know how scared you are Cat.*

Cat took the left tunnel, and it seemed like she had been walking forever. Her frustration began to build with each step she took. "Okay which way now?" Cat demanded, coming to another fork.

"Leeeeeffffftttttt," the eerie voice loudly whispered again.

"I'm so over this!" she huffed as she stormed further into the tunnel system.

"We're lost Leif, Cat must've gone the other way," Duffie whispered.

"Let's backtrack then, she wasn't that far ahead of us. How many tunnels could there be?" Leif's frustrated voice echoed in the stillness.

"Wait, I hear something behind us. Be ready for an attack, it might be one of the vamps tracking us," Duffie whispered in Leif's ear.

"Ahhhhh!" Duffie yelled as her flashlight beam caught a terrified little rodent, quivering in front of them.

"Duff, relax, it's just a mouse."

"Well I told you I heard something. Poor little thing. Look it's fallen over, but it's still breathing," Duffie replied.

"Come on, Cat may be in danger. Let's focus!" Leif whispered in frustration, pulling on her arm.

"Alright, let's move ahead," Duffie said, and then the two headed further down into the tunnels.

❦ ❦ ❦

"Where did they go?" Matt mumbled to himself. Coming upon the trap door, he hesitated. "They went down there? Really? Down there?" Matt moaned, thinking about every horror movie he had seen. Like Cat, he grabbed his bike's light, and before he could change his mind, bravely descended the stone steps. "Man, I think something died down here. Gross!"

When he reached the first fork in the tunnel, "What now?" He stood there and thought for a minute and then pointed his finger to the right path. "Eeny, meeny, miny, moe," he said going back and forth between the two pathways. Landing last on the left one, he continued down cautiously, careful not to touch the grimy walls. Even though he was totally grossed out by the sight before him, Matt was amazed at the tunnel system, and wondered how many people knew of its existence.

Hearing only his own footsteps echoing through the vast tunnels, "Just put one foot in front of the other Matt. You'll catch up to them soon, and hopefully find out what's going on. But something tells me I'm not going to like it," he whispered to himself, wanting to hear a voice just to break the quiet.

❦ ❦ ❦

Cat turned a corner and saw a light in the distance. Clenching tighter onto the bike light, she hesitantly made her way toward it. As she emerged from the tunnel into a large chamber, the first thing Cat noticed was the tall, pale man she met at the clearing two Halloween's ago. *The master*, she thought as she saw the three girls standing next to him, all grinning at her.

A moan off to the side drew her attention. At first she thought it was Mr. Pierson, but then realized the man was bigger. He was chained to the wall. His body leaned as far as his backwards stretched arms would allow, and his head was planted firmly on the ground.

"Welcome Catherine, to our modest home. I am afraid I cannot offer you any refreshments, as Mr. Pierson is a little low right now," Andrei quipped, bringing her focus back to him. "And I do not feel you would find Edgar Girven's too pleasant," he continued, gesturing to the figure chained to the wall behind him. "Ah, is that recognition in your eyes? You have met the Varulv councilman before? Of course you have. He is a good friend of your family. Is he not? Well, they're not really your family, but they have performed the part perfectly, now haven't they. Huh, to think a pack of mangy mutts would take in a filthy little half-breed like you." Andrei's malevolent smile made Cat sick to her stomach.

“Where’s Miss Amaya?” Cat’s angry voice resonated off the walls.

“Alas, I am afraid Amy told a little white lie. She is not here, only her phone,” he said, amused as the flush of anger became more prominent on Cat’s face. Another loud moan from Edgar on the floor drew their attention. “I hate to cut this visit short, but I have other arrangements. Please forgive me. Oh, and one other thing before I forget,” Andrei said, drawing a large silver dagger from beneath his long black coat. “Do you know what drives a Varulv mad with rage? Well, at least one that has been starved and tortured like our friend here? Vampire’s blood,” he continued and then proceeded to slice open his palm, letting the blood spill out onto the ground. “Oh, and you might need this when he changes.” Andrei sneered as he threw the dagger at Cat’s feet. The four quickly rushed into one of the tunnels leaving Cat behind, baffled. A painful cry from Edgar had Cat rushing forward, crouching down beside him.

“Mr. Girven, it’s Cat! Where are you hurt?” Cat became frustrated when he only grumbled. She reached into her pocket for her cell, “Damn, no signal! Mr. Girven, can you get up if I help you? I really don’t want to leave you here to go get help!” Cat gently lifted his head, pushing back his grungy hair to see his face clearly, wondering how long he had been down there.

His eyes were closed, his face bruised and battered. “What did they do to you?”

Edgar’s body twitched, causing her to gasp. His swollen eyes shot open, they were wild and glowing golden brown. She heard familiar crackling noises, like bones breaking beneath his clothes. Backing away, Cat watched as fur sprouted on his face and hands, his mouth elongating, and filling with razor sharp teeth. Saliva dripped from his mouth, and his tongue swept the moisture from his lips. As his body began to expand, she cringed at the sound of his clothes ripping. Her pulse raced, looking at the Varulv in front of her as he began violently thrashing toward her, trying to break free of the chains. Edgar let out a loud howl, making Cat cover her ears as it echoed through the open area. Suddenly one of the chains broke away from the old limestone wall. Cat moved away quickly, letting out a startled scream as Edgar swiped at her. Cat’s focus was on his huge teeth as they viciously snapped in her direction, and his eyes bulged as he strained against the chain. She could feel his hot breath on her skin. Touching the cold stone of the wall behind her, Cat realized she had backed herself into a corner. “Edgar! Why are you doing this? It’s me Cat!” she tried to reason with him. Edgar just snarled, pulling harder on the chain.

“Cat! What the hell is that?” Matt cried out.

Stunned, Cat turned to him, “What are you doing here?”

“I could ask you the same question! What the hell is that thing?”

“I don’t have time to explain, just go. Run!”

Edgar sniffed the air and then his eyes moved to Matt. He grinned widely, showing off his razor sharp teeth, and then let out a low growl.

“Cat, why is that thing looking at me like that?”

“Edgar! No, look at me! Matt get out of here!” Cat yelled as a shiver of fear ran through her, seeing Edgar’s attention fixed on Matt. Matt tried to move, but was frozen with fear. His mind couldn’t comprehend what was going on. “Matt don’t just stand there, run!”

“I can’t move Cat! I’m trying!” he yelled back, staring wide eyed at the beast in front of him.

Edgar gave one more frantic tug on the chain, breaking it away from the wall, and then charged at Matt.

“No! Edgar!” Cat screamed with desperation. Bracing for impact, Matt let out a loud yell, putt up his hands as a last defense, and shut his eyes. Cat shifted swiftly between them, grabbing Matt, and pulling him out of the way. Edgar flew by them, his teeth chomping inches from Cat’s face. Cat felt pain as the air was knocked out of her when they slammed into the ground.

Edgar let out a grunt as he hit the ground and rolled down the tunnel. He skid to a halt, and then raised his head, shaking off the dizziness.

"Matt…you need to go hide…now," Cat said breathlessly as they sat up. She could tell he was shell-shocked, and had no comprehension of what was going on.

"Oh…okay," Matt replied blankly. His eyes grew wide with fear as he saw Edgar's two golden eyes glaring at them through the darkness down the tunnel. He raised his shaky hand to point, and Cat followed his line of sight. She watched as Edgar slowly prowled toward them, grumbling in a low growl.

"Matt…I want…you to run," she whispered, helping him to his feet, and not taking her eyes off Edgar. The Varulv pawed at the ground while staring them down. "Go, now!" Cat yelled.

Edgar howled and charged at the pair as Matt took off down one of the tunnels. Cat faded to the side as Edgar leapt at her. Crashing into the wall, he let out a groan of pain. Shoving himself away from the wall, he charged at Cat again. She tried to fade out of the way, but Edgar caught her and knocked her to the ground. He pinned her under his paw, pressing hard on her chest. Edgar bent his head down, and roared in her face, breathing heavily. The heat from his breath was intense and smelled like hot garbage.

"Leave her alone!" Matt cried, poking his head back into the large central chamber. Edgar quickly turned toward Matt, saliva dripping from his chops. Stepping off of Cat's chest, he released the pressure, causing her to cough as she gasped for air.

"Matt…what are you…doing? Get…out of…here!" Cat called out breathlessly in frustration. Slowly raising herself to her feet, Cat noticed Edgar making his way toward Matt. "Leave…him alone Edgar!" Cat yelled out, trying to turn his attention to her.

Ignoring her, Edgar began to charge at Matt.

What the hell am I doing! Run Matt, Run! He told himself. Cat saw the dagger out of the corner of her eye and lunged for it. Grabbing it, she shifted in front of Edgar. He crashed full force into her, letting out a loud growl, and then a whimper. He fell limp on top of Cat. Pushing him over, she saw the dagger plunged into his chest. She looked down at her hands and shirt, and saw that they were covered in red. It was blood. Cat sat in shock as she realized what she had done.

A noise made Cat look up and she saw Matt emerging from behind the wall of the tunnel. He stared in disbelief and backed away from Cat as she approached him, his stunned eyes looking passed her. They both watched as Edgar Girven slowly turned back into his human form. She looked to Matt with sadness in her eyes.

"Cat you're covered in blood, are you hurt?" Matt asked, finally taking his eyes away from Edgar and focusing on her.

"Oh Matt, I killed him." Cat's voice trembled and tears filled her eyes as she sank to the ground sobbing.

"But you saved me," he replied shakily.

"Face it Duffie, we're lost!" Leif stated exasperatedly.

"I realize that Leif," Duffie replied, continuing ahead. "Wait did you hear that?" she whispered.

"What am I supposed to hear?" Leif whispered back in frustration.

"Voices, coming from over there," Duffie replied, pointing down the tunnel.

"I don't hear anything Duff, just face it, we've got nothing!"

Duffie put her index finger to his lips, "Will you shush and listen?" Leif rolled his eyes while humoring her. She smirked as the faint sound of a female voice came from in front of them. "Let's move," she ordered, pulling the black hood of her jacket down and over her face.

"Why does she always have to be right?" Leif muttered under his breath, following behind her.

"Damn, he locked us in here," Amy growled as she tried to push open the gate that led to the next chamber.

"Why did Andrei leave us? I don't think he's coming back," Becca whined.

"Oh shut up Becca! All you do is complain! And would it kill you to put a smile on your face Linda, you act like you just lost your best friend or something…oh right, I guess you did," Amy sneered. Linda grew angry.

"You're just mad because Becca's right! Andrei's not coming back! He's left us here to face that thing back there!" Linda yelled.

"Oi!" Duffie called out drawing the three's attention. "Evening ladies, so we meet again," she said coming into their view.

"Oh look girls, it's our mystery guests, right on time," Amy said snidely. "Come here to protect your little Cat huh?"

"No, we're just out for a nice little stroll." Leif nodded. Duffie watched the three girls, noting the angry flush on Amy's cheeks, the shock on Becca's face, and the tears drying on Linda's. "So are you three going to come quietly or are we going to have to force you? Either way, it doesn't matter to us," Duffie remarked, watching Amy clench her fists and bare her fangs.

"This won't be like the last time!" Amy roared.

"I agree, I came prepared," Duffie replied, pulling out a syringe. "A combination of nightshade, silver, and a splash of holy water. The perfect vamp tranquilizer!"

"Is that supposed to scare us?" Amy laughed.

"Let's find out shall we?" Duffie stated smugly. Amy growled and propelled herself forward.

Duffie waited until the last minute and side stepped out of the way, sending Amy flying past her. Landing on her feet, Amy yelled in frustration as she whipped around to face her again.

"Quit playing around and fight!" Amy demanded. Duffie smirked. Amy lunged at her, swiping at her face with her long black finger nails. Duffie ducked and swiftly moved behind Amy, shoving her away. Shrieking, Amy leaped into the air toward Duffie. Again she dodged her attack. "Why won't you fight me?" Amy asked angrily. Making her way toward her, Amy began to stumble and her vision became blurry. "What…did you…do to me?" she slurred, and then fell to the ground unconscious. Duffie held up the empty syringe, twiddling it between her fingers.

Looking over to the other two girls, "So who's next?" Duffie asked. Becca pushed her hand forward in a sweeping motion, sending Linda flying into Duffie's arms, and then tried to run. Becca's exit was blocked by Leif who quickly grabbed her. She let out a scream of protest as she bared her fangs and tried to bite him.

"We've got a wild one here Duffster," Leif commented. As he fought to keep Becca restrained, Duffie tossed him a syringe. After a moment of struggle, he was finally able to plunge the syringe into her neck, making her collapse to the ground.

"Now, are you going to tell us where Cat is?" Duffie asked looking sternly at Linda. Linda nodded.

"Follow that tunnel, and it'll lead you straight to her," Linda replied, pointing as her voice and hand shook. "Please hurry."

"We will, thanks," Duffie replied. Linda flinched as Leif proceeded to stick the syringe in her arm. He cushioned her fall and he laid her down next to the other two.

"Come on Leif, we need to find Cat."

"I can't believe I killed him," Cat murmured to herself in a melancholy tone.

"He would've killed me, if you didn't do anything," Matt replied, his eyes fixed on Edgar, his mind still not comprehending what he just witnessed. *Werewolves are real?* He thought to himself. Chains clanking in the distance drew their attention. "What's that?" Matt asked panicked.

"I don't know."

"Cat we need to get out of here! It's probably another one of those things!" Matt yelled, pointing at Edgar's body.

"*Help,*" a faint cry rang through the tunnels. Cat rose to her feet.

"Melvin! Is that you?" Cat called out.

"Melvin? Mr. Pierson's down here?" Matt asked confused.

"*Help,*" the cry sounded again, followed by chains clanging.

"It came from that direction," Cat said, looking at one of the tunnels. Matt slowly stood up with the assistance of the wall, as Cat began moving cautiously toward the tunnel.

"Wait Cat, you have no idea what that was!"

"It's Mr. Pierson, it has to be!"

"We should go get help. Not investigate it ourselves!"

"Then stay put, I'll be right back," Cat replied.

"You're not supposed to say that! People never come back after saying that."

"This isn't a movie Matthew. This is real life, okay!"

"Well if you're going, could you at least wait up for me?" Matt asked, hobbling over to her. "I want to go on the record, and say that I think this is a terrible idea."

Two sets of eyes watched as Cat and Matt went further into the tunnels. Duffie and Leif caught the tail end of the confrontation. They witnessed the death of Edgar Given by Cat's hands in self- defense.

"Come on Leif, we've got to go wrap our packages," Duffie stated.

"Well shouldn't we help them?" Leif asked.

"They'll be fine, there's no more danger here," Duffie said while looking at Edgar's lifeless body on the ground.

Retracing their steps, Leif and Duffie found their way back to the woods. Pulling out her cell phone, Duffie called Gerard.

"Melvin! Where are you?" Cat shouted out, listening for an answer. Hearing groaning around the corner, Cat and Matt peeked around it to find another open chamber. Three dingy mattresses were laid on the floor, and Melvin sat propped up on the back wall, chained, his head tilted to the side. His clothes were tattered and his face covered in spotty facial hair. The pale color of his skin worried Cat. "Melvin!" Cat cried, running up to his side as Matt stayed behind as a look out.

"Cat? Is that you?" he asked, raising his head slightly.

"Yes, it's me. We need to get you out of here." Cat could see the numerous puncture wounds on his neck and arms. Tears filled her eyes as she felt how skinny he was when she hugged him and lifted him to his feet. Matt watched on and became a little emotional as well.

Two cars barreled down the road toward the beach. “Aldon what else did the caller say?” Sam asked, sick with worry.

“I told you, Cat is in the tunnel system below town, and I was given the directions of how to get there,” Aldon replied.

“Are you sure they said that Catherine’s okay?”

“Yes Sam, that is what they said.”

“So you didn’t recognize the voice?” Dr. Bane asked, sitting in the back seat.

“I thought at first I did, but then when he told me about Cat, I stopped paying attention, because I was taking in all the details,” Aldon replied as he looked to Sam, not liking how pale his friend was. “Sam she’s fine, Ryan taught her well.”

I should’ve been with her tonight! It’s all my fault if she’s hurt! I hope the caller’s right and she’s okay, Ryan thought, sitting next to Dr. Bane and staring out the window at Olde’s Bay.

Coming to an abrupt stop, “We’re here,” Sam announced anxiously.

“We should wait for Lucien and his men before we make a move,” Aldon said, grabbing Sam’s arm as he tried to jump out of the car.

Lucien’s car pulled up next to theirs moments later and the two groups headed toward the clearing.

"Now let's go in quietly, I know the caller said that there was no danger, but now is not the time to throw caution to the wind," Aldon explained. "There's the trap door they mentioned. I'll go first. Harold, follow me, then Sam and Ryan. Lucien, your group will bring up the rear." Aldon's flashlight lit the way in the dark and dank tunnels. After a short trek, Aldon suddenly stopped and sniffed the air. "They went this way," he said, pointing down the left side tunnel. "Quiet everyone, I hear something," Aldon whispered, holding up his hand signaling for them to hold position.

"Matt hush, it was loose. I told you it was loose," Cat said.

"Uh uh, those chains were embedded in that wall! You yanked them out like they were nothing. What is going on Cat? Please tell me!"

"Just keep moving, we've got to get Mr. Pierson out of here!"

Aldon stood to the side, letting Sam rush past him toward Cat's voice. Cat's eyes lit up at the sight of her father coming down the tunnel. Dr. Bane moved quickly to relieve the pair of their burden. Sam grabbed his daughter, pulling her in close, holding on for dear life. The moment Sam let go, Ryan took his place, hugging her tightly.

“I’m so sorry. I’m glad you’re okay,” Ryan whispered, kissing her forehead. After smelling the blood on her, Ryan noticed it wasn’t hers and felt oddly relieved.

“How did you guys know we were here?”

“It’s a long story Cat. Are you okay honey?” Sam replied, hugging her again.

“No…I killed him,” Cat choked out.

“Killed who?” Sam asked puzzled.

“I’ll show you,” Cat replied, turning and leading them down the tunnel.

The group smelled death before they entered the chamber. Cat pointed to Edgar’s body lying on the ground. “It all happened so fast…I didn’t mean to do it…please believe me,” Cat pleaded, staring at what she had done.

“Of course I believe you honey,” Sam said as Cat clung to him, sobbing as if her heart was breaking.

“Mr. Colvin, I saw everything. That man was a wolf and he attacked us!” Matt blurted out, looking paler by the minute. With his quick reflexes Ryan caught Matt, before he hit the ground, passing out.

“I left my men to search the tunnels for the three girls the caller mentioned. What in the world?” Lucien Bancroft exclaimed as he made his way into the open area.

"It's Edgar Girven. From what I observe the poor man has been down here for a while. Held captive by these chains. The way he was tortured and starved would explain his actions tonight," Aldon said sadly, shaking his head.

"Uncle Aldon, I'm so sorry. I know he was…your friend. I didn't…mean for this to happen." Cat raised anguished eyes to her Uncle.

Taking her chin in his hand, "You have nothing to be sorry for, this was not your fault," he said kindly.

"Cat, one question. What is Matt doing down here?" Sam asked, looking at the unconscious young man.

"I don't know. He must've followed me or something."

"Lucien, we found the girls!" Ivan called into the room. "They were tied up, and knocked out, just like we were told."

"We need to make a decision about the boy's memory," Lucien said.

"You'll do nothing to his memory!" Cat said hotly, staring at her friend lying on the ground. "He's one of my best friends, and I won't sit by and let you do that. He'll never tell anyone about this, if I tell him not to! Dad you won't let them do this, will you?"

"I think Cat's right. Wait, before anyone protests, I trust this young man. And I trust him with my daughter's life. She's right, he'll keep this secret," Sam replied confidently.

"If you say that he will not divulge anything, then that is all I need to know," Lucien said, and then received a smile from Cat.

"Me too," Ryan piped up.

"Okay, so we agree. We shall not erase his memory," Aldon stated.

"Harold is tending to Mr. Pierson. Sam, take the youngsters to your house. I'll make arrangements for the body to be picked up and photographed for proof of the torture and starvation. And, I guess Druanna, Elsie, and I will be having house-guests for a while in our basement. I'll need assistance transporting the three girls there," Aldon explained.

"We shall take care of that matter," Lucien announced.

The phone rang in Blanche Caulder's quarters. "Hello, council woman Blanche Caulder speaking."

"It is done," Andrei said quickly and then hung up. Blanche smiled smugly in the knowledge that her plan had worked. She made her way to Reynard's office, the head of the Varulv council, with a bounce in her step. Knocking on the door, she impatiently waited. "It's Blanche," she said through the door when there was no answer.

"Come in," Reynard said, sounding distracted. Opening the door, Blanche saw him on the phone shaking his head sadly.

Hanging up, he raised his eyes to her. "We have quite the mess to contend with," he muttered.

"Whatever do you mean?" Blanche replied, attempting to look surprised.

"It involves the Colvin girl," he sighed.

"Has something happened to her?" she asked, trying to keep the glee out of her voice.

"No, not her. Edgar Girven. The poor council man is dead, and it seems she was involved. Aldon says it was self-defense. He assures me that he has evidence to prove this, which he plans to show at Catherine's council hearing…which is inevitable."

Blanche's eyes narrowed. The plan had backfired. *That stupid Colvin girl's still alive! How dare Andrei lie to me like this!* She thought as anger filled her.

"She killed him? Poor, poor sweet Edgar? I told you that girl was dangerous! But no, no one listens to me! Well, now maybe things will change," she stated.

"Blanche did you not hear me? If what Aldon says is true, and Edgar was starved and tortured in those tunnels, then someone must have planned on this happening."

"Do not be ridiculous Reynard. Who would have planned such a thing?"

"I have no clue Blanche, but my brother would not lie about something like this. That I can assure you," he answered.

"So, you do not think Aldon would be biased?" Blanche asked sarcastically. "I mean, why would he be, right? Even though he loves that little half-breed."

"I suggest you be mindful of where you take this conversation Blanche. If my brother has evidence, then he does," Reynard said, looking pointedly at her.

"Well, we shall see, of course. But I'm warning you Reynard, his evidence better be perfect! If not I shall ask for the harshest punishment for what she's done to our dear friend." Blanche declared, and then stormed out of his office not allowing him to have the last word.

Lisbeth stormed through the long, arched, white marble corridor leading to the observatory. Her angry footsteps were deafening in the large hall. The rage in her eyes was framed by the unruly and wiry black hair that hung in front of her face. Throwing open the double doors leading to the observatory, Lisbeth spotted Andrei standing in the glass enclosed balcony. He was drumming his fingers on the banister that surrounded the balcony, as he looked down at the Romanian village below. "Why didn't you tell me that my brother's condition improved?" she shouted. Andrei didn't answer. Crossing her arms, "I am waiting for your response!"

"Oh Lisbeth, I didn't notice you were there over the shouting, forgive me," Andrei drawled unenthusiastically. Lisbeth shrieked violently, slightly cracking the panes of glass surrounding them on the balcony. "You are infuriating, Andrei!"

"Uh, uh, uh, let us try and use our inside voices Lisbeth. I do not think Cain would be too happy to hear that we had to replace this glass for a second time," he commented smugly. Lisbeth gained her composure, and then smirked evilly.

"It is funny that you mention our master Cain. He has awoken. Oh, and I am sure he will love to hear that three vials of his blood have been taken from the vault," she said confidently. Andrei glared at her, but then became nervous at the thought of Cain's reaction to what he'd done.

"What are you talking about? I had no idea that those vials were missing!" Andrei replied vehemently.

"Why so defensive Andrei? I said no such thing. You better hurry though, you do not want to miss Cain's awakening ceremony," she said slyly, and then walked out of the room.

Andrei scowled at her. *You have really done it now Andrei! How could I be so foolish as to leave the evidence behind in Astoria! I have to fix this. Cain must never find out I changed those girls using his blood. After the dust settles I shall return to Astoria and finish what I started.*

21
Truth and Consequence

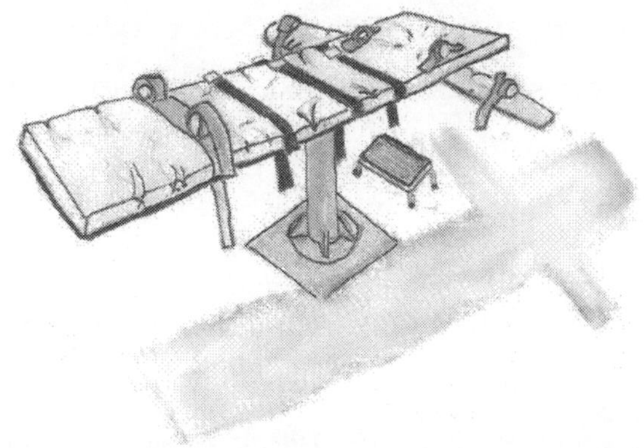

Rachel was waiting on the front porch as Cat arrived home after her ordeal. She rushed to Aldon's car as it pulled into the driveway and ripped open the passenger side door. Grabbing Cat in a hug, Rachel began to sob happy tears. "Oh Cat you're safe!" she wailed, squeezing her daughter tight. Taylor pulled Matt from the back seat and carried him into the house. As Taylor laid him on the couch, his dad filled him and Rachel in on what had happened.

Ryan helped Cat up to her bedroom and sat on her balcony while she cleaned up. Looking into her bathroom mirror, Cat didn't recognize the person staring back. She was covered in blood, and was as white as the towel she was using to wipe her face. Tears welled up in her eyes as she turned away and headed into the shower. As the water washed the blood from her skin, she watched as it swirled down the drain. *I'm a killer,* she thought.

Ryan heard the bathroom door open, and peered in at Cat through the open bay window. Seeing her strained demeanor he went to her side, took her hand, and led her to sit on the bright orange couch.

"How you holding up?" he asked.

"Isn't it painfully obvious?"

"I feel like I've let you down. I hate the fact I couldn't be there for you tonight."

"Ryan, I told you it's okay. I just wished Matt hadn't seen all of this. And if you had been there, you might have been hurt," she said, snuggling up close to him.

"Well maybe Matt should have his memory wiped then."

"I meant what I said. I trust Matt. He won't say anything. Speaking of Matt, maybe we should go downstairs and see if he's woken up yet. I wonder how he's going to take all of this."

Much to everyone's surprise Matt took everything pretty well. "Let me get this straight, you live with werewolves and you're a half vampire? But don't they hate each other?" Matt's forehead creased heavily as he pondered his question.

"It's true Matt. Like the movies, vampires and werewolves, or Varulvs, which is our true name, do not usually coexist. Some of us, who were tired of the old ways, moved here to Astoria. Cat's vampire father saved my life many years ago. So when Cat was brought to us as a baby, having lost both of her parents, there was no hesitation to make her our own," Sam explained, leaning forward in the chair, his eyes never leaving Matt's as he answered his question.

"So, there are like good and bad vampires and werewolves? Sorry Varulvs?" Matt asked and then Sam nodded. "And Ryan, are you a Varulv?"

"No I'm one of the other guys."

"Matt, *believe me*, I know this is a lot to take in. But people are out to kill me. And now that you know, they might come after you too," Cat said quietly, reaching for his hand and looking directly into his eyes. "Some wanted to wipe your memory of what happened tonight, but I told them we could trust you. I trust you with my life, and that's what's happening here. My life!"

"I know I act like a dork sometimes," Matt began and then noticed Cat's eyebrow rise. "Oh okay most of the time, but I know when to be serious. I don't want my memory wiped.

Remember years ago when we made that blood pact?" Cat nodded. "Yeah I know, it was kind of juvenile and all, but we promised we'd always be friends, no matter what. We'd have each other's back. I have your back Cat, and all of yours too," he stated, looking around to everyone in the room. I know it's hard for men to say the 'L' word, but it's not for me." Quickly looking at Ryan, "Just letting you know I'm not trying to take your woman, we're cool with that, right?" he was relieved when Ryan nodded his head with a slight laugh. "So Catherine Colvin, my best friend, I love you. And I'll protect you and your secret until the day I die. Which I hope is a long way off."

Cat hugged him tightly, "I love you too Matt! And I'm glad you've got my back!" she told him with tears in her eyes.

The small group stayed up most of the night talking, with Matt asking a million questions. Almost every question involved his movie impressions of both races, which had them all laughing heartily. After all the myths about vampires and varulvs were dispelled, and Matt's questions were answered honestly by both parties, they swore an allegiance to keep him safe. Matt found himself a little overwhelmed as he thanked everyone for answering his lone remaining question. Soon after, all of them finally found their way to a quiet, if somewhat restless sleep.

The final bell finally rang on the last day of school, and an exhausted Cat made her way to her locker to clean it out. Over the last week, she had been plagued with nightmares about Edgar Girven. Dark circles were painfully visible under her eyes. Ryan was standing there waiting for her, as was Matt. "Guess what the rumor mill is churning out today?" Matt whispered. "According to Marissa, you know in our English class? Who knows Courtney, who works at the Three Penny Brit? Duffie and Leif went back to England, due to a death in the family. Which explains why they haven't been here."

"Well that's a relief. I know that Mr. Bancroft said the tunnels had been searched, and they found no signs of anyone else down there. But I still had this horrible feeling that they might have been stuck down there."

"Well they're not, so you can quit worrying," Matt replied.

"I still would like to know why they followed you that night," Ryan interjected.

"Yeah it was kind of weird how they kept their distance behind you. I wonder why we never saw them," Matt said.

"Maybe they got lost. Which is probably for the best, if you know what I mean," Cat replied.

"Here comes Elle, act natural," Matt said as he nudged Cat.

"So what are you guys chatting about?" Elle asked inquisitively.

“How to celebrate our last day of prison, what else?” Matt joked. A goofy smile spread across his face as he saw Hannah heading toward them. “Isn’t she wonderful?” he said. Hannah blushed as everyone turned to look at her, her hands clutching her books nervously at the attention she was receiving.

“Hi guys, do I have something on my face?” Hannah asked shyly.

“No, you’re perfect!” Matt responded, and then went forward to grab her hand.

“So now that we’re all here, except for Amanda, who’s going to a gig with the Bombshells tonight. And Julie, who’s still battling a serious case of mono. What are we going to do to celebrate surviving another year?” Elle asked.

Cat put a fake smile on her face. “How about my house? Moviefest? You know, the usual,” Cat chimed in, trying to muster up some enthusiasm. She didn’t really feel like celebrating since she was still reeling from the events from the days before, but she couldn’t bear to let her friends down.

“Alright, but only on one condition, Matt doesn’t get to pick the movie,” Hannah joked, laughing as he lightly shoved her on the shoulder.

“Okay so movie night it is. But not too late, because you Cat, need some beauty rest,” Elle giggled. Cat laughed it off, *if only you knew*, she thought.

"Miss Colvin," Mrs. Rosenbaum called out to her down the hallway. Cat left the group and moved toward her. Mrs. Rosenbaum's tight mini skirt and high heels caused her to move like a model on the runway. "I'm so relieved I caught you. I found this little tid-bit stuck in my drawer, and wanted to make sure you got it. I know the grades have already been handed in, and it's a moot point now, but I thought you might want it back," she said, handing a stapled packet of paper to Cat. Looking at the front page, Cat recognized it as an essay she had written. It was entitled: *I'm Normal*. She also noticed the *A*+ circled in red at the top of it. Looking up at her teacher she smiled. "This is the first A plus I've ever given, by the way."

"Why thank you Mrs. Rosenbaum, I worked really hard on this," she replied.

Leaning in close to Cat's ear, Cat could smell her flowery, overpowering, and expensive perfume. "We both know this paper is a lie," she whispered, and then backed away with a smirk. "Have a nice summer dear. Don't do anything I wouldn't do."

Cat stood there staring in disbelief as Mrs. Rosenbaum walked away. *What did she mean by that? There's no way she could know, quit being paranoid Cat,* she thought.

Rounding the corner into the next hallway, Mrs. Rosenbaum scanned the hall cautiously before entering her empty classroom. After closing the door behind her, she hurried over to one of the many classroom windows that lined the far wall, and threw one open. She looked out the window suspiciously and watched as the last few students left the area. After slipping off her shoes, Mrs. Rosenbaum removed the sprigs of baby's breath that lay within. *Don't need that to mask my smell anymore, I prefer cinnamon anyways,* she thought as she tossed the sprigs out the window. Grabbing ahold of the necklace draped about her neck, Mrs. Rosenbaum chanted a few words in a strange language. Suddenly, her mouth shot open and a thick black smoke trailed from it, drifting its way toward the open window. Her body collapsed to the floor as the last of the smoke left her body.

Waking up, Mrs. Rosenbaum felt her head as a headache began to invade. *What happened*? *What am I wearing*? She asked herself, tugging at the skimpy outfit she had on. "Geez, I feel like I've been sleeping for months." As she rose to her feet, Mrs. Rosenbaum steadied herself with one hand on a desk. She began buttoning up her blouse to the top button, and then pulled her skirt down a few inches. "What was I thinking, wearing such a scant outfit? I look like a street walker."

A faint trail of black smoke, just outside the classroom windows, caught her eye, and she turned to watch it trail off. She rubbed her eyes, wondering if she saw what she thought she did. When she opened her eyes again, the smoke was gone. "Hrmph, you're losing it old gal," she murmured.

Ryan waited in the car while Elsie ushered Cat into Aldon's estate. "They're in the basement dearie, tending to those poor unfortunate souls," Elsie said in a solemn tone. "Do you really want to go down there Catherine?"

"I need to see for myself that Linda's okay. I haven't been getting much info from the adults," Cat replied.

"Don't be expecting too much my dear," she said, patting Cat's shoulder, and then moved forward to the basement's entrance. "I could come down with you, if you'd like?"

"I'll be fine Elsie, I know my way down there."

"Alright, but keep a stiff upper lip Catherine, no matter what you see down there dearie." Cat nodded. Elsie stood at the top of the stairs watching Cat. *I hope I'm not making a mistake by letting her go down there. I wish Aldon and Druanna were here,* Elsie thought while wringing her hands.

Cat made her way slowly down the stone steps, finally coming to the large, steel, soundproof door, which locked from the outside. She pulled the handle and was immediately met with painful cries coming from inside. She hesitated, but only for a second and then moved forward, closing the heavy door behind her. Aldon's basement was filled with numerous rooms, some furnished, some empty. She followed the piercing screams and took a deep breath as she reached the doorway to where the vampire girls were being held. Nothing prepared her for the sight that met her eyes when she opened the door.

The three girls were strapped to padded tables, each one attached to an IV pole with a bag of red substance hanging over their heads. All three were struggling to break free. Cat wanted to put her hands over her ears to block out the painful sounds they were making.

Dr. Bane and Lucien stood with their backs to Cat, in deep conversation. Dr. Bane sniffed the air and turned quickly to face the doorway. His handsome face filled with shock as he saw Cat standing there.

"What are you doing here? You shouldn't be seeing this Cat."

"What's wrong with them, why are they in so much pain?" Cat asked, ignoring Dr. Bane's question. Lucien moved quickly and took her arm.

"Let us go outside Cat and leave Dr. Bane to take care of them," Lucien said soothingly. As they stepped outside the room, the screams ceased.

"What just happened, are they okay?" she asked, turning to go back in. Lucien's grip on her arm grew firmer as he pulled her to his side.

"It is alright Catherine. Just before you came in Dr. Bane gave them a dose of sedatives. They're probably asleep now."

"Why were they screaming like that?"

"Well, they refused to take the capsules, so we had no other choice than to force the blood supplement into them. But something is not right."

"What do you mean?"

"They are having a reaction to the supplement, and it is not taking. Their bodies are rejecting it for some reason," Lucien explained, looking directly at Cat. "Don't worry though, we are taking good care of them. We will figure this out."

"But Linda-"

"Linda will be fine. Hurry along now, Ryan is waiting for you."

"How did you know he brought me here?" Cat asked.

"That boy is smitten with you my dear, and I would expect nothing less than him to be attached to your hip, am I right?"

Cat just gave him a hollow smile, and then made her way for the basement stairs. She felt a tinge of worry as she left the basement, thinking about what would happen to Linda if they couldn't get them to take the supplement.

As Cat reached the car, there was no need for words when Ryan saw her face. He immediately took her in his arms and hugged her closely for a few minutes until she stopped shaking, before starting the car.

As they pulled into Cat's driveway, Ryan and Cat groaned simultaneously as they saw Maude with Fredricka in tow, making a beeline for them. "Yoo hoo! Catherine, what a nice surprise bumping into you! I haven't seen much of you lately. Fredricka's missed you too, haven't you sweetie?" Maude mentioned and then flashed a glare at Ryan. "I wanted to ask you about last Friday night. You had your lights on awfully late, a party maybe? Did your parents know?"

"Oh nothing like that Mrs. Roberts. Taylor forgot to turn them off when he went to bed."

"I bet your parents weren't very happy about the waste of electricity. I know I wouldn't have been. I could've sworn it was a get together. But then again your friend Julie wasn't there, and I know you and her are like Siamese twins. Haven't seen those other girls much either. Amanda and Elle was it? Had a falling out, did you? Amanda's a little wild, I mean look at her mom and that crazy store she runs, *Squaresville*. What kind of name is that? She probably sells that marajuwana in there. One day the police will listen…I mean…wise up and raid that place. Oh Fredricka quit pulling mummy. Stop!"

Ryan and Cat kept straight faces as the little poodle kept dancing around and pulling with all her might, trying to make Maude move.

"Well it's always a pleasure Mrs. Roberts, but we've got to go!" Cat said, moving slowly away and pulling Ryan with her. "Bye Fredricka," Cat called out over her shoulder as she and Ryan made a dash for the front door.

"Okay, tell your folks I said hello, haven't seen much of them lately either," Maude said as the door closed. Stomping off in frustration, she yanked on the dog's leash. "Fredricka stop that! Just when I almost had them spilling the beans on what's been going on over there, you had to act up. I swear, we're going straight home, and there will be no special treat for you!"

Ryan and Cat collapsed on the living room couch, giggling. "I know this is so weird, me laughing like this after what I've been through, but I really think I needed this," Cat finally let out.

"I love it when you laugh. And they say laughter is the best medicine," Ryan said and then threw his arm around her shoulder, pulling her close. "I'm sorry for what you've been put through Cat. Linda will be fine. I trust Lucien and Dr. Bane to get to the bottom of this."

"Oh, dad, what are you doing home so early?" Cat asked, spotting Sam standing in the doorway to the living room.

"My last class was canceled."

"Everything okay? You're not sick are you?" she asked anxiously, seeing the solemn look on his face.

"No, I'm fine. What are you two up to?" he tried to smile, but knew it looked more like a grimace. Cat's expression changed to one of concern.

"We're having a movie night tonight, is that okay?" Cat asked, not liking the way her father was acting.

"Sure, sure…you guys have fun. I've got to go make some phone calls from the study." Cat and Ryan watched as Sam left the room and heard the study door close.

"Something's wrong with him Ryan."

"Maybe he's just tired. Like someone else I know," Ryan replied.

"It's not like I don't have a lot on my mind. Miss Amaya blames herself for the girls getting a hold of her cell phone. Matt doesn't know Hannah's a vampire. Elle doesn't know Brandon's a Varulv. My friends have no idea of this private double life I lead. I'm worried about Linda. I killed someone. And to top it all off, there are still people out there who want me dead. Sleep is the last thing on my mind at the moment," Cat replied bluntly, counting off every issue with her fingers.

"I mean there is one bright spot I guess. Mr. Pierson is making a full recovery, thanks to Miss Amaya nursing him back to health."

"We'll get through this Cat," Ryan said and then kissed the top of her head.

"I sure hope so."

It was only an hour before the end of the school year movie-fest, and Cat decided to call Julie and see how she was feeling. Not wanting to wake Julie, Cat dialed her home number instead of her cell. Looking out her attic bedroom window across the street to Julie's house, she saw the light was out in Julie's bedroom and her curtains were still closed, just like they had been for the whole week. Julie's mom answered on the fourth ring.

"Hi Mrs. Winters, It's me Cat. I thought I would call and check up on Julie."

"Oh hi Catherine, Julie is doing much better now. She's actually right here if you want to talk with her."

"Sure," she replied. Claire placed the phone onto the kitchen table as Julie leapt up onto it and plopped down in front of the phone, fur and all.

"Hey Cat, what's up?"

"We've totes missed you at school lately Julie. We're holding a movie-fest tonight in your honor," she replied.

"Aww! Sounds like fun! I'm sorry I have to miss out on all of this. I'm still a little bit under the weather," Julie said and then proceeded to go into a coughing fit.

"Julie? Julie, are you okay?"

"Yeah…sorry…mono is a nasty thing to get Cat," Julie replied as she glared at the offending hairball that she just coughed up.

"Well I'm going to let you go, sounds like you still need your rest. I will call you tomorrow, ok. Love you Julie."

"Love you too Cat, thanks for calling." Before Cat hung up, she heard a random succession of beeping sounds like someone trying to mash the phone's buttons on the other line, and then a dial tone. "Darn paws!" Julie chastised as Claire put the phone back onto the receiver. "Okay mom, I know that you wanted me to be patient and wait for Miss Amaya's spell reversal, but that was the last straw. We need to go to the ministry. I need my mortal body back, like pronto."

Cat opened one eye peering sleepily at her alarm clock. "What the…it's after noon?" she groaned sitting up. For the first time in a week, Cat had a restful night after the end-of-school-movie-fest with her friends. The house was quiet as she made her way downstairs into the kitchen to find something to eat. A note lay on the counter, it read:

Cat,

Please make sure you are home at 7:00 if you decide to go out anywhere. We're having pizza for dinner.

Love you,

Mom

"I wonder what's at seven? Like I really feel like going out anyway."

Cat spent the rest of the afternoon watching classic black and white creature features, not moving until she heard her mom call up the stairs that it was time for dinner. Following the smell of pizza, she entered the kitchen to see her family gathered.

"Hey sleepy head, you stay in bed all day?" Taylor quipped.

"I'm allowed. It's summer," she laughed hollowly. "So mom, what's this thing at seven? That I had to be home for?"

"Let's eat first, I don't want the pizza to get cold," Rachel replied.

"But mom, you like cold pizza," Cat stated.

"I meant for you guys," she muttered, not looking at her. Cat turned to her father and realized he hadn't said a word yet. She went to speak, but then decided to wait until after dinner.

"So what's with all the doom and gloom parents?" Taylor spoke up, his mouth full of pizza.

"What have I told you about speaking with your mouth full?" Rachel snapped at him. Taylor looked at Cat in confusion. Cat shrugged her shoulders and mouthed, "I don't know."

As they were finishing dinner, the doorbell rang. "I'll get it," Sam said, breaking his silence. He quickly left the room and Cat could hear muffled voices coming from the foyer. Before Cat could ask her mom what was going on, the doorbell rang again, followed by the door opening, and more voices.

"Could you two clean up, and then join us in the living room? I need to go meet with our guests," Rachel said before hastily leaving the room.

"What's going on?" Taylor asked. "I swear a person could get frost bite sitting with those two."

"Yeah, I know what you mean. Dad didn't look well when he came home yesterday. Do you think this is all about me?"

"Miss Red Freak, it's not always about you," Taylor tried to joke, but it failed miserably. "There goes the doorbell again."

"Let's go see what's up," Cat said in a worried tone.

The living room was full of familiar faces. Aldon stood at the front. "Catherine, Taylor, please come and join us," he said, seeing them poking their heads around the corner. A knock came at the front door. "Oh, Catherine, could you let

Matt in please?" Bewildered, she went to the front door and opened it.

"My mom told me to come right over. What's this all about?" Matt asked in a whisper.

"I don't know, but the only way to find out is in the living room," Cat said, grabbing his arm and pulling him down the hall.

"Ah good, Matthew. I believe you know everyone, right?" Matt nodded. "Well now that you're here, we shall begin," Aldon announced. Cat and Matt moved to sit by Ryan on the couch in the corner. "I have received news from the Varulv council. I am afraid they require an audience with Catherine for her testimony on last week's event."

Cat sank into the couch, the pizza weighing heavy on her stomach. Sensing her distress, Ryan threw his arm around her.

"Now young lady, do not fret, this is just a formality. With all the evidence in our possession, you have nothing to fear," Aldon said, and then flashed Cat a reassuring smile. "Matthew you are here because, as the only eye witness to the incident, you must accompany us. I'm afraid your parents will be made to believe you are at summer camp. We will discuss the details in a minute." Matt sat there shell shocked, not knowing what to say.

Taking a moment to collect his thoughts Aldon continued, "All the evidence that has been gathered points to a traitor in the Varulv council, who we feel conspired with this master vampire in a plot to kill Catherine. As such, we need to be vigilant. Here at home, and abroad. We hope to rid ourselves of this mess quickly with the council, and be home as soon as possible. With Sam and I gone, you will be in charge as usual, Roland. And if Lucien should require any assistance with my basement residents, I am sure you will be available to help. Now, we leave tomorrow. Are there any questions?" Aldon asked as he scanned the room.

Cat buried her face into Ryan's shoulder, trying to stop the tremors caused by the thoughts of what might lay ahead.

A proximity signal sounded through Robert Craven's mountain hide-away. He moved over to his computer monitor and saw it was Max, his long-time friend and agent, at the front gate, waiting to be let in. He hit the buzzer, and watched as the large iron security gate crept open. He observed, through several security monitors, as Max's car wound its way up the mountain toward his estate. "This can't be good, he's back early," Robert muttered to himself.

Robert waited at the front door, anxious to hear what had caused this unplanned visit. "Back so soon?" he asked as Max came toward him.

"You don't look happy to see me," Max stated.

"This is my intrigued look," he joked.

"So, are you going to let me in?" Max asked, pointing to the door.

"Am I going to like what you have to say?"

"Let's just say you won't be the happiest person," Max replied.

Robert's handsome face took on more of a somber look. "Catherine?" he asked.

"Yes," Max replied.

"Serious?"

"Very."

"Let us go discuss then, shall we? "Would you like something to drink?" Robert asked, opening the front door.

Max was always in awe every time he stepped into Robert's estate and saw the magnificent mountain view from the large, sweeping panoramic windows. "No, I actually can't stay long. I need to get back," he replied.

"Alright then, don't keep me waiting, what is this news you bring me?" Robert asked as he poured himself a scotch on the rocks, mixed with a shot of blood. It never failed to amaze Max that in all the years they were friends, and though Robert was a world renowned author, he was always to the point and a man of few words when it came to discussing matters.

"Catherine has got herself in to quite the jam," Max stated. "It has to be a setup. But never-the-less the Varulv Council is still going to hold her responsible."

"What is she accused of?" Robert asked.

"Murder."

"A Varulv? She killed a Varulv?"

"It would appear so," Max answered.

"Come on, she's only sixteen years old," he spat out.

"Robert, why don't you sit down, and I'll tell you what I know."

"I prefer to stand if you don't mind old friend," he replied and then raised his glass to Max before taking a swig.

"No old friend, I implore you to take a seat. For what I have to tell you will require you to again come out of hiding." The moment Max spoke those words Robert set down his glass, put on a serious face, and took a seat across from him. He listened very intently as Max told him everything.

A half an hour later, Max was on his way back down the mountainside to make plans for their trip to Austria.

22
The Void

The next day, the party boarded Aldon's private jet which was headed for Austria.

"You know I can't come with you Cat, for obvious reasons," Ryan said, and then kissed her softly as tears filled her eyes.

"I hate this. I want you to be there with me," Cat whispered as she placed her forehead gently against his.

"I know, but there's no way I can."

"I'll miss you," she replied.

"You have no idea," he stated sadly. "Well, you better get going. I'll be waiting for you, remember that."

Cat looked deeply into his blue eyes and smiled. "I love you," she said, and then embraced him in a hug.

"I love you too."

Cat stood there framed by the plane's open doorway, and stared at Ryan forlornly until it closed. She gripped the ring he had given her in her left hand and swiped away the tears with the other. "Be strong Cat, you've got to be strong," she whispered to herself.

As Cat took her seat next to Matt, she could feel his nervousness. "It's going to be okay Matt," she said as she buckled her seat-belt.

"I've never flown before. Heck, I've never left the state," Matt stated, gripping the armrest tightly.

Poor Matt, last night he looked like he was going to throw up after the announcement that he was coming with us. I feel terrible. This is all my fault, she thought. Cat reached over and put her hand on his, squeezing gently, trying to ease him.

"I'm sorry you have to go through this Matt."

"What was that?" he asked panicked, looking around frantically.

"We're just moving," Taylor replied and then rolled his eyes.

As Matt settled his nerves, "I kind of feel guilty about the little white lie we planted in my parents' memory. Since when have I ever gone to camp? But they actually believed it. I mean Lucien made them believe it, but still," Matt rambled on.

"It was for their safety and ours. You do understand that right?" Cat asked.

"Yeah, but that doesn't change how I feel about it though," Matt replied as he looked out the window and watched the tarmac disappear.

As the jet began to descend, the first thing Cat noticed was Austria seemed as lush as Astoria. There were forests of large trees and green fields as far as Cat's eyes could see. The only real difference was the glorious snow covered mountain range standing off in the distance.

It was raining, drizzling really, and a light fog trailed the ground. Two limos were waiting for them as they exited the jet, ready to transport them to their destination.

"I wonder how far we're going. This doesn't look like a main road." Cat said as the limos continued on a small winding lane toward the majestic mountains. "Have you been here before Taylor?"

"No, this is my first time," he replied, continuing to look out the window at the trees flying by.

"It's beautiful," Cat said, staring at the mountains ahead. She leaned back in the seat. "I'm glad we got our own limo. I still feel awkward around Uncle Aldon."

"Cat, how many times do we have to tell you? It wasn't your fault," Taylor replied, whipping around to look at her.

"I know, but I still shouldn't have taken off by myself like I did. It was a stupid thing to do," Cat murmured, fiddling with the clasp on her messenger bag that was in her lap. She looked over at Matt and saw him tapping his foot nervously while gazing out the window as if in a trance. She felt guilty that he had been dragged into this. "Matt, are you okay?"

"Sure, why wouldn't I be," he replied, not sounding convincing. "Is that where we're going?" Matt asked while pointing at a large castle nestled at the bottom of the mountain range.

"Maybe," Cat answered, shivering at the thought of what she may face behind its tall, dark, and grey walls.

"Never been to a real castle before…I kind of wish it was under different circumstances though," Matt laughed nervously, missing Cat's worried expression as they pulled up to the front doors of the massive structure.

Taylor reached across the seat, placing his hand on Cat's knee. "This will be a piece of cake," he said, wanting to ease the fear in her eyes.

The limos came to a halt. The drivers jumped out and opened the doors, waiting for their passengers to get out. The castle's colossal wooden doors creaked loudly as they slowly opened and a tall, thin figured man emerged from them. His face was stoic as he waited patiently for them all to approach.

"I want to go home. I can't do this," Cat said, her nerves getting the best of her.

Aldon approached the thin man as Rachel and Sam went over to the open door of the other limo. "Mom, I can't do this. Please let me just go home," Cat said tearfully.

Her mom knelt down, "We're right here Cat, there's nothing to be afraid of. Come on now, let's all go inside. The sooner we do, the sooner this will all be over."

As Cat exited the limo, the tall, thin man's stony gaze lingered on her, making her feel uncomfortable. "The name is Baroque. Please do come in. I will have Magda see you to your rooms. Dinner will be served promptly at seven," he stated to the whole group, his gaze still fixed on Cat. His eyes flashed golden as he smirked at her. Dodging his stare, Cat quickly focused her attention on her mom.

Magda was just as *warm* as Baroque, as she led the group down a long hallway lined with plush red carpet. She assigned everyone a bedroom, and Cat was relieved when she found out hers was between her parent's, and Matt and Taylor's, with Aldon and Druanna's room across the hall.

The inside of Cat's room was awash with rich autumn colors. Its focal point was a huge four post bed with a dark wood finish. Portraits of regally dressed men and women were hung on all the walls, seeming to be trapped in a time gone by. Their ornate gold frames didn't seem too gaudy, and fit in nicely with the room's décor. As Cat scanned the room while walking toward the pair of tall windows in front of her, she felt like every portrait was staring at her with their golden brown eyes.

While looking out the windows at the fairy tale like scenery below, Cat became entranced by the snow gently falling outside. She jumped when she heard a noise behind her. Turning, Cat watched as a man hastily left the room after leaving her bags just inside the door. Cat looked on as Magda, who had the looks of a cover girl, came slightly into the room.

"Is everything satisfactory Miss?" Magda asked coldly.

"Yes, thank you," Cat replied nervously as the beautiful woman stared at her.

"If you like, you may wash up in the bathroom behind the door. Someone will come for you when it is time for dinner." Not waiting for her reply, Magda abruptly left the room, and closed the door behind her. Cat lay down on the bed and curled up.

"I will not cry…I will not cry," she said softly trying to fight back the tears.

Dinner was a strained affair. The dark red wooden dining room table seemed to go on for miles. The food looked and smelled delicious, but Cat had lost her appetite. She spent most of the evening pushing her food around the plate with her fork. After dinner, Cat was relieved when everyone retired to their rooms. She was totally exhausted, partly from the travel and the time change, but mostly from thinking about what lay ahead. She had to reassure everyone several times that she would be okay in her room by herself.

Cat laid awake thinking about giving her testimony in the morning in front of the Varulv council. After many restless hours, exhaustion took over, and she finally fell into a deep sleep.

Cat's stomach growled as a small woman with wiry hair brought a tray full of breakfast food into her room. The woman avoided eye contact with Cat as she placed the tray on the end table, and then left without a word.

Cat had just finished getting dressed when her parents knocked on her door. Grabbing her messenger bag from the floor, she left her room, and was escorted downstairs where the others were waiting.

"You two ready?" Aldon asked. Cat and Matt nodded their heads. "Then follow me," he directed, and then led them down a long hallway, with Matt holding Cat's hand. No one said a word. Reaching the end of the hall, Cat looked at Matt, puzzled as it seemed they had reached a dead end.

Aldon reached out his hand and placed it onto the wall, concentrating. "Magie öffnen," he said aloud. As the wall began to shake, the wallpaper curled up and peeled away, exposing the brick foundation underneath. The sound of bricks grinding against each other filled the hallway as they began to rearrange themselves, revealing a hidden passage. It led to a cramped corridor that was lit by old fashioned torches.

"Wow," Matt whispered into Cat's ear as she squeezed his hand tighter.

The passageway seemed endless with many twists and turns and at the end was a huge, arched, wooden door. Aldon pulled it open by the large wrought iron handle, revealing a stone cavern filled with beautiful stalagmites and stalactites. Matt and Cat stood still, holding up the group as they marveled at the sight before them.

"Sorry young ones, the Council is waiting," Aldon said regretfully, wishing that all they had to do today was observe nature's beauty.

Traveling across the cavern they made their way to an iron door in the distance. Aldon knocked three times and then a loud grating noise echoed in the vast space, as the iron door slid open to the side. A guard stood at attention as they passed by, his uniform as dark as the look on his face. Cat kept her eyes averted but felt his gaze boring into her. A stone spiral staircase greeted them at the end of the torch lit corridor and Aldon began to ascend them. Cat stopped counting the steps after fifty and just kept her eyes on Aldon's back.

"Look another door. Will we ever get there?" Matt asked, his voice breathless from the climb. Entering the room, Cat scanned the large space, and noticed several ornate white chairs and a couch trimmed in gold meticulously placed about.

"Make yourself comfortable," Aldon said to the group as he pulled Cat to his side. "The rest of you will have to wait here for us. As only I can bring Cat in for her testimony. Don't worry, Cat will be safe with me."

"Be strong Cat," Rachel said, moving forward to hug her. "Remember they're just a bunch of old men and women. They may act mean but that's their job. We'll be waiting right here for you. Just tell them exactly what happened." Sam bent over and kissed Cat's hair, gently squeezing her arm. Aldon took her hand and placed it in the crook of his elbow, patting it softly.

"Ready Cat? Let's get this over with," Aldon said softly. After one last look at her family, Cat followed Aldon out of the room.

The doors to the main hall were enormous. They were made of old red wood and trimmed in gold. Two men stood guard on either side, their faces blank as Aldon and Cat approached. Each guard grabbed one of the golden door knobs and pushed the door open. A large chamber, with several stairways that led down to rows of plush stadium seats, lay ahead. Women and men were milling around, and as Aldon and Cat stood at the top of the stairs, everyone turned and stared, not a smiling face among them.

To her relief, instead of leading Cat down into the lion's den, Aldon turned left and led her along the edge of the room, above the crowd below. Across the way on a high stage, Cat saw a long, curved, marble table with thirteen empty high back chairs sitting behind it. Halfway around the room Aldon stopped at the entrance to a narrow walkway. The walkway led out over the crowd and directly faced the stage.

"Come Cat, you must walk to the end. Remember I am right here. Take your time answering their questions." He bent down and kissed her forehead and took the messenger bag out of her hands. Cat turned and nervously made her way to the end of the plank-like structure, and placed her hands on the banister to support her trembling legs. She kept her eyes on the stage, not making eye contact with any of the crowd below.

"Hear ye, hear ye! Please stand and recognize our wise and honorable council," a regal looking man bellowed. The crowd quieted as seven men and six women took their seats at the table on the stage. The last to take his seat was an exact replica of Aldon. *Must be Aldon's brother Reynard*, Cat thought.

"We all know why we are here today. We shall hear all the evidence before judgment is passed," Reynard's voice boomed in the vast room. *He sure doesn't need a mic*, Cat thought.

"Ms. Colvin?" Reynard repeated for the third time.

Cat jumped a little, and realized everyone was staring. "Yes?" she answered in a quiet voice.

"Please speak louder! We all have great hearing, but we prefer you to talk loud and clear," Councilman Rhys Darby ordered.

"Yes sir," Cat's voice seemed so loud to her she wanted to cover her ears.

"We would like you to tell us, in your own words, what happened a week ago this past Friday. And please do not omit anything," Rhys barked out.

"Where would you like me to start?" she asked, feeling a little bolder this time.

"Start when you…received the call from one, Amaya Phillips's phone," Rhys said as he read from a piece of paper in front of him.

Cat started her story and gave every minute detail about her trip to and through the tunnels, and what she found there. She described the three girls, their master, and the state that Mr. Girven was in. The gathered council hung on her every word. When she finished there was only silence.

"That will be all Ms. Colvin. Aldon will you please escort her to the holding room until all testimonies are finished. I think a break is in order. We shall now take a short recess," Reynard declared.

Aldon took Cat's arm and led her to a doorway opposite from where she had entered. When they were alone, Cat pulled Aldon to a stop.

"Why didn't they ask me any questions?" Cat asked anxiously.

"If they have questions after every testimony is heard, you will be brought back in to answer them. Do not fret child everything will work out." Aldon gently guided her along until they reached a small waiting area. It held a few chairs sitting on a large beautiful rug with a picture of a wolf woven into it.

"Stay here Cat, I must go and speak with Reynard, please do not leave this room. I will return after Matt's testimony." After noticing Cat's worried expression, "don't worry, you did well. This will all be over soon my dear," he said and then patted her cheek before he left.

A few minutes passed and the door to the waiting chamber opened. Cat clutched her messenger bag tightly as a woman entered, one that Cat recognized as a councilwoman from her hearing. She was strikingly beautiful with her dark brown hair pulled up into a bun, allowing for her high cheekbones to be showcased. Her eyes were cold, so cold that Cat involuntarily shivered.

"Catherine, please accept my apology if I startled you, but I must be quick. This trial is a farce. The council has already determined your fate, and it is not favorable. I have come to take you to a safe place where you will meet up with your family, and escape back to your home," Blanche whispered.

"But, Uncle Aldon told me-"

"He believes this will be a fair trial, and unfortunately his brother has no control over what happens. He is but one man. Quickly, we must leave. I must be back before the recess is up." Blanche grabbed Cat's arm, dragging her out the door and down several hallways until they reached the outside. The air was chilled and snow covered the ground. "Now Catherine, see those trees across that frozen river?" She paused as Cat nodded. "That is your destination. Here, take my coat. We wouldn't want you to freeze now would we?" she said, and then kindly helped her into it. "Now hurry before the guards spot you. Your family and friend will meet you just inside the woods," she continued, and then gave Cat a little shove. Moving toward the forest, Cat stopped and turned back to find the woman had disappeared.

"You! Stop!" A guard called out from behind her. Cat's eyes grew wide as she watched two guards hurrying toward her. Turning on her heel she sprinted for the frozen river. Hearing a loud howl, Cat glanced back. The two guards began running on all fours as they shifted into their Varulv form. An explosion of clothing shreds were left in their wake. Cat quickened her pace as fear surged through her. She could feel them nipping at her heels as they snarled just inches away. Her fiery red hair flew behind her, being thrashed about by the wind. She almost lost hold of her messenger bag as she picked up speed. Seeing the river just ahead, Cat reared down preparing to jump. Leaping into the air, Cat felt herself float up and over the frozen river, landing safely on the other side. She whipped around just in time to see the two Varulv guards skid to a halt at the river's edge. One began pawing at the ground, as the other paced back and forth. Both let out low growls as they stared her down. Confused, Cat continued her way into the forest as the Varulv's howls echoed in her ears.

***

"So, did the Colvin girl do as we planned?" Councilman Rhys Darby asked Blanche in a whisper, as they stood in an isolated office chamber during the recess.

"Yes, the guards informed me that she has indeed entered the void. Catherine Colvin will no longer be a nuisance to this council," she replied.

"Good, and what of our betrayer?"

"Andrei will answer for what he has done. He has deceived the wrong Varulv," Blanche Caulder whispered angrily. Rhys grinned menacingly.

"He will be hard to reach, being so high up in the Parliament," he stated.

"Leave that to me Rhys. You underestimate the pull I have," she said. Hearing the call back to order by Reynard, Blanche and Rhys returned to the great hall.

***

"Thank you Matthew that will be all. Aldon you may take him to be with Catherine," Reynard ordered.

Blanche Caulder sat at the end of the table smiling inwardly. *Oh how I wish I could be a fly on the wall when Aldon reaches the room, and realizes his beloved Catherine has flown the coop. Yes, today is a good day*, she thought, as she sat back and waited for the fireworks.

The door to the council chamber flew open and Aldon rushed in. “Catherine is gone!” he yelled at Reynard.

“What do you mean gone?” Reynard looked up worriedly at his frantic brother.

“I mean the room is empty. I specifically told her to stay put, and I know she wouldn’t disobey me. Somebody has taken her!”

“Only the guilty run!” a voice yelled out from the crowd down below, causing rumblings to run through the assembly.

“She’s not guilty, we have someone in here that is a traitor and planned on her death too, but it backfired. We must send out a search party.” Aldon’s face turned red with anger.

“Wait! We want to testify on behalf of Catherine Colvin,” A voice rang out from behind him. Turning, Aldon recognized them as two of Cat’s friends, Duffie and Leif.

“Who are you?” Reynard bellowed over the voices mumbling below him.

“The name’s Duffie Gibbs. I’m a hunter from the Upper Echelon Academy. And this is Leif Edwards. He’s a seeker from the same Academy. Our keeper, Gerard McNeil, sent us to speak before your council. We witnessed Cat’s, I mean Catherine’s, accidental killing of Edgar Girven. It was in self-defense. The varulv councilman seemed to be in a crazed and wild state."

"Well there you have it. These two cannot lie when speaking before this council. It is forbidden by their creed. Catherine Colvin is not guilty! You have your proof! Now let us go find her!" Aldon yelled. Reynard turned to his right, and then to his left, whispering to his fellow councilmen. He stood, looking out at the crowd below.

"The council recognizes that Catherine Colvin is proven innocent of all charges. We grant you the use of our guards to form a search party Aldon," Reynard announced.

"Thank you brother," Aldon replied and then hurried back to the holding area, as the crowd quickly dispersed. Rachel, Taylor, and Sam looked up as Aldon ran into the room. "We must make haste, Cat is missing!" Aldon stated.

"What? Cat's missing?" Rachel exclaimed.

"What are we waiting for? We need to find her," Sam yelled.

"Duffie, you and Leif must come with us. You two will be our only hope for finding her," Aldon said as Rachel, Sam and Taylor noticed their neighbors standing behind him.

"We'll explain later. For now, we must find Cat!" Duffie replied, looking at their puzzled faces. Moving past them, she made her way to the door which Cat had left from. The others quickly followed.

"I hope she's not hurt," whispered Leif as he caught up to Duffie.

"We must hurry," Duffie replied in a no nonsense tone. The group followed the pair across the open field, until they reached the frozen river. A dark, black, foreboding forest stood on the opposite bank.

"She went across there," Leif said pointing to the river.

Rachel stopped as did Sam, both with grim expressions on their faces. Aldon knelt in the snow shaking his head.

"What's wrong? Let's go get her!" Matt asked, puzzled by their actions.

"Mom, Dad, Uncle Aldon? Don't just stand there! We have to go get Cat!" Taylor yelled. Sam looked to his son with tearful eyes.

"We can't. The Void is a place very few have survived. Besides, there's a barrier of dark magics set in place by an evil coven of witches," Aldon explained. "The barrier prevents varulvs and vampires from crossing through. It must have let Cat cross over because she is still half human."

"Rachel, no, you can't help her now," Sam said, trying to sooth his wife as she began to tremble in his arms. Rachel ripped away from him abruptly and snarled, staring into the void. Her bones began re-shifting, and her body mass grew, shredding her clothes. Letting out a loud howl, Rachel charged toward the river. She hit the barrier and let out a small whimper as she was hurled back into the snow. Slowly climbing back on all fours, and shaking her fur, Rachel howled. “Rachel! Stop!” Sam choked out. Ignoring him, she charged once more toward the barrier with the same result.

Sam hurried over to her as she lay in the snow, slowly transforming back into her human form. “Someone get me something to cover her up with, please!” Sam ordered, tears in his eyes as he brushed Rachel’s hair from in front of her face. The crunching of snow made Sam look up to see Reynard and his search party running toward them.

“What’s wrong? Please tell me Catherine is not in the void!” Reynard looked at Aldon’s face, receiving his answer. Removing his robe, Reynard handed it to Sam to wrap Rachel up in. Rachel moaned in pain as she lay shivering in the cold snow.

She began to sob, “My baby, please someone help my baby.” Taylor knelt down next to her and placed his hand on her bare shoulder at a loss of words.

“There might be a way we can get her back,” Reynard started to say.

"No, there isn't! We can't go in! And now she can't come back out this way! She has to make it through the Void to get out! And how many have done that, and survived? How many Reynard?" Aldon yelled, his voice growing hoarse.

"Please brother, listen to me. There is someone among us who can go in after her," Reynard stated looking over at Matt. "A human can cross over."

"What? Me? In there? I mean, how will I find her?" he asked worriedly.

"There's no way we can risk Matt's life! His parents are our friends, and they think he's at camp," Sam interjected angrily.

"He won't be alone. We'll be with him," Duffie stated, with Leif nodding next to her.

"This may be the only way to save Catherine. I can't order you three to go in, but if I am right, you need no convincing," Reynard said, and then watched as Matt walked over to the Colvin's and bent down."

"We'll find Cat and bring her back. Omfffph," was the only sound that could escape his mouth as Sam drew him down into a tight hug.

"I know you will. Be careful Matt," Sam muttered as he squeezed him once more. Another's arms wrapped around them, it was Taylor.

"You better bring back my sister in one piece."

"I will," Matt replied.

"We need to get going," Duffie stated, tugging on Matt's jacket. "There's no telling how far she is now." Without another word the three teens stood on the banks of the frozen river, with Duffie in the middle, all holding hands.

"Be safe young ones," Aldon called out as he watched the three walk across the frozen surface, and were swallowed up by the darkened tree line.

"Dad? Dad? What's that heading toward the barrier?" Taylor asked, pointing to a trail of purple smoke soaring through the sky, and making a bee line for The Void. Sam looked up just in time to see the smoke disperse as it slammed into the invisible wall. There was no mistaking the woman with the bright red curly hair or green leather trench coat that was tumbling to the ground. Taylor was the first to react, running over to help Ròs to her feet.

"What was that?" Ròs asked, rubbing her forehead. "Taylor, what are you doing here? And where the devil are we? This is not Astoria! Where is Catherine? She called me, is she in trouble?" Ròs asked in a panic.

"Uh dad? Uncle Aldon? Some help here please," Taylor called out, steadying Ròs as she swayed a little bit.

“Cat called you? From her phone?” Sam asked as he left his wife’s side.

“No, from the locket I gave her,” Ròs began and then stopped as everyone looked at her confused. “Oh, never mind. Where is she? I sense she is in trouble.” No one said anything. “Why is no one answering me? Where is Catherine?

“She’s in there,” Taylor answered, drawing her attention to the wall of foreboding trees just beyond the frozen river.

“The Void…you let her go into The Void? What were you lot thinking?!”

“Now Ròs calm yourself,” Reynard said coolly.

“Will someone please explain what’s going on?” Ròs asked in frustration. Reynard quietly explained the events leading up to the point where Cat entered The Void. Ròs bit her lip to stop herself from screaming at the group in front of her. She was furious that no one had told her about what Cat had been going through. After he finished, Ròs focused her gaze back to The Void. “So, your idea was to send in three teenagers? A Class C hunter, a Class C seeker, and a mortal? The hunter and seeker are not even allowed to slay at their level. They can only trap because of their class limitation. Do you really feel that these three will be able to handle what they’re sure to face inside?”

“We must all trust that these youngsters will bring her out safely. They are our, and Cat’s only hope,” Reynard said, placing his hand on Ròs shoulder.

---------------- About the Authors ----------------

Carol and Adam Kunz are the mother and son author duo behind The Childe series. Their combined love of the supernatural and things that go bump in the night was what inspired them to write Cat's story. Dark Days is book two in this five book YA Paranormal/Fantasy series. The author pair currently reside forty-five minutes away from each other in the sunny state of Florida. If you would like to find out more about this duo and The Childe series, please visit these links:

Author Website- http://www.cakunz.blogspot.com
Facebook Author Page- http://www.facebook.com/cakunz11
Facebook Fan Page- http://www.facebook.com/thechilde

- A group of independent Young Adult authors who are dedicated to their craft -

Tiffany King, author of *The Saving Angels Trilogy*

Abbi Glines, author of *Breathe* and *Existence*

M. Leighton, author of the *Blood Like Poison Series*

Michelle Muto, author of *The Book of Lost Souls and Don't Fear the Reaper*

Fisher Amelie, author of *The Leaving Series*

Nichole Chase, author of *The Dark Betrayal Trilogy*

Laura A. H. Elliott, author of *13 on Halloween*

Amy Maurer Jones, author of the *Soul Quest Trilogy*

Shelly Crane, author of the *Significance Series*

Courtney Cole, author of *The Bloodstone Saga*

C.A. Kunz, mother and son author duo of *The Childe Series*

10932892R10306

Made in the USA
Charleston, SC
17 January 2012